Gold

into

Lead

Thank you for taking the time to help us out

Watt...

Gold

into

Lead

*Book one
in the
Alchemist Series*

Walter Brunt

Copyright © 2018 by Walter Brunt

All Rights Reserved

This book or any portion thereof may not be reproduced or used in any manner whatsoever without the express written permission of the publisher.

Cover Design by Kim West
using QuarkXpress 2018

ISBN 978-1-9994668-0-0
eBook ISBN 978-1-9994668-1-7

To my loving wife.

Thank you for giving me the time

to live my dream.

Gold into Lead

Chapter 1

A small transport glided above the contours of the barren landscape. Its hull, a multicolored patchwork of rust and camouflage took on an orange hue in the late afternoon sun. Beneath it, the tall dry grass parted then swirled as it passed. The hum and slight whine of its antigravity engine pitched as cross breezes rocked its sleek metallic hull. Kole, feeling the wind's nudges through his controls compensated, avoiding the sharp drops from turbulence. He pulled back on the throttle and looked out the port side window as he circled, watching his wash ripple across the surface of the grass, cautious of Trolls or camping Slavers. A healthy paranoia paid off in the wild. Too many people had thought they were alone when a Troll springs out of the bushes, turning them into a quick meal.

Kole's brown eyes glanced down at the semicircle of consoles around him, double checking his sensors for heat signatures and nearby vehicles. Satisfied that they were alone, he released the throttle and hovered long enough to extend the craft's short landing gear before touching down in the sea of grass. He cut the antigravity while his fingers habitually moved over the array of consoles clicking buttons and flicking switches setting the sensors to give alarm if anything approaches while he listened to the waning hum of the engine beneath him. He stopped, the engine still sounded too in-tune then decided to retard it a touch more before they picked their next destination because a good engine meant good parts, making them a target to bandits, or worse. In the waste if you get noticed, you'll draw a swarm of hungry humanoid scum to your door. He relaxed into his seat feeling the vibrations of the engine through the deck allowing his mind to drift, remembering those many years ago when he had pulled the engine out of an ancient excavator that he had found in the middle of nowhere, a forgotten gem from a time long gone half buried in some grassland. It sat weather beaten, reddish brown and pitted with its hover matrix rusted through, a home to a colony of vermin, a ghost of what it once was. He had no idea why it was there, but it felt pleasing to his touch and its bumpy surface took his imagination into the distant past where Humans would've manufactured it, perhaps even before the Purge.

The engine stilled bringing a moment of peace into his home that he embraced like a warm blanket on a cold night until he heard Eric over the intercom rummaging about in the rear gunners compartment reminding him why they were there. He smiled waiting for Eric, feeling the love of his home, but hating the fact that he had to slap mismatched chunks of scrap armor onto his baby in order to keep the illusion of riding in a junk heap. Though the cargo hauler looked like crap, it could slice through the air like a bird and he made sure that nothing was added that'd cause too much drag. All the precautions were to maintain the perception of mediocrity and his appearance was also designed to mislead. He always wore the same collage of faded patches sewn together to make coveralls, an eyesore valued less than a whole piece of cloth and holstered on his left hip was a cheap pistol to make for him to look normal while the weapons of his kind he kept hidden in a pouch on his right. Under his soiled undershirt he wore a necklace loaded with small charms next to his skin, carvings made out of various materials turned into tools that he could access with his inner power while his long unkempt brown hair matched his scruffy beard, adding to the ensemble by giving the world the impression that he was a wasteland scavenger.

"Eric," he called over the intercom that was always kept open to his young apprentice. "I think we'll be alone for awhile." He looked once again out the front window then added, "It looks cold out, don't forget your cloak." He clicked the button at the center of his chest releasing his safety harness then finished putting the craft into standby mode as he heard the rear gunner's compartment open with a slight hydraulic hiss and scratching metal. He turned, looking around his head rest to see the blond scruffy Eric stand in the doorway stretching his lanky frame. They made eye contact as Eric released a long exaggerated yawn that he didn't bother to cover replacing Kole's smile with a frown, but Kole chose to ignore Eric's familiar "I'm bored" protest then studied him a moment longer. Eric wore the same mismatched patchwork of clothing making Kole grateful that he didn't have to explain again why being flashy, or original would draw the wrong kind of attention from people who'd try to take what they want. Eric's baggy clothes flowed loosely over his gun belt which was barely being held up by his hips then Kole smile returned when he noticed the arms of his shirt were three inches too short which was perfect. He nodded approval then watched as Eric maneuver carefully through their galley slash bedroom avoiding the scorched and dented pots hanging from the ceiling to his locker retrieving his cloak. Kole worried about Eric's bouts of rebellion, not that he blamed him for something commonly called "Transport Fever" brought on by being cooped up in a small space with little stimulation. They spent most of their time deep in the wilderness with no one new to talk with and to Kole, the young always seemed to have a strange desire to show the world who they are which draws all kinds of trouble to them and if they survive long enough they'll be glad to be alive, living unnoticed.

    Eric wrapped himself in a dark blue cloak throwing it over his shoulders before fastening its clasp. He walked to the entrance then hit the red button waiting for the door to recede, quietly sliding open to allow him to stand at the edge of the entrance. Kole watched him thinking about how he was going try not to lecture him about why they're there, listening to the wind whistle outside as it washed over the hauler's armor plating and gun ports.

Eric's light blue eyes scoured the horizon before he sighed releasing a long protest that danced on the cold breeze before he flopped his head to the side facing Kole looking bored. "You're right," he sassed. "We're south of the middle of nowhere. There is nothing out here. No rocks, trees, or anything to look at."

Kole gave him the look that told him to stop complaining, but Eric moaned once more in defiance then dramatically pulled the hood of his cloak over his head. He grabbed the edges of his cloak and wrapped himself in it as tight as he could before stepping off to land in the grass allowing the door to close. Kole pushed himself up and twisted his muscular frame, sliding out of the cockpit ducking under some low hanging consoles then went to his locker to retrieve his cloak, pushing the folded hammocks hanging on the wall aside. He took a moment to mull over visiting the closest town to throw Eric into a social setting, but knew the citizens would want him to make projectile gel as barter for their stay. He didn't mind being put to work, but sometimes it was nice just to share food and relax hiding among the Commoners. He closed his locker, draped his thick cloak of filthy wool over his shoulders feeling the scratchy material drag across the back of his neck then opened the door and jumped into the dry grass. For him it wasn't as cold, his mind and body has been beaten by time and hard living, but wasn't surprised that something in him enjoyed watching Eric shiver after his yawning protest.

Eric saw his smirk. "I'm cold," he defended then shot him a partial glare, daring him to say something sarcastic then yielded, "Let's get this over with. What are we doing out here anyway?"

Kole shifted his gaze to the grass before him, allowing his cloak flap in the breeze pretending he was unaffected by the weather causing Eric to pout and turn away. He fought the urge to grin, but his smile could be heard in his voice, "This place is as good as any to teach you about our people. I know I could've taken you anywhere, but cheer up, we're outside and this place is out of the way, besides no one ever comes out here so it should be relatively safe from the Soulless." He cleared his throat. "In the beginning…"

Eric groaned dropping his head interrupting him. "I've heard this story a bazillion times since I was five. It was boring then, but now I'm certain it's a way to inflict some form of mental torture on me. Over the years I've even tried to interrupt you, but oh no, you have to have it your way."

Surprised by Eric's reaction, Kole realized that he didn't have to lecture him at all. "Well then, tell me what you know," he quizzed.

"At the start of our kind," Eric informed. "The Universe gifted the Human race with alchemy which changed civilization taking them in a new direction of science and medicine, drawing them back to the balance of nature until everything went wrong." Eric dramatically waved his hand then embellished, "Oh, the madness, an impact to the Human psyche." He hunched and his voice deepened, "Oh, manipulating matter wasn't enough." He shook his fist. "Humans have always battled their pride, arrogance, but there will always be balance, light to dark and as they manipulated the spark of life and its manifestation of the genetic code, like a computer program being altered, Humans were twisted it into new creations."

Kole chastised, "Tell it right and stop being a turkey."

He straitened. "I'm the one telling it now and my way's not boring," he said then spun to face Kole, squinting one eye. "The other races were born and no one understood the scope of what was being done." He clawed his hand reaching to the sky. "Evil, evil, the unbalance to creation, the horrific beauty and awe inspiring tragedy as Humankind rose from the dirt to become as the great as the supposed gods and being drunk on the praise of the Commoners, the Alchemists changed people into their desired bodies, men into women, women to men then Elves, Dwarfs, Orks and Trolls became popular choices."

Kole groaned in annoyance not liking Eric's dramatized rendition.

He shivered then thrust his hand under his cloak. "New languages, entire cultures sprang up and everyone was screaming for the new "in" thing, sending everything spiraling out of control. There were no laws or regulations keeping the Alchemists in check and with the backing of corporations, the Alchemist stepped further into the realm of evolution, creating new patented life. The Soulless were born." He became serious. "Were they really soulless?" he inquired. "They were made from twisted DNA. I mean life is life, right?"

It was Kole's turn to glare.

Eric cleared his throat then dramatically continued. "The public went wild over creatures of fantasy becoming reality. A fad as faerie folk were caged and sold as pets while the public blubbered praise over their delicate beauty, but there'll always be balance and even though the world's genetic code was being altered giving birth to new forms of life that were never meant to be, something seeped into the Human psyche dropping a hammer as…" He declared, "The Madness swept through our kind. Alchemists clamored, clawing, competing to top one another. It became a race to make new creations, some twisted and evil, others military funded. Vampires, Werebeasts and new diseases that no one had a cure for seeped out of the military bases then to top it all, they animated the very dead in the quest for immortality. Oh no, it didn't stop there folks because with the creation of the new races it was discovered they possessed longer lives. Elven fetuses became the fountain of genetic youth in a bottle and no one cared that life became a cheap product, manufactured overseas to a world whose morality was struck blind. "Forever Young" was its brand. Insanity twisted the world, uniting Humans and those who used to be Human for a brief time as a host of other creatures poured off the assembly line to become slaves to the five self proclaimed superior races. Designed to make life better, their new creations were affordable and semi intelligent wasting away as beasts of burden. Shortly after, small wars broke out releasing the diseased Vampires and Werebeasts into contained areas. The world was enthralled by change, ignoring the pressure building under their feet." He smiled pausing for effect. "Don't give me that look," he argued.

Kole challenged, "What look?"

"The scrunched up frowny face look." But before Kole could respond, Eric continued his theatrics, "Arrogance, pride, jealousy and fear manifested as the Commoners woke from their drunken stupor to find that the proud Alchemists had separated themselves into a new class of demigod. They jumped onto a pedestal demanding worship and in the Commoner's confusion the world quickly changed, plummeting like an anchor into the cold darkness as the new spark of enlightenment was snuffed out. In that moment the slaves took a chance and started a slaughter that would last hundreds of years reshaping the surface of the world. Billions died and in the following thousand years, the Commoners hunted down the Alchemists of old, destroying their work and knowledge sending the world into a new Dark Age. Alchemy was confused with science and technology as self-righteous zealots sized control, furthering their interests and thrusting people deeper into ignorance till the races fractured. New nations were born, slaves were freed and as time passed the Commoner's anger subsided allowing the new Alchemists in hiding to slowly surface, humbled they crawled from the rubble with timid care as they went to face the weary masses." Eric proclaimed, "Then calm returned," finishing the story.

"Yes," Kole approved. "Not bad despite your theatrics and the reason we're here." He pointed to the ground. "Is to show you an example of balance working all around us, from the large to the small and a thousand years ago, this spot was the center of a city with a population of…" he dramatized, "six million people. Can you imagine so many people working, living together in a coastal city on a planet that scholars say was covered by two thirds water? Imagine all that water teaming with life now gone, the city burned to ash, evaporated into the wind with all those people, leaving us standing here in the middle of one of our five continents."

"Yeah, no one really knows what happened back then," he countered.

"It doesn't matter what actually happened. The point is that life on this planet had almost ended."

"I know, but I mean who said it was the Alchemists that went mad? It sounds like propaganda to me."

Kole grunted dismissing his opinion. "I wouldn't put it passed people to twist things to their advantage, but I'm not talking about that. Changing an object allows us to access the energy between its atoms transmuting matter allowing it to remain in balance with its environment. Water into fuel or air into gold is simply the recombination of atoms, but the madness comes when we reach passed what is to touch the genetic code and warping it into a new creation. Altering the host's DNA warps the psyche and damages their soul, the inner totality of that person. That's why the races became what their bodies were, the bulk of Humanity transmuted, lost forever in an idea of what being an Ork, Elf, Troll, or Dwarf should be."

"At least they still have souls," Eric pressed. "They're radios that have been tuned to a different station unlike those black eyed Pixies."

"Yes, those damned Pixies!" Kole spat. "The person who made those vile little things should be shot! I have no idea how they were made and you can tell when you look into them and hear their oily vibration that their souls aren't real. I think someone manufactured those bastard things from scratch and if the people of the past had seen what those little bleeders are capable of, they wouldn't have been sold as a child's pet!"

Eric's teeth chattered. "Kole, I'm freezing. I've learned my lesson, can go now?" he asked.

He calmed down listening to the wind stir the grass then considered Eric's feelings. "There's something else I've been thinking about. We've spent too much time in the wastes visiting small outposts and caravans. I think it's time we went to a town."

Eric grimaced. "Do we have to?" he pleaded. "I'm sick of the fearful glances from the old people, but mostly the looks of disgust from the girls. Remember a couple of years ago, those girls I wanted to get to know who had always seemed to travel in small packs whispering to each other shooting quick glances over their shoulders. It was hard enough to say hello to just one of them, but being an Alchemist in a world taught to hate our kind, it was awful." He shrugged deflated. "We can make our own food and fuel. We don't need them." He pointed back to the hauler. "We already live lower than vermin so we don't scare the Commoners. It isn't fair."

"Eric," Kole soothed, "Human contact is a good thing and the right girl won't treat you that way, besides I'm sure you're tired of looking at my face by now." He glanced back at the hauler. "That's our home, not a nest for vermin. We must remain humble, or we may be tempted to repeat the World's mistakes without you even realizing it."

"I…" he forced a smile and sounded more enthusiastic. "Could use fresh surroundings, but out here away from the bigger cities, they're not so friendly to our kind. I'd rather just wait until we migrate into Alchemist friendly territory."

He stepped closer placing his hand on Eric's shoulder understanding his reluctance. "I know how you're feeling, I was once just like you, but we can't stay isolated forever. It's now time to serve the Commoners because it lessens their fear of us and removes the negative myths that cloud their perception." He reassured, "I know we can be self sufficient, but that leads us down the wrong path of separation and look at the other races who have embraced their Alchemists, they flourish together, united in song while we on the other hand remain apart and any sort of separation breeds hate."

"Oh," Eric perked. "Can we can go to the Elven nation?"

He dropped his hand. "Elves hate Humans and there'll be no difference there. They won't shoot us on sight, but it's still hate no matter what form it takes besides Elves are too prissy for my taste. All we'll end up doing is working the fields altering their grapes so they can make their precious wine. They don't even think we're good enough to walk down their streets so we'll be living in a shack on the outskirts of some outpost."

"I think working in the field is better than being a cleric for the Orks," Eric mused giving a slight smile. "I can learn what your teacher taught you, patching up their wounded on the front lines in a simple border dispute." A gust of wind caught his cloak opening it blowing it around his shoulder.

Kole felt a shift in the weather, a subtle charge in the air signaling the beginning of a storm then pulled on his cloak gathering it up, allowing it to fall around him. "I was a child and shouldn't have been there," he regretted, but smiled at his overall experience with the Orks. "I did learned a lot, but they don't like it when you try to leave." His mind went back to when he was around four feet tall and his teacher took him into Ork territory. He remembered what he called "The Night of Blood" in a torch lit triage shack made of twine, pelts and small logs where the thick smell of blood was almost palatable and the clashing of steel and popping of gunfire raged in the distance. He'd never been more scared in his life and couldn't do any real alchemy back then, just accidental stuff. He waited in the corner shivering, his patchwork clothes stained and wet with blood, sticking to his skin as he prepared bandages on a crude wooden table. There was nothing that he could do to make his hands stop trembling, or to tear his eyes away when the Ork soldiers carrying in their wounded on animal hide stretchers, in what seemed to be a steady stream of horror. The sound of metal and flesh crashed on the ground in a loud hollow thump as the soldiers in a hurry to get back into action dropped their wounded carelessly on the dirt floor. The injured howled in pain, their deep meaty screams for revenge rolled out of their slobbering maws stinging Kole's little ears as their pale green faces adorned with white war paint flashed between pain and rage. Kole's teacher, a tall lean Native man in a blood soaked robes hurried, working furiously to close their deep gashes and alchemically seal any bloody stumps where a limb used to be.

An Ork squirmed then his legs spammed. His long scraggily black hair knotted with mud and dried blood hid his lupine ears and as the light from distant explosions stretched, flashing through the tent's flaps, the light flickered across the tusk canines of his lower jaw that were stained pinkish white from an enemy he had bitten. The Ork jerked, kicking his legs off the stretcher, burying his heels into the ground as his dented and worn black plate armor over Kevlar scrapped steel on steel. The rows of small spikes that stretched across his shoulders looked menacing in the candle light.

Kole shook his head ending the memory that had given him nightmares for many years after. "They're not the brightest, but they sure love to fight," he jested.

Eric pulled back on his hood then spat out some of his hair that the wind had blown into his mouth. "If the Orks don't like us leaving because we're useful in a fight, what can we do against an army of angry Orks?" he wondered then spat again. He brushed his fingers against his cheek collecting the fluttering strands of hair then tucked them behind his ear.

Kole's face hardened. "Nothing they'd like, but no Alchemist wants to be pushed that far because the Commoners fear us enough already for what little we show them, so push those dark thoughts out of your mind because we don't need another Purge, besides we're not invincible. Orks are technologically retarded, but they do have some of the ancient weapons used to kill our kind scattered throughout their land."

Eric turned away from his gaze and let out a nervous laugh. "I was teasing," he confessed. "You don't have to get so serious, besides it doesn't really matter because we're like the Trolls, tribal, roaming in small packs and inside ourselves we hide underfoot like the Dark Elves. How can we make a good impression out here when they think we're a secret society?"

"We're not a secret society," he lectured. "We're nomadic, and that's because if we're not, they'd have a better chance at hunting us down and killing us in our sleep. Alchemist are not made, they're born. Some people drown their children if they show signs of the gift." He looked at Eric thinking back fifteen years ago when he had traded Eric's parents a rifle and a box of ammo for him. Kole had just finished collecting all the trinkets he'd used for trading, putting them into a duffle bag then placing them into one of the holding compartments of his two manned armored hover cycle, preparing to leave camp. The cycle wasn't special, a flying metal box with a dome top, just a couple of chairs mounted to a hover matrix encased in armor. He had parked with the other small makeshift vehicles on the outskirts of a small walled farming community when an angry man stormed up to him. The man's tall frame shook with rage as Kole mentally went over all the things he had done in the past year that might have called for revenge, but couldn't think of any and didn't remember seeing the thin blond man before. The man wore a light green short sleeve shirt and brown jeans carrying a round tan hat in his fist. Kole noticed the signs of wealth and almost pulled his weapon in defense when the man stopped a short distance away.

The man's face blotched red as he visibly regained control of himself before blurting, "You." His face contorted in disgust then he pointed the rim of his hat at Kole. "I have your kind's taint in my seed.

My people have shunned my family and the only way for redemption is to get rid of my spawn and never have any other children ever again. My other children are to never procreate and have been blacklisted from the breeding list. My blood line has ended. I'm ruined, my life has been destroyed and my marriage may not survive all this because of that little bastard. I thought my wife had cheated on me, but the tests…" His fist tightened on his hat whitening his knuckles. "I don't deserve this curse and I shouldn't have your kind's stink on me. I was going to kill the thing before anyone found out, but someone in the community did and now I'm ruined. The damage is done and its mother promised to stay with me if I trade it to one of you. It must be worth something to your kind."

Kole had been chased out of several small towns by people hemorrhaging racist crap and at the time he didn't care about the man's emotional state, or opinion, but violence was already diverted so he went straight into negotiations remembering the story of how he was traded to his teacher. "I need to see the child and if it's healthy and strong, I'll give you what I was traded for," he insisted.

The man looked him over then nodded. He turned then waved his hat in the air, Kole tensed feeling his charms hanging around his neck against his skin, thinking he was under attack only to relaxed when a short brunet with long strait hair and nice round curves shown off by her white summer dress walked out from her hiding spot behind a small transport. The woman slowly approached holding the hand of a small boy in one hand while wiping the tears from her eyes with the other.

Kole watched the way the child move checking for defects and didn't see any. "How old is he?" he wondered.

The man turned his back to the woman and child declaring, "It's four and in good health. What will you give me for it?"

"A pristine hunting rifle and a box of ammunition," Kole offered then opened the door to the passenger compartment he used for storage, retrieving the rifle and ammunition holding them out. The man took the rifle inspecting its sites and mechanics then grabbed the ammo. He then spun around and walked by the woman nodding once to her.

She knelt then wrapped her arms around the boy squeezing him in a tight hug. "It's time to go with this man," she explained, her voice tightening. "He'll take good care of you." She released her embrace then wiped her tears away.

"I don't want to go," the boy begged trying to force his way back into her embrace. She quickly held his shoulders as his little hands tried to find a grip on her arms to pull her close. His legs pushed forward, but her grip held as his little body bent backward. His sobs grew louder as snot slid down his face then he choked between screams, coughing.

Kole could no longer remember his parents and watching this woman with her child wondering if his mother loved him as deeply then found himself sympathizing with her choice, the only decision she had to save her child. He watched for a moment longer feeling horrible then walked over, reached around the boy's waist and with anguish etched on her face, she let him gently slide out of her outstretched arms.

Frenzied, the boy screamed, kicked, slapped, pinched and clawed at Kole, but Kole held him tight. The woman looked up him then back to her son horrified. "Go," Kole reassured between the boy's screams. "I'll take good care of him, I promise."

She stood, staring at the boy as if to burn his face into her mind then as more tears filled her eyes she turned around and ran. The boy stopped for a moment watching her then flung his head backward, but Kole moved his face out of the way. He then became as straight as a board, dead weight almost sliding out of his shirt and Kole's grip.

Kole had enough of the child's tantrum and swept his legs up, lowered him to the ground and held him face down, his little body trembled breaking Kole heart, but he held him until the boy was too tired to protest. "I forgot to ask. What's your name, boy?" he asked, but the boy didn't answer, even refused to speak for a long time after that. Kole eventually named him Eric, after a hero he once read about in a children's story.

Kole came out of the memory. "Some are lucky and find their way to us, other aren't."

"Lucky like us," Eric complained. "Abandoned and traded to a stranger like a piece of property. To a stranger who wasn't, but could've been a pervert or worse. All because of the fear of what we may turn into." Tears welled in his eyes. "It didn't really mater!" he spat. "I don't remember my dad and only the smell of mom remains, I think."

"My teacher never told me about my parents, said it was unimportant, but I know your mother loved you very much and yes, we also go to these villages to find our kind. Children left to rot in the streets." He sighed clearing his mind not wanting to think about all the lost children. "We've gotten off topic. I want us to hunker down for a couple of years so you can develop socially. I taught you how to fight, use our weapons and survive, but not how to live. I know I haven't been the best teacher, but I've passed along what I was taught."

Eric looked down, wiped his tears away then pulled his hood over his head. "We're living."

"You're old enough to understand the responsibility that comes with the power you're going to wield and I've slowly introduced you to the basics, but your emotional body isn't as mature as your physical one, which is my fault. I've been a little over protective and may not have been as emotionally balanced as I'd like to think I was."

"There's nothing wrong with me," he hissed then angrily tugged his hood over his eyes.

"I know that there's nothing wrong with you," he defused.

"Then stop treating me like a child!" he yelled and turned his back to Kole.

Kole knew Eric wasn't angry with him. "The past can sometimes hurt. I'm just trying to have a serious conversation with you. We're the only ones out here and…"

Kole, startled by their alarms, froze. A moment later they were sprinting through the grass back to the hauler. Eric, always being quick on his feet, arrived first grabbing the side handle and thrust a foot into one of the recessed steps. He punched in the door code then jumped inside. Kole followed then turned and grabbed the cockpit chairs sliding under the hanging consoles into his seat. He slapped the standby button killing the alarm then strapped in as the antigravity wound up. He glanced at his sensors. A contact was approaching fast. He then turned on the rear view camera, grabbed his controls and took off retracting the gear.

"Eric, what do we have?" he inquired into the intercom then maxed out the throttle. "Take your time. We'll be fine."

"It's a small battle barge flying the banner of the Jolly Rodger."

Kole cursed. "Slavers of course, why wouldn't they be out here?" he brooded. "Tell me about them."

"Who designed those things? Barges look like flying triangles with soft edges. Oh, they're in jamming range and... There it goes, external communications are down. The barge itself has a greater estimated mass then it should, but it's still advancing meaning they have a retrofitted engine and slave pens with all the fixings, most likely located in a hind quarter."

"Just one barge?" he questioned, probing Eric's ability to think beyond what's seen.

"They could be in single file with other vehicles out of sensor range, waiting to flank us?" he pondered. "They could also have three man hover bikes for boarding. I suggest we slow and alter course to see if we can visually spot anything else."

"Well done," Kole approved then slowed, turning and waited for Eric's report.

"It looks like they're alone and there's no air support," he noted.

"It's not like them to attack one on one I guess they think they'll win. We're a third their size, what do you say we take them out?" he offered, thinking about the front and back gun nodes that won't do much against the barge's armor then decided the hidden cannon running the length of the hauler under the deck would do the trick. With just the two of them the cannon was equipped with an automatic reload mechanism, but the armament still seemed a little light so he added two guided missile launchers, one on each side facing the rear to give pursuers something to think about. He also wanted to be able to do some light damage so he added two forward grenade pod launchers, one on each side loaded with smoke, drones and explosives.

"If they're alone, we can run," Eric countered. "But if they call for backup we may not make it to a town that'll help us, ammunition is precious and no one likes defending strangers. Besides, Slavers are bastards they'll just chase us down, so I say we fight and maybe we'll rescue some prisoners, or discover why they're out here. Some Intel would be helpful in avoiding patrols from a new base."

Kole agreed reasoning, "We can fight and if we run the next target they find may not be as well armed as us. So let's get busy." He reached over and pushed the number three on his stereo for what he called battle music then adjusted the internal speaker volume. A mixture of Ork love ballets and Elven punk played. Kole smiled to himself then flicked the external speakers on setting them to max, blasting the music so everyone within a kilometer could enjoy it. The Ork songs, guttural language centered on love, blood and battle while the fluid Elven words harmonized with their electric wood instruments in a soaring flow of music. His head nodded with the beat then shouted into the intercom, "We'll see what happens. Hit them with the tail guns to lure them in then give them the hardware. I'll try to keep it steady for you."

Kole then banked right firing smoke canisters and thermo drones. The barge slowed turning to face them as a wall of smoke and false heat signatures went up between them. Kole jerked the controls putting the throttle down as a cannon round exploded where they used to be rocking the hauler, launching it sideways into the air within a cloud of dirt, rocks and chunks of grass. They landed a short distance away bouncing once, sending the pots and loose items in their small galley crashing onto the floor. He cursed at the ear piercing noise then checked his sensors and banked again circling back. Out of the smoke, the front of the barge emerged like a wild animal leaping from the fog. Painted grey like the face of a wolf with wicked eyes on the sides of its wedge shaped body. A gun nest mounted in the front, sat between its white jagged teeth that stretched across its dome front and the color of dried blood along its flat bottom. Other gun ports held in place with nasty messes of armor jutted out each of its sides and the black one way window of the cockpit formed the wolf's nose. Railings ran around its top deck caging in an anti aircraft gun and Kole could make out a mixture of Ork, Troll and Humans holding the railing pointing their guns and various edged weapons at them screaming death in anticipation of their kill.

The Slaver's forward gun opened up in flashes of yellow crosses spraying hot rounds up the front of Kole's hauler sounding like metal rain washing over the armor. He instinctively jerked to the side as the last rounds fractured the passenger side bullet proof window then focused his mind, tuning out the noise. He closed fast clicking off his weapon's safety then fired both grenade pods, lobbing their modified rounds onto the top of the barge which exploded in a cascade of orange flashes tossing dismembered Slavers into the air as he sped by. Kole heard the thumping of the barge's side gun over the Orkish music and felt his hauler shake while he read "Death's Fury" painted in flames down the barge's side. He jerked sharply veering away then pulled back on the throttle slowing to keep under the trajectory of their cannons and watched the rear monitor as the barge turned then suddenly his hauler lurched forward as Eric fired the hidden cannon and one of the guided missiles.

Kole compensated for the sudden thrust and watched a trail of smoke race out obscuring the rear camera's eye, but was able to see two filtered explosions confirming hits then turned to watch the destroyed flaming front end of the barge drop plowing into the ground. Taking advantage of their confusion he began an attack run squeezing the triggers firing grenades at their side gun and watched a series of explosions fall short but race toward the barge striking the gun emplacement in a flash of brilliant light spraying chunks of metal and glass in a cloud of bellowing black smoke. He slowed coming alongside the barge waiting for it to come to a stop as the barge's antigravity failed dropping its back end to the ground with a loud screeching moan.

Kole extended the hauler's gear and landed. "I'm boarding to rescue slaves," he blurted over the intercom. "Get up here and take over, be ready to get out of here if something goes wrong." He released his harness then pulled himself out of the cockpit and stepped over the scattered mess of galley almost slipping on a ladle to reach the door. He took a moment to calm himself then ran his hands down the front of his cloak straightening it. He reached into his right pouch grabbing a one inch diameter, six inch long wood dowel and a tarnished silver knuckle buster. Eric emerged from his compartment as Kole slipped his knuckler onto his fingers feeling the alchemical programming within them. He concentrated creating his kinetic shield that encompassed his body forming a bubble over his clothes.

Ready, he hit the door's button, wishing he'd turned off the blaring music then flashed Eric a reassuring look before jumping into the grass. A howling gust of wind blew between the hauler and barge flattening the grass blowing his cloak open, but Kole didn't feel the cold, his shield protected him. Adrenaline flowing through his pounding heart warmed him. He ran toward the smoking hole of twisted metal in the side of the barge then slowed hearing the music change to a fast paced Elven song fitting his mood making him want to rush into certain danger but stopped short. He gathered his cloak around him hiding the dowel wanting to use what he was as a surprise then looked up at a fierce Ork wearing red mismatched plate armor over black Kevlar peering out the hole with white war paint smeared across his face.

The Ork's guttural laugh and slobbering maw sent a chill up Kole's spine as the Ork showed Kole a large gruesome one-handed axe in one hand and an odd looking rectangular barreled gun in the other. The Ork jump into the grass landing with a thump then slowly straitened to twice Kole's size. His long black hair flowed over his shoulders as his hot breath danced like smoke in a breeze. The Ork's red eyes shining with excitement as he pointed his gun at him then with a meaty battle cry, Kole felt the pressure of the weapon's discharge. Kole jumped to the side narrowly avoiding a blue bolt of energy as it tore a hole through his shield almost collapsing it. He nearly fell to his knees as the power of the weapon stole his breath and right then he knew what that weird looking gun was and how much trouble he was in. He then heard an explosion behind him, but before he could look the Ork sprang forward swinging his axe in a powerful downward stroke. Kole defensively re-empowered his knuckler then stepped forward dropping under the Ork's heavy blade forcing it to glance off his shield. The Ork twisted taking a tight step back to bring the gun to bear. Kole felt the pressure again and lunged forward shrinking his shield to get close to the Ork as the blue bolt shot by harmlessly absorbed into the ground.

 Kole held the charge within the knuckler then concentrated to empower the destructive power within the dowel willing, it forward as he collided against the Ork. He pushed the tip of the dowel through his shield and touched the layered plates stretching across the Ork's abdomen then released its energy. He felt a quick vibration in his hand then heard a wet slap as chunks of armor, bone, guts and blood exploded out the Ork's back. Kole side stepped ignoring the gore at his feet and turned to watch the Ork collapse, but before he could think a shadow crossed his face. Surprised he looked up as a figure leapt out of the sun off the top of the barge. Stepping back with the sun stinging his eyes, Kole carelessly dropping his Kinetic Shield and reached out, open handed with his busters hanging loose fingers as he felt the power in the air around his Human attacker. On impulse he squeezed his fist and with a loud woomph the Slaver burst into flame. The Slaver screamed a short high pitched yelp before slamming into the ground with his smoldering body armor melting into his flesh.

 Kole gasped in horror not believing what he had just done, but before he could think another Human Slaver with a shaved head and filthy brown body armor stood in the burned out side gunners compartment screaming obscenities about Kole's mother while unloading two pistols at him. Surprised and unprotected, Kole couldn't think with all the bullets speeding by and the loud music pumping out of his speakers. He threw himself backward hitting the ground then reformed his shield grateful the Slaver was a crappy shot, but angry at himself for being so careless. He looked up to see the Slaver rush to the edge of the hole. His eyes burned with intense hate as he aimed then fired another volley at Kole, but the rounds were disintegrated by his shield. Kole raised his dowel and fired an orange bolt of energy that punched deep into his chest spraying chunks of ribs and blood in a small explosion that tossed the man into the ceiling, slamming him hard. For a second he stayed there, his limbs bent in the wrong directions before falling with a wet slap against the metal floor.

Angry at himself for being isolated, out of practice and for dropping his shield, almost getting himself killed, Kole released any contemplation about the incineration. He felt foolish for wanting a moment to think in the middle of a fight then remembered why he was there. He rolled onto his feet and climbed into the side gunner's compartment then cautiously moved along the wall to the hatchway. He didn't know what other weapons they had and cautiously peeked into the dark quiet hall. His shield protected him from gasses, cleaning the air, but Kole imagined the smell of warm sour stink of poorly recycled air distracting him from the heap of burnt flesh outside. He put his dowel away then pulled a rock out of his pouch and configured it for a timed explosion. Ready, he tossed the rock into the passageway toward the cockpit. The rock tapped, bouncing off a metal walls and floor then with a bang, sharp tiny fragments sprayed out finding home. Men cried out signaling Kole to move. He pulled out his dowel, stepped over his last kill avoiding that Slaver's pooling of blood and looked into the passageway. Sun light steamed in from the cockpit through the thick cloud of floating dust showing that at one time the walls were painted white, but now rust and mold stains run from the ceiling to the anti slip floor. Two Slavers with lacerations over their exposed hands and faces quickly pulled themselves off the floor, ducking into two adjacent doorways for cover.

The first Slaver peeked around the corner seeing Kole's dowel then dropped his pistol into the passageway. "We surrender," he sputtered then raised his hands before stepping out. The other Slaver squatted, leaned around the corner and aimed his pistol at Kole's face, but the first Slaver quickly added, "He's an Alchemist you idiot."

Kole cautiously leaned around the hatchway not sure what type of pistol the Slaver was holding, but before he got a good look the second Slaver, he reluctantly surrendered. "Are there any others?" he demanded.

They exchanged sour looks before the first Slaver spoke. "There's just the wounded."

Kole half smiled thinking how they hate him for winning when the fight could've gone the other way then relaxed still aware of his surroundings, but not sure what to do with his new prisoners. "I assume you have slaves. Take me to them," he ordered.

He glanced at the body behind him regretting the waste of life and wished there had been another way. His heart felt heavy as he stepped back over the body into the gunner's compartment allowing his two prisoners to pass. They shot him mixed looks of fear and doubt seeing their charred companion then led Kole down the passageway to the rear of the barge.

The Slavers pinched their noses shut then opened the last hatch. There was a hiss of air pressure then the second Slaver gagged, almost puking on the first. The first Slaver reached in and clicked a switch turning on a yellow light set into a wall mount at the end of the room. Kole looked over the Slaver's shoulder to see five men in torn soiled clothes sitting on filthy blankets thrown over a straw floor. Across from them in another cage a small group of women shielded a cluster of children. The slaves became still and Kole was relieved to see a glimmer of life in their eyes. A man in the back covered his mouth then coughed breaking the silence.

Angry at the savagery of the world, Kole commanded, "Release them and stand aside!"

The first Slaver rushed in and opened the cells fearfully looking back at him, but the slaves didn't move. They stared at him through the bars with a renewed crazed peace in their eyes.

"I'm here to free you. You can all go," Kole calmly reassured the slaves, but no one moved. "Get in the cell with the men," he ordered the Slavers. They complied and quickly moved to the far corner. "You men," he said to the slaves. "Go to the women." He wanted to reassure them and tell them that he meant no harm, but there was something creepy about the way they were reacting. The five men slowly moved in a cluster against the back wall into the other cell closing the door behind them confusing Kole, but he ignored their behavior and walked to the Slaver's cell. He placed his hand on the lock configuring the metal to fuse shut, locking the Slavers in then the sound of rustling straw caught his attention. He turned to watch a young boy walk up to the other cell's bars. His matted hair matched the color of his ripped and soiled cloths.

The boy tilted his dirty tear marked face up at him. "Are you an Alchemist?" he challenged with the fire of hate in his eyes.

Confused by the boy, Kole nodded.

Suddenly the boy's face contorted with disgust. "My dad says your kind made this world," he seethed. He wrapped his little fingers around the bars. "I'd rather die than be helped by your kind!"

Shocked at the intensity of the boy's hate, Kole looked at the adults behind him to see that some had the same feelings reflecting in their eyes.

"Jacob!" a sandy blond woman scorned, her long matted, wavy hair fell over her tattered summer dress leaving little of her thin frame to Kole's imagination then her expression softened before she rushed forward wrapping her dirty arms around him. "Now, say you're sorry," she coached.

Kole's fingers tightened around his dowel and his arm twitched upon hearing her voice. His first instinct was to blast a hole through her, but was able to stop the impulse before he acted. Surprised and horrified that he was a split second away from murdering an unarmed woman he quickly searched for an answer discovering there was something really wrong about her. Her lips were still moving but he could no longer hear her and the more he watched her the more he saw the oily taint of a Soulless. His mind reeled at the impossible concussion, that an Alchemist had made her. He felt faint and forced his eyes to look away to regain his composure.

The boy stared up at Kole through his greasy bangs. "I'm sorry for saying those things," he said in the low steady tone of a veiled threat.

Kole returned his gaze to the woman feeling sweat gathering on his forehead trying to give himself time to understand why he instinctively wanted to kill her.

The woman straitened to a proud, unashamed pose, holding the boy against her. Her green eyes looked into Kole's. "We don't hate you.

You can't help what you are. You see, my husband and two children were killed when the Slavers attacked our caravan, but I was spared. We have chosen to give the Slavers what no one else has, redemption."

"What?" he asked confused.

Her face filled with compassion. "We can't bring back the old world. We can only unite to build a better future and helping the Slavers find redemption will start us all on a brighter path." The group of slaves smiled, looking at her with glistening eyes filled with admiration. "That's why," she continued, "we're here and some of us are a little upset at you for ruining our plans. You can now understand how we would see your interference as a bad thing."

A light pressure rolled over his body making him want to vomit. Her words were toxic, pooling energy under his skin and all he could think was there was a fabricated Human standing before him, but he didn't know what to do. Other Soulless didn't affect him this way, but they weren't Human. "How does my rescuing you from an existence of slavery and misery ruin your plans?" he managed to ask while trying to stay centered and fight off a forming headache.

She gave a warm and forgiving smile, which Kole thought was condescending. "We don't expect you to understand, but every other race has a home and the bigotry against the original Human has kept us low. When Alchemy polluted the world, no one wanted to be Human. "We…" she waved her hands to the people around her, "have chosen to bring change to the Slavers. We suffered through the attack loosing loved ones, but out the chaos I saw a plan to save the Human race." She slowly raised her hand to the ceiling and spoke with conviction, "We are to act by giving love to all those who've lost their way." She returned her hands to the boy's shoulders and looked disappointed. "That is until you, interfered." She sighed. "I'm sorry. I'm a little upset with you right now."

He stared at her dumbfound and almost laughed at the thought of her being a true Human. He'd heard many strange things over the years, but never from the mouth of someone on the verge of being used as a party doll in a Slaver's den.

One of the five men stepped forward. "It's time for you to leave

Alchemist. You'll never understand us because you're not a pure Human."

Kole watched the boy turned around and wrap his arms around her hips in a hug as she smiled down at him. The other slaves gathered around her, hands reaching out touching her. She raised her gaze meeting Kole's. "What is your name Alchemist?"

"Kole," he said, dumbfounded.

She gave him a soft smiled. "My name is Sarah. You may now go, Kole."

He backed away then shook his head trying to shake the sick feeling polluting his body and wondered why he risked his life trying to save them in the first place. "I'll send help," he offered. He turned walking back through the barge to the smoldering cockpit ignoring the two half burnt corpses strapped into their seats. Through the hole of twisted metal he heard another Elven punk song streaming in from outside. He paused listening to the music realizing he was in a foul mood and wished he'd turned that damn noise off when he had the chance. Looking over the broken monitors to the burnt consoles he found a functioning terminal to splice into then quickly downloading the Slaver's information. Unfulfilled he left the way he came.

Jumping into the grass he took a moment to shake off the icky feeling Sarah gave him then looked at his hauler remembering the first shot the Ork took that missed him. He was surprised to see some rough scoring the size of his head in his baby's armor. He cursed knowing that the damage could've been worse, but couldn't shake his dark thoughts as he went over the day's events. Everything started off good but now it's spoiled. His eyes found the Ork's corpse. The red body armor wasn't hard to find in the dry blood splattered grass. He knelt beside it and rummaged through the grass ignoring the gore. It didn't take him long to find the pistol. He slowly stood, gripping the strange weapon designed by Alchemists for the Commoners to kill Alchemists, but something about the weapon irked him. He pushed his senses outward feeling the alchemical programming within the weapon's power pack that was far beyond his ability. He couldn't touch that level of alchemy and that worried him. He was talented and stronger than most, but the person who made this power pack was far greater than him. He searched for a clue, but couldn't get a sense of the person who had made the pack. He had once seen this kind of weapon before. The weapon he remembered was ancient and barely worked, not brand new like the one he held. He rotated the gun in his hand which grew heavier by the moment. It was a bad omen and looking at the small dimly lit display, eighty seven percent of the power remained. He ejected the metallic clip to see a strip of high impact glass with an electric blue gel within then noticed that all the weapon's components were manufactured. He smirked thinking he should've known because you can't use alchemy to house something that destroys alchemy and that realization created more questions. He slapped the power pack back into the weapon and tucked it under his belt then returned to his hauler.

Eric slid across to the passenger seat. "Well, what happened?" he urged looking around the head rest at him. "It looks like you've seen a ghost. Was it that bad?"

Kole shut the door, stepped over the mess of pots on the floor then sat in his seat. He turned off his battle music. "I want you to analyze this information," he requested holding up a data stick.

Eric took it and inserted in into his secure terminal. "What did you see in there?" he asked and fastened his safety harness. "Were there slaves, or…?" His expression soured. "Was it a Troll's kitchen?"

Feeling safe, Kole collapsed his shield then put away his knuckler and dowel. He strapped himself in and didn't want to burden Eric with what he saw, or strengthen his argument to stay away from civilization. "Trolls, you always go to the worst scenario. Don't be silly, let's just get out of here." he said checking his sensors before lifting off. He retracted the landing gear as he sped away watching the barge grow smaller in the monitor.

Eric went to work tapping his console. He selected an entry. "It turns out the Ork you killed was the captain and a couple of days ago they hit a small group of merchants who were camping for the night. They took slaves even though they were on the run from the Elven Navy with dwindling supplies. Their captain thought that a successful raid was what they needed to boost morale." Eric laughed then cursed. "You should read this guy's broken English. He even misspelled Ork and his description of how they slaughtered the Humans and plundered their camp is disgusting."

Kole glanced at him. "Stop cursing, I didn't raise you to use that language!"

He looked away then crossed his arms and glared out the window. "I can curse if I want to. I'm not a kid anymore."

He realized that he was venting on Eric and didn't want to continue their earlier argument. "I'm sorry. I've had a bad day. Tell me about this captain."

Eric slowly uncrossed his arms pouting. "The Captain was trying to secure a buyer for his new slaves because two week ago the Elven Navy with their air ships destroyed the Slaver city of Pontiac on the Pacific coast." He laughed. "Awesome news and the survivors went to ground making their way to the other coast." He looked at him. "So, you did rescue the slaves? There were slaves in there, right? You came out alone, I'm just wondering."

Kole was silent organizing his thoughts barely hearing Eric's questions. "There was a small group of slaves that I let out of their cage, but I think they were crazed. They spewed some crap making me feel bad for saving them." He hissed and tightening his grip on his controls feeling tension building in his shoulders fueling his headache. "There was a woman, a clone, a Soulless Human."

Eric stopped reading. "What? You mean she looked like a pixie, or fairy?"

"No. She looked like a real Human, but without a soul, a fabrication."

He sat in silence then laughed in disbelief. "You're making me think, testing me. The other races were once Human, but no one has done that in forever because of the laws before the Purge and such. Besides no one's stupid enough to do it now, the world would rise up and crush them."

"No test. I looked into her makeup and she's a Soulless."

"That's creepy. I can't imagine how weird that'd look. What did you do after you let them out?"

"I left because she had a following of Humans adoring her and her death would make things worse." He shook his head. "I've never seen anything like it. What could I have said to make them believe me? I have a feeling something bad is coming."

"Commoners are so narrow minded, choosing not to listen to anything outside their hate and if any of our kind says anything, it doesn't go over well because to them, we're the bad guys." Eric smiled and leaned back into his chair. "There was nothing you could've done, so let it go."

"I'm not sure I can. I don't know how long Sarah has been alive. If she's new, then there's a dick head Alchemist out there stirring things up." Kole dismissed the questions milling in his mind, for now. "I guess we've both been out here too long. We'll be near a town by night fall and I'll tell them that they have some people to pick up."

Eric pointed to his monitor. "One last thing and it's hard to make out, but I think a Soulless traded the Captain a gun near Pine View as payment to attack the merchants. I'm paraphrasing. The English isn't clear and looks like gibberish."

Kole tapped his fingers against the controls. "Pine View it is, maybe we'll find some answers there."

Chapter 2

In the distant land of Koresgen within the Dark Elf Capital of Nezrum Talhor, Byron Sims ran his hand over his long wavy brown hair then grabbed his pony tail, draping it over his shoulder before crossing his muscular arm. He fell back leaning his tall frame against a slightly warm wall in the market district. He waited watching the crowd, his green eyes slightly glowed red from moving his sight into the infrared spectrum as Grey Dwarves, Orks and the occasional Troll milled about buying and selling from one of the many small kiosks. Their weapons and body armor were easy to see against the heat of their bodies and not much was hidden, seen against the walls and floor. The market and streets weren't that big, everyone was forced together grinding away their patience speaking in low grunts and tight whispers in a place where the only law is, don't do it unless you can bribe, or fight your way out.

A smaller man in body armor, wearing night vision goggles walked out of the crowd and stood beside him, his lips close to Byron's ear. "I hate this place," he hissed. "Crossing the lava fields, the smoke and black clouds before we even get here. Just so I can be your message boy."

"Do you have it?" Byron demanded, uninterested in the man's

whining then pulled his kinetic shield tight against his body.

"Yes, but this is the last time I'm coming here. We're inside an active volcano and that freaks me out. I have nightmares of darkness and being burned alive."

"I pay you well and we're alchemically protected here."

"Yeah, well my greed is all filled up and those bastard Dark Elves think they're better than us living over head while we ground dwellers choke on their spicy perfume."

Byron looked up through the haze of incense at the square buildings hanging from the ceiling of the huge cavern and the longer that he looked at the upside down buildings, the more he felt that he was the one on the ceiling looking down. The only thing breaking the illusion were the bridges stretching between the dwellings. "Incense," he corrected the man, "and it's better than sucking on the massive stink of muggy body odor. What does it matter? You don't live here."

"I'm glad I don't live here, I'd get lost. All these tall building looked the same with their posh ornate windows. This place is all one large piece of black stone that looks fragile. One earthquake and everybody's dead."

The man's complaining was wearing on Byron, but as he thought about it, he realized that that's all the man ever did. Every time they met it was about food, heat, cold, cramped quarters, the stink of something, or his bullet wounds. "Are you a big bad Slaver, or whiny little imp? You're sounding like the latter to me."

"Well, look at you all done up in your burgundy silk shirt and designer tan pants looking like a Dark Elf's boy toy. You're lucky you're an Alchemist, or I'd…"

"What?" Byron interrupted, his voice taking on a dangerous tone. "You mentioned a message. Hand it over and if you tell anyone about dealing with me, or what I wanted, I'll hunt you down and make you wish you died before we met."

The man handed him a data stick then backed away disappearing into the crowd leaving Byron fuming. He cursed under his breath knowing anger didn't look good on him then watched the glowing multicolored walls, heated by the volcano making a huge artistic display shaped by the different densities in the stone creating slow shifting patterns, murals and merchant signs. He was no one's toy and knew he looked good. He designed his clothes himself to accent his body heat and make himself look more attractive to the Dark Elf women. Remembering the smoothness of Elven skin as he ran his hand down their legs made him feel better and helped him to finally calm down. Now excited, he decided that he needed to blow off some steam before meeting with his teacher.

He tucked the data stick safely away thinking he'd get to it later then made his way to his favorite brothel passing its bouncer, a large Troll in a filthy Loin cloth. He hated that stinking Troll and was sure the feeling was mutual, but what happened all those years ago wasn't his fault. When he had first arrived in the city he was looking for a place to relax and ran into the Troll who knocked him around forcing him to use Alchemy. Instead of using charms his teacher had taught him to write the power into his bones and being inexperienced, he wore night vision goggle making the Troll think he was a Commoner. It all happened so fast.

The Troll's glowing red eyes peered down its long pointy nose at Byron before it said in a deep rumbling voice, "No Humans allowed."

Never being so close to a Troll let alone hearing one speak before, he froze. His first thought was that he was grateful his nose and sinuses were already saturated with the Dark Elves incense, or he'd smell the rotting flesh loosely hanging from its lanky body. The Troll then without warning pummeled him, grabbing his throat and pinning him against a wall forcing him to defend himself. His shield was tight against his skin and the Troll didn't know what it was holding and in a few quick moves he brought the towering Troll to his knees. From there he had to show his dominance and make an example for all to see, so he forced the Troll eat his own eyes, which later had regenerated. Now, every time he passes through those doors the Troll just glares at him. That is until today.

Byron passed through the doors into the foyer then stopped, thinking he saw a slight smirk on the Trolls lips. That little observation gave him a bad feeling and his foul mood resurfaced, but he dismissed the thought of blasting a hole through the Troll in favor of spending some quality time with a dancer. He had time to fully enjoy the morning before meeting up with his teacher. They'd discuss all the boring plans, but sometimes he'd get the odd exciting assassination or like his last task, to pay off the Elven Prince after he'd ordered his fleet to sack the Slaver city Pontiac.

He requested his favorite girl from the painted Dark Elf Matron who told him that she'd been sold to a different brothel and Monique, a new girl would take her place. He knew all the girls and requested another, but the Matron insisted and assured him that he'd have the pleasure of being Monique's first client which heightened his paranoia after seeing the Troll's smirk. He'd made many enemies over the years and among creatures that live extremely long lives, revenge can take decades to manifest. He has little patience for that, but they seem to feed on the anticipation, savoring each year as it rolled by, stalking their prey until the day came when their hunger was too great and come for blood. Playing along with the Madam, he negotiated a cheaper price then went to a private room closing the door. Layers of silk drapes hung elegantly from the ceiling covering the walls partly shielding the wall's heat, creating patches of black and the alchemically altered patterns in the wooden stage made from Purple Heart gently shimmered as heat was released from its surface.

He sat on the padded loveseat made from a soft anti slip fabric that faced the stage and was careful not to touch its surface with his skin, unsure of how clean it was then waited for the music to start. After his first experience he didn't have to wait long and made sure they knew that they weren't being paid to make him linger. He wasn't patient enough for the excitement, anticipation or titillation of the art of waiting. The gentle chimes and rhythm of the wind instruments introduced the dancer who was adorned in layers of body paint that shielded and accentuated her body heat highlighting her erogenous zones. She moved with a grace he'd never seen before, sure the other dancers were good, but she was great. In tune with the music her sleek body almost rippled and her strait shoulder length hair flared from the sudden shifts of her movement.

He was captivated, lost in his desire to touch, taste and consumer her. In his yearning he almost forgot why he was there then undid his pants and motioned for her to approach. She bound forward to the edge of the stage then arched forward flinging her hair over her face, but between the strands he saw murder in her eyes. She sprang off the stage landing inches from his legs and out of nowhere a knife was in her hand. Surprised he pulled his hand out of his pants and from behind a battle axe bounced off the top of his head. Before he could think he rolled off the love seat to stand facing his opponents. The dancer stabbed at him her knife deflected off his shield and the Troll bouncer with his crude, chipped battle axe backed away his expression was almost apologetic realizing their attempted assassination had failed.

Byron's pants fell around his ankles making him feel stupid which pissed him off more than their attempt to kill him. He grabbed the dancer's wrist with one hand while palm striking her face with the other. As she fell back he took her perfectly balanced ceramic knife then wondered where she had hid it during the dance. Feeling exposed he reached down and wiggled his legs while he pulled up his pants. The Troll looked at her then turned to run, but Byron dropped his infrared sight and summoned his power channeling the energy into a bone within his hand releasing bolt of energy that punched deep into the Troll's back. The Troll lurched forward off balance slamming into the wall. The Troll struggled to find his balance clawing at and ripping down some of the silk drapes as he collapsed to his knees. Justified and no longer feeling stupid, Byron lashed out with a stream of flame engulfing the Troll, controlling the flames intensity making the Troll's flesh scream and pop. The Dancer whirl around scrambling onto the dance floor, but Byron focused on his infrared sight, grabbed her ankle and pulled her back, spinning her around then stabbed the knife between her esophagus and jugular pinning her to the dance floor.

He looked at her face and was certain he had never seen her before, but her eyes burned with such passionate hate he couldn't help but feel aroused. No one has ever looked at him with such powerful emotion, he was enthralled. He wanted her and only her, no other dancer would do. He collapsed his shield so he could feel her soft skin and lean body against his. The stench of burnt Troll over powered the Elven incents and as the drapes burned, he grabbed her wrists tight then forced himself between her legs to finally take her.

Later, on his way out the Matron didn't look happy, but backed down once she looked into Byron's eyes. He knew that she had a part in his assassination, but didn't care. She now owed him and he didn't bother paying for Monique, or the mess he'd made. He stepped close grabbing the Matron's arm hurting her then whispered through clenched teeth that if Monique disappeared he'd do horrible things to find her again. After he made sure that she understood he left. Walking through the crowded streets, his head buzzed and all he could think about was Monique's eyes. In them he saw her intensity, power and passion that he'd have to cultivate and harvest. He didn't even realize that he had walked into his teacher's office until the room's lighting hurt his eyes and brought his sight into normal vision.

He squinted hating to come to this cold tomb that lacked any of the outside beauty. A series of recessed lights shone down robbing the walls of their patterns making them look empty and just black while the tacky cream colored tiled floor made his boots click with each step. His teacher, James Ashwood sat behind an ancient oak desk at the end of the room with two hard wood chairs facing him. Byron hated those chairs, always hurting his ass and creaking under his weight. James' desk was always kept bare except for a console and lamp. Today, James wore his short black hair slicked back accenting his designer Dark Elf suit made for his average, but thin build. He looked relaxed and comfortable nestled in his padded leather chair.

James looked at him then his blue eyes slightly widened. "What have you done?" he challenged. "You came here covered in blood and hooker paint."

Byron looked at his clothes not realizing the Troll had got blood spatter on him. "Don't worry. People would think I did this on purpose to make my heat look good, its fashion."

James chuckled. "Fashion," he mocked. "Some of these people have lived their whole lives in darkness and can spot blood splatter…" He shifted his gaze to his pants. "And semen a mile away."

He didn't like the way James was looking at him, like he had done something wrong. "It's Troll blood and Monique is not a hooker, she's a dancer. I killed that idiot Troll in self defense."

James regarded him for a moment. "You're losing it, Byron and you've made a lot of unnecessary enemies."

He waved away James' concern. "It's just the bouncer from a long time ago that I made eat his own eyes, besides everyone knows I'm with you and you'd want heavy compensation if someone took my head."

He sighed. "Byron, lately you haven't been professional and I've looked the other way a couple of times. Now your enemies are gambling that I'd look the other way when they come for you. The cost for my revenge on your head is dropping. This is getting serious."

Byron groaned hating politics and rules made by the weak to control the strong. "I'm an Alchemist, what can they do against me?"

James regarded him for a moment before answering, "Sometimes immortality can be hard on the soul. I've seen it before. A person survives while the ones they love die of old age. They end up aimlessly roaming the world stuck in the past while the world grows around them." His leather chair creaked as he leaned into it. "You've worked for me for a long time now and everything we've planned for is coming into focus. Another Purge is coming and the weapons to kill our kind will once again be available. I don't think Jax will forget that you killed his son and when he came for compensation, you refused to pay then killed his wife out of spite. That was bad business."

Byron cursed then rubbed his temple feeling a headache coming on. "I was high that day and no, I'm not tired of living."

"Is it the drugs? Is your head getting a little fuzzy?"

He cursed again. "I'm fine!"

"You're fine? You still have dead hooker all over you. It takes two seconds to break down the blood, cum and paint that's all over you. When I mentioned it, you didn't even bother. You look psycho."

James' ignorance was starting to get on his nerves, always talking down to him like a child. "It's Troll blood and Monique is a dancer. She's special. She's the only one for me now and I don't care what I have to pay to see her again. I have a plan. I'm going to make her love me."

"Are you listening to yourself? You need to stop, maybe spend some time in the sun."

"You mentioned our work, our plan, but it's all you. All I do is go here and there killing people and staring wars. I've been busy for the last five hundred years blackmailing, extorting and killing. Our plans," he repeated rolling his eyes. "I'm your puppet, lackey, minion, or whatever."

"Where is this aggression coming from? I thought you were on board. We're creating a new future for the world. You're not having fun anymore? Or are you acting out because you feel guilty?"

"Acting out? Stop treating me like a teenager. As for guilt, I just don't feel anything anymore and I don't know how to fix it. Things are just getting worse, but today…" He touched his chest. "Monique made me feel, I don't know what, but it was awesome."

James looked confused. "How did a stripper make you feel?"

"She's a dancer! She was already naked, there was nothing to strip," he corrected. "I needed a little relaxation after my meeting with my Slaver contact…"

"Wait," he interrupted. "You got the very important message I've been waiting days for, so important that I had it hand delivered, then went to a brothel instead of coming straight here?"

"I had the time before our meeting," he lied. "I was in a hurry to see you, that's why I forgot to clean up."

James closed his eyes and sighed heavily before looking at him. "I don't believe in experiencing anger, but sometimes you try my patience. Why do you bother lying? We've known each other for so long I can tell. Your lips twitch when you fib and that tells me you had no intention of seeing me right away. What did the message say?"

He pulled out the data stick and held it between his fingers. James had that fire in his eyes telling him something bad was about to happen. "I haven't looked at it yet."

James laughed through a cold smile. "You're now two steps away from pissing me off and I hate getting angry. It's bad energy that clamps down on my mind clouding my thoughts. See, right now, this is what I'm talking about. You're losing it. Did you even bring a data pad to read the stick?"

His face flushed hot. James had already had pissed him off, treating him like an idiot. What did it matter if he forgot a data pad? And if James wasn't such a dick he'd be able to remember things. Byron wanted to throw James' precious data stick as hard as he could and bury it deep in James' fore head to teach him a lesson. But, instead he walked up hating each click of his boots on the stupid floor and slid the stick across the table to him. James' dead eyes and cold smile set off Byron's instincts warning him that things have just become serious. A tinge of fear ignited within him. Maybe he should be worried, but the fear quickly faded leaving him empty. His thoughts returned to Monique and what she made him feel, filling him with longing.

James took the stick then inserting into his console and read for a couple of minutes.

Byron grew impatient watching James' eyes move. "Well? Is it good news?"

He shook his head. "No, it's tragic. We're so close to saving this world, but everyone around me is struck with some form of stupidity that I've never seen before. Cid, that ignorant bastard, instead of handling the mission himself, he hired an Ork Slaver to capture Sarah. Thank the stars she wasn't killed in the attack. She's now on her way to the new Slaver city, but he used a Ripper as payment. We need that gun back. First, I want you to meet with Cid and remind him that he still works for me. He needs to maintain a low profile and to stop giving away our weapons. If he fails to comprehend what you're saying, put the bad puppy down. Second, find the gun. Its existence in the world is going to cause problems. Kill anyone who's seen it, spoke about it, or even heard about it. And find out what has happened to Sarah."

Byron summarized his orders, "Go kill." Excitement for the hunt trickled through part of him, but for a second he remembered who he used to be before he met James, the Dark Elves and the drugs. Another feeling crept up from his belly. It was warm, irritating and make him want to think about what he was about to do.

James cleared his throat. "Is there a problem?"

"No," he replied. "Talk to Cid, find the gun, eliminate all those who can interfere with the plan and find Sarah." He took the warm feeling and crushed it, burying it deep in his darkest place.

Chapter

3

Kole leaned on the throttle speeding away from the wrecked barge, but no matter how far away he got he couldn't shake the dirty feeling crawling over his skin. To leave the slaves unprotected, though miss guided, left a sour taste in his mouth. And that woman Sarah, the way the other slaves looked at her, almost worshiping her, worried him. And worse, that "thing" told him that he wasn't Human when she's the frigging clone. She was even upset that he tried to rescue them, like he planned to ruin their lives as doe eyed slaves. He fumed in his thoughts and his anger told him he made the right choice as the last speck of the barge faded from view.

He slowed, extended the gear then landed. Tightening his grip on the controls, he released a long heavy sigh, draining the tension in his shoulders then set the alarm, putting the hauler into stand by. Feeling a sense of calm return, he unstrapped then instructed Eric to tidy up while he went out and assessed the damage.

He slowly walked alongside the hauler running his fingers over the plating remembering all the work he'd done to make his home look undesirable, wishing he could show the world the beauty in his machine. An unmodified hauler would've been severely damaged if not destroyed by the Slavers, but with the tender help of an Alchemist a frame could be fused into one solid piece and armor can be made dense with all the force directed to the places that can deal with impact stress.

He smiled to himself thinking he'd have to replace the fake armor that was blown off, more camouflage to show welds and corrosion. He then climbed up the front and touched the passenger side window, reconfiguring the impact resistant glass to remove the cracks then jumped down to examine the damage the Ork's weapon made in the armor plating. Thinking back to what his teacher had shown him, a weapon that destroys altered materials and Alchemists. He gently ran his fingers over the sharp jagged edges of torn metal then closed his eyes, pushing his awareness into the hauler looking the molecular programming of the metal plates. He strained his mind knowing he was touching the metal, but it alchemically looked void like it wasn't there. All his work was ripped away, erased, leaving nothing to work with. He tried, but couldn't manipulate the plating to patch his baby's wound and knew he needed clean materials to transmute. He pulled his hand back and ran his fingers through his knotted hair cursing the wind then thought back to when he was a child. His teacher had a weapon like the Ork's, but extremely weak, which Kole was grateful for. He was five, playing with some wood blocks minding his own business when he felt a pressure, the release of the energy within the weapon from somewhere behind him. The first couple of times he didn't understand what was happening then the pain would come, like having your guts ripped out and your skin tore off. It even burned for an hour afterward and instead of offering comfort, his teacher would say, "You should've moved." He learned fast to fear the weapon and to get out of its way.

Kole knew his teacher was old, but his body looked young with his long strait black hair pulled into a ponytail, his dark eyes looked cold against his tan skin. "This weapon," he lectured, "was made by the Alchemists of old before the Purge. Its science is long gone, but there will come a time when you'll see it again." He slowly shook his head lost in thought. "Most of these weapons, if not all have been destroyed over time, turned to dust, but if you see a new ones, know that a great evil is rising and the end of the world is coming."

Kole felt a chill run up his spine breaking him free from the memory. He looked into the sky at the waning sun and saw the blue formation of the mountains in the far distance. He frowned, thinking about the slaves who are waiting for either friend, or foe to find them and wanted to rush to the closest town and get the people there to rescue them, but the following thought of how dangerous it is to rush off into the night unprepared made him think twice. He felt jumpy and didn't like the feel the Ork weapon was giving him.

"A great evil," he whispered and watched his breath disintegrate in the wind. "Could it be Sarah, or the one that made her?"

He didn't want to dig up Eric's past especially when he was the guy that did him harm, but he knew what had to be done. He put his compassion aside like he did those years ago and filled himself with grim purpose then walked to the door opening it. Eric was bent over collecting the last of the pots with his cloak in a heap on the floor. "Eric, pass me a pot and grab your cloak." He couldn't let Eric's dismissive behavior slide. "Your cloak should be hung up. You need to take better care of your things." Eric huffed then grabbed a small pot and thrust it to him. Kole nodded thanks. "Come out, I have something to show you." He turned and focused on the pot alchemically reinforcing its metallic structure then threw it a fair distance away into the grass as Eric landed beside him. He then pulled out the Ork's gun and fired in the vicinity of where he thought it had landed, but missed.

They both felt the pressure, but Eric jumped away from Kole to evaluate the person pulling the trigger, like he was trained to do. "It's safe Eric," Kole soothed. "I'm not going to shoot you this time." Eric glared at him and forced himself to relax. Kole didn't want to think of the times he had hurt Eric, like when his teacher had shot him, but the act was necessary he told himself. He aimed at the spot where the grass wasn't uniform and squeezed the trigger exploding the pot in a flash of yellow light.

Eric groaned. "That was my favorite pot."

"Why did you give me your favorite pot?" Kole inquired, tucking the gun back into his belt.

"I didn't know you were going to blow it up," he whined. "And I wasn't going to give you a warped stupid pot."

Kole shook his head in frustration not wanting to argue. "Forget the pot. You remember the little gun I used on you when you were a child to teach you to avoid being hit?"

"I remember the pain, the hours of crying and that you said weapons like the little gun should no longer exist, which made me wonder why you hated me so much."

He groaned. "I never hated you. If I didn't learn about the pressure when I was a child we'd both be dead. An Ork Slaver in the middle of nowhere had this gun," he stated pointing to the gun's hilt protruding from his belt. "It's brand new and unless he found it perfectly preserved for the last thousand years someone out here made it." He paused to let the implications sink in. "Guns like this one were used to kill Alchemists during the Purge and my teacher saw this coming. Knowing this now makes me wonder if he was murdered because he knew something. When I found his exploded corpse draped over a heap of dead filthy pixies, the energy matrix of his body was void, like the hole in the front of our hauler. At the time I didn't understand how it could happen, but seeing the power of this weapon it all makes sense. If I could only remember what this weapon was called." He ran his fingers through his beard gently tugging, feeling the pull on his chin. "It was like terror, or render… no I remember, it's a Ripper. It's no coincidence that a clone and a Ripper show up at the same time. Something bad is coming."

"What are we going to do now?" Eric wondered.

"Get me a stupid pot so I can destroy this Ripper and safely release the programming within it."

Eric nodded then hesitated. "Why are you going to destroy it? If something bad is coming, won't you need it as proof?" he offered. "And as much as I hate it, it's a powerful weapon that we can use."

He placed his hand on Eric's shoulder feeling his cloaks scratchy fabric then pressed the point, "This is a weapon of fear and many people will want to do a lot of bad things with it. And no matter how careful we are at concealing this weapon, it will demand to be used."

"But, what if we hide it in the transport? It'll be use it to reassure our minds that it's there, if we ever need it. That way it's being used and we're all happy."

He laughed then shook his head. "No."

Later, satisfied that he had successfully destroyed the gun, Kole helped Eric clean up before he replaced the spent missile. With everything secure, they sped off toward the Human town of Winter Haven. The town used to be called Rivet Village, a small trader's outpost that provided a safe place to sleep for Elven merchants on their way inland to the Human cities and traders heading south. That was until a group of Anti-Alchemists took over, pushing out what they called "Altered Races," but to their credit they fortified the outpost making it grow into a village then a town, spreading their influence to the area. Now it's a safe haven for Humans, a pretty umbrella for racist scum.

Night came and they sped on, running dark like everyone else, not wanting to light the way and draw attention to themselves. Kole watched the screen at the passing terrain colored in the different shades of grey provided by the low light sensors. Beside him, Eric yawned and stretched the best he could in the confined passenger seat then undid his harness, climbing out of his chair to start his bedtime ritual by going to the small washroom beside the gunner's compartment. After he pulled his hammock across the galley and went to sleep. Kole continued to watch his screens as they rode along until he saw the dark rectangular shape of a walled town on the horizon. Knowing there may be a frosty reception he changed course turning south not wanting to get in range of their artillery then opened communications with the town's automated beacon. The com pulsed, buzzing until the round face of a dark haired man appeared. His huge bushy beard dominated the screen until he leaned back into his creaking chair revealing a white flag with a broken red cross within a circle and a dot at its center on hanging on the wall behind him. Kole always thought the Anti-Alchemist flag looked like an angry crosshair which he felt suited their beliefs.

"What can I do for you?" the man asked looking away, the light of a screen reflected off his face as his large shoulders moved with the rhythmic sound of typing.

Kole looked back at his screen watching for an ambush, not that he expected one so close to town, but it was more out of habit than paranoia. "I have news of a downed Barge with Humans on it." He sent the coordinates encoded into the transmission.

The man looked down his nose at him and continued to type. "We don't have anyone in the area traveling in a Barge."

Kole knew they kept in touch with those under their protection. "They were attacked about a week ago by Slavers and were rescued. I don't know what they were traveling in before that. They probably didn't even tell you they were coming."

He stopped typing and rolled his eyes. "We know a lot of things and have captured an image of your transport. It shows recent battle damage and our scans show that some of your plating isn't welded on which is proof of alchemy. We don't support Alchemists."

Kole glanced at the screen with a sour expression, knowing the town's sensors could've picked up the damage, but are not sensitive enough to pick up the conditions of any welds.

The man laughed. "You got me, I lied. We have records of you and your transport. You are the Alchemist, Kole and you travel with Eric, your apprentice. You have a good reputation in the wasteland for providing good service and excellent product. That's to be commended. You wouldn't believe how many Alchemists pump out junk and expect hard working salt of the earth Humans to take it." He looked at the other screen and read out loud, "Anyone in the area." He groaned hitting a single button Kole assumed was the backspace.

He didn't want to be baited into an argument, but didn't know why the man was being so condescending. "You've been spying on us?"

The man stopped typing, sneered at the screen and informed Kole, "We've been collecting information on your kind for over two decades."

Kole couldn't believe what he was hearing and the attitude of this arrogant bastard. "All you people do is sow hate and mistrust into the world upsetting the…"

"Balance," he mocked, interrupting him. "We know you believe that the Orks, Dwarves, Elves and Trolls are Human, but the truth is that, you're not. You only think you have a soul, that you're Human. But we're the only pureblooded Humans on this planet and we're keeping tabs on your kind. One day there will be another Purge and we'll cleanse the world in righteous fire returning…"

Hearing enough hate for one day, Kole cursed interrupting the man on his screen then growled, "Listen up tubby…"

The man gasped. "You did not just go there! I can't help my weight! I have a glandular problem." He leaned closer making his face appear larger.

Kole wished he didn't get so personal, but he need this guy who'd obviously never missed a meal in his life while the rest of the world starved, to cooperate. "I'm sorry. I'm trying to do the right thing, but you're all insane. I was wondering why the nut jobs back in the Slave Barge didn't want to be rescued by me and why they were giving me weird looks. It's because of guys like you get off on spreading hate."

"We don't care about the Barge," he balled. "We think it's a trap to lure us into an ambush. We know how your kind thinks. You're probably planning to feed us to Trolls."

"Now you're just being ridicules." Kole no longer wanted to be in the conversation and missed the silence of the open fields, but he told the slaves he was going to send help. "Why don't you go out there and see if I'm lying. You can add it to my record and pass it around to all your racist buddies."

The man leaned back in his chair seeming to recover from the personal attack. "That would be a waste of time and if it's an ambush, a waste of pureblood."

Sick of hearing the man's propaganda, Kole scoffed. "If you don't think the people are that important, you could always salvage the Barge before someone else does."

He looked thoughtful. "Fine, we'll check your report out and I'll put this conversation into or files." The screen turned black as he disconnected.

Tension in Kole's neck mounted giving him a throbbing headache making him wish he didn't care if they send help, but knowing there's a lot of hate in the world especially towards Alchemists, he couldn't add to it. Everyone blamed his kind for the collapse of civilization, but this blame shifting was getting old and no matter how much good he did, people seemed to keep pissing down his back. He couldn't beat the fairytales being told to children as they're tucked into bed about the wondrous cities of light and glass in a time long gone when Pirates, Slavers and Bandits didn't exist. A child's dream when humankind was one race before the time of manipulated evolution, or what is commonly called the "Rise of the Alchemists." That type of brainwashing never goes away quietly and the thought that the Anti-Alchemists keep personal records on all the Alchemists, threatening them with another Purge, just adds more fuel to the world's hate. Now just to heat things up, he found a Ripper on an Ork Slaver who just happened to bag some pure blood Humans who didn't want to be saved. Kole didn't like the crap he was wading into and speculated that's what the Humans want, to pick a fight with the Alchemists to show the world how dangerous they are so they could rally support under the banner of hate and fear to manifest another Purge. He shook his head not wanting to think of his kind as different because separation on any level breeds hate. His mood darkened and he attacked his thoughts in a different direction. You can justify anything and the Anti-Alchemists don't need public support to start killing, getting drunk on hate would be enough. Which reminded him why he hated politics, but the Ripper and clone were made by a powerful Alchemist. There's another player out there using them.

    He continued to speed over the grasslands entering a sparse forest. Kole yawned and his eyes grew heavy, but his anger over powered his logic refusing to get Eric to take over. Hours passed and fatigue wore away the dark thoughts as well as his headache and soon the morning rays of sunshine stretched across the forest piercing his tired eyes. The forest thickened forcing him to slow down until he found the remains of an ancient highway leading to a town.

    His com screen beeped as an automated beacon initiated contact. He touched the screen and a thin red headed man with a bushy mustache wearing a tan cowboy hat appeared. "Hello sir, welcome to Pine

View," he greeted with a drawl. "My name is Roy and we picked you up on our scanners heading our way. You look like a trading kind of fella and we want to encourage you to pop on by. We have many services that can aid you in your endeavors, or provide you with a safe place to rest." He looked at another screen. "Our remote sensors show that you've seen a bit of trouble and by listening to the oscillation in your engine, you could use a tune up." He returned his gaze to Kole. "What do you say, friend?"

Kole's foul mood lingered thinking that the man would never shut up, but was too tired to negotiate. "I'm Alchemist Kole and I do seek shelter. How much gel do you require?" His voice sounded rough in his ears.

Roy's eyes brightened and he took off his hat revealing a dome of curly hair. "An Alchemist you say? We haven't seen one of you for awhile. We charge four liters of projectile gel a night for one room and to start things off we'll provide a cash card as payment for a second jug, a total of eight liters. If you're looking to stay longer we could also use the raw materials to construct munitions."

Kole nodded. "The price sounds right, but I can also make the munitions."

He laughed. "Not that I don't trust you," he pointed a skinny finger at him, "but I don't. Part of our economy is based on building the stuff other people need. If you come along building everything, you'll take away all the jobs. You'll make what I tell you and you can stay."

Kole understood all too well. "There'll always be balance," he stated. "I won't disrupt what you good people have built here. So with all that out of the way, I'd like to stay for a couple of days."

He clapped his hands together in excitement. "Excellent. I'll have a cash card made up for you and a couple of gallons of water waiting for transmutation. We'll test the gel to see if its weapons grade, if not we'll have to come up with another form of payment. The last Alchemist that came through wasn't too bright and provided defective goods."

Kole could now see the walls of the town through the trees. "I'm coming up on our town, send me a map and show me where I can set up camp."

"Here you go." The com screen beeped again. Roy nodded. "I look forward to seeing what you can do." He ended the transmission.

Kole brought up the map and found the main entrance, glad he'd thought about visiting instead of passing through like he always had. He slowed, approaching the wall not wanting to get too close and be accused of scanning for weaknesses, remembering a tale of a rich town that had the best made walls and defenses. It attracted caravans of traders from across the land and was a nexus for all the races, but its wealth also caught the eye of several bandit hordes. The bandits knew they couldn't take the town, so they slowly infiltrated the city sabotaging their weapons and defenses making it ripe for the taking. The town was razed and its story told a hundred years later to warn people not to trust anyone, or look like a target.

Pine View's wall was a mess of concrete, bricks, steel plating and electrified stainless razor wire. It didn't look too bad to Kole and the gun entrenchments showed signs of some progress, but not enough to attract a serious threat. Guards patrolled the perimeter in enclosed lightly armored attack hover bikes that some call flying coffins. Rectangular shaped with a smooth body, flat bottom, curved top and armed with one cannon and two forward gun pods. He smiled to himself thinking about the bike he earned after his teacher had died. It wasn't as nice as the ones patrolling town, but there was something about zipping around the country side hugging the ground, it was the closest thing he'd ever felt to flying. Remembering looking out the arched front window straddling the bench seat and using his body to control the antigravity controls gave him goose bumps. He approached the huge main gate that was large enough to permit a full sized trade barge, but only opened enough to let him through. There were half a dozen other visitors in the allotted camp ground, different shapes and sizes of makeshift crafts, all aerodynamic in their own way, but most of them were large heavily armed trade vessels, larger versions of the Battle Barge.

Eric stirred, throwing his blanket over his head as he groaned at the light. "Where are we?" he murmured.

"Pine View," Kole replied reaching over and flicking the landing gear switch.

"We've never been here," he said now fully awake. He rolled out of the hammock, hit the floor with a slap then sprang up and looked out the front window. "Can we rent actual rooms where we'll have beds, maybe even bathtubs?"

The mention of bed reminded Kole of how tired he was. "A bed sounds good. An actual bath sounds better and we'll use two apartments in the visitor's building. It'll cost us double, but I'm sure Roy won't mind."

"I get my own room without you?" he gushed too excited to care if he was answered. "Who's Roy?" he quickly added.

Kole landed on the bare ground. "He seems like a nice guy, but we'll see his true face when we deal with him." He looked over his shoulder at Eric. "Lock everything down and set the sensors. Let's make sure no one tampers with our baby while we're in town." Eric nodded then spun on his heels heading to the gunner's compartment. Kole smiled at his sudden enthusiasm then adjusted his sensors and released his safety harness, glad to see Eric in a brighter mood. He pulled himself out of his seat then opened the door. A tall man with strait brown hair dressed in the town's green fatigues stood a short distance away holding a glass jug of water in each hand.

The man walked forward and placed the jugs on the floor just inside the door. "Here's the water."

Kole knelt then took them, placing them on the narrow small stove top. "There's a slight change. I'd like to use two, one bedroom apartments while we're here."

He nodded. "We can arrange that and if you transmute those jugs of water, I'll get another. Here's a card," he offered presenting a white card.

"Thanks," Kole said slipping the card into his pocket then closed the door. He picked up a jug and alchemically looked into the water at its molecular bonds. He tilted the jug holding its cool glass with both hands lifting it to eye level then waited, willing the transmutation to take place until the water turned a pale pink. He placed the jug back on the stove then glided his fingers along its contours of the second jug watching its water transform into high grade projectile gel.

Eric closed the gunner's door. "Did you get a card? We always get a card, right?" He cupped his hand in front of him greedily wiggling his fingers.

Kole groaned knowing exactly what Eric was thinking then decided he was old enough. He'd done his best to instill his knowledge into Eric and it was time to see if he could fly. He reached into his pocket then handed him the card. It was about time he caved to the demand, Eric had asked for the card in every town since he was thirteen. "If there's a guy out there with another jug, tell him I'm still transmuting. I'll be an hour."

"Sure," he beamed, staring at the card in disbelief. "I'm going to dump my extra clothes in my new room then make sure this card works."

Kole yawned thinking about a soft warm bed. "If you need me, I'll be sleeping." Then added as a second thought, "Stay out of trouble."

Eric opened the door and announced, "He'll be done in an hour." He jumped down and closed the door behind him.

Kole looked at the jugs then cursed not wanting to wait the hour, but wanted them to think it took a lot out of him, to appear less of a threat then cursed again realizing he'd have to wait another half hour on top of that to transmute the last jug. "Screw it," he whispered to himself, feeling the weight of his fatigue. "No one will notice." He opened the door and took the other jug transmuting it. The quality of the gel checked out and he was permitted to enter the town. He put his cloak away, grabbed his overnight bag and passed through the personal gate, noticing the absence of litter and debris. In a lot of other towns filth was a sign of a low or broken moral with people just looking out for themselves, not that he blamed them, but coming into a place with happy people filled with purpose made him feel good. The town was big with its cobble stone streets, well manicured lawns, brick houses of various sizes and fenced off anti-aircraft guns. A control tower stood in the center of town reaching high above all the other buildings surrounded by the militia's barracks and artillery units. The streets rippled out from there, running toward the downtown core consisting of the produce market, restaurant, pub, arms dealer, clothing and general store. Residential housing surrounded the core with the visitor's apartments overlooking the farmer's fields.

He walked along the sidewalk carrying his bag over his shoulder passing people who smiled and greeted him with a nod. They wore whole pieced clothing, not scraps sewn together sold to those who couldn't afford better. Even through his fatigue Kole felt their sense of community and knew if he made one person angry, they'd all share that person's opinion. He continued up a path across the grass to the apartments and found a man behind the front desk holding a key waiting to greet him. With everything out of the way he went into his apartment not caring about the dusty rose painted walls, linoleum flooring and kitchen with all the appliances or a living room with a pink flower pattern couch and matching chair. The bedroom was just as plain with a double bed covered with light grey blankets and an adjacent pine nightstand with a telecom sitting at its center. He dropped his bag at the foot of the bed, crawled onto its mattress wanting to take a second to test the pillow before he got undressed, but fell asleep.

Kole's eyes shot open, but he couldn't discern why he woke then the heavy pull of sleep beckoned him. His eyes closed then he heard a series of raps on his door. "Eric what are you doing?" he barked forgetting where he was then became alert. He cursed realizing it was still day time and that someone was knocking on the door. He got up feeling dirty from sleeping in his clothes, readied his dowel and slipped on his knuckle busters creating a shield before opening the door.

Roy stood in the hallway with a grim expression. His tan cowboy hat cast a light shadow across his face and over part of his beaded suede jacket that hung loosely on his shoulders. "Your boy got himself into a heap of trouble last night," he stated and held out a new pair of shoes.

Confused, he replied, "Last night, I just went to sleep, it's still light out."

"It's the next day. You must have been very tired yesterday from all that transmuting. Here," he said pushing the shoes toward Kole making him take them.

Kole awkwardly held them. He collapsed his shield, fumbling with the shoes while he put his knucklers and dowel away. "I don't want, or need these shoes."

Roy pulled up his expensive denim jeans and wiggled his foot inside his cowboy boot to loosen his pant leg. "The shoes are for Eric, he lost his. You see he drank to excess, got into a fight with an Ork youth then evaded my men while taking off his clothes and running through the streets naked. We decided to stop chasing him and let him run out of steam because no one really wants to catch a naked man. He ended up climbing into a dog house and passing out. The dog's name is Beth, she's pretty old and probably enjoyed the warmth, but he probably earned a few slivers when we dragged him out."

Kole closed his jaw not realizing it was hanging open. "Is he okay?"

He nodded. "Oh yeah, we wrapped him up and put him in the drunk tank, but he also lost your town credit card. We've collected a portion of his clothes and there was damage to the bar. He'll live, but may die from embarrassment because a couple of kids followed him around on his reign of terror with recording devices. It's already posted on the local net if you want to watch. That's the good news, the bad is I've drawn up a bill and you're not allowed to leave town until all your debt is paid."

Kole lowered his head feeling embarrassed for Eric. "Can we remove the recording?"

Roy put his clammy hand on his shoulder. "Don't worry. We have rules about what gets posted. They blotted out his genitalia."

Kole rolled his eyes. "That's not what I'm asking. Can you take it down?"

He slowly shook his head. "Not really. It's not offensive, just a guy running around making a fool of himself screaming at the top of his lungs that he's an Alchemist and one day he'll learn how to make wings and leave all of us sorry ass dirt chucking peasants behind. I think he meant our farmers."

Kole cursed.

He agreed. "That's what I said when I saw the evidence this morning. I feel for your boy, I really do, but there was also damage to a corn field…"

"No," he interrupted. "He's a good kid and there's no way he could've done that much damage." He pointed at him trying to sound angrier then he was, "You're trying to fleece me!"

"Watch the recording," he said then flashed a smirk. "There's also emotional damage done to Old Lady Mary who fainted. We thought she broke her hip hitting the ground the way she did, but she's okay." He took off his hat. "Poor gal."

Kole frowned trying to remain pleasant. "Enough. Give me the bill and tell me how much it will cost to remove the recording."

He smiled. "It's included on the bill. You look like a caring father who'd want an embarrassing night like that out of the public eye. Not that it's going to help since nothing new happens around here, so a juicy bit of comedy spreads through here like wildfire."

He looked at the bill. "It'll take me six months to pay this off."

Roy shook his head looking sad then clasped his hands together. "Another part of the bill is going to help heal the emotional damage of all the witnesses and a portion of payment is also included so you can live. We don't just need projectile gel. A man of your quality can do other things to quickly clear your debt."

Kole surrendered. "Take me to my boy."

He looked him over. "Did you sleep in your clothes? It's a bad habit to fall into, but while you're here we have a clothing store that sells high quality merchandise as you can tell by looking at our fine citizens. There's no need to hide who you are here, you could treat yourself better. Get yourself a nice hot bath, haircut, shave and a little pampering. Heck, we might even get you to make us some bolts of silk."

Another headache started to grow between Kole's temples. "Can we please go see Eric and don't worry we're not going to leave until our debt has been paid."

Roy backed into the hallway allowing Kole out to close and lock his door then they proceeded to walk down the hall. "I have no doubt.

You have a good reputation out here." Roy chuckled. "Even those Anti-Alchemist types said some nice things about you. That in itself speaks volumes."

Kole rolled his eyes then followed listening to the clicking of beads as the fringes of Roy's jacket swayed with each step. They walked out into the morning sunlight and moved down the streets watching small hover vehicles glide by. The police station sat behind the barracks at the center of town and Kole wasn't sure how to react to Eric. The boy wasn't hurt, but he could've lost control of his power even though Kole had only taught him the basics. Children under the right conditions have accidentally cause serious damage. Moving into the shade they arrived at a brick building with a steel door. Roy flipped a false brick open then punched a security code into the hidden console and waited as the door opened with a magnetic click. They walked down a long cool hall into a sparse office with a cement floor passing an armed guard sitting behind a green desk watching a monitor that displayed the interior of the cells. Bars enclosed six narrow cells each equipped with a steel toilet missing its seat, a steel sink and a narrow bed with a thin mattress. Kole and Roy came around the corner to find Eric sulking in his underwear sitting in the fetal position on the bed wrapped in a grey wool blanket. He was in one piece, but looked miserable with a black eye and messy hair. Kole stopped. He could smell a mixture of stale alcohol and the faint scent of vomit coming off of him.

Eric glanced up at Kole returning his gaze to the floor. "I'm sorry, it was an accident. I don't know what happened."

Kole nodded to Roy who pulled the keys from his pocket and unlocked the cell. "No more drinking for you until you can hold your liquor," Kole scorned realizing that Eric would need to drink to build up a tolerance so he could hold his liquor, but didn't care. "Do you know how much?" he paused choking on his anger. "Do you know how long?" he paused again wishing he could stop. "You lost all our money and now we're here for the next four to six months. What happened?"

Roy pulled on the bars opening the cell, but Eric wrapped himself tighter in his blanket. "I don't know."

"How can you not know? You were there and you're the one who did it." Kole released his anger in a long hissing sigh knowing he wasn't going to get a straight answer out of him. "Roy, can I get another cash card so I can buy him some new clothes?"

Roy nodded. "I kind of figured you'd need a new one. I took liberty of adding this to your bill," he said then calmly walking back down the hall whistling a sad tune.

Kole ignored Roy, annoyed at the man's opportunistic behavior.

"I bet you wish you never bought me," Eric blubbered.

He looked at him stunned then shook his head. "Bought? Is that what you think?"

Eric glared. "I don't have to think it. It's what happened." He stood, his hand clasping the blanket draping around his shoulders. "Are those for me?" he asked pointing to the shoes Kole forgot he was carrying.

Kole handed him the shoes wondering how long Eric carried this resentment. "You've seen enough of the world to know how things work."

Roy came around the corner holding a new card. "Here you go," he said handing it to Kole. He looked at Eric. "I don't want to see you in here again." He smiled looking back to Kole. "Take your time and leave the way you came." He turned and sauntered back down the hall.

Eric finished tying his shoes. "Can we go?" he pleaded.

Kole didn't want to continue their conversation in the cells and motioned to Eric to follow. He led him outside and down a sidewalk into the warm sun away from eavesdroppers then stopped. Eric almost walked into him squinting from the light. Kole turned to him and sympathized saying, "You're not alone. I was traded too. The sooner you let the crap in your life go, the sooner you can move beyond it. I'm not trying to be a bastard and it sucks you've had to grow up faster in some ways, but you have to understand what you're doing." He pulled out the bill.

Eric pointed to the piece of paper. "Why are you catering to that?

You can make a whole lake of projectile gel and get out of here."

"If we did that the Commoners would figure out that we don't need them." He held up the paper. "This bill doesn't matter and it's all part of the game. They think they have us cornered, look around, the townsfolk don't care that you made a total ass of yourself. All they see is an opportunity to get an Alchemist to work for them, to be normal like anyone else. They bring us water, we make it look hard to do the small things, they think we're being helpful and everyone gets along. The truth is we need them because they're our humanity. You see there're two sides to separation. They'll fear us and we'll lose all empathy toward them. We'll lock ourselves away in magnificent buildings surrounded by anything you could ever want until we repeat the past. The Commoners will bind together out of hate and fear to create another Purge. In the end, another set of people like us will be standing here in a more desolate world having the same conversation all over again."

Eric rubbed his eyes complaining, "If none of this is real, why did you get so angry with me over the money I lost?"

"You have so much power in you, but you have no control. I haven't even started teaching you in case you throw a tantrum and incinerate a city."

His face soured. "Like when you incinerated the man at the Barge the other day? I saw what you did. What else do you have in your little bag of dirty tricks?" Eric asked in a petulant tone.

Kole shook his head hoping he'd get him to understand. "You can get accustom to having power flowing through you and in a split second a stray thought can unleash terrible destruction. I can't say I lost control, but in a flash of a second I couldn't see him properly with the sun in my eyes, so it triggered a fight or flight response," he reasoned. "There's a lot more at stake here than just us and sometimes I forget to treat you like a regular person. Burning that guy was a stupid thing to have happen. I dropped my shield leaving myself vulnerable. We can only use two tools at one time and your body is the most important tool you have. It's a limitation and some people know it. Under the right circumstance we can be hunted down and slaughtered, granted it would take a lot, but it can be done. We also need sleep."

"You!" deep voice shouted.

Startled, Kole turned to see a young male Ork Eric's height standing across the street. The Ork spoke with a slight slur, but didn't have an Orkish accent and wasn't dressed in the traditional hides. The Ork wore dirty combat boots, tan cargo pants and a black T-shit that stretched across his broad chest. His black hair, a symbol of Orkish virility was even shaved down into a short buzz cut.

Eric turned and let out a surprised scream then pointed at his eye. "You did this to me!"

The Ork flashed a justified grin. "You grabbed my sister's ass and told her that you wanted to take her home and bounce her like a pleasure girl in a Dark Elf harem," he said then punched his fists together. His red eyes gleamed menacingly in the sunlight. "You're a slippery little guy," he sneered. "You can't shed your clothes to escape this time."

Eric raised his hands in surrender, dropping his blanket around his feet and Kole was glad he was wearing underwear. "Can we make a deal?" he implored.

"I'll take a pound of flesh and a quart of blood to go. How's that for a deal?" he mocked grinning, showing more of his lower jaw canines. "Please," he added finishing with a low growl.

Eric flashed his best smile then bolted, sprinting down the sidewalk.

The Ork grunted then followed in a slower, but even pace.

Kole cursed. "At least he didn't hide behind me," he reassured himself knowing the Ork probably wouldn't kill Eric then thought about what might happen if things went sideways. He groaned wanting Eric to handle it, but his dark thoughts made him run after them, chasing them away from the core into the market. Stunned shoppers quickly parted for the screaming half naked man frantically running through the crowd almost tripping over a stack of bagged potatoes. Some shoppers shook their heads in disbelief, others laughed, while the younger adults shouted for him to run faster. Kole ignored their snide comments directed at him for being a disgraceful parent and the shouts that he should discipline his miscreant son. Kole ran around the corner of the general store and found Eric standing over the unconscious

Ork. He skidded to a stop almost tripping over the Ork then slammed into Eric's clammy chest. He pushed off Eric of then took a step back looking at the Ork worried that Eric had done something drastic. "What did you do?" he croaked between laboring breaths afraid the Ork was dead.

Dazed, Eric stared at the Ork. "I stopped." He took a moment to breath. "He attacked and I did what you trained me to do. I think I knocked him out."

Kole gestured to Eric to move away then knelt, checking the Ork's pulse. "He's alive," he said. "Go back to the apartment, get dressed and wait for me. I'll wake him." Eric nodded and ran down the alley. Kole regained his composure taking a moment to look at The Ork's numerous small scars from cuts and burns on his hands, arms and face then lightly slapped The Ork's cheek until his eyes fluttered open. Kole stood then backed away giving him room.

"What happened? Where's the runt?" he asked then sat up, rubbing his chin.

"I sent him to his room," Kole said. "Are you going to be alright?"

"The little bugger beat me," he whispered to himself. He looked up at Kole saying, "You never know how a fight is going to go. He was lucky and I didn't even get a chance to bite him."

Confused by his calm attitude he wasn't sure what to say. "You don't seem to be angry anymore."

He stood then dusted himself off. "I was never really angry, besides your boy's very offensive." He smiled. "It's only a matter of time before I'll get a rematch and then I'll taste his blood."

Confused Kole watched the Ork walk away. "What is wrong with the kids these days?" he pondered. His stomach rumbled telling him how hungry he was. He glanced around making sure he was still alone then closed his eyes feeling his body's needs then pulled a black lemon flavored protein ball the size of an orange from the air. He shrugged dismissing his thoughts then took a bite of the ball before walking to the apartments. His mood picked up with something in his belly and rethinking the day he decided that things weren't as bad as they had first seemed. No one had died. He asked the clerk sitting behind the front desk which room Eric was in then walked to a door then knocked. Eric answered looking depressed dressed in his second set of mismatched clothes. Eric dramatically spun around swaying with each step then slumped on the couch at the end of the living room with his hands stuffed between his knees. Kole walked in not surprised that their rooms were identical and closed the door behind him.

Eric took a deep breath then stammered, "Did I hurt him?"

"I don't think so." He thought for a moment then added, "He's an odd Ork. I don't think you even hurt his pride. What happened between you two last night?" Eric took a deep breath, but was interrupted by a knock on the door.

They gave each other looks saying neither was expecting anyone then Eric got up and opened the door a crack then slammed the door bracing it with his body. "He's come to kill me!"

"What?" Kole motioned for him to move. "Let me?" Eric looked uncertain, but backed away allowing Kole to open the door just wide enough to fit his face.

The Ork casually stood in the hall with his arms crossed. He cocked an eyebrow and nonchalantly said, "Hey."

"Hey," Kole responded. "Can I help you?"

He changed his posture and dropped his arms to his sides. "Last night we didn't start things on the right foot. My name's Nick."

"Nick?" he puzzled. "That isn't an Orkish name."

"Yeah, it's a long story. The name was given to me. I wanted something cool translated from Ork like Blood Fang or Death Fist, but all I got was Nick and it kind of grew on me."

"Well Nick, I'm Kole and…" he said then nodding toward Eric. "You met Eric."

"I had fun today and last night. I was hoping Eric would come out and have some drinks with me and my sister, nothing sinister, promise."

"One sec." Kole closed the door.

Eric stood slack jawed. "Is he serious? He just wants another shot at me."

"Nah, I don't think so. He's a little odd, but I think his intent is good. You should go out. In fact, here," he insisted pulling the second card out a belt pouch and forcing it into Eric hand. "Try not to lose this one."

"What?"

But before Eric could refuse, Kole opened the door and pushed him into the hall. He flashed a smile at Nick then shut the door, locking it. He pressed his ear to the door listening for fighting thinking about Eric's emotional development, happy to have found the town he was looking for.

Chapter

4

Byron left James filled with a renewed purpose, but with each person he bumped into, grinding his way back to his transport, dissolved his resolve. The crowd was thick today, he didn't care why, but they were beginning to piss him off. He stretched his awareness to the outer edge of his shield wondering how many people were sticking poisoned blades into his back testing him as they brushed by. He thought about the weird look James gave him. It told him that it's only a matter of time before James ends him. A part of him didn't care, but a louder part didn't want to go out at the hands of that evil prick. Making him feel stupid and worthless, it was James' fault that his life had turn into crap. But James is the strongest Alchemist on the planet, how could he be ended? Byron's anger sputtered out and all he could think about was the fire in Monique's eyes. He wanted to see her again, gather her into his arms and tell her that everything was going to be all right.

He pushed his desire for Monique aside and entered his small transport, an alchemically made flying cockpit mounted to a powerful engine. It was long and narrow made from a black metal that Byron had dreamt up. He slipped into his plush seat that at times he used as a bed then turned on the monitor setting it to standby. Data filled the screen telling him that no one was foolish enough to strap a foreign object to his temple that he kept immaculately clean, for his Godhood. He smiled, glad he didn't have to teach a lesson of pain to some mundane, instead he brought his second home to life, turning on the very best electronics and enhanced sensors. He didn't bother with defenses and the thought of using weapons in battle sickened him, he was the weapon, the hand of death that destroyed people by will alone. Warmth filled him as he became aroused at the thought of leaving a small town in ruin then Monique's eyes crept back into his mind, but she'd have to wait till his return.

He left the city traveling past the lava fields out of the city's sensor range then slowly pushed back on the throttle. He knew the terrain and found his favorite hiding place, a small dip in the land large enough to hide in then lowered the landing gear coming to a rest. He tried to push the thoughts of Monique away, but she was compelling him to return to the city. He could have her and she would love the real him that's lost in the darkness within, but James was in the way. He wanted to turn around and return to the city. His fingers tightened around his controls as he fought to calm himself down remembering that he had to do a few tasks. He needed to clear his mind and think of a way to do those tasks without traveling away from Monique. He wanted her more than he could handle, but his mind was filling with the noise of James' voice cutting him down. His mouth became dry and perspiration built on his forehead. He let his fingers find a secret compartment beside his chair and pull out a small baggy full of green powder, a steel card and a black obsidian disk. His hands trembled as he poured some of the powder onto the disk. He let out an excited exhale while forming the pile into a line then held the disk up to his face and snorted the powder. In his youth Byron believed that there was an art to Alchemy, a beauty that's personal in everything you do and his dealer made the best drugs, a talent that he no longer cared about. He dropped his hands to his lap, closed his eyes and let the cool drug roll down the back of his throat.

Multicolored triangles swirled on the back of his eyelids, a dance that filled his eyes and he knew to keep his eyes closed to avoid the side effects. He didn't want to see the thick white trails his hands made, or his environment vibrate while it felt like his skull was being ripped open. His body was heavy and if he moved, it'd feel like his limbs were mud sliding off a mountain resulting in him vomiting. So he waited to be pulled out of his body and be taken away from his pain and problems. Then it happened, he was in another place floating among the stars hallucinating. James drifted below him through space on a small island made of rock and dirt. James lifted his hand and the Earth the size of a beach ball appeared before him.

James grinned, clinched his fist and commanded, "Burn." The Earth burst into flames. He thrust his hands downward and his clothes rippled off of him like water. James, now naked and erect grabbed the flaming sphere, sinking his fingers into it then impaled on his penis. He pounded his hips against the world till the flames died and the planet turned into chocolate cake which James devoured while hysterically laughing.

Confused, Byron whispered, "What in the?"

James stopped and looked up at him. He was drifting further away, but when he spoke it sounded like his words traveled through a tunnel of rushing wind, "You know what I'm doing. For a thousand years I've made war with all the other races, but Human."

Byron wanted to back away, shake away what he was seeing, it wasn't a normal trip. He felt tingly inside and there was a high pitch hum in his ears. To escape, he managed to open his eyes. His cockpit vibrated, everything was fuzzy and the lights from the consoles painfully penetrated his skull. He moaned and brought his heavy cold hand to his face. A thick clear tracer followed as it felt like half his body was falling off. He leaned to the side and vomited with painful heaves, wishing he ate something before he threw up. Finished, he wanted to wipe his chin, but was pulled back into darkness.

He tripped that he was in the brothel, standing in a private room waiting for Monique to begin. He smiled feeling warmth in his chest and when she came out in body paint he stopped himself from jumping onto the stage to embrace her, but she walked funny, slightly off. His smile faded.

She looked at him with empty eye sockets and spoke with James' voice, "Do you think I would let you be with her?" Her skin grew hot and sparks popped from her flesh releasing flames that enveloped her body rolling up and across the ceiling incinerating the room.

The room fell away to stars, but Byron's eyes still hurt. He was floating in the void of space staring into a bright white sun. He closed his eyes, but realized that they were already closed. He forced his eyes open and was back in his transport. He vomited again with deep heaves, but had nothing to throw up. "Poison," he whispered then tried to create a pitcher of water, but couldn't focus his energy. His cockpit was fuzzy and the lights were too bright. He closed his eyes and tripped that he was back in James' office sitting on the ass buster chair looking into James' blackened eyes.

James leaned back into his chair then brought his hand up resting his fingers together. "I said this before, but you never listen, foolish man. There are no secrets within the Universe, you just have to ask the right question and be strong enough to carry the answer within you."

"What does that even mean?" he implored. "It doesn't matter. I'm going to die in my transport covered in puke."

James smiled. "It looks that way, but if you dig deep enough, past all your emotional garbage you might find the drive to survive and I'm saying, true knowledge is power. Everything is vibration and when something powerful is added to you, it changes you. If you have the strength, it will trigger self evolution, but if you don't, it will crush you, perhaps turning you mad."

"I have the drive to survive and when I do, I'm going to look at my stash, see who altered my drugs then kill them."

"That's one way to go. Do you know why Karma is such a party pooper?" He frowned.

Byron moaned. "I'm sure I'm poisoned and this isn't real, but you sure lecture like James."

"You have seen knowledge and it has crushed you. The life you're living is destroying you and your Karma will echo into your next lives until you stop avoiding your crap and render your soul into gold."

"What the hell are you talking about? I'm sick of your shit. I might just die so I don't have to listen to your crap anymore." He closed his eyes whispering, "Wake up."

"Everything is vibration including your deeds and what you think you know. It is all the totality of your soul."

"I'm not interested. I want to wake up."

James agreed then said, "Some of my words are not for you Byron. What I've said has become a part of you that will travel through time into your next lives until they find you ready. Be careful what you add to yourself."

Byron woke vomiting onto his lap. Through the heaves he felt a warm trickling between his legs and smelled the stench of puke, but didn't understand what was happening. He peeked through his tear soaked eyes as his body finished its rhythmic motion and realized how close to death he was. He moaned then whispered, "Water. I need water." A voice in his mind replied, "No you don't. Just rest and you'll be okay." A string of drool poured out of Byron's mouth as he tried to move, but his body fought him. He cursed then pushed his will through a layer of crap that was hijacking his body to force himself to sit up. "I need water," he moaned calling upon his primal will to survive and forced a glass of water to manifest in his hand. He hungrily consumed the water then tried to put the glass on his console, but his arm created a thick clear trail that made his head spin. The glass fell off the edge of the console, bounced off his knee and landed at his feet. He closed his eyes not wanting to throw up the water he fought for then slipped into another hallucination.

He was in darkness looking at a naked overweight bald man sitting at a banquet table gorging on food. Byron watched as the man violently shoveled handful after handful of food into his filthy face. The man's bulging eyes shifted from the food to meet his, but his hands didn't stop grabbing the food that was now a mixed pile resting against his belly. "You disgusting pig," Byron spat realizing that the Pig lived within him, devouring his thoughts and feelings. He then understood that the Pig was the one hijacking his body trying to kill him. He stared into the Pig's eyes wondering how much of his life was actually his and how much was influenced by the Pig. "What have I done to myself?"

He woke and threw up the water, thankful he had something in his stomach. "I need to move," he said. His body didn't move. "Relax you don't need to go anywhere." Hearing the voice again put a picture of the Pig in his mind. Just the thought of that bag of crap winning pissed him off. He clenched his teeth and pushed through the Pig's influence forcing his body to move. He ignored the trails and his spinning head to pull himself out of his chair. He fell and hit the cold floor, but he refused to give in pushing himself onto his knees. He sat slumped against the wall summoning more strength to stand so he can get to the door. He took two deep breaths then stood only to stumble to the hatch slamming his hand against its release. The hatched opened and he fell, landing on his face. A flash of light and pain filled his head. He cursed and his mouth filled with dirt. He choked then rolled onto back spitting out the soil. He thought his eyes were closed, but it was either night or he could no longer see. "No," he said. "I'm not going to die like this." He rolled onto his belly and crawled out of his hiding spot forcing his body to come alive to fight the poison. Gaining momentum he crawled into the fetal position and looked within, summoning alchemical energy to negate the toxin feeling the wave of life return to his aching body.

He rolled onto his back and sprawled out staring into the night sky. He'd never seen the stars so bright or the taste of the night air so clean and crisp. Enjoying the moment of survival, he pushed away the dark thoughts of revenge because he decided that he had enough time to find and brutally kill all those responsible. He laughed, for the first time he knew himself and felt peace.

Chapter

5

Kole woke with a sore back, not used to a soft bed and thought about how much of his time he'd spent in a hammock, but was grateful nothing happened during the night that'd add to his bill. After stretching he sat on the edge of his bed then reached into his overnight bag and grabbed a ration pack. After eating he swept the crumbs off the bed then went back to his hauler to erect a walk in tent beside it, creating a place where he could do his transmuting in private. He'd just finished setting up a fold out table when he spotted Roy through the tent flap walking toward him. Kole didn't expect a face to face thinking that they'd chat over the com about what was needed then remembered he'd forgotten to bathe.

"Good morning," Roy said tipping his hat, stopping at the mouth of the tent. Kole nodded a greeting. Roy continued, "I'd like a two of bolts of silk transmuted today. I'll have the cotton bolts brought here for you."

"Cotton to silk," Kole said hoping he stood far enough away not to be smelled. "I can also do bamboo. It's soft, antibacterial and exotic. You can roll it up, throw it at the bottom of a bag, pull it out later and it won't stink of mold."

Roy stepped back, leaned against the hauler and thought about it.

"I don't know if I can sell it to the tailor, or how difficult it is to use. I'll tell you what, make me one of each and I'll base the price of the bamboo on what my guy says."

He nodded. "Fair enough, I'm sure your tailor will love it. Is there anything else?"

"I've heard some good news from our trading caravan up north. The projectile gel you made for us two days ago fetched a good trade. We'll also want more of that quality."

Kole laughed at the hypocrisy. "You traded the gel I made to the people who hate everything alchemical. They're the very people who blame my kind for destroying paradise."

Roy shrugged not seeing a problem. "They didn't ask where it came from, I'm sure they know because the technology to make the gel is lost. Besides they're not stupid." He chuckled. "You buzz by their town heading our way then all of a sudden we have extra gel to pass along. You know how it is. They tell me what they need and what they'll trade for it and I get it from you. You're helping two towns stay out of the hands of the Slavers."

Kole frowned, wanting to tell Roy to shove his system up his ass, but knew it was just his hurt pride welling up. "I just don't like being shunned from a town then used, but I guess it's just my kind's lot in life to draw people together, even if it's out of hate."

Roy smiled and walked closer to place a comforting hand on his shoulder, but stopped then took two steps back. "People like to live their lives under a certain light and your presence casts a shadow on them." He waved his hand brushing the conversation away. "Forget about them, I know what'll cheer you up. At the general store a woman sells scented soap and bath oils that she claims can pull the stress right out of you. After you're done today, pick up some freshly brewed beer and soap then have yourself a warm soak." He smiled waiting for acknowledgement.

Kole laughed at Roy's polite way of telling him he stank. "You're right," he concluded releasing his wounded pride and put on his game face. "We Alchemists enjoy serving society and helping more than one town at the same time is a bonus."

Roy rubbed his hands together in excitement. "Like ripples in a pond." He grinned then pointed at him saying, "I liked you from the first moment I saw you and I'm a good judge of character. You're helping out a lot of people and everyone knows it. I'll send the supplies with some extra water, bricks for ingots and steel to be made dense. It'll keep you busy for a while and as your reputation grows here you can make some money on the side doing odd jobs for our citizens." He turned and walked away with a bounce in his step.

Kole didn't have to wait long before his tent was half filled with materials, but all he thought about was Eric and how much he'd grow here. He foresaw himself getting wealthy within the walls of the town, but wasn't sure if he could handle the confinement. He shook his head, closed the flap on his tent and transmuted the two bolt of cotton before Eric showed up, opening the flap and walking in. It took Kole a moment to recognize him clean shaven with his hair cut and wearing new clothes. Unable to shake his surprise, Kole blinked thinking it was a trick of his mind, but Eric was still there in his jean jacket, black shirt, jeans and black steel-toed boots.

Eric smiled. "Nick isn't a bad guy. He has a friend named Kyra who picked all this stuff out for me today then called me a denim warrior. She even took me to a barber that was tucked away in an alley beside the bakery. Did you know this town also has a gambling den?" Kole's expression soured then he quickly added, "We didn't go in, I know it's bad." He smelled the air. "Speaking about the barber, I can show you where he is. After a bath you can get cleaned up, maybe even meet a nice woman."

Kole dismissed his hint, nodded then chose his words carefully not wanting to upset Eric and create a fit of rebellion. "Gambling, like everything else is good in moderation. Unfortunately people can accuse us of cheating, or even make it look like we were cheating so they can extort our abilities. It's not hard to transmute cards into what you need and they make sure they point that out, but if you're interested in learning how, play with a group of friends or people who you trust."

He shrugged. "I don't want to gamble anyway, but I was thinking about this." He reached into his pocket, pulled out his cash card and held it between two fingers. "What stops anyone from adding to this card?" he asked. "Could someone buy the whole town?"

Kole thought about it, remembering his experiences in different towns with similar systems. "The economy in this town is its own little world and for arguments sake let's say Roy runs it. You can pick a philosophy, but the economy isn't about money, it's about bringing order to chaos. Look around at all the unified people who have common goals." He pointed to Eric's card. "And that piece of plastic is a physical representation of an account on a computer's mainframe where a program watches the amount of money in circulation and if the flow falls below a certain percentage, it'll give Roy some money to inject into the town's economy. There's only so much money in circulation and there'll be hoarders sucking it all up, so the economy isn't about population, but is affected by it. The town has ways of hiding how the economy works and scavengers that go into the waste sell what they find to Roy. Roy then gives them money that can only spend here, which increases the flow. Some people may not have work or be able to, so Roy implemented a welfare system which also injects new cash into the system. It's a physiological circle and if people don't see money flowing into the town hall, but only see it going out, the system collapses because people will think that Roy is making it up to trick them. If the system collapses the money will no longer hold any value in the mind of the masses and to prevent this they have town tax on sold goods. Now getting back to counterfeiting, the reason they want to prevent it is not because it upsets the economy. Added money just winds up being horded anyway. It's because if counterfeiting isn't stopped, more people will do it until money doesn't have any physiological value."

Eric put the card into his pocket. "You're saying the economy is an illusion?"

Kole disagreed. "It's an adequate, but necessary system that manifests a united frame of mind. Without it people would fall back into bartering for the essentials, but at that point you lose mass unity. If this economy here collapsed who'd have time, or the desire to clean the streets? If someone needed food, but had nothing to trade, they may turn to theft and once down that road it's hard to come back. In the end, there'll always be chaos and corruption, but this system is built to fit most personality types. A common goal, or enemy will unify the masses and acquiring money is a strong objective."

"So it's about controlling the masses?" Eric asked trying to see the point.

"No, more like guiding them, but think of Human history. How did this system evolve? It's built to increase and unify the population, but also creates division within it. We can talk about this another time. I've finished my work for the day and was thinking you'd like to practice your alchemy on a cup of water."

Eric brightened. "Sure, I'd like that. What should I turn the water into, fuel, gel or booze."

Kole grabbed a cup off a pile of materials and dipped it into a bucket, filling it with water then placed it on the table. "I was thinking of turning the water into different color…" He looked at the multicolored patches on his pants then pointed to a triangle piece of burgundy. "Like this one."

Eric nodded. "Sure I watched you transmute before, it shouldn't be too hard."

"Remember you were born with the ability. All you have to do for now is see the color in your mind and find the part of the water that'll be changed to suit your needs. The rest will take care of itself. Transmuting is an art, a reflection of the Alchemist's soul and if you're not properly balanced, it'll be reflected in whatever you alter. So if you made something and I knew you, I could tell you made it, like a finger print. The ability is also a product of your mental state, the last Alchemist that passed through town wasn't too bright and his product was garbage, Roy made a point of telling me, but for now he's happy with my work. Now, give the water a shot and take your time."

Eric stepped forward and placed his hands on the cup while Kole watched him interact with the water, mentally poking, probing its essence, clumsily grabbing at it. Kole quietly stepped forward, not wanting to break Eric's concentration and looked into the cup at the colorless water. "You can't control, or make it happen. You have to allow it to," Kole suggested.

Eric strained. "That doesn't make sense. I've seen you do it hundreds of times. How can I change something by allowing it to be?" A bead of sweat gathered running down his temple.

"You'll understand later, but since everything is connected to your personal well being, your abilities are slightly angry. To get better you'll have to clean yourself up emotionally, doing so will teach you about balance and responsibility, besides when you watch me your mind interprets what it thinks is happening not necessarily what is. Perception is a window and we can only see what is filtered through the glass."

Eric slammed his hands onto the table in frustration almost tipping the cup. "That's all you talk about! Balance this and that, but I want to feel." He turned and clutched his chest. "I know you're trying to protect me, but I have to learn some things on my own, be my own man and do my own things."

Kole knew that eventually he'd have to allow Eric to make his own mistakes and grow up. "When you're ready," he soothed. "I'd be happy to show you more, but remember you're blessed and cursed." He watched Eric for a moment then decided it was time to let him go and trust he'll survive. He smiled. "Tell me about the girl?"

Eric relaxed leaning against the table. "It's a horrible story, but she says it made her tough. Her mother was in a trading caravan that got raided and in the carnage was captured then later sold into slavery. She escaped after Kyra was born and fled to a city on the east coast where she gave Kyra up to a foster home. Kyra grew up with a lot of orphans, but didn't want to talk about it. She later escaped with Nick and together they learned to survive." He changed the subject saying, "People in town had their fun poking fun at me, but now say they've seen worse. They mainly ask if were thinking about staying."

"Tell me about Nick," Kole said in a cheerful voice, but the whisper of paranoia erupted in the back of his mind. He hoped that they weren't using Eric to gain access to free alchemy.

"Nick is half Ork and believes that his mother was Human because he grew up in a Human foster home. He now owns a modified trading vessel that they used to get here."

Kole smiled. "And what are they doing here? Are they working for Roy?"

"Right now they're scavenging to buy supplies. Nick also wants to come by and hire you to inspect their vessel. He said it's not the best, but they couldn't afford much and that it's badly damaged. He tried his best to fix it, but said his welding was just good enough to get them here. He also said there are fractures in the plating and a major crack in the frame. He knows it won't survive a heavy assault, so it's built for speed like ours."

"Sure, he can come by," he said sounding supportive.

"Really, I'm surprised. I figured you'd tell me that they were using me to get free help, or steal from us. I'm glad we're going to stick around for a little while instead of heading back into the wilderness."

Kole laughed trying not to look guilty for having those thoughts. "You're your own man and I trust you," he encouraged. "I'm happy that you met some good people and I can't wait to see Kyra. I'm done here, but I can wait for Nick to come by, so I can check his vehicle."

"Perfect," he beamed. "I'll tell him right away. I'll be in the pub, but don't worry I won't drink too much." He held the flap opened and the cool outside breeze purged the warm stale air refreshing the tent. Eric turned flashing Kole a thankful smile then left.

Soon after, the sun was higher heating his work area, but Kole relaxed into the warmth. He waited becoming board then looked for amusement. He picked up the cup of water looking into it then transmuted it into Orkish Ale then back into water. He poured the water back into the bucket then put the cup down. It wasn't long before Nick announced his presence outside the tent prompting Kole to open a flap and invite him. He waited for the flap to close before he spoke. "I'm happy you came by. Eric has told me a little about you and said you have a problem with your vehicle's frame."

Nick gave a slight smile and a shrug then looked around the tent. "The local mechanics told me that it's not worth fixing and to junk it." He frowned. "I can't do that. It's our home. We can gut it and turn it into whatever we want once we get some funds. It has potential."

Kole smiled relating to him. "There's no harm in me taking a look at it."

Nick agreed and held the flap open for him then led the way toward the town's vehicle entrance. They passed a couple of sharp looking two story heavily armed trade crafts. The crafts rested almost identical with their faded paint in shades of yellow and orange, the colors of their caravan. Their hulls, peppered with impact scars and burns from a recent battle had very little rust, signs of a successful merchant. They were new additions since Kole had arrived. They also passed a medium transport that looked in good shape, but when they came around the corner, Kole flinched. A rundown junk heap sitting on broken uneven landing gear lay before him. He hoped it wasn't the one, but Nick stopped and smiled warmly at it. It was a smaller version of a battle barge with mixed patches of color dotting its rust pitted hull. Patches of poorly welded scrap made up its armor and Kole wasn't sure if the scrap was there for protection or to keep the hull from buckling. On a good note, it had most of its weaponry except for its left side gun which had been patched over. At first Kole, wanting to give the benefit of a doubt, thought the rest of the loose fitting junk was camouflage, but on a closer inspection it was as it appeared. "Where did you get this?" he asked, trying to hide his revulsion, picturing them finding it at the bottom of a ravine, or junkyard.

Nick crossed his arms. "It runs."

Kole didn't want to let it go, but didn't have any words to express what he felt. "It looks like a bigger Barge puked its guts out onto yours and you couldn't get it clean. Scrap it. You can buy a new one for less than the cost of repairing this one and I'm being nice." He cursed. "You guys are very brave to travel in this." He pointed at the barge. "I'm surprised the engine didn't rip itself free and take off without you."

Nick's words took on an icy tone. "Not everyone can afford to buy a decent vehicle, so stop wasting my time. I get mocked enough at the pub."

"I'm sorry. Vehicles in this condition are salvaged and melted down, but I'll see what I can do." He touched a painted part of the hull, not wanting to get any rust on his hand and pushed his awareness into the

Barge. He instinctively picked out the frame and mentally pictured it, seeing the cracks, dents, metal fatigue and stress points. He visualized looking closer at the modifications and felt the porosity and slag within the welds from past repair jobs then looked at the hull. Not surprised, it was corroded and ready to buckle and a direct hit to certain spots could rip the barge in half. Kole dropped his hand and spoke over his shoulder, "Ten thousand for the frame, twenty for the hull, fifteen for the armor and thirty to redirect the stress. I can look at the engine, weaponry and pluming if you want, or even the electronics, but that's where it gets real expensive."

Nick cursed brushing his fingers over his hair. "What should be done first?"

Kole faced him. "I'd say the hull. The frame can wait and hold out a little longer, but even if you slap on new armor, once you get a rupture you'll be torn in half. It's up to you, but if you have time to make money and avoid physical confrontation the frame is a better bet." He sighed. "I can also divide up the work, but I suggest you save your money and downsize, there's only two of you. I'm sure Roy can find you something. Even picking up two hover bikes would be better than investing in this wreck."

Nick's face soured. "Thanks for your honesty, but I'm having a problem with junking her. She's the first real taste of freedom I've ever felt in my life. I've talked to the mechanics here and they said the same thing except for the downsizing part. They want my money and work, so I have to think about it. How much can be salvaged?"

On a whim, Kole thought about how long it'd take him to resort the barge to new and the unlimited options of changes he could make, but shrugged fibbing, "I have no idea." He remembered he had to hide his ability no matter how honest he wished he could be. "You'll have to talk to Roy." He smiled. "I remember my first ride, she was also a junk heap, but I worked on her until I could trade up."

"I originally wanted to increase its cargo hold, hire a crew and run supplies, but I know this barge isn't safe and not worth repair. But saving up, we'll be here working for Roy forever." He looked at the other vehicles. "What do you know about Werewolves?"

"That's an odd question," Kole said then saw the information flash before his mind's eye. "The disease isn't too contagious, but a bite can transfer it and you'd have to get the cure before the first transformation. If not treated, the full moon triggers a chemical release in the brain, much like in certain people who act crazy during that time. That release forces the body to shape shift. Once that happens, it's permanent. Coincidentally, the very thing that makes it possible for them to change makes them highly allergic to silver. Even touching silver can cause a reaction and having enough contact with it will send a Werewolf into anaphylactic shock. I'm sure you don't need to know their history, or origins, but some of their behavior is interesting. Though Human, they tend not to live among regular people. I talked to one once, she said that when she was first turned her instinct was almost overpowering. She could barely control herself. Certain people looked so damn tasty to her. She didn't want to leave town, but if she smelled something wrong with someone, like an illness, she'd have a powerful urge to kill them, for no other reason, like nature culling the heard. In the beginning, her transformations were so traumatic to her psyche that she blocked them out until she was able to come to terms with what she was. Now she can resist the moon's call, shifts at will and lives with a small pack of her kind, even adopting wolves as pets."

Nick looked uneasy. "They're still Human then?"

"Yes, as much as you and I are." He wondered where the conversation was heading. "If you know someone who's been bitten, I can cure them before they change, if they want it."

He looked puzzled. "No one has been bitten, but who would want to be a Werewolf?"

Kole thought about the people in the ancient past that had changed themselves into one of the other races. "There are many roads leading to the same decision making it impossible to answer why, but the simple answer is that people wanted change in their lives."

"The reason I asked is because Kyra and I are thinking about taking a job from Roy. He's paying a lot of money to hunt down and kill three Werewolves. A month ago, before the full moon a team was sent out to find wild game on the outskirts of town. When they were overdue, Roy sent another team looking for them, but all they found was their vehicle, shell casings, a lot of blood with a mixture of wolf and Human prints on the ground. It came to everyone as a shock because there hasn't been Werewolf activity in the area for at least fifty years."

"A month is a long time to wait. Why is Roy doing this now?"

Nick leaned closer and lowered his voice. "It's kind of a cover up because someone infiltrated the clinic, hacking security and destroyed the Werewolf antitoxin. Without it no one wants to take the job because they fear catching the disease. Roy's trying to acquire more and it's taking time, but now you're here so you can replace it."

Kole thought about charging Roy a steep price to cut down his debt, but knew that Roy would just turn around and exploit those who need it, blaming him for the steep price. He then wondered who destroyed the antitoxin in the first place. "Did Roy catch those responsible for the antitoxins destruction?"

"No, but he suspects the Alchemist who passed through a while ago. There was a witness who saw him sneaking around, but there's no proof."

Kole had a bad feeling and trying to discern the motives of an Alchemist without investigating is hard enough, but sending a small group of people against one is suicide. "If an Alchemist is suspect, I can see why Roy covered it up. If you're going to take on this suicide run, I should go with you. I'll contact Roy, make up a couple of batches of antitoxin and meet you when you're ready."

Nick looked surprised. "I'm glad you want to go, we could use your experience and if things go well we can team up again for better pay. I'll head back and make arrangements before you change your mind. We'll be at the pub, come by later and meet Kyra." He turned speaking over his shoulder, "I think we're going to have a lot of fun together."

Kole nodded then returned his gaze to Nick's junk heap. "We'll cram into my hauler," he decided.

Later, Kole strolled down the sidewalk basking in the warmth of the setting sun. He turned a corner and saw the pub at the end of the street, a converted two story house with yellow, red and black patterned stained glass windows. The square cobalt blue building looked tall with its high arched black shingled roof and brick chimney. A wisp of smoke rose into the air vanishing into the slight breeze and as he walked closer he heard voices coming from a small group of older people sitting at one of the outside tables on the wraparound wooden porch enclosed by a rod iron railing. From the sidewalk, a path made of grey bricks ran down between two flower beds filled with daisies to the oak front door. He grabbed the carved handle, pulled it opened and walked into the dimly lit rustic cabin. Iron chandeliers hung from chains high in the rafters and the light scent of smoke from the smoldering fire gave the pub a cozy feel. Various landscape paintings hung on the wall above the red leather booths with black table tops that ran along the edge of the room to the brick hearth. Square tables and their steel arm chairs seemed randomly placed making space off to the side for a small dance floor and in the center of the room sat the bar. The faint sound of Elven folk music playing over hidden speakers was almost drowned out by the hum of conversation from the many happy patrons.

    Kole took his time meandering around the tables absorbing the feel of the place while casually looking for Eric. The odd person sitting at a table would acknowledge him with a nod or raised glass making him feel that the pub was the heart of the town. Through the crowd he spotted Eric sitting on the inside of a booth with Nick while an attractive young woman with shoulder length brown hair sat across from them. Kole stopped and watched them laugh and smile then shifted his gaze to an older woman with a withered face standing behind the bar wearing a soiled white apron over a baggy red shirt. Most of her grey hair was pulled back into a bun, but some strands escaped and hung randomly in the air. As he approached she turned, staring at him with one eye bigger than the other, waiting. He looked up at the menu hanging above the bar, but didn't like the choices. "Can I get an empty wine bottle filled with water please?" She crossed her arms knowing who he was, but before she could tell him she didn't like people bringing in their own alcohol Kole added, "If you give me two bottles, I'll pay by making you a fine bottle of Elven wine."

    She smiled a toothless grin, left the bar, went into the back room and shortly returned with a narrow bottle and one three times its size. "The smaller one's yours." Her words whistled through her lips.

Kole looked at the bottles. He didn't need her, he could create whatever he needed out of the air but she was a flavor, an experience, a vibration he could share like two merging streams. He could argue over the price and call her a cheat, but this is her house and the harmony of the place would be disrupted. Everyone who has invested energy in the moment would be adversely affected and it was time to play the game, to govern the energy of thought, to use and be used by another, in a nice way, all for balance. He rested his hands on the bottles then asked, "Do you have a private place where I can do some work?"

She smiled again pointing her long boney finger at the broom closet in the back corner. Kole returned her smile wondering if she was a little crazy or just treated everyone badly then walked around a small group of people who were collecting their things getting ready to leave. He weaved his way around the tables to the closet then entered, closing the door behind him. He found the light switch, glad the closet was tidy and well organized with its various cleaning tools then knelt. He placed the bottles on the floor and filled hers with a rich purple liquid then focused on his. His bottle wasn't large enough for everyone, so he doubled its size. After filling his bottle he returned to the crone hiding his altered bottle by his side while placing the larger one on the bar. She wrapped her scrawny hand around the bottle's neck then cackled a dry laugh before putting it under the counter.

"May I have four wine glasses please?"

She grabbed a tray, slid it onto the bar and placed four glasses on it. "The bottle you have is too small for four people, unless you want to be cheap? I'd be happy to give you a deal on a fine bottle of Elven wine I just happen to acquire, say for the low sum of two hundred. I even know the Alchemist who made it. He's a good guy."

Kole laughed at the thought of buying back the bottle he'd just made. "You're funny."

She leaned close enough for Kole to smell her rancid breath. "In my youth I used to have an Alchemist lover and I know you can make things out of the air. He had such wonderful hands, but sad eyes, the kind of eyes you can get lost in, like yours. You're not like the twit who passed through here. He was dumber than an anvil and didn't practice the game. I bet that it took every ounce of mental power he had just to take a crap."

"I've heard a lot about the last Alchemist who passed through town since I arrived," he mentioned changing the subject to side step her advances. "What did he do to leave such a poor impression on everyone?"

She reached over and slowly wrapped her fingers around his sleeve grabbing hold. Leaning close, she licked her lips before saying, "He didn't do too well with trade as you know, so he went out to scrounge. We were all hoping he wouldn't come back, but somehow he survived out there. No one else cared to noticed, but he didn't come back the same. It was as if he was enveloped by a cold creepy shadow. After, he didn't see me like before when he was a bumbling moron. It was like he lost something out in the waste, like something reached inside and stole a piece of him." She jerked Kole's sleeve pulling his arm closer. "He came back haunted with dark eyes full of contempt."

Kole smiled almost buying into the crazy woman's ghost story. "I'll be going into the waste and I'll look for that revenant for you. If he's still around I'll get him to move along. Will that make you feel safe?"

She reluctantly released her grip. "Yes, I'd feel safer if you and I shared a warm bed, at my place. I know you have some alchemical tricks to please the women." She grinned and chopped her gums together. "I can be fun to."

The look of lust in her eye made his skin crawl, but he was able to hide his discomfort behind a pleasant smile. He searched her cloudy eyes for the joke, unsure if she was messing with him then realized that she was serious. "Bad granny," he stammered shaking the image of her naked body out of his head. "You're a bad granny." Unsettled, he quickly put his wine bottle on the tray and carried it toward Eric's table listening to her cackle over the noise of the crowd. He nodded to Eric's group, put the tray down then slid in beside Kyra. She shifted her curvy, muscular frame and make room for him.

Eric smiled and handed out the glasses. "What's in the bottle?" he wondered. "You've never shared a drink before."

Kole regained his composure from the crown's creepy advances and pushed the thoughts of her naked body out of his mind. "I share drink," he protested but couldn't remember the last time. "In my youth I spent a little time on the outskirts of the Elven Nation working the wine fields learning how to make their finest. I figured it would be a nice treat for everyone."

Kyra looked at Kole with her whiskey colored eyes and thanked him then took a sip. "I've never had this before and it tastes very nice."

"A little sweet for my taste," Nick complained. "How much would you trade for a keg of your finest Orkish ale?"

Eric over looked at the bar. "Don't they sell that here?"

Nick laughed. "No one this far north knows what it tastes like, so they mix all the left over swill together, probably a little piss too, and try to pass it off as ale. The crap they sell here is rot gut."

Kyra scoffed. "I once heard a story about a man who thought unicorn urine held medicinal properties, but when he got a mouth full, he said it tasted like Orkish ale. You can't compare this exquisite wine to that."

Nick chuckled. "All this time and I didn't know you were such a booze expert."

Kyra flashed a mock glare and everyone laughed.

Kole took a sip. "In the case of Elven wine, altering the grapes is much like magnetism where there's only so much flux a piece of iron can contain and once we've learned how to create the wine, it's skill alone that makes the best. In other words, we change the grape to make the best then memorize what we did to reproduce the effect. It's also about knowing that each race tastes things differently. Ork Ale tastes very earthy to Humans, but spicy to Orks. Dwarves like the taste, but hate the texture and something that's dry and bitter to Humans is rich and fruity to Elves."

"Sounds complicated," Kyra noted then slightly turned to Kole. "Did you learn to made ale from the Orks?"

Kole's mind flashed back to the different triages he had been in filled with bloodied Orks howling in pain. "No, I did learned how to make the best, but not from them and since everyone loves alcohol my teacher insisted I learn most culture's drinks so if I'm ever in need, I can use it for barter."

"Sounds like a good idea," Kyra agreed. "But I'd love to see the Elves fabled flower gardens. It's too bad they're so snooty about letting non-elves into their country."

Eric finished his drink. "Kole has seen the flower gardens."

Kole laughed. "No," he corrected. "They brought some flowers to me, so I could learn to make more." He thought of all the rules he had to agree to before they let him stay. "Xenophobic is putting it nicely. They didn't even let me into their smallest village."

Kyra's eyes beamed. "Can you make me a flower?"

He smiled. "I will, but most of their flowers are given under special occasion and have specific meaning. If you can't say it with words, say it with a flower. Of course there is also the raven's claw, a black modified pansy which says I want you dead. The Elves aren't without a sense of humor."

Her face puckered. "I don't want that flower."

"Well," Nick said. "I think we should take our Barge tomorrow. It's larger, more menacing…"

Kole laughed interrupting him. "I'm sorry," he said, regretting hurting Nick's pride. "We can all squeeze into my hauler."

Nick thought about it for a moment then disagreed. "I know your transport is better, but we have a lot of gear and it'll be a tight fit. We don't know what we'll find out there so, I'd rather have everything at hand than be short the right tool."

Eric nodded. "Kole let's go with them, what can it hurt?"

"Alright," Kole conceded, deciding to relax his anal need for safety and to trust Eric's instinct. "Let's finish this bottle and I'll pay the crone for the other, then I'm off." He smiled, enjoying their company wondering what tomorrow will bring.

Chapter

6

Byron woke on his back baking in the morning sun. The heat and the sound of buzzing in his ears drew him out of sleep's darkness into a bright annoying light. He moaned then lifted his head out of the dirt that pulled on his long hair. He blinked his sticky eyes trying to focus, seeing the top of his transport where he'd left it, ignoring the small swarm of flies crawling over him. He dropped his head back into the dirt relieved that he was still alive. He closed his eyes then slung his arm over his face to block the light. He was hot and itchy all over, but too worn out to move. He lay there for as long as he could then struggled, gathering enough strength to sit, disturbing the flies. His muscles ached and quickly tiered as he fought against his crusty, rotten smelling shirt that stuck to his chest. He moved his legs for balance then cursed in pain, his pants had pulled then ripped out a section of his leg hairs. He gagged, sometime during his high his bowels had released, but it wasn't the first time that he'd awoke this way. He managed to stand then almost puked while he waited for his head to stop spinning. He then focused his mind and transmuted his filth away, cleaning his clothes and freshening himself up. He remembered the hellish night before then staggered his way back to his transport that sat open, infested with flies. The stench hit him like a wall that he tried to peer around while looking through the hatch into the transport. And for the first time in his life he was disgusted by what he'd become. The night before he'd puked over the consoles, walls and floor and leaving foot prints of urine and feces that had run down his legs.

He remade his shield then placed his hand on the hull transmuting his filth away then altered the atmospheric pressure within, forcing the flies out. The transport that he was so proud of now felt somehow tainted to him, it no longer felt like a home. He'd changed overnight and the feeling pissed him off. He picked up his baggy of drugs and the thought of getting high again disgusted him. He tightened his grip on the bag crushing its powder, angry that some jerk off stole his pleasure away. He shifted his awareness into the bag and saw that everything appeared normal. He looked deeper and found an obscure compound and worked on it like a puzzle until he realized that it was designed to interact with his body chemistry to create the poison. His dealer tried to kill him.

His body was too tired to hold his anger. "Tell me Bishop," he whispered to the bag. "Should I hunt you down and kill you, or let it go? Perhaps I deserved it? I'm not the nicest guy. I could bail, grab Monique and disappear." He imagined being somewhere nice with Monique on his arm, but a nagging feeling brought him back. "No, I can't let this go, Bishop. I'm going to have to spank you and make you suffer like I have." He dropped the drugs into his hidey hole then powered up his transport. He was about to close the hatch when a large pop and a whistling noise distracted him a second before an internal explosion tore his transport apart.

He was in darkness wrapped in metal, protected by his shield and only one word sounded in his mind, "Enough." Anger filled him to the point of bursting. He extended his awareness pushing outward ripping apart his smoldering cocoon of debris in an explosion of fury. He floated, lifting himself out of the wreckage. He felt the Battle Barge before he saw it and watched it fired its dorsal cannon missing, exploding behind him. Hovering there, he let out an animalistic cry then fired himself at the Barge, crashing through the cockpit and into its interior. He wanted them to know him, wanted them to feel his rage. He extended his shield around his hands making claws then ran back to the cockpit and ripped the pilot and co-pilot apart. He didn't hear their screams or feel the gore. All he felt was floating millimeters above the deck, seeming to move in slow motion. The crew fought him and he brought them swift death until a word punctured his mind, "Recognize."

He dropped a body to the floor then looked down hall at a man holding a pistol shooting at him. "Recognize." He burst forward and was in front of him. He knocked the man's gun aside, grabbed him by the throat and lifted him off the ground. "Recognize." His mind cleared enough instinct away for him to remember his message boy, who was afraid of being in the Dark Elf city. The man grabbed the arm holding his throat and put the gun to Byron's forehead then pulled the trigger, but the round ricocheted off of Byron's shield shooting the gun out of his hand.

"You," Byron hissed still holding the man struggling to breathe.

He choked, "Let go."

Byron dropped him to the floor allowing him to gain his footing, but held him. He laughed. "Let go," he mocked.

The man gripped Byron's forearm with both hands. "Don't kill me Byron. We can make a deal."

"Okay," he doubted. "Wow me."

"You understand, I got paid a lot of gel and armaments to make sure you were dead. The guy, who hired us, said you'd be dead, or too weak to fight. It was business."

"Who hired you?"

"The price is my life."

Byron agreed with a nod.

"An Alchemist named Bishop."

He tightened his grip on the man's throat and with his free hand he flicked his wrist, cutting off his ear.

The man screamed holding his wound. "We had a deal, Byron!"

"That was tax for trying to kill me," he growled. He leaned in face to face. "And the next time you try to put on a pair of sun glasses, you'll remember not to screw with me." He let him go and the man fell to his knees, picking his ear off the dirty floor. Byron dismissed him then made his way back to the cockpit. He concentrated on flight lifting into the air, committing almost all of his energy to do what only a few could.

He shot himself high into the air. The black sand and lava fields blurred beneath him, but he didn't feel the cold on his skin or the wind in his ears and a couple of hours later, he was over the prairies. In the past, flight had always made him feel a little scared, the chance he'd lose focus and fall, seconds before splat, but his shield would've protected him, taking away the fun and his connection to life. He hadn't flown or took a breath without his shield since he'd learned how to form it. Now without it, the feeling of being naked was overwhelming and in time the fear of flight, falling, and death had vanished. He wanted to feel again like when Monique was in his arms, her warm soft skin against his. Now James is on him and people are trying to kill him. He wanted them all to go away, wanted to feel the beating of his heart once again. He dropped his shield, accelerating. The cold howling wind numbed his face, knotted his hair and frayed his clothes. Tears welled in his eyes almost blinding him as he raced for across the sky feeling free, alive, naked and terrified. He entered a mountain pass then slowed, raising his shield and flew that last few Kilometers feeling his heart pounding in his chest and listening to the thumping in his ears.

Bishop's cave sat at the base of cliff in a valley where an ancient battle had scarred the land. Now, thick slabs of concrete and a bright red door marked the cave's entrance. Byron lowered himself gently landing on loose gravel at Bishop's doorstep, but before he could kick the door in, it opened.

A dirty short round man dressed in filthy grey coveralls leaned against the doorframe. "I think we should talk," he said then brushed his long thinning brown hair out of his facial stubble and away from his cold blue eyes.

He probed Bishop's defenses and felt the power to destroy him flow down his arm and pool in his hand. "I'm here to kill you Bishop," he declared.

"You're a lot stronger than me, you can kill me after, but I didn't run, I could've." He raised his hands defensively then continued, "It's important, you can kill me after, if you still want to."

Byron's hand vibrated, coursing with the energy meant to blow Bishop's ugly face apart, but he managed to hold back the impulse. "Not only did your drugs almost kill me, but they made me never want to do drugs again. Do you know what that means for me? And you want me to listen to you after you've wrecked that part of me."

"This is big," he defended. "I had to do something."

"You don't do anything!" he spat.

Bishop backed away then beckoned him closer. "Come inside and I'll tell you everything."

Curiosity held him. The thought that this spineless vermin was taking a stand for something surprised him. But the whisper of paranoia told him that this was a trap and to splatter him. Since Bishop was still backing away and he hadn't killed him yet, he reluctantly followed.

Byron stepped in and walked along a waist high path made from stacks of miscellaneous garbage that lined the walls. The path split when he entered a large room filled with lab equipment, stasis pods, more garbage, spare parts and all manner of junk. He looked at the mess. "You live in this crap heap?" he asked.

Bishop waved his hand dismissing him. "Come," he said climbing a small stair case to the next level that held a computer console and lab equipment then rummaged through a stack of debris clearing a spot for Byron to sit. He sat in his leather swivel chair beckoning Byron to come over.

Remembering waking up in worse filth, Byron sat. "All right Bishop, what's this about?"

He licked his lips. "I guess I'll start from the beginning. Shortly after you became a client of mine, I had a visit from the most powerful Alchemist I'd ever seen. He wanted tons of chemicals, and I don't mean a lot, I mean metric tons. I didn't think anything of it, making chemicals is my gift and it was one hell of a payday, in advance. It took a long time to do it right, but I completed the contract. I had to cook portions of each of the 10 chemicals, I couldn't just manifest them.

He wanted it all to be natural, no signature. I did wonder why such a powerful person needed me, but I couldn't resist the money. Periodically slaver types would pick up the shipments and that was that. One day Pooza, my pet mixed some of the chemicals then ingested them."

"You mean that impish Troll ugly looking thing that I once saw?"

"That was her. I used her eggs to make permanent children of the different races."

Disgusted, Byron raised his hand stopping his dribble. "You create and sell children…" he searched for something vile to say, but was too worn out from the drug trip. "That's sick," he finished.

He nodded agreeing. "I used to sell kids and even though they weren't the real, it was still quite lucrative." He frowned. "Don't look at me like that you prick, you're no better than me. After all the evil shit you've done, this is where you draw the line, besides I just sold them, I didn't use them."

Byron sighed dismissing the argument.

"They were my best creation lasting fifty years and they never grew up. People paid a lot for that and I never asked why they wanted them, I just like making things." He scrubbed his chin stubble. "You've upset me and made me go off topic. Now where was I?" he pondered. "Oh yeah, after my poor Pooza ate the chemicals she became sterile and I had to put her down. All those years of work, wasted. I looked into what she ate and discovered that over time and after eating different combinations of my chemicals, a new compound was made within any Non-Human causing sterility. My Pooza was a freak, so it happened faster than it was intended, but if she wasn't such a glutton I would've never of known."

"You're losing me."

"Just wait. Through my various contacts I found out that the man who'd hired me is your boss."

"If this is about James, then why did you try to kill me?"

He scoffed. "I can't kill James. I can't even kill you. But I can slow him down by killing his minions."

"What did you just call me?"

"Hear me, James is going to commit genocide and kill off every

Non-Human on the planet."

Byron chuckled. "Do you have any proof?"

"No, but you can find out the truth."

"I've heard what you've said and now you hear me. Your story tells me that you're pissed because you lost that miserable pet of yours and are no longer able to sell children. You have no proof that James was ever here, or that he hired you. Now, I'm going tell you what I think is going on. I think that everything that you just said is a lie to save your pathetic skin. I think the Troll bouncer was a diversion and you were the true assassin."

"Troll? No, you have to believe me. James is too clever to leave a trail."

With a quick motion Byron thrust his hand forward releasing a tight yellow bolt of energy and with a thump it punched through Bishop's shield and buried itself into his chest. Bishop moaned then toppled off his chair landing onto a pile of garbage.

Byron sighed. "I should've asked him who'd hired him." He moved to Bishop's seat to access his computer system and place a call.

The console lit up and an old unshaven man with long scraggly grey hair answered, speaking with a Russian accent, "What is it now?"

"Cid, we're not very happy with you. You were supposed to attack Sarah's caravan and be selective on who dies and the Ork you hired with a Ripper messed everything up. I trust that you've found the factory. Those weapons aren't yours to flippantly give away. What were you thinking?"

The man laughed from his belly. "You didn't tell me we were looking for Rippers. I pulled all my kin here and now I think I don't have to listen to you anymore."

Byron rubbed his face then complained, "Why today?"

"Not today, I've been planning to betray you for years. You are weak inside and James talks saying nothing."

"You idiot," he fumed. "We rescued you and helped build your family."

"I remember, but you use us to attack the races, starting wars. We are now even, I'll be your slave no more."

"Cid, I can't let you have the factory. How many guns did you put into the world?"

"Just the one to get your attention and I keep the factory."

"You could've called to tell me all of this. You're being a dick."

His face got bigger on the screen. "I want you to wake up. I want your passion when I face you. I want to look you in eye when I cut your stomach open, reach inside and pull your guts out."

Byron growled. "All right, I'm on my way," then terminated the call. He then pounded in another number and James' face appeared on the console's monitor.

"How's everything?" James asked sounding pleasant.

"I hit a couple of snags."

His voice tightened. "Do you need help?"

"My dealer tried to kill me, but before he died he said that you ordered a shipment from him."

"I don't need drugs and you don't have time to be fooling around over there."

He wanted to argue that it wasn't drugs that he ordered, but felt defensive. "I was on my way to talk with Cid, but I was ambushed and my transport was destroyed. I took a detour to take care of my dealer, but I did manage to call Cid."

James studied him for a moment making Byron feel small then inquired, "How's the excavation coming?"

"I don't know. Cid just told me that he's keeping the factory and he wants to kill me."

"I see, crazy is a lot of fun until it bites you. It was only a matter of time before that bastard turned on us."

"I'm going to head down there, take care of him and do the usual. I'll put one of his underlings in charge."

"No. Things have changed. We have time to deal with Cid later, he's not going anywhere. Sarah and the weapon are connected, find her and you'll find the weapon. That's more important."

"That's only one gun, Cid can pass out more."

"He won't, he just challenged us. He'll want to consolidate his forces so we have at least a week before he gets restless and demands our attention again, besides Sarah is worth more now. Find out why she hasn't reported in and if you have to, help her get into position."

"I lost her last known. Send it and I'll be off as soon as I make a finder."

James nodded, sent the information then disconnected the call.

Chapter

7

Morning came fast for Kole and as he walked down the street he mused at his new sense of belonging. Feeling good, he decided not to question his mood and took a deep breath to enjoy the fresh morning air then indulged in the warm sun on his back as small birds chirped in the distance. Playing the game and all those years of sacrifice had finally paid off. He was now a member of a community. He passed by the other Barges then stood in front of Nick's and was surprised that he was anticipating today's adventure. Nick's Barge wasn't that bad of a junk heap and made plans to make small adjustments here and there, things that no one would notice. He felt deep in his gut that today was going to be a great day then walked along its side and found Nick dressed in body armor waiting for him beside the hatch.

"Good morning Nick," he said, offering him a verbal handshake.

Nick smiled. "You're chipper. I thought you'd change your mind about riding with us."

"No, I think it'll be fun and I'm sorry for reacting badly the other day."

"Don't worry about it. The guys at the pub teased me a lot that morning and I was a little sore," he admitted.

"Forget them. Once you get the money you can restore your

Barge."

"Yeah, and if we work well together, there's plenty of room for you and Eric," he offered.

"We'll think about it. Is Eric around?"

"He's inside chatting with Kyra. "Oh," he remembered then handed Kole an earpiece. "Here, it's short range and tuned to our head sets."

"Thanks," he replied then nestled it around his ear.

Eric, still wearing his denim ensemble emerged from the darkness and stood in the doorway. "I thought I heard you. Isn't this Barge great, Kole?" he asked. "I know it needs a little love, but it has awesome potential."

Kole agreed then climbed up the recessed steps and stepped in the hall smelling poorly recycled air.

Eric reached past him and hit the light switch then waited for the circular ceiling lights to flicker on. They brightened then dimmed, shining with a slight buzz revealing a narrow hallway. Its walls displayed two amateur murals, one of forested landscapes with patches of green fields, another depicting a battlefield of blade wielding Orks fighting Dwarves.

Kole expected rust and water stained walls matching the outside, but was pleasantly surprised to see more artwork, making the interior artistically chaotic, but interesting. "There's plenty of food for the eyes in here," he commented.

"It's okay," Eric said. "I didn't get it either until Kyra explained art to me. In a way we're artists, but without the creative expression. We make copies of what already is."

"As it should be," Kole agreed. "In the past, creative expression in Alchemy unbalanced the world manifesting abominations from the darkest parts of our imaginations." He frowned. "Like those damn Pixies."

"I know, I know," Eric teased. He miss quoted Kole and added some dramatic flair, "It transported the Human race through the threshold…" He curled his fingers into a claw holding his hand above his head. "Into madness and godhood they went, destroying the world." He thrust his hand down finishing his miss quote, joking, "The Pixies, born of darkness, scrambled to spread their trickery into the world. Gleefully they giggled while they undid shoe laces and farted on babies. And that's why we suppress our artistic side."

Kole fumed. "You bugger!" he spat. "You have no idea how evil those little bastards are! Farting on babies, I've never heard such crap in my life!"

Nick peered through the open hatch. "What's all the fuss about?"

"Nothing," Eric said. "Kole's going off about Pixies again."

Kole ignored Nick. "Eric, do you think this is funny?" Eric smirked almost making him loose it. He pointed his finger at Eric. "You think this is funny, pushing me. I'm out, go hunt Werewolves without me." He turned to leave.

Eric quickly moved around him blocking his path. "I'm sorry," he apologized. "I was playing. I didn't mean to make you mad."

Kole wanted to be there for him, but Eric's flippant attitude towards those blasted Pixies pissed him off and he was having a hard time calming down. "Get out of the way, Eric."

"Don't go," he requested. "Can we clean slate?"

"Fine," Kole agreed. "What type of gear do they have?" he asked changing the subject.

Nick climbed up and they made room for him. "We have full suit body armor, rifles, blades, a med kit, a scanner and some grenades," he answered.

Eric grinned. "I'm going to be in the rear gunner's compartment, Kyra in the side and if they had the extra side gun, you could've taken that position, but Nick wants you in the cockpit with him." He brightened. "I'm glad you dragged me to this town and I know I haven't been making things easy for you, but Kyra has explained a lot to me. I like them, so try not to embarrass me."

Nick laughed.

Kole thought for a moment convinced that he'd never embarrassed him before then watched him walk to the end of the hall and disappear around the corner.

"Come on," Nick said leading him to the cockpit door. He hit the button, but nothing happened. He chuckled. "It's a little sticky, but it will work," he reassured then hit the button a couple of more times until the door screeched open. He entered then slid into the pilot's seat leaving Kole standing in the entrance of the four man cockpit.

Kole stepped in and grabbed the headrest of the closest brown armchair, spinning it around. It wobbling with a long squeak and he wasn't surprised to see a large tear across its bottom cushion were soiled foam darker than the chair protruded from the rip. He grimaced and sat on the lumpy seat then read the instruments flicking some switches to rout communications and various sensor readings through his station. Nick joined in with clicking of his own and together they worked the controls, bringing the Barge to life. The floor plating vibrated as the antigravity wound up lifting the craft off the ground.

Nick retracted the landing gear and backed out of their spot then communicated his intent to leave with the town's control center. He passed through the main gate and increased speed once they met the road. He clicked a button that brought up a topographical map of the region then plotted a course for their two hour ride through dense forest and hilly terrain.

They traveled for almost an hour and as they approached a point on the map, Nick pulled back on the throttle then slightly turned forcing the anti-gravity to level out as the Barge dipped over a ditch toward a path that had been logged for hover crafts. At half speed they traveled over old stumps, decayed logs and underbrush through the narrow path of trees winding its way into steeper, rockier terrain toward a distant network of abandoned mining camps. They passed the first open rocky plateau and followed the path as it wound its way back down into a valley through more forest.

Kole could see the distant snow covered mountains tops between the trees and enjoyed the beauty of the dark green treetops against the deep blue sky. He relaxed into his chair that made half his ass fall asleep then closed his eyes reaching out with his awareness feeling the molecular vibration in the rock beneath them and the energy of life within the forest. He breathed deep letting the raw wild power of nature flow over him washing away the feeling of domestication. He was about to fall asleep when a large explosion rocked the Barge. His eyes shot open as the sharp sound of creaking and tearing metal reverberated throughout the halls like a metallic howl. He frantically brought up the sensors as a secondary explosion ignited warning beeps from several alarms across the various consoles. Information flooding across his screen, then with an electronic pop and the smell of burned wires his station died. Kole cursed then watched Nick fight with his controls, pulling back as the nose dipped toward the ground. Kole grabbed his armrests waiting for the antigravity to respond, but nothing happened. He then locked his chair, bracing himself a moment before they hit the ground spraying dirt, grass and rocks across the windshield. The Barge shuddered, moaning in protest as parts of the hull buckled, shearing bolts in a popping cascade of dreadful noise then jerked to the side as the last of its momentum partly spun the Barge around. For a second everything stopped then the back end dropped with a loud bang of denting metal pulling the nose out of the ground. The lights flickered and the alarms dropped pitch as the last of the power drained away.

"It must have been a mine," Nick guessed as he quickly unstrapped. "I didn't see anything on the sensors."

Kole sprang to his feet stumbling as his sleeping leg gave out. He grabbed the wall and rode out the sharp tingling sensation erupting throughout his leg. "It was artillery," he replied, taking a couple of slow steps to reach the door. "Sensors would've picked up a mine, besides they said that the initial impact came through the upper deck into the engine room." He opened the small compartment in the wall and pulled on the release lever opening the door a crack.

Nick put on his helmet. "No one said anything about artillery being out here."

Kole heard his muffled voice thought the earpiece then laughed as he widened the door. "I bet you wish we took my hauler," he teased. He slipped through the door and peered into the darkness using the dim light streaming in through the jagged cracks in the ceiling. He activated an amulet allowing him to see in the dark then hoped that Eric had used his shield and was safe. He ran down the hall, turned a corner and almost collided with a portion of buckled wall then quickly looked through the gaps to the other side making sure no one was trapped or crushed.

Nick grabbed his shoulder. "It's blocked, let's go the other way," he urged.

"What hit us," Kyra demanded over the headset.

"Artillery," Nick answered. "Is anyone hurt?"

"I'm good," Eric replied.

Kole had forgotten about the earpiece and was relieved to hear Eric's voice.

"I'm all right," Kyra said. "Time to go, we won't survive another hit." She came around the corner fully suited with two rifles slung over a shoulder, a backpack and a weapon belt over the other. She handed Nick his weapon and belt then readied her rifle.

Eric joined them. "The main entrance is blocked. We're going to have to leave out the top."

Nick led them to a door then forced it open exposing the ladder to the outer deck. Kole returned his vision to normal then looked at the sky through a portion of ceiling that the explosion had torn away as Nick jumped into the narrow passage and climbed through floating specks of rust that had been shaken loose. Kole went next, the damage was more extensive than he'd imagined. The last wisp of the smoke rose up then disappeared on the warm afternoon breeze allowing him to look over the edge of twisted and torn metal into their scorched engine room, but he didn't linger long. He grabbed his dowel, slipped on his knucklers then manifested his shield before stepping over a long crack that ran diagonally across the outer hull. He jumped, landing with a thump in the knee high grass. He took a breath unable to smell, but sensed something sickly like the alchemical smell of Pixies, but fainter. He didn't like the strange feeling creeping up his spine and ran to the tree line. He heard the others behind him, but ignored them, looking into the thick underbrush for movement.

The forest was beautiful and unnervingly quiet. Streams of sunlight penetrated the forest canopy as tree tops swayed in the breeze, shifting the shadows, making the light dance to the sound of rustling branches. The others gathered around Kole as he led the way running low across the uneven ground out of the grass into the tree line then crouched not wanting to reveal their position to possible snipers. They fanned out, alert, expecting confrontation and a barrage of artillery fire, but the forest was void of Human and animal noise. They stopped at the bottom of an old shallow crater filled with dry branches and pale pine needles and hid behind two fallen rotted out trees. Kole turned to make sure Eric was following then focused on a charm beneath his shirt, channeling its energy to enhance his hearing, tuning out the creaking tree tops, listening for the rhythmic pounding of feet. Kyra leaned her assault rifle against a log then dropped her backpack to the ground. She pulled out two silver hand axes and tucked them under her belt then thrust her hand once more into her pack, pulling out a foot long stainless steel cylinder with a sensor dome at one end. The group waited for her to extracted the sensor's legs and place it on the ground then to grab the remote pad from a side pouch on her belt. She initiate the device and Kole watched her gently tap the pad then looked away to scan the quiet forest. Something felt wrong, eerie, like the forest was coated with a faint odd smell, or a strange static permeating the air that confused the senses. He reached out listening in the direction of the silence to hear the rumbling of foot falls as the sensor dome beeped, picking up movement. "How many Werewolves are we hunting?" he asked, fearful of the truth. "I think we just entered a large pack's territory."

Kyra cursed then tapped the screen once more. "Incoming," she growled confirming Kole's fear then pointed passed the logs at the crest of a hill toward the silence.

Tightening his grip on his dowel, Kole looked up the hill between the trees, over the grass outcrops in the sea of needles. He relaxed his shoulders, feeling the alchemical programming within the dowel waiting to be used, wondering how many they'll be facing. He felt troubled, what he knew of Werewolves was they were more into hiding their presence than using artillery, but things change and motives are sometimes hard to discern.

Eric was the first to react. He reached over the log releasing a bolt of bright yellow energy from the end of his dowel at the smoky mass of moving fur and flashing teeth from the half dozen wolves running over the crest of the hill. The wolves barely parted, springing away in mid run as the ground exploded in a flash of brilliant light, singeing their fur, spraying them with dirt and broken needles. They yelped in surprise, but didn't slow, scattering behind trees, darting in and out of the shadows. Nick and Kyra, moved in beside Eric opening up with their assault rifles in short bursts, spraying hot silver at the shadows, tearing up the ground, fracturing tree bark before they punched into their target's flesh.

Kole covered his sensitive ears feeling his dowel and knuckler against the sides of his head and watched a wolf fly sideways into a tree in a puff of fur, blood and bone. It yelped, crumbling into a shredded heap, skidding across the bloodied ground. Kole stepped back away from the noise, watching both Nick and Kyra find the same target leaping between the shadows. The wolf in mid flight looked at them as they fired, shattering its front leg sending it into a spiral, the remainder of their burst rupture its side pushing it away as it fell into the thick brush while the rest of the pack vanished into the foliage.

"Watch the perimeter!" Nick ordered, his voice crackled in Kole's earpiece. Kyra repositioned herself to cover the rear, kneeling, peering over the lip of the crater.

Kole saw what they planned and grabbed Eric, pulling him back to the center as a bush rustled a short distance away. He listened, stretching his senses outward trying to grasp at any sound until a low chorus of animalistic moans and popping joints broke the silence. A bead of sweat rolled down Kole's temple as he realized he was listening to them transform then released his hearing charm and readied his dowel, knowing what to expect, but had never seen it.

Kole could feel the nervous tension in the air as they listened to the noise escalated into loud throaty growls and snarls. A branch snapped to their left, bush rustled to their right and the sound of claws rending tree bark came from the rear. Unsettled Eric stood tall, pointed his dowel with purpose at the moving bush and fired three bolts in quick succession extinguishing the shadows between the trees then exploded in the ground behind the bush, but the rest held their fire until a large black blur jumped between the trees. They shifted in unison, Kole stood, extending his arm as they all opened fire in the shadow's direction, chewing up the trees and bushes, spraying bark, dirt and leaves into the air, but missing their target as the other Werewolves attacked the opposite flank.

Kole heard heavy footsteps and snapping branches behind him. He spun to see two massive humanoid creatures three times his size charging them. Their black haired muscular bodies with canine heads swayed with each step, arms swaying with their clawed hands ready for blood, but all Kole could focus on was their burning yellow eyes and white teeth begging for a throat. He fired at the lead Werewolf's forward leg trying to slow it down, but it leaped high into the air over the bolt, extending its arms then brought its claws together as it dove toward him, ready to rip him apart.

Squeezing his fingers together he felt his knuckler, confirming there was power flowing through it then dropped low under the Werewolf, allowing it to slide over his shield before he pulled his dowel close, firing upward twice at the Werewolf's exposed abdomen. His rounds burned into its chest and belly, exploding, punching deep into the wolf's body showering its blood and guts against Kole's protective barrier. Disgusted by the blood splatter and various bits of entail running down his shield, he watched the Werewolf land on its head bending backward as it crumbled unconscious onto the ground.

The second Werewolf avoided Kole and went for Eric. Eric looked back, his eyes wide with surprise. Kole felt him try to form a shield, but failed as the Werewolf lifted him off the ground biting deep into his weapon arm. Eric screamed as the Werewolf jerked him back and forth shredding his bicep then held him, twisting its massive body to hide behind Eric as Kole tried to get a clean shot.

Kole heard Nick's loud war cry coming through his earpiece, but ignored him seeing Eric's gore soaked sleeve and blood dripping from his fingers sending Kole's mind into a place beyond fear and rage as he watched the Werewolf cowardly hide behind his boy. The Werewolf bounced from one leg to leg taunting him in a sick dance, jostling Eric until he managed to lift his legs. Kole without hesitation fired two bolts of energy, one into each of the Werewolf's kneecaps shattering them. The Werewolf dropped to the ground howling in pain onto its useless knees then fell on top of Eric crushing him. The Werewolf reached out, digging its fingers into the earth ready to push itself up, but Kole didn't hesitate. He aimed then blasted a hole into the top of its head blowing its skull apart.

Chapter 8

As the Werewolf leapt into the air attacking Kole, Nick and Kyra came together on the other side of the crater to form a firing line while two other Werewolves charged them, muscles pumping, running in single file. Kyra was quick to act, firing a burst of silver into the first Werewolf's neck, blowing away chunks of its meaty flesh, almost severing its head. The Werewolf tried to yelp, gurgling on its blood and clutching at its missing throat before it collapsed sideways into a tree.

The second Werewolf leaped into Nick knocking away his rifle then slammed its powerful hand over the top of his head grabbing him. Nick dropped under the heavy blow then was picked up off the ground and whipped high into the air over the Werewolf's shoulder. The Werewolf then dropped its weight running its claw down the face of Kyra's helmet and shoulder pushing her back. She hit the ground almost dropping her rifle, but managed to bring it up in time to impale the Werewolf on it barrel stopping it from clawing at her throat. She pulled the trigger then watched the Werewolf flail, stumbling backward spraying gore with each hit until it finally fell. She didn't realize she was screaming until she took a deep breath then heard the clicking of her empty rifle. She focused staring at the smoke emanating from her barrel before she released the trigger.

She sprang to her feet to protect the group thinking that there were more monsters, but didn't see any. Thinking about Nick, she ran past Kole who was on his knees beside a dead Werewolf and grabbed Nick's rifle lying on the crest of the crater. "His rifle is here and…" she trailed off studying the ground. "Where did he go?" She pulled out her data pad to check for movement then looked for the motion detector that had been trampled during the fight. The pad beeped, she checked it then spun around running into the forest finding Nick sprawled out on the ground rubbing his neck.

Chapter 9

Kole slid his dowel into his belt pouch then dropped beside the headless Werewolf. He thrust his hands under its ribcage thinning his shield to let its course oily fur slip between his fingers then tried to roll it onto its back to free Eric, but the Werewolf was too heavy. Frantic, he dug his feet into the ground and lay on the carcass, summoning his strength to try again. He lifted and pushed with everything he had barely moving the corpse then remembered his charms. Calming his mind, he put away the thought of Eric bleeding to death with each passing second then concentrated, empowering his strength charm, pushing, freeing Eric. Kole froze, his heart pounding in his chest. Eric lay still, pale, his arm matted with blood. Kole feared he was too late. He placed his hands on Eric's bicep, moving his awareness into his arm transmuting the savage wound, closing his torn flesh and repairing the muscle. He felt Eric's life force, weak, but still flowing. Lycanthropy hid in the back ground ravaging Eric's immune system, but Kole was relieved to be in time to save his life. He looked to the sky as tears ran down his cheeks, but disgusted by the blood and entrails covering his shield, hovering inches above his head. He grimaced at the mess forgetting it was there then moved a short distance away before releasing his shield, careful to make the gore slide off raining on the ground before he reenergized it.

Eric's eyes fluttered open. "Those things stink," he whispered.

Kole smiled letting his fear, worry and regret flow away. He placed his hand on his chest. "I'm going to remove the disease," he said. With ease, he dismantled the virus.

The sound of popping joints and creaking bones caught his attention. Disgusted, he witnessed the Werewolf's corpse twitch and jolt, slowly shrinking as it reverted back into a chubby naked male. He didn't have to worry about that one coming back, his head was already missing. He got up and found the other, a lean Human female with short black hair lying on her side. Her back was to him and though unconscious she was already starting to regenerate. He knew that it wouldn't take long for them to regenerate without silver in their blood and dug his dowel out from the bottom of his belt pouch. He aimed at the back of her head and fired, thankful he had never seen her face. After he made sure that she was gone, he walked over the crest of the crater looking for the other fallen Werewolves.

Their bodies had fully reverted to humanoid form revealing a young filthy Dwarven man and slender Elven woman who looked around Eric's age. They looked dead and would stay that way as long as the silver rounds remained in their bodies for the next three days. Kole aimed his dowel at the girl's face, a pretty angel with her long curly blond hair wrapped around her naked body. He wondered how they transformed and kept their hair, but dismissed the thought not wanting to identify with those in sleeping death at his feet. He closed his eyes reminding himself they came to kill them then tried not to think that what he was about to do. All he had to do was remove the rounds and they'd recover, continuing their lives, but they are evil and attacked without provocation. He opened his eyes and pushed the guilt weighing heavy on his heart away then fired two rounds, finishing what they started, burning the horror of the moment into his mind.

Kole rejoined the group. "Are the others taken care of?" he asked.

Kyra nodded. "They will be," she quipped spinning an axe handle in her hand.

"Fine, let's get it over with then get out of here. We'll take their

DNA as proof for Roy."

"Roy, that bastard!" Nick fumed. "That's the last time I'll trust him when he tells me there are only three Werewolves out here."

Kyra turned her back scanning the forest for movement. "No one knows what's out here, especially him, sitting behind his desk. You should've known better to believe anything he says. Besides we can now demand more danger pay and bounty for saving the town from a potential attack."

Nick groaned then kicked at the ground. "I don't care about the money. We just lost our home to a pack of mutts! How are we going to carry all our stuff back to town?"

"At least you still have stuff," Kyra grumbled. "My room got torched." She sighed. "All my beautiful dresses are gone. My first real dress after we escaped and my shoes were to die for," she complained. "All of my shoes, that took me years to gather, my treasure, gone."

Nick scoffed. "All your crap took up so much room. What did you need all that frilly stuff for? It was a waste of space."

She slung her rifle over her shoulder then spun and punched him in the kidney. "You just don't get it!"

He grunted. "You didn't have to hit me that hard," he whined rubbing his side. "Now I'm going to piss blood for a week."

She nodded in satisfaction.

Eric laughed then flexed his bicep. "Kyra, I'm sorry you lost all your things, when we get to town we'll come back and salvage what we can then go shopping."

"I don't know about that," Nick disagreed. "We don't know who owns the artillery and if these Werewolves were working for them, or just looking for an easy meal. I think we should press on and take out the artillery then come back for our stuff, or they'd just shoot us again." He readied his rifle. "But then again if they have artillery then they must have transportation and since they tried to kill us, I don't feel bad about taking their gear."

Kyra brightened. "We might get a new home and we'll be making this area safer for everyone."

Nick looked back over his shoulder. "Kole, in all your extensive knowledge, do Werewolves operate this way?"

"No, but they're still Human," he stated. "These guys don't seem to have back up, so we're probably dealing with two groups."

"Are you okay, Kole?" Kyra asked. "You seem a little off."

"I guess my conscience is bothering me. I just killed three people in cold blood."

Nick grabbed his shoulder. "You did what you had to and we can't have them at our back."

"That sounds great, but if I throw life away so easily, it won't take long before I'm living only for me," Kole said, unsure they'd understand.

Kyra shrugged. "This is the world we live in, it's ugly but it's all we got. You are who you are and if you're worried about becoming bad, it's too late because your conscience would've stopped you. You're struggling with remorse and beating yourself up for doing what you know is right."

Nick cleared his throat. "Are we going after these people, or what? Because we're losing light talking about our feelings and the crap we lost, so let's move."

"You just want their stuff," Eric said then laughed.

"Okay people, we're the hunters now. We'll assess their strength and if possible take them out. Kyra take rear, I'll take point. We'll follow the wolf's tracks until they deviate from where we want to go, who knows they might lead us strait there. Oh, and Kole, stop pulling your punches. We understand that you think you'll lose yourself to your power, but one day you'll have to trust in who you are, like everybody else."

Surprised by Nick and Kyra, Kole thought about what they said then released his guilt and followed Nick at a steady pace deeper into the forest through a sea of waist high leaves.

Chapter

10

Byron left Bishop's in the morning and flew to where Sarah's merchant caravan was ambushed then took a gamble and changed course heading toward the closest Slaver outpost. He flew high surveying the landscape looking for the Slavers, or more wreckage then spotted movement. He kept his distance, hovering, watching two hover cycles patrolling, circling a small Battle Barge and a crew of salvagers working on the fresh wreckage. He lowered himself into the tall grass and thought about how he wanted to play the game. He decided to use a story instead of violence to get information then walked to the wreckage. He passed the two hover cycles as they buzzed by then strolled up to the Slaver's Barge noticing a line of bodies, Slaver types that were placed a short distance away. The small Battle Barge then slowly turned to point its forward gun at him as three men in body armor armed with rifles took position on its deck.

He stopped and waited for a darker skin man with curly black hair to meet him. "Hey there," Byron greeted waving.

"If you can't count, you have three rifles trained on you. Anything happens, you're dead."

"That's not necessary friend, I'm unarmed," Byron soothed raising his hands and slowly turning around to show them.

"What do you want?"

"I can see that you're in the middle of salvaging. How much are you going to leave behind?"

The Man looked around then asked, "Where did you come from, friend?"

"Oh. I'm traveling with my wife and two children," he lied. "I've hid the transport and walked in. If anything happens to me, they run."

"I'd do the same," The Man said then pointed his thumb over his shoulder. "We're taking it all."

Byron whistled. "There's a lot of damage. Did you guys do that?"

"No, these Slavers had a run in with an Alchemist."

Byron cursed. "Damn Alchemists, I guess it doesn't matter how far you travel you'll never be away from their kind."

"What do you have against them?"

"I'm an aspiring merchant, you can tell by my attire," he boasted, glad he hadn't repaired his clothes after he had flown without his shield, flavor for his lies. "I used to be a salvager then I saved up trading for my transport and some valuables to get me going. Then an Alchemist showed up, ruining it."

"They do that," The Man said.

"You said Slavers. Did the Alchemist rescue any slaves?"

"No, he left them to rot. We saved them."

"Good for you guys. I never trusted those bastard Alchemists. Where are you all from?"

"Winter Haven to the South and if you're interested in setting up a business dealing with pure Humans, your family can register your genetic code and get a trading license."

"You'd take us in just like that?"

"If you're pure, yes, we have to stick together and we can always use good breeding stock. We're fighting for our existence and we need good people."

"I'm glad I stopped," Byron said. He pointed at the row of bodies. "Do you have any weapons to trade?"

"That's one good thing about Slavers, they're well equipped, but you missed out. We've already sent their gear and valuables back to town."

He gestured to the Ork Captain. "An Ork, would you believe I've never been this close to one."

"Who wants to be?"

"What was he using? I bet it looked savage."

The Man laughed. "It was an ugly looking hand axe, the kind used for chopping bodies more than wood. We'll melt it down into something useful."

Byron nodded then looked around. "I'm sure you guys have everything under control, but I just had a thought. I can help out for a modest finder's fee. I have a G One automated scanner that can find anything lost in this tall thick grass. It'd be a shame to miss something priceless out here."

"We have a "Gone" scanner," he stated. "I'm sorry friend, there's nothing here for you."

"You got to try. Oh, one last thing. Do you know where that Alchemist went? They're trouble and I don't want my family near one."

"I heard he's in Pine View," he answered, but Byron's expression begged for elaboration. "It's further south, but Winter Haven is Alchemist free. Think about the safety of your family before deciding where you want to be."

"I'll talk it over with my wife, thanks for the invite," he said then left the way he came before flying low over the grass toward Winter Haven.

Byron took his time reaching the city's fortified walls, avoiding patrols and sensor drones then found a blind spot between their weapon platforms and hopped the wall. Landing, he waited for an alarm telling his that he was spotted, but none sounded. He casually walked through the back allies to the town's center and blended into the crowd. The town felt odd to him, the energy was high with a lot of people bustling in the streets. A passerby nodded a hello to him as a group of children ran by laughing and playing, but he couldn't place why everyone was in such high spirits. The buildings were poor quality, made from the standard mismatched materials and litter was strewn across the worn out walkways. People were being good to each other and their happiness annoyed him. He thought about putting them under his boot, in their place, stealing their contentment, but then felt her presence. He followed the feeling then saw her meandering through the crowd. Sarah wore a white robe with thin gold trim and was being followed by a young black haired woman in a similar robe.

Byron stepped out of the crowd blocking her path. "Hello."

The young woman sprang to her side. "Sister Sarah, he looks dangerous. I can fetch the authorities," she offered.

Sarah gave her a warm smile. "No, he's lost and wants to be found. Run ahead and prepare my tea." The young woman bowed then glared at him as she passed.

"I was wondering why you hadn't reported in, but seeing you and your servant... mystery solved," Byron mocked.

"Lord Byron," she sassed, bowing. "I've been waiting for you, hoping that you'd find your way out of the brothels."

He ignored her comment. "I think you ran off and didn't want me to find you, or you would've reported in."

A dark haired woman in miss matched clothes interrupted them, stepping close to Sarah. "Thank you Sister Sarah for the medicine, my son recovered." She cupped Sarah's hand in hers. "What can I do to repay you?"

Sarah gazed fondly at her. "Release your fears, live in joy and aid your fellow Human."

"Thank you," she blubbered. "I will. We are blessed to have you." She brushed by moving on.

"Byron, I didn't run off," she corrected. "James would've extracted me and started over judging this town to be too small, but my attire and servant were gifts from the people proving that the plan is still in motion."

"I hate to say it, but James' right. There aren't enough people here. You were supposed to infiltrate the Slavers, gather the Humans and lead them to safety."

"I have a better plan that'll gather the Humans here."

Byron regarded her. "Let's see if I've figured out what you've done here." He made quotations with his fingers. "Sister Sarah."

She took a breath then relaxed. "Mocking doesn't suit you, my

Lord."

He glared at her then gave his best smile noticing that the passersby were paying attention to them. He also noticed that the crowd wasn't milling into them, or forcing them into a wall, instead they were giving them room, privacy.

A man in light blue coveralls entered their space carrying a cardboard tube, ignoring Byron and spoke to Sarah. "I was waiting at your home and your servant said you were here. I've secured a power system from one of our neighbors. We can now build the equipment to make medical supplies. Thanks again, it's going to help us out so much and draw more trade here."

"Medicine is just the first step. After everyone here is taken care of we can reach out to those Humans in need and together we're going to make Winter Haven great."

"I'm so excited I can't wait. If you don't mind me asking, where did you get these plans?"

"I've carried them for a long time," she lied. "I knew they were valuable and protected them, waiting for a home to share them with."

"We're blessed that you're here. Thank you," he beamed. He hurried, disappearing into the crowd.

Byron changed his mind about Sarah. "James is crafty giving you those plans and you've set yourself up as a holy woman so that men can't touch you and women won't see you as a threat. You're trying to be a beacon of light and hope to these Commoners."

"You've almost got it. I already have enough influence to sleep with everybody here if I wanted and they'd all want more, the other women would even applaud me, but that's small minded and self serving."

"All right, I'm curious. What's your plan?"

"I need a broadcast tower and a steady supply of beacon drones. The drones will carry my signal into the waste and be programmed to seek out other Humans. My recordings will do the work for me and people will come in droves. With the medical supplies we'll trade for everything that we need."

"You're starting to scare me."

"I'm doing what I was made to do. I'm using what James gave me to protect the Human race. I will gather them, elevate them out of the mud, give them purpose, a safe place and together we'll create a new nation."

"Whatever. Tell it to James," he said.

"No, right now for this to work I can't contact anyone. I'm influencing the psyche of everyone here on a level and they're watching everything I do without realizing it. Look around Byron, everyone on this street is watching us and wondering who you are and what we're discussing."

"Fine I'll pass along your request and one last thing before I go. The Slaver captain had a Ripper, where did it go?"

"Once we were freed I looked, didn't find it and it's not in Winter Haven. The Alchemist Kole must have it."

He searched her face for lies. "Or you kept it for yourself. You're going to gather a lot of power here and want to protect it from us."

Her warm smile irritated Byron. "I don't need the Ripper and as long as I'm doing what I was made to do, James won't harm me. For now, Kole is in Pine View and our records show that he doesn't stay in one place for long, if you hurry you can catch him before he disappears into the waste."

He glanced at the people who were pretending not to be watching realizing how tense he was. He relaxed again, smiling. "I don't take orders from you. Don't forget that you're a clone…" His face contorted as he searched for the correct insult. "Crap on my heel. You'd be wise not to forget your place."

"I am what I choose to be and you can't change that."

"What does a clone know about anything?" he dismissed her. He left the town through its gates then walked into the sparse forest looking toward Pine View and planning his next move. He smiled deciding that he'd find the Ripper then use it on Cid to punish him for his arrogance.

Chapter

11

Kole followed Nick along the trail of broken twigs, flattened brush and paw prints gradually leaving the valley, climbing higher into rockier terrain to another section of hovercraft road. Nick cautiously approached the tree line then knelt, leaning against a tree for cover before he raised a fist signaling them to stop.

Kyra knelt turning her back to them watching behind. "What do we have?" She asked, lowering her rifle to pull out her motion detector.

Eric cocked his head listening. "It's quiet like before with that same weird feeling in the air."

Kole crouched then shuffled to Nick's side. He listened to wind brush the tree tops then focused on his hearing charm, reaching out listening to the faint sound of footfalls surrounding them. The eerie feeling thickened and he knew they were in trouble. "I'm sorry," he said. "It seems my knowledge of Werewolves is incorrect."

Kyra finished setting up her detector, hit her pad then cursed. "There's a lot of movement out there flanking us. Please tell me they're not what I think they are."

They all turned, looking at Kole. "They know how to hide," he said then thought for a moment about what Nick and Kyra had said earlier.

"You want me to stop pulling my punches? Do you have any hovernades?" he asked.

Nick reached into his belt pouches pulling out two six inch cylinders and handed them to Kole who subconsciously allowed them to pass through his shield. He examined the weapons having a small hover matrix at one end and a pin with a small data pad at the other.

"Those aren't going to do anything if they're Werewolves," Nick said dryly. "I'd like to think we're facing Slavers, that way we'd have a chance."

Kole placed hovernades on the ground as Kyra reached into her bag and pulled out two square boxes. He quickly took the boxes opening them and put eight more with the others. Kole looked into them seeing how they worked and using the molecules in the air, he increased their size, explosive yield and changed their shrapnel to silver."

"That's the weirdest thing I've ever seen," Nick commented.

Kyra agreed. "So that's what it looks like. A vibrating mess of colors, one second one thing, the next another. That's crazy."

Eric's jaw dropped. "He's never transmuted anything in front of outsiders before. We must be in real trouble."

Nick sighed. "Yeah, I think we're all going to die, but I'll decide for sure after we see what we're up against."

Kole worked the pad on each hovermine adjusting their settings. "Kyra, link these to your data pad and position them half way between us and them." Kyra nodded and Kole watched the mines quietly speed away.

Eric lifted his head sniffing. "You all smell that?" he asked. "It's faint, but it smells like tobacco."

"Very good," said a man with a Russian accent over their com channel. Kole thought about his shield, making sure it was still erected. The voice sounded Human, but only Elves and pirates transverse the oceans and traveling with Elves is very expensive. The man continued, "My pack and I have been watching you for over an hour. We're trying to decide on what to do to you for killing our kin. Their ideas are very gruesome, but I told them that I personally get to take care of you. Do you know what I'm going to do?" His silence begged Kole to answer, but before he could, the man snapped, "Of course you don't! I'm going to spill your guts then eat your heart!" He laughed a cold belly laugh which Kole could also faintly hear through the forest a hundred meters away. The man calmed. "Your friends will join my family to replace the fallen. They're smart enough to wear thermo protected body armor unlike you and your apprentice. You both show up like flares against the cool forest floor."

"This has all gone too far," Kole said. "You fired upon us then tried to finish off the survivors. We were defending ourselves, so it's your fault your people are dead. I urge you to disband your pack and leave this sector before I'm forced to kill you and the rest of your family, bringing you all final death."

The man grunted. "Disband, leave, final dead, I'm old," he said, "but very strong. I've spent fifty years on General Postick's torture table." He sounded proud, but Kole was lost to his reference. "I lost count, over three thousand times I died and I don't feel pain the way others do. They say it has made me a little crazy, but I have moments where I think I'm crazy and that makes me sane." He cackled making Kole feel uneasy then took a drag off his smoke, slowly exhaling before saying, "I don't fear death, haven't in a long time, but now let's get to the, as some say, posa and potatoes of our talk."

Kole cringed at the Troll word "Posa", meaning Elven meat. "Gross," he whispered.

"I challenge you to hand to hand combat, on the road, no guns. I want to rip your guts out with my bare hands and feel the warmth of your blood on my skin."

Kole wasn't sure if the man was trying to intimidate him, or was just caught up in the moment. "Yes," Kole agreed in a calm dangerous tone. "You're crazy. What do you think is going to happen, I walk up the road meet you and we'll duel?"

"That's exactly what I think is going to happen," the man confessed. "You're going to say yes, how can you resist my charm and the thought of a challenge? Your kind has everything easy and you look for ways to make your lives have meaning. You live a personal quest for glory and there's nothing wrong with that. We all search for meaning to who we are. Some embrace their destiny, while others play the martyr and fight themselves all the way to the grave. As for me, I am what I am and I'm enjoying myself." He chuckled then growled allowing a hint of anger and madness to surface.

"I don't accept your challenge, but I do want to meet you. Reconsider disbanding your pack and leaving the area before we both choose the wrong path." Kole took his ear piece out and adjusted it before putting it back. "Synchronize your helmets to alternating frequencies and dig in. It's going to get rough." He looked at Eric giving him a reassuring smile. "Keep your head down and stay safe. I'll be right back. I'm going to see if I can change his mind."

Kole walked onto the logged road through the underbrush and stood on a relatively flat outcropping of rock. He took note of the positions of some loose rocks and sticks, thinking of the different alchemical combinations he could use to make weapons in case things went sideways. Further up the road he watched a naked man in his fifties emerge from the forest. The man was Kole's height, but twice as thick with hairy shoulders and a round pot belly. He walked toward Kole grinning with his long scraggly grey hair flowing over his shoulders. Kole felt the warm flush of adrenalin course through him in anticipation of combat then watched the man step over a log. He noticed his feet and at first thought the man was wearing some form of homemade mud caked sneakers then realized that he was barefoot. The man stood at the end of the outcrop close enough for Kole to see his tobacco stained teeth. The man's grin widened revealing more plaque. He held his hands before him, his yellow fingers curled into claws showing off his long cracked nails telling Kole he had access to a steady supply of tobacco. He cringed inside at the thought of being bitten by him.

The man said, "You are Kole and I'm Cid. Our spies in town said you were coming and they told me to let you run around my territory even though we possess the weapons to lay waste to your kind. I'm not just talking about these hands." The man admired them. "They're strong and my nails are sharp." His eyes shifted, partly obscured by his bushy eyebrows, making eye contact with Kole as a menacing expression washed across his face. "For centuries my kind had to be small, huddled in the corner afraid of being hunted, but now my pack is the largest this world has ever seen, gathered from its darkest corners."

"You have special weapons? That's funny because I took one off an Ork Slaver."

He laughed. "You found it. Sadly you're not the Alchemist it was meant for, but I'll still have some fun." Cid eyes widened, his pupils dilate turning bright yellow and his jaw clamped shut grimacing in pain. He stepped back then hunched, flexing his arms, moaning a deep rattling noise as his muscles trembled increasing in size.

Kole watched fascinated by Cid's transformation, suddenly knowing what to do. "Screw this noise!" Kole growled then fired three bolts of energy into Cid's chest.

Cid staggered back falling off the outcrop as patches of grey hair erupted over his body.

Kole ran closer, aimed his dowel at Cid's face to end it quick, but a pressure from behind forced him to jump sideways as a blue streak shot by.

Cid arched his back, his face elongated and his bones creaked and popped as he took on the lupine form.

Kole spun around looking for the Ripper.

Cid sprang to his feet then barked, almost howling each word, "I'm going to reach inside you, grab your guts and squeeze the crap out of you!" He rushed forward, his maw open in a silent scream swinging his claws at Kole.

In the flash the world slowed and a calm enveloped Kole. He stepped forward under Cid's arm allowing his shield to flex then struck Cid's ribcage with his knucklers searing his flesh. Kole heard sizzling then on his second strike he pressed hard dragging the knuckles, watching Cid's skin blister and hair smolder. He expected Cid to move away, or slow down so he could attack again, but Cid weighed into his attack further searing his flesh as he drove his elbow into Kole's shield.

Cid sprang away. "Hit this prick and drop his shield!" he commanded.

A mud encrusted naked man with a Ripper peeked around a tree, but Kole was faster. He shot and took the top of his head off. "That was your plan?" he mocked turning to face Cid.

Cid laughed in grunts. "You got me. He wasn't to die. I was always going to kill you and add one friend to the pack."

"I have a good team and you only want one?"

He flexed his body adding a deep rumble to his voice. "World be given back to Humans, everyone else, meat."

He looked him over stressing the point, "You're not Human."

He thumped his chest with his fist. "Soul, Human, all that matters in end."

"You think it's possible to be normal again?"

"Of course," Cid barked. "One man made this world. His thought to break, to remake."

He raised his hand to silence Cid, no longer listening to his propaganda. "Stop what you're doing here and disband your people, or all your mutts will die. I can't have you murdering innocent people."

"Fool!" he spat. "You hear, but no listen." He tensed then released a loud howl that vibrated through Kole.

Kole fought the urge to cover his ears and when Cid finished, snapping branches and the pounding feet erupted around them. Their eyes met and Kole saw a hint of mischief in Cid's yellow eyes a second before the Werewolf sprang forward, wildly clawing at his shield. Confused, Kole held his ground knowing he couldn't be hurt then felt the pressure of another Ripper behind him. He dropped to his knee as half his shield was blown away and in his mind's eye he imagined the crazed Cid ripping him apart. Terror flooded through him igniting the deep well of power within. His fingers touched stone instinctively transmuting the area under Cid into a bed of long silver spikes that shot through Cid's body elevating him off the ground, impaling him. Cid yelped then whimpered as the silver boiled his blood and seared his flesh.

Kole felt like he was floating, instinctively spinning to face a wave of Werewolves running on all fours. A black carpet sweeping across the landscape, never in his life had he heard of or seen such a nightmare. He felt the pressure again. He dove toward a grimy half naked man in green camouflage pants as the blue bolt narrowly missed him, absorbing into the silver spikes impaling Cid. The spikes exploded spraying needles of shrapnel into the tree line, a thunderous rumble that dropped a line of Werewolves. Seeing the effect, Kole had an idea, but he needed those guns. He slapped his hand down reaching through the earth into the tree beside the man, creating a silver branch that punched through his skull. The man went limp dropping his Ripper.

Kole reset his shield then ran, grabbing then man's pistol. He didn't have time to think, or to wish the day went differently. The Werewolves were almost on him and Rippers were back. He reached out as far as he could turning trees among the rushing hoard into silver. A part of him screamed for him to stop, to find reason, but he couldn't let his friends die. He ran to the other Ripper, reduced his shield exposing the ends of his guns' barrels then fired at the trees.

Chapter

12

Nervousness crashed through Eric making his hands slightly tremble. He didn't want Kole to leave and meet the pack leader, but it wasn't the first time Kole had left him behind. He understood why Kole did it, but staying back didn't make him feel safe and what unsettled him the most was the primal tone in the Werewolf's voice. He reassured himself thinking that Kole knew what he was doing and shrugged away his uncertainty then focused on the forest, calming himself, relaxing his muscles so they'd react faster. In his opposite hand, he reached into his pocket and rubbed a small stone charm with his thumb feeling the carved lines that made a crude picture of a bullet, making sure his shield was erect. He couldn't let fear or surprise defeat him, destroying his concentration dropping his shield, not like last time.

He lowered himself closer to the ground thinking of the possibility of snipers locating them then crawled forward pushing a leafy plant to the side and leaned against the base of a tree. His eyes casually found Kyra. She knelt, working on the hovernades exuding a quiet confidence occasionally checking her motion detector. Even with her body armor he could see the nice curves of her ass and the strength in her legs. He indulged in the fantasy of grabbing her hips and taking her right there, but wasn't sure how. He smiled at his active imagination then piped up, "Kyra, do you think Kole will end things peacefully?"

She glanced down at her detector then her muffled voice came through his earpiece, "I think this whole meeting thing was to buy time for them to surround us before they attack."

"I should've thought of that," he scolded himself. "I was distracted by my feelings." He looked in Kole's direction then blurted, "We need to warn Kole."

"Kole's not stupid," Nick soothed. "He's divided their numbers and more will attack him, or us."

"I hope it's the former," Kyra said. "He's the bigger threat and I'm sure he can handle himself."

"Out there he has enough room and doesn't have to worry about hurting us," Nick commented.

Eric grimaced. "What are we going to do if these guys have kids?"

Nick looked into the forest. "A better question is. What can we do with a bunch of Werewolf pups? Put them in a kennel?" he quipped. "Give them away as pets? Or, should we release them into the wild and let nature take its course?"

"It's a waste of time thinking about that," Kyra said. "We'll decide what to do when we have to."

Nick snorted. "The safest thing for everyone is to remove the problem." He was quiet for a second. "That sounded bad. On second thought, if we let them live they'll be someone else's problem, if they become evil that is. It might not happen."

Kyra finished programming her enhanced hovernades. "It's not their fault, they're just wired funny. Eventually their brain chemistry will drive them to kill."

Eric watched the hovernades disappear into forest. "I think Kyra's right. We'll decide when we have to."

Through the trees Eric watched an old naked man step onto the rock platform to meet Kole. His nudity surprised Eric, most pirates dressed like Slavers with spiked blood stained body armor to intimidate their victims, some even like flamboyant shirts and fancy guns, but this old guy was filthy as if he had never taken a bath. The man displayed his hands to Kole, but Eric couldn't make out what he said then the man tensed and in a quick motion Kole fired first. The man stumbled back then fell, his skin darkened, body increased in size and hair quickly grew covering him. Witnessing the painful transformation unsettled Eric and he found himself agreeing with Nick.

The Werewolf then attacked mingling his body with Kole's in a quick violent dance that ended with Kole unharmed. They started talking again.

"Stop talking and kill him you idiot," Nick complained.

"What's happening?" Kyra asked.

Eric turned to watch the forest. "I think the old bugger's stalling."

"Kyra, what does the motion detector say?" Nick asked.

She glanced at her pad. "I didn't want to say this again, but there's a lot of movement out there and Kole's right, they're really good at not being seen."

"How much movement, like ten, fifteen blips?" Nick hoped.

"I don't think we have enough ammo."

Nick cleared his throat. "You're kidding, right?" Her silence was deafening. He shifted his position to tighten the group then checked his rifle. "Stay calm, control your burst and we'll make it out of here. I do have some bad news though. I don't think Roy has enough money to pay for all this."

Eric laughed then heard a loud howl before feeling the pressure of a Ripper discharging. Fearful memories flash in his mind making him dive to the ground. He didn't know if he was the target, but he had to react. Many times as a boy he was caught playing and was shot in the back by Kole's practice Ripper. Eventually he learned to feel the pressure and move, but when he failed the intense pain left him hugging himself in the dirt screaming. Anger quelled the fear within. He pushed himself onto his knees to see that Kole had suspended the Werewolf on a bed of long silver spikes. Kole then ran into the forest and Eric felt the pressure again from two sources behind him. He spun onto his feet then dove, rolling to safety.

Nick yelled, "There!" He aiming his rifle at a naked man smeared with camouflage paint hiding behind a bush then fired a burst into his chest.

Kyra found the second man as he went to hide behind a tree then fired her rifle taking what she could. His exposed arm, shoulder and knee were torn apart with a section of the tree and as he fell, Kyra squeezed her trigger again placing another burst into the side of his neck and head.

Eric watched the two men fall then heard the rumbling of the charging Werewolves surrounding them. The snapping and crashing sounded ominous. He didn't want his new friends to die, but didn't know how to save them. He looked for a way out. A black wave of moving fur bound between the trees then a glittering caught his eye. Trees were turning into silver, Kole's work, but before he questioned it, he spotted Kole running toward the Werewolf horde firing a Ripper. Eric fought the instinct to move away from the pressure then saw a tree explode with such force that it tossed the closest Werewolves into the air, spraying chunks of silver into their flesh. He realized Kole's plan then ran to get the other Rippers, but stumbled when Kyra's mines went off. The ground shook and the smell of burning flesh was carried on a gust of warm air. He sprang to his feet and found the Rippers.

He turned. Kyra and Nick came together kneeling back to back preparing to be overrun. Eric didn't hesitate. It was the first time he held a Ripper and he swore he'd never use one, but watching his friends fight for their lives changed his mind. He wanted protect them and to be there for them. He ran and with each step he released his fear, knowing his shield would protect him.

The Werewolves were on him. He spun sliding sideways and pulled the triggers unsure what would happen. He felt the pressure and hoped he didn't waste his precious time, but when the weapons discharged, the Werewolves' torsos exploded into meaty chunks. Surprised, the gore slapped against his shield and every time he pulled the triggers after that he thought about what a Ripper would've done to him. All those times Kole had shot him, how he learned to avoid that death. Now understanding Kole's lessons after all these years released a wave of confusion, pain and resentment that he didn't know was there. Hot tears blurred his vision and streamed down his cheeks, but he kept firing knowing he'd live, he'd save his friends and that he was built to survive.

Chapter

13

Kole stopped running. His Rippers felt hot in his hands. He slowly turned calming his heavy breathing trying to slow the pounding in his chest, searching for movement through the shattered silver trees, but nothing stirred. He listened for Human noise, but the decimated forest was quiet. He thought of the others and felt foolish for leaving them, but at the time he wanted to protect them by quickly disposing of the monsters as fast as possible. He imagined them wounded, or needing his help and ran back avoiding the various sized silver spikes carpeting the ground. Once Werewolves, now naked bodies lay scattered mutilated, burned and poisoned by silver. He ran up and around a small stump to see Eric pointing two Rippers at him, standing in solemn confidence a short distance away from the others who stood back to back decorated with blood and gore. Kole noticed that it took Eric a moment to recognize him. Eric's pale face wore a grim expression, but his eyes brightened when he recognized him and for a moment his body slightly trembled as relief replaced readiness. He lowered his weapons and it was obvious to Kole that Eric used the Rippers on the Werewolves. The bodies around them were torn asunder.

Kole wished none of this had happened. It was supposed to be a nice walk in the forest ending in the death of some bad guys, not bloodying his boy's soul. He didn't want to be his teacher, exposing Eric to trauma to coat him with a thick layer of emotional scars so he'd no longer feel, but now he'd be able to do what was needed to survive. "Is anyone hurt?" Kole asked, his voice sounded forced even to his ears.

Nick spoke, "There's no way we're going to decapitate all these bodies."

"I don't think we have to," Eric muttered. "There's too much toxicity from all the silver."

"We still need to gather samples for proof of death, if we want to get paid," Kyra commented.

Kole looked around. "What a mess. I guess I could've made a silver mist for them to breathe, but I didn't think about it."

"Oh, that would've been so much better," Eric agreed.

"Kole," Kyra said. "I'm grateful to be alive, but just one of you did all this. I didn't know this was possible, I guess I should've, but now I understand how the old world ended."

Kole could hear them, but with the danger gone he relaxed and felt energized, clean and free from his mental chains. He'd always kept his power in check, even today he held back, doing just enough, but it felt so good to stretch. He went big instead of small and wanted to do more. His mind race to find an excuse to let his power flow, but the years of discipline pounced on those growing thoughts, pinching them closed. He swallowed, controlling the chaos within. "Add the right elements and things can get out of hand. It isn't hard to lose yourself because the mind enjoys addiction."

Kyra chuckled. "I'm not addicted to anything."

Nick snorted. "Tell that to your shoe collection."

Kyra moaned. "For a moment I had forgotten about them. They made me feel good."

Nick slung his rifle over his shoulder then held out his hand. "Eric, pass me one of those shooters, will you?"

Eric smirked. "Are you going to use them on us?"

"No, we're family now."

"Yeah," Kyra said sounding chipper then collected her motion detector.

Kole shook his head finally feeling normal. "We all need some sort of therapy." They all looked at him then laughed. Eric passed Nick a Ripper.

"Who's sane in this world?" Nick asked. "Maybe there's some hermit out there untouched by the world somewhere in the mountains, you can talk with him." He thought for a moment. "On second thought, like he'd want to hear all your crap, so no therapy."

Eric walked around the gore to meet Kole. "It's nice to talk about our sanity in this mess, but I'd like to get this day over with so I can take a bath."

"You should get a suit like ours," Kyra suggested. "We don't smell a thing."

"No," Eric disagreed stepping over a body. "That's negative manifestation. Suits mean you have something to protect and you'll attract a reason to need your suits, besides our shields protect us."

Nick laughed. "That's your propaganda. Like saying being a pacifist will attract violence so you can prove how much of a pacifist you are."

"What?" Kyra asked. "That doesn't make any sense."

The group met Kole. "We can discuss philosophy later. Let's find their base and remove the rest of the threat, especially their artillery."

"What if there are pups?" Eric worried.

Nick nudged him.

Kole looked around. "We'll have to terminate them. They were raised and felt safe in a large pack. To feel safe again they'll be motivated to gather another one. It'll take time, but the thought will be running in the backs of their minds. They'll also stick together, so if you find one you'll find them all."

"That can't be true," Kyra stated. "They're just kids, like they'd know."

Kole didn't want to be the one to do it. He pointed to the corpses then said, "Look around, this will happen again because the monster within them will make it happen."

Nick pushed passed the group. "We don't know if there are any pups and if it comes to it, we'll draw straws to see who does the deed, until then we're burning daylight. Let's go."

Chapter

14

After infiltrating Pine View, Byron transmuted his clothes into a pair of grubby coveralls and worn leather boots. He ruffled his hair then dirtied his face and hands before walking down the sidewalk, nodding a hello to passersby. There weren't as many town's people as Winter Haven, but they were calm and spoiled with clean streets and spacious housing. Creating a cover story he asked around about Kole discovering that Kole was well liked then found his apartment. He broke in the old fashioned way so he wouldn't leave an alchemical finger print, but didn't find the Ripper. Eric's room was the same except for an incomplete deck of nude Elven playing cards. Byron smiled to himself as he thumbed through the cards thinking of Monique and how all other women couldn't compare to her. The fire in her eyes, silky skin and long soft hair, he missed her so much it hurt. He put everything back the way he found it then went to the port. The town wasn't that big and everyone knew each other's business and asking the right question the right way revealed much. He learned that Kole left on a mission with another crew leaving his transport unattended.

Kole's transport was where they said it'd be, but Byron looked around at the other vehicles before examining Kole's. He walked into the tent, crossed his arms and leaned against the transport sending his awareness into its hull. There were many modifications that Byron used to feel Kole's strength and personality. Kole was the stronger Alchemist and could be more talented, but the way he wove his creations together showed that he restricted himself, lacking the imagination to be great. If he had to face Kole, he'd rely on speed and creativity to beat him, imaginative expression would be Kole's downfall. Satisfied that he knew Kole, he felt his way through the transport looking for the void of a Ripper, but only found the shape of a kid's toy gun. It wasn't anywhere near the strength of a Ripper, but it was hidden well. It was worth a look, but before he moved to pick the lock and dig out the pistol a man entered the tent.

"Hey there, my name's Roy and I don't think we've met."

"No sir," Byron said then offered his hand. "My name's Sam," he lied.

He shook his hand, but didn't let go. "Well met Sam, but I meant that I don't remember seeing you around town either."

"You know everyone who goes through town?" he doubted.

"We're in the middle of nowhere and it's prudent that I get a good look at everyone coming and going. You never know who's truly a friend."

He slightly smiled. "I guess that's a good thing, not creepy at all. To answer you, I've been working on the Venture's antigrav matrix the whole time she's been birthed here."

"Captain Bith didn't mention you."

He rubbed the back of his neck with his free hand looking sheepish then explained, "I'm new to the crew and I didn't meet the Captain. Honestly, I didn't ask names. I just needed to get out of Winter Haven and to prove my worth they stuck me with a damn near impossible task. Now I need an Alchemist to mend a part that I can't replace."

Roy let his hand go. "Is that why you've been asking all over town for him?"

"Is that what this is about? Well yeah, I needed to get a sense of him. You just don't blindly hire an Alchemist without knowing his rep. Is what they say about this Alchemist Kole true?"

He nodded answering, "Yes, he's fair and does fine work."

"I really need the part mended. Will he be back soon?"

"He's doing a job for me."

"Oh, he's in town? I guess I missed him. With your permission, can I borrow him for a minute?"

"No. He's in the waste."

His face scrunched in distaste. "What's he doing out there?"

"He's taking care of a Werewolf problem."

"Werewolves, here, that can't be true?"

His mustache twitched. "You said you're from Winter Haven and want to hire an Alchemist?"

"That's why I needed to leave Winter Haven. Those Anti-Alchemists are okay if you're Human, but they're full of venom. Somehow they figured out that I don't hate Alchemists, or blame them for everything wrong in the world. One thing led to another and now I needed a safe place to live. That's why I'm here." He faked sadness then complained, "I didn't even get a chance to pack. I need to get far away from those people."

Roy grabbed Byron's shoulder then led him out of the tent to where six security guards waited. "Why don't you go into town, enjoy yourself and when Kole gets back, I'll send him your way," he suggested.

"Thank you. That sounds fun and I could use the rest."

Roy gestured to the exit.

Byron happily strutted to the door then looked back to see Roy watching him while talking to the guards who all turned in unison to look at him. "Prick," he murmured knowing he had triggered Roy's suspicion. It didn't matter how it happened, some people are just paranoid.

He stepped through the exit closing the door behind him then ran up the grassy slope to the outer wall where he risked being seen leaping over it. Landing, he crouched low before flying to the tree line where he hid behind a tree almost being seen by a passing patrol. He then manifested a data pad and hack his way through the town's beacons into the mainframe where he deleted all their surveillance records. He tried not to make it personal but that nosy self-righteous Roy irritated him and before he logged out he deleted Roy's bank records and emptied his account leaving him with a single credit, a thin middle finger on his console screen.

Satisfied that he had taught Roy a lesson in manners, he dissolved the pad then flew through the forest to an old road and followed it to a hovercraft path. He followed the path higher into the mountains then found the smoldering wreck of a Battle Barge. He lowered himself into the grass then placed his hand on its rusty hull thinking that the lost Ripper might be inside, but there wasn't any sign of alchemy or bodies.

Kole didn't do anything for his team. Sure, they had survived, but he could've done something, anything to protect them. It was luck that no one was killed, and it seemed that Kole would've let them die in this rusted out junk heap. "Why?" Byron asked himself when they had left a perfectly good transport in town. He wanted to get to know Kole. He had seen Kole's anal alchemy and heard about his barter relationship with the people of Pine View instead of owning his power. Now, seeing that Kole risked the lives of his team to force them into his delusion of balance instead of protecting them made Byron pause. Kole could've lost his team right here, but he would've survived to continue the mission and soldier on leaving them to rot.

He followed their trail of flattened grass to find mutilated bodies and shell casings, but there was still no evidence of the Ripper making Byron believe, that out of fear Kole must have destroyed it. The thought that someone would throw away that much power hurt his mind. He rubbed his forehead slowly cutting through the haze of drug abuse and remembered a school of thought he'd heard about ages ago. He dropped his hand once the memory solidified.

"Alchemy to serve the people, to limit oneself for the masses, or some nonsense about losing your humanity," he mocked. "I thought that school died ages ago." He closed his eyes and focused his thoughts. "Wait, wait, wait, thought is energy and those that think the same gravitate together, layers of realities stacked on top of each other. If you're an honest person you won't see the criminal world. And I don't think like them so I won't touch their reality, but the other races in one form or another enslave their Alchemists in gilded cages, exchanging status for performance to keep the peace." He laughed. "I get it now. Kole is a fanatic hiding in plain sight so he can stay close to the Commoners, exchanging power for humanity. What a looser."

He shook his head dismissing his thoughts then followed Kole's trail climbing higher into a silver forest. Exploded trees and naked bodies littered the ground adding up to a colossal waste of resources. It took James years to quietly gather such a force just to have Cid throw everything away in one day, tragic. He needed to find Cid to make him pay for his stupidity, if he was still alive and Byron knew he'd find Cid at the heart of this disaster. Byron had lost Kole's trail, stepping over bodies and pointy chunks of silver then found himself on another section of the hovercraft path where movement caught his eye.

Byron smiled then mocked, "Cid, did you pull yourself off those spikes? Did that Alchemist spank you? You look awful. Those black puncture marks look like blood poisoning, you should have that looked at. Wow, those are some wicked looking chemical burns."

Cid rolled onto his back then squinted, looking up at him. "Byron," he croaked. "Friend, I think I might die this time. You can save me."

"You're one tough prick Cid," he admitted. "I'll save you if you answer my questions," he lied.

"Hurry, please, I hurt."

"You're pale with black veins, eerie. Just looking at you hurts me. Now pay attention like your life depends on it, because it does. Did the Alchemist who did all this have a Ripper?"

"No," he choked, confirming Byron's suspicion.

"There's Ripper damage here. How did that happen?"

"He took ours."

"Yours, you mean James'?" he corrected. "How many did you give the Alchemist?"

"Four," he wheezed. "Hurry and we can face them together." He coughed then begged, "I hurt."

His story didn't add up. "With all your people, you only attacked with four Rippers?" he asked, but knowing Cid only one thing made sense. "You didn't find the factory did you?"

"No factory. Four's enough to scare away Alchemists, so we can find factory later."

He closed his eyes as his anger overwhelmed him. "You idiot!" he snarled. "The level of your stupidity boggles my mind. You threw away years of preparation for nothing. The Rippers were never for you and even if you had them all, I could still kill you from miles away." Seething, Byron wanted to make him hurt, to share the pain Cid forced him to feel. He knelt and placed his hand on Cid's clammy forehead transmuting his skull into silver. Cid moaned then clutched Byron's ankle. His voice shook, his body convulsed and his eyes rolled back into his head a second before they both popped out releasing puffs of steam. Byron watched Cid twitch, his face etched in pain, but killing him didn't sate his anger. Byron's shoulders tightened and his mind clouded. "Why did you make me hurt you Cid? You were dying anyway, but you had to make me kill you."

He needed to calm down. He grabbed at the thought of Monique. Her lips, soft skin and the way her eyes shone with passion the day they had met. He smiled remembering her then felt better when Cid finally stopped twitching. He felt satisfied that he had taught Cid a lesson he'd remember in his next life. The forest was again quiet and had a graveyard peace to it. He soaked up the peaceful feeling then felt his shoulders relax and his mind clear. He missed Monique and thinking of her filled him with warmth, like she was the one he'd always been looking for. She was his fire and the other girls had been cheap stops on the way to finding her. And her smile, such a beautiful smile. She did smile? "Of course she did, we're in love," he said reassuring himself as his delusion took hold.

Chapter

15

Kole urged everyone forward abandoning stealth, knowing they reeked of blood, showed up on thermal scans and had made enough noise in the last fight to alert everyone in the valley. They followed the Werewolves' trail higher around the rocky crown of a small mountain then dipped into a denser section of forest. The group pushed on as the sky faded into night then slowed when they came upon light streaming through the forest. They quietly drew closer to the light source creeping in the shadows of the underbrush to the crest of the small hill. Down the other side the trees thinned to a clearing at the mouth of a large cave where a man with a black haired mustache waited. He wore a light purple suit and top hat. The man stood strait, almost arching backward with his nose in the air. Around him, yellow electrical cords ran out of the cave to two flanking stands supporting four large banks of blinding lights.

Kyra's helmet slowly moved into the light. "There could be snipers behind those lights."

Nick nodded. His smile could be heard in his voice, "Only an Alchemist would dress so garish and I believe he's the one that passed through town."

Kole stayed in the shadows looking passed Nick pushing his awareness outward, brushing against the man's suit to study the quality of the Alchemist who made it. From a distance the suit looked sharp and of good quality, but on a closer inspection anyone could see its many flaws. He frowned not surprised by the man, knowing his reputation of being a poor quality Alchemists. People like him were flashy and of weak character, those who'd profit off the reputation of their betters, trading garbage for the real thing. He sighed.

Nick half turned to him. "Do you know him?"

"I don't know him," Kole whispered, "but I've met many like him. Why would the pack send him out, they know we're coming? He's fake, weaker than the real thing. His kind usually runs when a true Alchemist shows up."

Kyra crept up between them. "A crappy Alchemist is still an Alchemist. If the Werewolves were smart, they would've had spies in town and probably know he's a looser. Most likely they didn't tell him who was coming and left him here to slow us down."

Eric snickered a little too loud agreeing with Kyra.

"I hear you," the man in purple shouted into the darkness. Eric cringed forgetting his kind could enhance their hearing, but before he could whisper an apology the man continued, raising the pitch in his voice to the point of arrogant superiority. "I'm a powerful Alchemist and you better leave, or I'll lay waste to you!"

Kole moaned, embarrassed. "Its guys like this that gives Alchemists a bad name."

Kyra nudged Kole. "Are you going to go and take care of him?"

"I guess I'll go talk with him."

"What?" Eric whispered. "If he was a Slaver he'd be dead already."

"He's weak, but he can still serve society, maybe as a guard."

"So can Slavers," Eric stated. "But they don't. A guard, look at this guy. He's too full of himself to be anywhere but here, he's evil and we're the good guys."

"You're right," the man shouted, "I am evil and there is no good, now run off before I get mad."

Nick laughed. "Someone, please kill this guy, I can't listen to his whiny voice anymore."

Kole placed his Rippers on the ground and took out his dowel. "Eric, look after these guns. I'm going to have a chat, I'll be right back." He stood in the light with his hands up then slowly walked through the underbrush toward the purple suited man.

The man stepped back taking a fighting stance and waved his gun in front of him. "Stay back! I have a Ripper and you should know what I can do to you!"

Kole kept walking. "You can see me, you know who I am."

"Yeah, I see you," he sneered. "I've been beaten up and chased away by enough of your type." He pointed his Ripper at Kole. "This time!" he screamed. "You will leave my territory and never return!"

"I can't do that," he soothed. "I've now seen six Rippers within a week. I destroyed the first one I found because I thought it was the only one. The existence of these weapons will disturb the balance of the world and bring about another Purge."

"You destroyed it?" he asked dumbfounded. "Of course you did. You wouldn't want a weaker Alchemist to find it and take your power, making you feel lower than garbage."

Kole stopped a short distance away from the man. "You don't get it, and your teacher should've explained this better to you, but power doesn't come from your hands it…"

"Shut up!" the man screamed interrupting Kole. "You don't know!" He fired his gun.

Kole felt the Ripper's pressure and sprang to the side avoiding the blast. And before the man could react, Kole flicked his wrist releasing bolt of energy that punched through the edge of the man's shield.

He shrieked recoiling as a part of him was torn away. He spun on his heel looking over his shoulder at Kole and ran into a tree. He hit the tree hard enough to knock his hat off and throw his gun into the bushes. He spun again dazed, but found his bearings running into the night.

Kole retrieved the man's gun. "How many of these things are there?" he wondered.

"Well," Nick said walking up behind him. "There's one for me and two for each of you of course." He slung his rifle over his shoulder then held his Ripper up, admiring it.

"Aren't you going after him?" Eric asked passing Kole another gun.

"No, he's just lost and confused."

"I agree with Eric," Kyra said looking in the direction the man ran. "Even the weakest Alchemist can raze a town. If he does anything bad from now on, you'll wish you ended him here."

Kole rubbed his fore head trying to chase away a budding headache. "Are we all broken? Kill, kill, kill, I've killed enough today."

"All these people are evil," Eric stated. "Ending them now saves the future."

He regarded Eric. "You've been poisoned. You need to let today go."

Eric snorted.

"I'm serious," Kole countered. "A weapon made will demand to be used and if you hold violence in your heart, violence is all you'll find."

Eric crossed his arms. "Peace can't exist without violence. In order to let go of violence you have to first let go of peace."

"I'm not talking about peace. The idea of peace is the waiting for disruption. I'm talking about contentment and a bowl that's full is full, but a bowl that's empty can be filled with anything. Empty the violence within your bowl and don't succumb to duality."

"What the hell are you two talking about?" Kyra asked.

"Yeah," Nick agreed. "Are we going to take the cave, or sit out here jerking off all night?"

Eric cursed. "We're going to take the cave and kill everything in there, but we let that dickhead go. It just shows that you can justify anything."

Kole ignored Eric's argument and felt the weight of the Rippers in his hands. He calmed his mind remembering that these guns were supposed to be rare if not extinct, yet his group possessed five. This was bigger than him and maybe Eric was right, he should've ended that Alchemist and buried the secret of the Ripper's existence on this mountain top.

Continuing on, Kole embraced the darkness at the mouth of the cave while the others cautiously hung back giving him time to listen to the reverberations of dripping water from farther in. He rubbed his chest with his thumb feeling a charm under his shirt that allowed him to alter his sight to see in the dark then, satisfied that they were alone, strolled in. The quiet of the cave was broken by the odd stone bouncing off his shield, clicking, skittering across the floor and bouncing off the walls as the cave narrowed. He came to the end then squeezed through a fissure entering a larger cavern that had been converted into a living area. In the dark, Kole could see yellow wiring stapled to the rock walls running to all the lights hanging among the stalactites and the many tables and chairs clustered in what looked like a cafeteria. Scattered across the floor were odd bits clothes and a little ways further in he found a messy kitchen in a smaller side cave.

"What a dump," Eric commented after coming through the fissure.

"I've lived in worse," Kyra admitted.

"These guys have been busy," Nick said looking around. "Eric, I got a feeling there's no kids here."

Kyra sighed in relief. "That's great news. I don't want any more bad Karma."

"Wait up, Kole," Nick called.

At the other end of the cavern Kole stood at the mouth two tunnels. Yellow cords ran from one into the other supply power to small drilling and excavation machinery. "It looks like they were drilling down this tunnel, but initially came from the other. I wonder if they knew that this cavern was here."

"Does it matter?" Nick asked. "They could've been here for years quietly plotting revenge against all those who've spurned them and this cavern could've been filled with a mountain of treasure guarded by the fattest Troll you've ever seen who ate too many children and could no longer fit it's fat ass through the fissure to get out."

They laughed.

"Gross, I hate Trolls," Kyra said.

"Yeah," Eric agreed. "I pictured something like a pointy nosed witch with leprosy hunched over a boiling caldron."

"You guys," Kole interrupted. "We've all seen Trolls, and they're not like that. Remember they're people too. Not all of them eat babies."

They laughed again.

An odd feeling was pulling Kole down the newer tunnel. "Eric and I'll go this way. You guys see where the other tunnel goes and stay alert."

"Do you think we should split up?" Kyra asked.

"I'm here Kyra," Nick reassured her. "What can go wrong?" He then held up his Ripper. "Besides we got these now."

"Be careful, we don't know what else is in here," Eric warned.

"Come on Eric, let's go," Kole said then took his time moving passed the smaller machines toward a large man driven burrower at the end of the tunnel.

Nick moaned then said something, but his voice crackled with static before cutting out.

"What's that Nick?" Eric asked, but there was no reply. "I guess there's too much interference."

"I wonder if he found some loot."

"Maybe we should go back and see what's going on," Eric suggested. "It's a dead end, there's nothing here."

Kole studied a section of wall. "Don't you feel it?"

"Feel what?"

"This section isn't real."

Eric walked up and touched the cave wall. "It feels real to me."

Kole smiled, touched the wall then pushed his hand into it. "See."

Eric recoiled. "What? How are you doing that?"

He pushed into the wall up to his elbow. "I feel the other side. I'm going to stick my head in."

Eric grabbed his arm and pulled him back. "Are you nuts? What if you can't get your head back? What if there's no air? It could be a trap. You just don't stick your head into stuff."

Kole thought about it then tucked his Rippers under his arms. "You're right." He looked down then grabbed a rock transmuting it into a tube. "Now I can poke it through the wall and have a look."

He nodded. "You're the one who's supposed to be practical, not me."

He shrugged then sunk the tube into the wall. "I can't be perfect all the time."

Eric shook his head. "You're never perfect."

"And don't you forget it. I know I've made mistakes raising you. I just don't want to hear you crying about it later."

"Whatever. What do you see?"

"Give me a sec, I haven't even looked yet," he said then peered down the tube. "It's a hallway and I can feel air on my eye, so I think it's safe."

Eric tapped the butt of his Ripper against the wall. "I don't get it. Why can't I do it?"

"You can do it. Your mind just won't let you."

He dropped his hand then pouted. "I don't want to hear another lecture about why I'm failing."

Kole gave a warm smile then had a thought. "Grab the end of this pipe," he instructed. "I'll go through then pull you in. Sound good?"

He shook his head. "No!"

"Come on, it'll be easy, just don't freak out and let go."

"Why?" he asked, stalling, not wanting to be pulled into a solid wall.

"Now, if you let go, your mind will decide on what happens to you."

He sighed impatiently. "I don't mean to sound dumb, but I am my mind."

Kole grunted. "Hold the end of this pipe. If I let go it'll fall."

"Fine," Eric grumbled, tucked a Ripper into his belt then grabbed the pipe that felt embedded in the wall.

Kole stepped through the illusion onto a pile of loose rock, cracked plaster and shattered wood to stand in a lit hall with mint green walls and an inch of dust on the floor. He walked past the debris and scraped some dust away with his boot uncovering a checkered pattern of white and green tiles. Cobwebs hung from the ceiling across long mercury and gas filled tubes that had been transmuted to last forever running evenly spaced down the center of the hall. He turned around and saw Eric looking worried and holding the pipe with the tunnel behind him. He released his charm that allowed him to see in the dark then pulled on the pipe. Eric fought him for a moment tensing. He closed his eyes then inched into the illusion until he made it all the way through almost slipping on the debris.

Eric opened his eye blinking. "I don't like these lights. They have a funny hum and hurt my eyes." He took the pipe and leaned it against the wall.

Kole agreed. "I've never seen anything like them. Take a look behind you."

Eric turned. "The wall's gone. How is this possible? The light goes into the tunnel, but we couldn't see it. What is this place?"

"Intense, isn't it?" he said feeling his chest swell with excitement and hope that he'd find something that'd change the world for the better. "I've never seen or even heard of Alchemy like this. Let's take our time and explore."

Chapter

16

The air chilled and the sun had set deepening the shadows of the forest as Byron came upon Cid's small fleet of transports and small Battle Barges. He strolled with his hands behind his back whistling a sad tune trying to draw out some guards, but there weren't anyone around. Disappointed, he shifted his sight to combat the darkness then half smiled thinking they'd all got themselves killed, but the smile faded tasting sour. Annoyance nagged him filling his gut, making him feel heavy and it was Cid's fault. The bastard had forced him go through so much trouble and Byron found himself wishing he could kill him again to alleviate the growing pressure. All the planning and time it took him to move pieces into place to assemble this force had been so boring and mentally painful because James didn't allow him to manifest what he needed to get this fleet together. He had to acquire all the parts legitimately without leaving an alchemical trace leading back to James, or himself. But, on a bright note, it's not his master plan that's shattering, it's James' and that thought made him feel better. Still, this guy Kole is tripping all over it. He wanted to think about what it meant, what the Universe was saying, but Monique popped into his mind distracting him. The fluid movement of her slender Elven body, the fire in her glowing red eyes, like rubies in the sun and her soft lips that tasted sweet made him want to abandon his mission.

He stopped in mid step, his mind stilled and his whistling slowly died when he'd found something new. A long rusted metal transport used to carry livestock sat with its cargo doors facing the mouth of a small cave. Something about it tugged on his attention tearing him away from his escalating bondage fantasy with his sweet Monique. He then smiled at the thought of her safe phrase, "I love you." It didn't matter if she whispered or screamed it, but the thought was very exciting. The remnant of his fantasy faded into emptiness when he noticed two steel re-enforced walls set to funnel the transport's contents into the cave and as he walked alongside the transport he understood why. The meaty moans of desperate hunger and fleshy thumps against the transport's wall told him what the cargo was.

"Zombies," he hissed trying to expel the word's bitterness. If his shield wasn't on he would've smelled their flesh long before he found them. "Cid, this wasn't part of the plan." A loud thump beside his head made him recoil as their moaning escalated into a rhythmic, almost hypnotic noise. His breath quickened and body tensed as two long rotting fingers with chipped and cracked nails protruded out of an air hole stretching to touch him. He stepped back, remembered his shield then fought the urge to incinerate the transport blasting the rotters to ash. "What would James do?" he asked himself then answered, "He would use what the Universe has provided and annihilate his enemies without leaving a trail back to him."

His instinct cried out to destroy them, but he had a better idea. He laughed dispelling the creepy feeling their moaning gave him then stood on a platform at the end of the transport. He reached, grabbing the door latch and opened the doors, but after all their commotion the Zombies had made, nothing happened. Byron expected them to crawl over each other trying to get to him then imagined being swarmed by them, their grubby fingers pressing against his shield trying to penetrate him and sample his flesh, but his expectations quickly faded as he waited. Bored, he leaned over the wall and peered inside thinking there was a second set of doors, or that he needed something extra to entice them to come out, but saw them slowly shuffling forward. Horrid, naked husks of people that had once lived, loved and laughed, but are now trapped inside a glistening pasty grey monster with missing chunks of flesh. With their cloudy eyes half closed and their heads tilted back they followed his scent. With each step their bodies jerked, shifting like an awkward pile of books, slowly making their way down the ramp and into the cave, but some lingered staring up at him, jaws open with rotting teeth sniffing the air, but all Byron could see were hijacked bodies being ran by an alchemical virus with the need to spread.

Byron shuddered almost feeling their ravenous hunger that'd never be sated then thought again about setting them free by burning them all, but that'd be wrong. The Universe gave him a gift, a way to rid himself of a problem named Kole without leaving a fingerprint. To throw this gift away would only manifest more gifts he'd have to throw away and he'd lose his manifestation battle with Kole. He thought for a moment then walked away wondering who Kole was actually fighting with. It wasn't Byron's plans being screwed with and the flow of the Universe may be against James. His mood darkened, annoyed that he was thinking about the larger picture, but before he could clear his mind of infinite variables, a man in a purple suit tripped over a root and fell in front of him.

Byron discerned him to be a low grade Alchemist with a shattered shield. "What is your purpose here?" he demanded, thinking the Universe has given him another gift.

Startled, the man looked up with fearful eyes. "You're Byron," he said then groveled on his knees. "Cid said you'd be coming and he wanted me to kill you. He gave me a Ripper, but I didn't want to do it," he said, but his eye twitched telling Byron that he was lying. "I thought Cid would kill me if I said no." He begged, "Don't hurt me."

Byron forced a warm smile wanting to mine the potential of the experience. "Calm down, everything will be all right," he lied. "Cid's dead. I found his body and it looks like an Alchemist killed him. Do you know who did it?"

"Yeah, it was that guy," he blurted then pointed the way he came. "An Alchemist I'm sure, he took my Ripper from me and made me run away. He said he was looking for you. I don't think he wants to talk, there's evil in his eye. If you see him, don't think twice. Kill him."

Byron saw through his lies and wanted to kick the weakling in the face with the flat of his boot, but held his verbal mask and sympathized, "I know, the man's dangerous. You're lucky to be alive. You should've seen what he did to Cid, his body looks awful. Now, you said he took your Ripper, how many does he have?"

Tears ran down his cheeks. "He laughed at me when he took mine then boasted that he now has five. I was so scared."

"I know," he soothed. "This other Alchemist had five, but how many Rippers did Cid find?"

"Cid found half dozen in a case. He gave me and Ork Slaver one and kept the rest for his men."

"Did he have six or five? Try to remember, it's important."

He wiped his cheeks. "You're right. He said that he accidentally destroyed the first Ripper he found. He overcharged it and it exploded, but he was glad he had them all, he was hunting them. You have to stop him. He wants to start his own empire."

"I will," Byron said. "I have a problem though. You know too much about what's going on out here, but I think you're an innocent victim in all this."

He nodded profusely then whimpered, "I am a victim."

"I'm going to give you a choice. I kill you right now, or give you a fifty-fifty chance of survival."

"You don't have to do this," he pleaded. "I won't say anything."

Byron disagreed, "Yes you will, your kind always does."

He sighed, "I'll take the fifty-fifty."

He smiled. "When you land, walk away and don't come back, or I will kill you."

"Thank you, I will," he whimpered then confusion crossed his face. "Wait… land?"

Byron wrapped him in a tube of alchemical energy then fired him high into the sky like a mortar round then listened to the man's scream fade into the distance. "If you calm your mind and fix your shield before you hit something, you'll most likely live." He laughed, but a part of him despised his weakness in letting the man live, thinking his good deed would come back to bite his ass.

He waited standing there in the dark listening to forest testing his luck wondering if the Universe was going to give him another gift, but nothing happened. Giving up, he squatted under a tree and casually manifested a data pad. He found a weak signal allowing him to access the factory below. He used the security cameras to find Kole and Eric on the administration level. He listened to their conversation and was surprised that they're truly stumbling onto James' plan. Intrigued, Byron followed Eric's trail through the files and watched what they did then put the pad down. He looked up through the trees to the stars above and thought about how many centuries James has moved in the shadows keeping his identity a secret only to have some ass clown from out of nowhere end up on his trail, but James is still the strongest Alchemist Byron had ever seen. He thought about confronting the two to preserve James' plan and was sure he could quickly kill Eric and have a good chance at beating Kole because Kole's mind was too ridged, but something nagged at him, a feeling that Kole was destined to stop James. He felt strange as emotions broke through the nothingness within. Almost like a warm panic attack, perhaps it was hope, joy, or something nice, but it became an uncomfortable energy. He needed something to do to sort his feelings, his fingers tapped the pad and he activated a storage container on a lower floor to seed the thought of conspiracy in Kole's mind then disintegrated the pad. Somewhere he knew James wasn't going to allow him to keep Monique and that all his past Dark Elf bitches were in danger. He thought for a moment, if he fought Kole and lost he'd know the Universe's plan, but he'd never see Monique again because he'd be dead. If he let them go, he could watch them from the shadows and when the time was right, he could point them in the direction he wanted them to go and be the hero he was always meant to be.

Chapter

17

Nick walked backward watching Kole and Eric move down the other tunnel then spun around keeping pace with Kyra. He hummed a tune and readied his Ripper then moaned. "I got this stupid Dwarven song in my head," he complained.

"Which one's that?" Kyra asked sounding mildly interested to pass the time.

"It's the one about swinging your axe to chop down Troll trees."

Kyra laughed. "I know that one, it ends…" She sang in a burly voice, "Smashing your mugs together, spill some ale and burn the fleshy timber so it never grows again."

"Yeah, that's the one," he said then thought about it. "Trolls are disgusting things, but extremely flammable and they're good to have around when you want to start a fire, you just peel a strip off and woomph, better than fuel. And those Dwarven songs are crazy. They don't seem to end because the end flows into its beginning."

"All their songs are like that. They're interchangeable and the Dwarves don't repeat the same song during one of their drinking campaigns. They just keep singing and drinking, that's what the mug part is for."

"That's right," he said remembering being at a Dwarven pub. "They drink after they say drink."

She glanced at him. "You didn't notice? They're all professional drinkers."

He shook his head. "I guess I was too drunk at the time, but now that you say it, it makes sense."

"That song's about killing Trolls and what you need to do with them after. They have songs about everything, but my favorite is about drinking and using heavy machine guns."

Nick laughed. "The flamethrower one is hilarious."

Kyra sang, "Hunker down, wait your turn, take a swig, clack, clack, clack and don't overheat your barrel. Smash your mugs and drink your ale. Let the bullets fly, aim a little low and hit high, clack, clack, clack put one in their eye. Take a swig, drink your ale…"

"You know," Nick interrupted her thinking that it was a terrible song. "They sounded a lot better in my head, or when I'm drunk."

"Everything sounds better when you're drunk, besides I don't think those songs were meant to be sung sober. I think they rely a lot on drunk memory."

"Yeah," Nick agreed then wanted to sneak an idea in. "You know, we left a lot of silver back there. After we get the reward for killing all those Werewolves we can buy a small hauler and collect it all. I don't think Kole cares about the riches he abandoned on the hill, or the bodies. After we get all the money we can hire a crew, travel the world and sell booze to the different races. You know, take a shot at being respectable merchants."

"No," she cautioned. "I like most of your idea, but it's been tried before and the only drinkers are the Dwarves and they love their ale. Orks won't buy it if they can take it, Elves like their wine and Humans are casual drinkers in comparison. Running booze is high risk with a lot of travel time for very little profit."

Nick frowned and thought about it. "You're right, I just want to keep our luck going and we're going to need food, fuel and trade to keep our lush life style going. We're never going back to being cold and hungry. I want to die warm and cozy, perhaps even cuddling with someone nice."

"That's gross. Imagine being the guy who wakes up next to your cold clammy pale green corpse, that's already starting to stink. Also we're not kids anymore, we'll never be that hungry again and if we ever bottom out, we'll be bad guys and take what we need. Nothing was free for us and we don't owe the world anything. We have enough in the pain bank to dish it out to anyone who deserves it."

He shook the image of his dead body out of his head. "I always thought I'd leave a pretty corpse, but I guess you're right, I would start stinking. That's how I roll." He felt the weight of the Ripper in his hand and his rifle on his back. "We now have the will and the means to be anything. For now we'll be good guys. I guess our moral compass is a little bent."

"A little, but whose isn't? We now have new friends and if we take care of each other we'll make sure that you can fulfill your dream to die in a warm cozy bed with some young men keeping you warm at night."

He corrected her, "A king sized bed."

She echoed, "A king sized bed."

"That's the nicest thing anyone has ever said to me. I love you."

"I love you too. Now talk about something else, remembering our childhood depresses me."

They passed by a large well loved drilling machine that still had some of its original yellow paint among the rust. "All right, what are you thinking about?"

She mourned, "My shoes, my wonderful collection that took me years to build, then whoosh gone when our Barge died. I know it's petty and I didn't wear them much, I just really liked looking at them."

Nick sympathized, "I'm sorry we lost our stuff and I understand what you're feeling. Your collection made you feel rich and gave you a sense of peace in this damaged world. I never questioned your obsession to find those shoes, some you went to find based on rumor and during a mission I might add. But those were fun detours and I just went with it, but now we have Alchemist friends who can make perfect shoes for you. You can even show them off and make the other girls jealous without worrying about wrecking them."

"My shoes didn't make me feel rich," she disagreed. "They were like a steam of sunshine in the darkness…" she trailed off then asked, "Did you fart?"

"No," he said. "Not this time. Besides you shouldn't smell anything unless your filtration system is damaged."

"I don't know," she teased. "It smells like you after one of your meatapalooza weekends."

"Meatapalooza, is that even a word? I don't know what you're talking about," he lied.

"You know exactly what I'm talking about, when you pig out on all types of meat."

"Pig out, that's racial," he huffed.

She snorted. "Whatever. You lounge back, get slop all over your shirt then balloon out. Then you have the nuggets to laugh as you gas me. I can't be in the same room with you for a week after, it's disgusting. Now that's an example of feeling rich."

"Geez," he snorted then patted his stomach feeling the size of his belly beneath his armor. "I didn't mean to piss you off I just thought there must be a reason you like those shoes so much. I was trying to support you."

"Don't assume. If you're curious about something, just ask and talk to me like a person. You make me feel like I'm some kind of a shallow shoe crazed bitch."

"I'm sorry," he apologized in a tone she'd heard a thousand times before. "I guess what's really on my mind is how easy it was for Kole to kill all those Werewolves. I mean physically, Kole has the power to create and destroy."

"Alchemists aren't the only ones who have the power to do that. One person can incite a war that'll kill millions, another can build cities. Kole just killed in a way you weren't used to, so it freaked you out. Me, on the other hand, I think of death all the time. I don't know how it'll happen, maybe a kid with a gun or a Dwarf with a missile, who knows. What I'm trying to say is that Kole carries a big gun and right now it's not pointed at you. One day he might want to kill you and you might come out on top, but in the end, one day you're going to die."

Nick cursed. "When did you get so depressing?"

"I'm not depressing. You just can't deal with life. Are you sure you didn't fart? The smell is getting worse."

"Yeah I'm sure. I think you farted and your suit's broken. You're chocking on your own stench."

"See that?" she warned.

Nick stopped then aimed his Ripper down the tunnel at a half naked man staggering around the corner. The hair on the back of Nick's neck stood up as he watched the man shuffle his feet, jerk his shoulders then tilt his head up, jaw open, smelling.

Kyra called out and the man and he answered with a deep moan then quickened his pace.

Nick licked his lips. "Can he see?" he asked watching the man fumble his way toward them, shuddering with each step. "He's creeping me out."

"I'm getting the same vibe," she worried. She tensed, took a step back then called out again, "Answer me now, or I'll blow your face off!"

The man didn't slow as more people in a thick crowd jostled around the corner, their heads back and arms outstretched, hands clawing. Their moans resonated into a loud penetrating noise that Nick felt deep within his chest. His legs felt light as a wave of their putrid smell hung in his respirator chocking him. His mouth watered and a pressure in his stomach quickly grew. Nick yelled clearing his throat then fired his Ripper at the man. A wet slap, his round blew apart half of the man's torso releasing a dark congealed mass that rolled out of his skin slopping on the floor followed by his severed, still twitching arm. The man gurgled, not slowing, reaching for them.

Nick gagged, felt a wave come up out of his guts then threw up into his helmet. His warm vomit flooded his respirator, wrapped around his head stinging his eyes and filled his ears and nose. Blinded, he pulled his helmet off with his free hand wanting to gasp for air, but retched a second time into his helmet before falling to his knees.

Kyra screamed, "What are you doing? Shoot dammit!"

In the tunnel, her rifle fire was deafening as hot shell casing rained on the back of Nick's head. He finally cleared his mouth and nose then gasped, filling his lungs. He wanted and expected cool soothing air, but the powerful inhuman stink burned his aching throat and filled his lungs with prickly fire. He screamed pushing away the pain building within him. He envisioned the hoard of near Humans diving upon him and ripping him apart. Hearing their mouth noises and shuffling getting closer filled him with horror. Panic overcame him, he pushed himself onto his knees, knocking away his helmet then pointed his Ripper toward the noise and blindly fired.

Behind him, Kyra yelled a string of profanity then abandoned her short controlled bursts to unload everything she had. Her war cry told him how much trouble they were in. She leaned her leg against his back telling him she was there till the end.

Tears from his stinging eyes rolled down his cheeks and his scream joined hers, he fired blindly hearing little over the echoing popping of gunfire.

"Aim higher," she screamed while reloading.

He desperately pulled the trigger hoping he was helping then felt something grab his ankle and tug. He instinctively moved like a wave bringing the butt of the Ripper down onto something round and hard then felt a snap as its surface gave way releasing a spray of warm fluid over his hand and face. He didn't want to know what happened or think about it, didn't want his disgust to well up in him and make him get sick again. Still pulling the trigger, Kyra grab the back of his collar and heave him to his feet.

"We're punching through these assholes!" she yelled through her helmet into his ear.

He stopped and she grabbed his forearm then dragged him stumbling down the tunnel. He tripped and landed on his elbows then slid across the slick floor saturating his body armor with cool fluids. He flailed trying to find traction as Kyra grabbed him like a piece of baggage, pulling him up against her hip dragging him kicking. He ran for a number of steppes then heard the snap of teeth and a moan next to his ear a second before something grappled him, knocking him out of Kyra's grip. His head smacked against the rock wall igniting a brilliant flash of light in his eyes. His strength rolled out of him and his knees almost gave. Terrified, he brought his forearm up and lodged it into his attacker's gnawing mouth. His attacker pressed in coiling around his leg and shoulder, latching on, tightening its grip in pulses trying to take him down while its head thrashed, teeth tearing into his armor.

Nick didn't want to die. He cursed through clenched teeth and in desperation he stabbed the muzzle of his Ripper under his attacker's ribs and pulled the trigger. A wet slap, a pop and its cool innards splashed onto the floor washing over his boots. He screamed in utter disgust, tangled in entrails, frantically shaking his arm and kicking his leg to dislodge his twitching attacker. Finally free, he flung the corpse away then fired blindly down the tunnel venting his raw sour emotion.

Kyra grabbed his arm. "Stop shooting," she commanded sounding fatigued, but relieved, telling him that they were safe for the moment. She dragged him along, quickly guiding him out of the tunnel and into the light.

The fresh outside air felt good on his face encouraging him to take a deep breath, but the stink wafting off his armor stung his nose igniting a sneezing fit that drained his sinuses leaving him a blubbery mess. He wiped his nose on the inside of his arm then dried his eyes.

"Open your eyes and stop screwing around," she growled.

"They burn, I got puke in them," he rasped then heard her undo her canteen.

"Here," she said then gently grabbed his head tilting it back. "Blink it out," she instructed before pouring water in his eyes.

"Oh, thank you. That's so much better."

"What happened to you back there? We almost died."

He blinked his eyes clear then said, "I know you totally saved me, don't tell the guys." He quickly took in his surroundings and looked into the back of the empty transport.

"Don't tell the guys?" she repeated, heat returning to her voice. "That's what you're worried about?"

He placed his gear on the ground. "I got that gunk in my hair and all over my face," he whined then started to pull his armor off.

"What are you doing? We're still in deep shit here. Stop it!" she barked then leaned in and slapped him. "What is wrong with you? Put your shit back on right now!"

The side of his face stung and it hurt a little that she had hit him, but he didn't stop until he was free from the gore that had ruined his favorite armor. "Ah," he sighed. "Much better, but my armor's ruined. I'm never going to get the smell out."

She cradled her head in her hand. "You're naked. You're so disgusting. You don't wear anything under your armor?"

"I've always been naked," he informed her. "It fits better that way besides, don't worry about me, I'm not into you."

"I don't care that you're not into me, put that thing away."

He cupped the lower part his belly with his hands and giggled. "Some people find my belly sexy."

She cursed. "I'm not talking about your gut. I swear I'm going to beat you down if you don't cover up. Grab some gear and help me get our asses out of here."

"I'm not going to cover up, my twig and berries are beautiful."

She dropped her rifle then stepped in, grappling him, taking him to the ground before he could scream. They wrestled until she got the upper hand then repeatedly punched his legs while yelling, "Why... do you... make me... hurt you?"

Pinned to the ground, Nick screamed with each strike, but couldn't help but laugh and gasp between hits further aggravating Kyra. After the beating she grabbed the back of his head and pushed his face into the ground while she got up. She calmed herself then grabbed her rifle and waited for him to collect himself.

Nick lay in defeat face down in the dirt. He turned his head and looking up at her with one eye. "I'm sorry Kyra," he blubbered. "My mind popped. I'm not sure if it was the way they moved, or their smell, but they hit me sideways and I'd be dead if it weren't for you." He cried, "Thanks for not leaving me."

She sighed. "You big dummy, of course I wouldn't leave you."

"My mom left me," he sobbed. "She threw me away, I'm ugly."

"You're not ugly," she moaned. "You're doing this now? We're still in danger."

"Mommy," he wailed. "Why didn't you want me? I would've shown her love."

Kyra knelt beside him and placed her hand on his back. "You don't know her side."

"It doesn't matter, I was hers. In the tunnel, all I wanted was her to hold me and protect me."

"I know," she consoled.

"In that horrible place," he wept. "When they put me in the dark, I always imagined her taking me away, but she never came. She didn't want me because I'm a thing."

"You're not a thing, Nick," she said. "It's too bad that she missed out on how wonderful you are." She stood then motioned with her hand for him to get up. "Give me a hug."

With wet and puffy cheeks, he gathered himself off the ground. He ignoring the dirt and twigs stuck to his face and embraced her in a firm hug that lifted her onto her toes. He held her there for a few seconds, her coarse armor felt scratchy against his naked body, but he didn't care. He released her. "Thank you, I feel better. Let's get me something to wear and together we'll find a way out of this mess."

Chapter

18

Kole led Eric down the mint green hall to the first room. Its steel frame and door was painted flat white and on the left side a rectangular window sat above a leaver with a key hole. Kole felt around the wall for an activation button, but couldn't find one then gave up. He peered through the window into darkness then placed his hand on the leaver slowly turning it until the door opened.

"Did you break it?" Eric asked as the room's automatic lights flickered on.

"No… it's on hinges," he said pointing to the doorframe. "It's built this way," he complained. "Just to open, these doors take up so much room." He looked into the small room and saw a glass cylinder sitting on a dusty pedestal in the center of the room. Feeling safe, he walked in past a computer bank and noticed a terminal against the far wall. He brushed away the glass cylinder's cobwebs then leaned closer. "What is that?" he asked, not believing what he was seeing.

Eric nudged him aside and stuck his face next to the jar. "It's a brain with its eyes still attached," he stated. He squinted then jumped back, hiding behind Kole. "Its pupils dilated, it's still alive!"

Kole leaned in again. "Interesting," he said examining the electrodes inserted into the brain that ran to the bottom of the jar into the pedestal. He stood back then brushed away some dust covering a plaque beside the jar with the number 372 engraved into it. "See if the computer terminal is working."

Eric smacked the monitor with his sleeve creating a dust cloud then coughed. He dusted the keyboard then went to work. "I'm in, what do you want me to look up?"

"The number 372 for starters then we'll find out what this place is and when it was built."

Eric worked the keyboard then waited. "It's slow, give me a sec, oh wait here it is. 372, was an Alchemist captured a thousand years ago and place into a transmutation tank for the purpose of creating an illusion to protect the underground entrance to the Ripper and Battle Barge production facility. Wait, we can do that? Put thoughts into people's heads making them see what we want? I don't believe it." He continued to type. "I'm accessing the mainframe," he said as his hand came to rest. "The facility was brought online prior to the Purge for the purpose of arming The United North American Coalition."

"I've never heard of anyone able to create illusions, but we just witness it," he said. "That's all we need, people claiming that an Alchemist made me do it. We'll be blamed for everything, from adultery to murder." He thought for a moment then continued, "And the idea that we can do that is too dangerous for the world. We must never mention what happened to us. The thought that it can be done will make people want to try." He fell silent thinking of the implications. "Who was this Coalition against?"

"There's some racist propaganda, but it seems they wanted to wipe out the impure, which means the Alchemists and all the other Non-Human races."

"Maybe they were the start of the Anti-Alchemists?"

"I found a personal log made by the led scientist. Want to watch?"

Kole looked again into the jar at the floating eyes wondering what substance they were suspended in, but decided it was unimportant. "Sure, let's see it," he said thinking about how long this man was sitting here trapped in his own head. "I wonder if this guy is still sane."

Eric looked up from the monitor. "Would you be?"

"Cut out of my body and thrown into a jar, probably not." He laid his hand on top of the jar sympathizing with the brain then moved to watch the personal log over Eric's shoulder.

The video showed a thin clean shaven man wearing a white lab coat enter what looked like a staged room with framed diplomas hanging on the wall. He walked past a tall plant over to an office desk then casually sat on its edge. He adjusted his short dark hair then folded his hands across his lap before saying, "I'm Science Officer James Ashwood of The North American Coalition. A decade ago I was working a serum to increase the efficiency of our soldiers' intelligence." He placed his hand on his chest and continued, "I worked long and hard on the project sacrificing my personal life and the two chimps, Molly and Spud that I was experimenting on didn't show any signs of progress." He sat in silence for a moment. "After the last failed experiment I released Spud to a different department and was about to have the entire project scrapped because the brass was crawling up my ass for going over budget." His eyebrows furrowed. "They said I was over spending, but they couldn't see my genius and raw power of what I was proposing." His face contorted. "The small minded idiots!" He took a breath and regained his composure. "Anyway, Molly was fine and I took her out of quarantine, but a few days later I walked into the lab to see her sitting in her cage, still and quiet. I watched her for a bit to see what she was up to because I had a weird feeling then she made a banana appear out of thin air." He paused lost in the memory then laughed. "I almost defecated in my pants. I was so disturbed by what I'd witnessed I ran to my desk without thinking, grabbed my gun and shot her in the head." He placed his hand on his chest again then said, "As brilliant as I am, I still react like a normal person. I wish I didn't panic the way I did, I could've shot her in the chest and dissected her brain. Also in that moment I should've thought of Spud, but my first thoughts were of my serum and how the military would destroy it, or bury it in some warehouse."

He lowered his hand as his face darkened again. "I knew it was too much for their little minds to handle. They'd never use it because they'd lose control over the men and if it got into the population." He licked his lips. "At the time, science was at its peak. We'd discovered the twelfth planet in our solar system and as a society we'd evolved beyond flashy colors. Fashion was in the past, an indulgence of the weak European Alliance. Individuality was sacrificed and any form of negative stimulation such as games, television, books and sports were removed because it was proven to evoked strong emotion. Harmony was said to be the goal of all the new laws. Then they outlawed the use of natural herbs because ingesting plants caused negative chemical reactions in our brains. Emotions were chemically suppressed and slogans like, an honest employee is a calm employee or my personal favorite, which allowed the government to strip away our basic rights, if you're not a criminal you won't mind. All these things impacted the Human psyche and created a collective mindset."

He sat a moment in silence. "We had gone through a series of wars, the last one ended badly and the public was sick of the emotional backlash, so they gave up everything to be calm. The politicians were the ones who started those wars and the people made it easy for them to take away our collective identity. But that's not my story. There I was holding my serum and I thought, at any moment they'd kick down my door to steal my work. I wasn't thinking clearly and Spud was in a different department, for all I knew my serum didn't work the same on him. It's funny now, but at the time I had an image of Spud manifesting a mountain of bananas in front of the Brass. I kind of freaked out and administered myself." He smiled. "Obviously I survived, but later found out that Spud had died without manifesting anything. That worried me and what happened next is kind of funny. It turned out that my serum had mutated into an airborne virus within Spud and over a couple of days infected the world's population. Looking back, I think the chimp cooked up the virus using his body for materials, deliberately poisoned the world." He raised his hands in defense. "I didn't know this at the time, or I'd have stopped it, but I was busy tripping. My head felt like it was being ripped open and the things I seen and understood with my new intellect blew my mind wide open. I slowly understood the mechanics of the universe and because of my genius I was stable." He placed his hands on his lap and smiled then continued, "I finally sobered up and found myself on the floor in a puddle of my own vomit, thankfully I didn't choke to death and after I cleaned myself up I decided to destroy my work." He laughed.

He put his hands in his pockets. "Curious, Spud just quietly sat there until he died. I couldn't believe I thought it, but the damn chimp must have changed my serum using his body as a catalyst, so I incinerated both Molly and Spud to protect my secret as the world fell apart. You see, not everyone has my type of mind. I am a genius after all. There are some unsavory and downright psychotic lunatics running around out there. In short, a lot of lower end people died and it wasn't my fault because if they were more intelligent, they might've survived and I wasn't going to take the fall for a stupid chimp's idea. In the end the world's governments covered it all up. No one knew the truth that I was responsible and I was okay with that. Sometimes it's necessary to sacrifice the few to enhance the many."

"The governments of the world had no choice but to embrace the "Blessed" in their attempt to control them. They spun the story that God, in our time of need returned us to Eden. So the Blessed were sent out to clean up the world's pollution which bottomed out my shares in the Fresh Breath, bottled oxygen and the H two Oh Corporation. They also fed the starving people of wherever, destroying my Chem Food shares. Regular people would gathered around, wanting to touch them like they were the Pope, it was embarrassing to watch. No one knew it was my genius that saved the world, but I had to wait to see what was going to happen. I knew something bad was coming, they weren't as smart as me and power in their hands has never been a good thing. All of it was designed to give the Blessed purpose so the governments could test and catalogue them." He chuckled. "I requested to study the changed, but it was above my pay grade, dumb bastards."

"The first racial transformations happened in Europe... not surprising. They have decadent ideas and celebrate free thinking, breeding weakness into their society. They've always been overindulgent in negative stimulation, selfish, self serving and have forgotten their responsibility to their country. They've always have been about the individual, but the fad caught on. Knowing what we know now, what they did back then was the first step in undoing the world. For example, Orks became what the world believed Orks to be, stupid, lumbering animals because of perception. The psyche has a way of shaping us and the physical transformation made them become, inside and out, Orks."

"Here we are now. I'm the one who has the pure serum within me, not that mutated crap Spud made, polluting the Human race. This world belongs to actual Human beings not those pointy eared freaks. In this facility I've designed weapons to kill the Blessed and big heavily armed hover tanks to clean the world of the abominations that plagues it. The world will return to the way it was, of course under the rule of The North American Coalition, which I'll take over, being the only one who truly is intellectual enough to guide the people onto the correct path. The dullard politicians have had their fun, now it's time for new management." He smiled, stood then walked off screen.

The video ended and Kole didn't know what to say.

"What's a chimp?" Eric asked.

"That narcissistic sociopath made Alchemy then instigated the Purge?"

"Well, Spud gave Alchemy to the world, but this can all be a fabrication. We weren't there, so we don't know the truth."

He placed his hand on Eric's shoulder. "Let's go, I want to check the rest of this place out." He turned to leave.

"What do you want to do about the brain?"

"Leave it for now. I don't want Nick and Kyra stumbling onto this place. This is all bad for our kind. If the Anti-Alchemists found this place their beliefs would spread over night and there'd be no stopping another Purge. We'll take care of Brainy when we come back this way." He went to the next door, the office held nothing of interest, so he quickly moved on. He wanted answers, but the rest of the rooms along the hallway were almost identical with desks, chairs and office paraphernalia. At the end of the hall was a set of elevator doors with one button and a stairwell. He pressed the button and heard the screeching of metal on metal then a large bang from behind its doors.

"Maybe we shouldn't," Eric said then opened the door to the stairs releasing a puff of cold stale air that made him to cough. "The air smells funny." He coughed again. "Maybe they filled the lower parts of this place with gas and we wouldn't know it till we were about to suffocate."

Kole walked passed him touched the concrete wall then closed his eyes searching with his awareness, feeling for the air. "This place isn't as deep as I thought, but the air's good, just hasn't been circulated for a long time." He smiled. "I like your paranoia."

Eric laughed. "Thanks, your mistrust is infectious."

Kole grabbed the red handrail and looked over the edge, following the concrete ledge that descended the square stairwell. "Funny, no one likes a smart ass."

"Yeah, but everyone hates a dumb ass."

Kole ignored him then slowly descended the stairwell while Eric followed, playing, plowing the dust off the handrail as they went. Half way down they found a door labeled organic storage and when Kole walked into the large rectangular room he stopped, alerted by dust particles floating in the air and large webbed foot prints on the floor. Across the room the lights flickered buzzing loudly progressively worsening leaving the opposite side in darkness. Various sized metal boxes lay strewn across the floor, but some remained stacked allowing Kole to imagine what the room looked like before something big rampaged through it.

"Do you see this?" Eric asked pointing to the elevator doors to their left. Something big had caved in the doors leaving streaks of smeared blood across its metallic surface.

"Shush," Kole whispered. "We're not alone…" A flash of pink shot from the darkness sticking to Kole's shield then the room sped by pulling him into a giant glistening mouth. The mouth snapped shut and it took him a moment to process what had happened. He sat like a pill protected by his shield as a creature tried to digest him. He almost laughed at the thought then fired his Ripper upward and being surrounded by alchemical flesh, the pressure from the weapon was almost unbearable before the creature finally exploded. The meaty pop was deafening as Kole was flung upward through the tiled ceiling, smacking against the concrete above then falling to land in a large pile of guts. He lay cradled in half a carcass.

Eric shouted his name then frantically ran by the rows of stacked boxes. He crawled to the top of a pile kicking and flinging smaller boxes aside then stopped when his foot slipped, flipping a box, losing his foot down a hole, but breathed easy when he saw Kole. "Are you alright?" he asked. "What was that thing?"

Kole carefully stood not wanting to fall then shifted his shield, encouraging the gore to slide off. When he could see he looked at the remains, an eye, partial jaw and the two legs. "I'm fine. It was a giant toad… I think."

"How could that thing live down here all this time?"

His feet sank deeper into the toad's guts, though his shield would keep him clean, watching the guts form around his feet still grossed him out. "There's something against the back wall." He climbed down and together they found a large stasis freezer. The large steel door was magnetically sealed and the rectangular window at eye level was frozen over.

Eric scraped away the frost. "It's empty." He stepped to the side and accessed the freezer's controls. "This console was activated less than an hour ago."

Kole moved closer touching the wall, reaching out to follow the circuitry to find the command. "The mainframe was accessed via remote. That means someone knows we're here."

"The Werewolves were trying to find this place and someone's trying to protect it?"

"Or, protect it from us," Kole stated. "Some Werewolves may have survived."

"I guess that makes sense," Eric said. "You realize that someone went through a lot of trouble to keep the place hidden and probably for good reason." He confessed, "This has gotten too hard, it was supposed to be a fun day out, but it has turned into a nightmare and I'm done. Let's get out of here. We've seen enough."

"We just got here," Kole soothed. "This is a link to our past and there's so much to learn here. Usually you're the one who's excited and it's not the first time people have tried to kill us."

"That's what I'm talking about," he urged. "People are trying to kill us and you don't even find that rude." He shook his head calming down. "No, I've seen this before. You're just saying that because you're in one of your energized moods, like a high frequency static in the brain after transmuting all day. This has not been a good day for us and I'm worried that the extreme level of alchemy you used out there has…" He searched for the right words, "struck your sensibility."

Kole studied him for a moment and saw how emotionally drained he was then placed his hand on Eric's shoulder. "I haven't crossed the line into madness. I assure you, I know the difference."

Eric huffed. "I'm not saying that you're mad, I'm saying that you're high."

Kole almost laughed at the accusation then scuffed Eric's hair. "We need to figure this place out and take what we need then blow it up so no bad guys can't use it," he said then pushed passed him moving around the toad's remains back into the light to an undisturbed stack of boxes. Eric followed and Kole could feel the heat of his disapproval on his back. He tucked his Rippers in his belt then picked up a small box, dusting off its top. Its surface was smooth looking like stainless steel. He flipped it around looking for an opening, but it appeared seamless. He held the box closer looking for a trick to open it because the thought of a room full of metal cubes seemed silly. He peered into the box's alchemy, but couldn't perceive within. It looked as if the box contained a void, but he knew better, someone much stronger than him made its contents. He felt Eric's presence beside him. "I have no idea what these things are, or how to open it," he said handing it to Eric.

Eric held the box and shimmering light blue words appeared to hover just above its surface. He read, "DNA recognition, Human Alchemist. Experiment 1409 is alive." He gave Kole a smug look. "View contents." The surface of the cube became transparent revealing a miniature winged person with blonde hair dressed in elegant green and gold embroidered clothing. "That's a pretty Pixie," Eric commented.

"What," Kole fumed then peered into the box. He informed, "That's a Fairy, but they all got wiped out by those filthy Pixies during the Fay War when I was a boy."

"Weren't Fairies the good ones?"

Kole moaned and slowly shrugged. "That all depends if you piss them off, or not. It was the totality of the perception of their creators that made them. People thought that Fairies were more good than bad and Pixies were more mischievous, darker." He pointed to the Fairy. "See the round ears and Human features. The psyche sees similarity and makes the creature more good than bad, but Humans can be both, so Fairies could also be both. Pixies on the other hand have pointed ears, sharp features and darker eyes which told the psyche that they are more evil than good, so that's what they became."

"We could let this guy out, find a female and their race could live again."

He thought of the Balance. "There is a reason why they went extinct."

"Yeah, they were butchered," Eric countered. "It's not like nature tried to wipe them out."

Kole laughed. "We are connected and it may have been time for the Fairies' extinction. Letting this Fairy go may have massive repercussions across the planet."

"Oops," Eric said a moment before a hiss of cold mist escaped the box as it opened.

Kole closed his eyes and swallowed his fury. He wanted to beat the boy who never listened, but he needed to think clearly and calm himself, before an Eric induced headache spawned.

Eric reached into the box and gently cradled the Fairy in the palm before putting the box down. "Look," he bubbled. "He's so cute. He has little pointy boots."

Disappointed, Kole released a long loud sigh. "I hope this doesn't bite us in the ass later on."

"It won't," he assured. "Look, he's breathing. Here," he said then passed the Fairy to Kole. "I'm going to check the console for the invoice and see if there are any more."

Kole groaned then looked into the alchemy of the Fairy as Eric ran back to the entrance. He didn't know the person who had created the Fairy, but could see that the Alchemist had a different relationship with matter than he did. Their style looked bold, commanding and fearless bordering on arrogance. Its shifting pattern was unlike anything he had ever seen, or even thought of doing, almost moving backward. "Impossible," he whispered, but the evidence lay in his hand. He then realized that what he was looking at was an original Fairy not one who had been born.

"Eric," he said. "The specimens here are originals. With each generation their environment would influence their alchemy altering their original pattern till the race was its own, but I can see their creator's alchemy."

"Yeah," Eric said over his shoulder as he worked the console. "That sounds great."

"Let's stuff this thing back in its box and blow this place up."

"No!" Eric stomped his foot. "You don't let me have anything. You're the one who wanted to investigate. I wanted to go, but I found something, and I want it."

"You don't understand what this thing is."

"It's a Fairy and I've found more of them."

"No," Kole pleaded. "It's the physical manifestation of a thought that died out during the Purge. If another Alchemist finds and studies them it will bring about another wave of terror."

"You're so negative. You never see the good in anyone."

He placed his hand on the hilt of one of his Rippers. "I don't want to fight you on this, don't make me kill you to save the world," he threatened feeling himself darken. "Listen," he implored. "This Fairy is an instruction manual on how to create living creatures limited by one's own imagination."

Eric raised his hands. "Kole, calm down and think. If you believe in the balance and that everything is connected then these Fairies are still part of it. They may be in stasis, but their vibration is still part of the clock and as Pixies were used to make them extinct, we are here to make them live again."

"You're twisting things."

"Am I, you psycho? It was pure fate that we investigated that one box. I opened it and it felt right. I found more and want to help them. I'm even risking my life negotiating with you when I know that you're two steps away from killing me." He bit his lower lip as tears welled in his eyes. He took a shallow breath then continued, "Don't you feel that it's a little arrogant to think you're the only one who can fulfill the manifestations of the Universe? If you're going to kill me, I want you to know that I think you're high and suffering from delusions of grandeur."

The room filled with silence and Kole struggled to think clearly.

"Kole, I don't want to be an Alchemist. Look at you, if you had the power to create organic matter you could cure disease and mend bone, but you jump right into monsters. If you actually look at the balance, none of us have any say in anything. We're all just ships on a massive ocean trying to survive thinking we're getting somewhere, but were not. It's a joke. I've had time to think about this sitting in the back of our tin can running around the plains. If you have a disease and I have the cure, should I cure you? There's a reason that your vibration aligned with that disease infecting you and here I am in all my arrogance taking away what the Universe gave you." He laughed. "You're going to kill me over a thought, a whim, that's very self righteous of you to think that you know the will of the Universe."

Kole calmed. "That's an old argument. What are we supposed to do? We have to live."

"That's the answer. We live and move through the world doing what we feel is right and the Universe does the rest. The Fairies are back and a stone is thrown into the ocean, the ripples are amalgamated into the whole… done."

"But we have to take responsibility for what we do, or there will be chaos."

"Look at it from the Universe's point of view. It doesn't care if the life on our planet winks out, it'll just make something else. If we're too stupid to exist, then we don't deserve to. We are only responsible for ourselves. If some dickhead is placed on our path then we do what feels right."

"Where is all of this coming from?"

"I'm sick of living in fear. We run around afraid of what people will think of us if we don't play the game. Who are they? They don't have any authority over us and if we try to make the world a better place, they rip it down. That tells me that the Universe doesn't want us to meddle in other people's business. Let's free the Fairies, blow this place up and live our lives to the best of our ability, screw the rest of them."

The idea of relaxing or even taking a decade off from trying to save the world felt nice to Kole, but he didn't want to be lazy, or apathetic to the world's needs. He thought about his conflicting emotions and took a hard look at himself. "All right, we'll buy a house in Pine View and make whatever we need for ourselves. But be warned, when you are content you want nothing."

Eric smiled. "You'll find that's all people really want from us. They'll even forget that we're Alchemists."

It was Kole's turn to laugh. "How would they forget what we are?"

"Stop being so self-important, you have to let them. Everyone is wrapped up in their own crap and all you have to do is blend in, dress the way they do, go shopping and shave."

"You want to throw away everything that we are?"

"What are we? No one wants our help. The big..." he said making quotation marks with his fingers, "game you're playing is so people tolerate us while we stick our dicks into their pie. They can't wait for us to go away so they can return to their own crap. Trust me, they don't care about us. We can have peace if we just leave the world alone."

He raised his hand. "Enough. We'll try it your way. Wake the Fairies then we'll finish looking around before we destroy this place. That feels right to me."

"Thank you, Master," a tiny voice said.

He'd forgotten about the Fairy. "I'm no one's master."

The Fairies wings fluttered making a mixture of metallic green and purple haze behind him as he slowly floated to eye level. "I can tell by your aura that you're a creator, therefore you are my master."

Eric came closer, examining him. "You're so cute."

"Thank you, Master. My maker kept her best work for herself and I was her first. She made many types of creatures, all beautiful and kind, as was her heart."

Kole looked at Eric who wore his I told you so expression then closed his eyes looking for an escape route for the Fairies. "There's an air vent in the ceiling that'll take you and your kind outside. You're free now, but beware that your kind was hunted to extinction by the Pixies, it'd be best to hide from everyone."

The Fairy saddened. "Pixies were made by the dark one to do his bidding, sour hearts to do sour deeds. Their teeth are sharp and hunger for the throats of many creatures."

"Well," Eric sang then clapped his hands together. "Behold, container 4762 illuminate." The wall near the toad's guts reflected a light blue glow. "Eww, it stinks back there," he whined.

Kole shrugged. "You wanted the Fairies."

"Oh please Master, I'd like to see my friends again."

Eric looked at the Fairy and his face softened. "Come with me and I'll set your friends free." The Fairy cheered with a fist in the air.

Kole groaned at the Fairies' cuteness then walked back to the door, ignoring the noise of Eric rummaging through to boxes and thought about their argument, feeling foolish for wanting to harm him. He thought back to when he was a boy when his teacher told him to rise up against the darkness and to make the world a better place, but Eric had some points, but why now? The reemergence of the Rippers was the sign he'd been waiting for his whole life, but now Eric suggests that they bugger off. He sighed then decided that if the Universe wanted him to do something about it, events would converge on him and shape his path. He spoke over his shoulder though their com link, "Hurry up, you're done messing around. And don't tell me that you found something else to free."

"I'm done. Their so cute using their tiny hands for pillows, you should come and see them."

Kole walked into the stairwell and waited for Eric before descending to the deepest level. Kole looked through the door's window at a scarcely lit factory floor. The automated arms, conveyer belts, presses and work benches sat waiting for power and instruction. Kole walked in and though everything was covered in a thin layer of dust he could see hundreds of Rippers in all stages of construction and as they explored they found several crates of finished product.

"What is that?" Eric asked pointing at the back end of a large battle barge.

Kole was so fixated on the production line he had missed it. "That," he educated, "is a pristine war machine made at the height of technology."

"I call dibs, it's mine," he cheered then ran laughing to the Barge's entrance climbing in.

Kole groaned then followed, thinking of the ripple that'll be caused when that monstrosity entered the world. Though the Barge was pretty, Kole could see seams and rivets across its shiny unpainted hull. He closed his eyes then touched its side and peered into its structure finding nothing but natural parts. He searched deeper and found something odd, an alchemical field in the heart of the craft.

The door quietly slid open and Eric's head popped out looking at him. "It has a shield and a cloaking system. Wait till Nick and Kyra see this."

Kole was about to protest, but Eric cut him off.

"No, you're not going to take this away from me. I claimed it."

Kole clinched his teeth and glared.

"Why? What's wrong with it?" he asked.

He sighed, hating to disappoint Eric. "I found something and once you see it I think you'll change your mind."

Eric pouted. "Fine."

He led Eric through the roomy primer painted corridors and up a set of stairs to the second floor. They continued to a security door that Kole had already bypassed and into a room lined with computer banks. "See," Kole said gesturing to the two pedestals in the center of the room each displaying a brain in a jar.

"If we get rid of the brains, can I keep it?" he asked.

Kole shook his head. "The brains are wired into everything. I really hope that this is one of kind because it's a pure predator. This thing is fused, alchemy and technology."

"If you knew how to manipulate matter you could rebuild the brains' bodies and learn from them. You never know, they could be sedated and still sane."

"I really don't want to clean the glass and see their floating eyes looking back at me."

"They may not have bodies, but they're still alive."

Kole imagined the best then worse case scenarios before making a decision. "I know you mean well, but they could probably restore their own bodies if we took all the hardware out and I have no idea what they would do. I think we should terminate them just to be safe."

"No wonder you don't make any friends."

Kole frowned, upset that Eric had finally sparked another headache.

"I have a solution," Eric suggested. "Let's rig this factory to blow then come back here. There's Rippernades in the armory and we can rig this room to disintegrate the brains if they turn out hostile. There's a chance everything will be fine and we can make some new friends."

"The odds are that they're insane and something bad can happen even if we take every precaution. We should just end them and forget about it. It'd be merciful."

Eric disagreed. "How do you know? If you we're stuck in a jar, wouldn't you want a chance to live again?"

Kole cursed giving up. "Reviving the brains is a stupid idea and I'd like to stop you right here, but I hope I've given you the tools to survive in this world. You're old enough to make your own mistakes. All that I want is to be here for you. I'll help you revive the brains, but this decision might be fatal."

"Kole, everyone ends and all we can do is live," he said then rubbed his hands together in excitement. "So let's get to work."

It didn't take long for them to manifest and place the powerful implosion devices, setting them for remote detonation. Kole wanted to take his time, stalling, trying to think of a way to persuade Eric that he was right and Eric was wrong, that they should destroy the brains, but Eric's excitement thrust them along and before Kole knew it, they'd finished rigging the computer room of the battle barge with Rippernades. Kole stood before the brains and couldn't think of anything other than bullying his point, proving that he didn't trust Eric's instincts. He knelt before the first brain, opened the pedestal and retracted the hardware setting the brain free. The brain trembled as splotched of black grew across its surface, its eyes clouded over and optic nerves shriveled to thin strings.

Eric lunged forward clutching the sides of the jar watching the brain shrink to a black raisin a quarter of its original size. "What did you do? You did that on purpose," he accused.

"No," he gasped. "I hit the right code. Let's try the other one." He moved to the other brain and Eric hovered over his shoulder while he punched in the code. The hardware retracted setting the brain free, but this time a swirling cloud enveloped it. Kole stood then backed away bumping into Eric while the cloud grew floating upward, forming bone and musculature until a tall, thin woman with pale skin hovered naked before them. Her lips turned blood red, the color seemed to hover over her skin and with her eyes closed, her head arched back sprouting a long mane of strait blond hair that cascaded over her shoulders and down her back stopping at her waist. She opened her deep blue eyes looking first at Kole then Eric before she looked at herself.

Kole glanced at the blushing Eric then watched the woman create layers of a grey silk robe that hung elegantly off her shoulders, but before he could say anything she took a step forward and collapsed. Kole rushed forward catching her then waited for her to collect herself. Her alluring eyes fixed on his sending a shiver down his spine. He had never sensed such a presence that radiated such life and power. Her hand reached up gently penetrating his shield to caress his cheek. Her sudden warm and soft touch set off his paranoia, screaming for him to drop her, grab his Ripper and blast her into her next life, but as if hearing his thoughts...

She whispered, "I didn't mean to startle you, my child. I mean you no harm. My name is Enora."

Eric cheered then leaned closer to Kole and whispered in his ear,

"I told you so."

Kole wanted to drop her and slap him, but all he could do is stare into her eyes.

She broke their gaze and stood. "I've forgotten how to move, but my new body is responding well to my will."

"Then you know where you've been?" Eric asked.

She smiled slightly then looked at the first jar.

Eric stepped forward defensively. "We didn't do that."

"His name was Mason and don't worry, he took his own life."

"How do you know?" Kole asked placing his hand on his Ripper.

"Try having everything taken from you including all but one sense and see what choices you make. You can accept it, maintain your sanity and learn what you can, or delve deep into pain and darkness wishing in every agonizing second for death."

Eric sympathized, "That sounds horrible."

"If you're not laughing, you're crying," she commented.

Kole put his back to the door then asked, "Do you know how you ended up here?"

She faced him then looked at his hand resting on his Ripper. "You're too loud, trying to control everything. Let's do away with your fear, shall we?" She opened her hands and his and Eric's Rippers were pulled from their belts, hovering, dissolving before them until four blue orbs floated toward the wall like the eyes of an invisible demon that had perched on the top of a computer bank.

Kole stammered, "How did you… you couldn't have… impossible."

"My child, it was simple, I created a molecular membrane that controlled an air cushion for the anti-alchemy orbs to rest on. Seeing them, I can also protect myself from the explosives in this room and now that you've been disarmed, can we speak truth to each other?"

Kole sighed releasing his stress. "What are your intentions?"

"Wrong question, you're not strong enough to stop me, so knowing my intentions does what for you? Out of fear you're trying to place yourself into a position of authority over me, get me to explain myself." She slowly blinked. "Know your heart."

"Enora, how did you end up in a jar?" Eric asked. "I'd honestly like to know."

She studied him a moment then explained, "It doesn't matter now, but an eternity ago a group of my friends and I stumbled onto a plot that would plunge the world into war. Billions were slated to die and at the heart of it was an evil man, pulling strings from the shadows. My two friends and I confronted him, but he was stronger. It was terrifying having our alchemy blocked and bodies torn away. It took me some time to deal with my fate and to put away the memory of his cold soulless eyes."

"Wait," Kole said. "You're talking about the Purge?"

"The Purge, that's right. That's what he called it."

"What, only the three of you tried to stop the Purge?" Eric asked.

"Before that, he had killed most of my friends and we were the only ones left. No one else wanted to believe us and in their complacency they refused to think that the Commoners could harm them. They were too busy chasing fame and personal glory to be concerned or threatened by the thought of the Purge. But small things were being put into place to topple it all."

Kole gave her a warm smile. "I can't imagine what you've went through and I'm sorry for all your suffering." He knew there was nothing he could do to stop her if she chose to hurt them. He offered, "Let's get you out of here."

"Yeah," Eric agreed. "You can meet Nick and Kyra, they're good people. And there's one more brain up stairs, maybe it's your other friend."

Kole led them across the factory floor, up the stair well back to the security room with the brain as Eric matched Enora's pace asking her questions about the time before the Purge. Kole stood beside the brain and waited for their discussion to end before asking, "After telling us what happened to you, do you think this person will be stable? Don't get me wrong, but we seemed to luck out with you and since you've disarmed us, I don't think we'd be able to stop this person if they turn out to be destructive."

She gave him a slight smile. "Can't you feel his pain, his sorrow? He doesn't wish revenge or destruction."

"How can you tell what its feeling?" Eric asked.

"He may not have a body, but his soul is still there and if you know what to listen for, you can hear him too."

Kole knelt, opened the pedestal and retracted the brain's hardware. It took a moment before a whirling cloud of particles enveloped the brain, disintegrating the jar and forming a small deformed hairless body. His skin stretched across his hunched back, protruding spine and mismatched limbs then he dropped, falling heavy to the floor. Kole backed away as he pushed himself onto his knees to look up at Enora. He blinked, focusing his black beady eyes.

"I thought he was a Human, not an imp," Eric stated.

The man looked at his elongated fingers then felt his long pointed nose, sharp facial features and pointy ears then cried out a heart wrenching noise.

Enora's face softened. "Hello old friend."

Tears rolled down his cheeks and between sobs he blubbered, "I'm so sorry I betrayed you and Masson. The man who did this to us approached me and offered me everything. All I'd have to do is tell him when we were coming, that's it, and he'd fulfill all my dreams. I thought we'd beat him, but I wanted so much more. He lied to me, his offer made me want us to loose, and when we did he took us apart. I didn't fight as hard as I could have. I'm so sorry, forgive me."

"What's done is done," she soothed. "I forgive you old friend."

"Thank you," he whispered. "Tell Mason, I'm sorry." He arched backward as his body dissolved with a long low hissing scream into a swirling grey cloud until nothing remained.

Eric cocked his head puzzled. "How could you forgive him after what he did to you?"

"What you saw here, that pitiful creature wasn't his original body. We transcended our original form to reflect our inner self. The person that he was within his heart was handsome and pristine, standing tall and sure. In that moment of weakness he damaged his soul. There was no amount of revenge that I could've sought that would've mutilated him as much. And in torturing him I'd only harm myself. So, there are only two things that I could do, forgive him and let go of the bruise that his betrayal had made."

Kole looked at Eric. "That's very wise, I'd do the same."

Eric scoffed at Kole. "I'm sorry Enora. I didn't mean to wreck the moment."

"You didn't," she assured. "Shall we go? I'd like to feel the sun on my skin once again."

Chapter 19

Byron stood on a branch high in a tree watching a woman in body armor work the legs of a naked Ork. He liked the way her armor hugged her body then enhanced his hearing to listen to the pitiful Ork pour his heart out. Sick of his whining, he almost groaned disappointed that the Zombies hadn't killed anyone then thought about killing them both and making it look like the Zombies had got them, but still wasn't sure how Kole fit into the flow of things. If he interfered and killed Kole's friends it may change Kole's direction and he'd stumble deeper into James' plans. He waited, watching the Ork gathered his weapons and the two of them climb over the wall, out of the Zombie funnel. They fluttered around the Werewolves' transports that were parked in the forest and finally focus on one.

"Kyra, this is perfect," the Ork said. He climbed onto a large flat deck Barge. The Barge's engine room and compact crew quarters were up front with the forward and side guns, leaving the armored lump of the rear gun in the back.

The woman spoke, her voice muffled by her helmet, "Nick, that's perfect. They also have mining equipment we can use. We're set for life and maybe we can employ Kole and Eric."

"Yeah they can help us and we'll all be rich."

Byron smiled at the thought of Kole getting tangled up with those two, glad he decided not to kill them, but there's always a chance he'd be drawn back to James' plans. Byron relaxed and released his negative thoughts not wanting to pit his manifestation against the Universe's will and create a giant cluster bomb centered on him. He thought a moment longer then decided that the flow was working for him and all he had to do is sit back and watch the positive enthusiastic energy of the two Commoners sway Kole to stay.

His responsibilities waned and boredom choked Byron, high jacking his mind, creating an enticing dream of Monique, the way her face softened when she whispered into his ear that she loved him. Her words had tickled his ear and he was sure that she had said them, or did she? The memory felt so real, he was sure that it had happened. He smiled to himself and was grateful when Nick finally cleaned himself up and found a pair of tan slacks, black shoes and a long blue shirt in one of the Werewolf's transports. He was tired of watching the naked Ork run around, pretending to mark everything he was going to loot and dry humping the odd transport. More time passed and he was about to create a data pad to search the factory for Kole when they walked out of the cave and into the light. But, there was something unexpected, a woman that he hadn't heard about in Pine View, or seen on camera walked out with them. She opened her arms and basked in the late sun. He focused on her trying to remember, thinking that he must have heard about her before because there was no one else in the factory. He then reached out and looked into her for signs of lycanthrope thinking she was a Werewolf that they took pity on, but couldn't sense any signs of the disease. She dropped her arms and looked in his direction startling him. He abandoned his probe and froze waiting for her to look away, unsure if she had found him. Kole moved distracting her then made a hole in the Zombie wall large enough for them to walk through. They found Nick and Kyra loading some of the mining equipment onto the flat deck of their Salvage Barge.

"Hey guys," Nick called out. "We were just about to come looking for you," he openly lied flashing them a toothy grin. "What kept you so long?" He looked at the woman and his lips moved, but Byron could no longer hear him.

He strained to hear again then Eric pointed his thumb over his shoulder asking, "Did you guys make that mess in the tunnel back there?"

"Yeah, my Ripper made short work of those Zombies," Nick bragged. "Unfortunately, I lost my body armor. There's no way I'm going to get the stink out, but with all this silver salvage out here, I'll buy a new set."

"I can clean your armor for you," Kole offered.

He shook his head declining. "Thanks, but I can't wear that set anymore, I'll always smell them even if you get all their stink molecules out."

"Hey guys," Kyra greeted, strolling around the front of the Salvage Barge with her rifle slug over her shoulder.

Kole laughed. "I see you guys made yourselves at home."

Nick slapped a compact yellow laser drill. "Their stuff may smell like wet dog, but it's all in good condition. How can we pass up our good fortune? We're planning to lay claim to all that silver you made, do you want to join us?"

Kyra nodded toward the woman, but Byron heard nothing then knew that somehow the woman was blocking him. She knew he was there and he knew he should flee before the group found out, but he needed to listen in a little longer to see if Kole was heading in the right direction.

"What?" Kole mused. "You want to claim my silver, harvest then sell it?"

"Yeah, we'll get the whole town involved taking a cut on what everyone mines making it legitimate commerce. They're not going to want it if it comes directly from you. You have to create jobs that get everyone working. That's why I'm going to do you a favor and claim it all. You and Eric can work for me. Heck, I'll pay you well."

Eric laughed. "Come on Kole that sounds fun. We don't even have to work that hard. When the silver runs out, we can make another mine and live off the percentage. We can buy a house and have normal things, like a bed. We can live quietly instead of fighting off Slavers and thieves."

Kole didn't look convinced. He argued, "We help people in the world."

Nick hopped off the deck and landed in front of him. "You'll still help everyone by supplying the caravans. You can find out what's needed, make it, we'll salvage it and sell it to Pine View. They'll sell it to the merchants and it'll ripple out to where it's needed. People will love it."

Kole regarded Nick. "I've never thought about it that way, but it might be worth a try. You can be the face, no one will know that there's an Alchemist involved and we'll all get what we want."

"It's nobler this way," Kyra reasoned placing her hand on his shoulder. "You'll be helping the world one salvage at a time."

Kole flashed a smile. "We'll work for you Nick on the condition that you give me your Ripper."

Nick's fingers brushed the pistol's grip. "Why do you want him? I just named him and we've been through so much together."

"I'm sorry Nick, but I can't allow that weapon to exist. Let's deal, I'll trade you all the silver for that weapon and Eric and I will help you salvage it."

Nick looked from Kole to Eric. "Wait, where's your Rippers? Did you lose yours and now want mine?"

"No, they were destroyed and I'm going to destroy yours."

Confusion flashed across Nick's face, but he dismissed his argument. "Deal, it's a good trade." He handed Kole his Ripper, grip first saying, "You can have my Billy Ed."

Eric laughed. "You named your gun Billy Ed?"

"What's wrong with that?"

He snickered. "I just thought it would be more Orkish."

"Just because I was born an Ork doesn't mean that I am one, you dick. I happen to like finer things and I speak good English."

Eric laughed again. "Well, aren't you swanky? I guess I speak bad English then."

Byron smiled, returning his hearing to normal, convinced that Kole was out of the picture and ecstatic that the flow was in his favor. Kole was contained, the Rippers destroyed, Sarah was on track and Cid was taken care of. He floated down from his hiding place landing in a small clearing. He made a data pad and tried to access the factory's server, but failed to connect. He had a silly notion that Kole, drowning in goodness destroyed the contents of the factory in an attempt to save the world from potential disaster. He hesitated knowing that James wasn't going to be happy about that. He was starting to like Kole's predictability and the thought of manipulating him from the shadows. He could put Kole on the path of his choosing and that pleased him. He knelt touching the earth, sending his awareness into the factory confirming what he already knew, everything lay in ruins. He walked through the forest thinking of what to say to James then sat under a ginkgo tree, an oddity for the area. He modified his data pad then connected with James.

James' face appeared taking up the entire screen. "Any luck?" he asked.

Byron nodded. "Sarah is in Winter Haven and is proceeding, the Ripper problem has been taken care of, but there's been a snag." Byron waited, but James said nothing. Byron continued, "Cid and his people are all dead and the factory has been destroyed."

James cupped his face, his hands looking unusually large on Byron's screen. "That factory has been hidden for a thousand years and now it's gone. Its weaponry was irreplaceable. I'm not happy. Did Cid do it?"

"No, an Alchemist named Kole was hired by the town of Pine View to look into a small Werewolf problem. He followed Cid's trail back to the factory and seeing what was there, he feared for the future of humanity and destroyed it."

His hands slid down his confused face. "He destroyed all of it?"

"I got close enough to confirm it."

"You let him live? He's seen too much."

"He assumed that Cid was making an army and was trying to loot the factory. He personally believes that he can better the world by serving the masses and an army of Werewolves threatened everything.

Besides, the factory was already gone before I got here," he lied.

"That factory was a big part of my plans. In a couple of years Sarah would've collected enough Humans to make an army that would've expanded across the planet. Now I'll have to strengthen my other plans, so the Humans will come out on top." He looked away from the screen and Byron heard typing. "Kole was Carl the Mad's apprentice."

"Carl the Mad, that name sounds familiar."

"It should. You armed a tribe of Pixies with a couple of Rippers and had him assassinated."

Thinking back, Byron remembered more. "I replaced him. He used to work for you and the first task to prove my worth was to find and kill him leaving no trace back to us. He tried to warn the world about you before my time then went into hiding because without proof, they all thought he was crazy and laughed his warning off. He was a hard man to find and I remember Kole, he was a nothing back then."

"And now here he is, with an apprentice. This news worries me. I fear that they are a manifestation of Carl the Mad."

Byron had never seen James worried before, but hid his surprise. "It's a coincidence that he has found what he did. Now his friends have convinced him to make a life with them. He's no longer a problem."

"The clock ticks and the gears move. There are no coincidences." James studied Byron. "Why are you arguing with me? Go kill them."

"If they go missing, others will investigate and right now they'll be heroes. Once word gets out that they stopped the Werewolf apocalypse, the convergence of everyone's platitudes will anchor and divert their state of being on the path of self righteousness. They'll forget about what has happened here and be swallowed up in the expectations of others."

James sighed. "Fine, but that distraction may only tie them down for a time. For now the flow protects him from us, but if Kole gets in the way again, we'll have to take a closer look at him."

Satisfied, Byron asked, "Shall I come home?" He itched to see Monique again. They'd been apart for too long and he missed her touch.

"Some influential people haven't forgotten the mess you left in the brothel and your psychopathic stroll through town. That whole Troll and hooker thing has come full circle and I'm not going to be able to stop them. I need you to stay away for a little longer and give people time to cool off and forget. It's for your own good."

He growled under his breath. "Since when do we listen to them? What can they do to stop me if I want to rip their hearts out, use it as a paint brush and paint their dying expression on a wall? And for the last time, Monique is not a hooker, she's a dancer."

James' expression relaxed then warmed. "I can see that you're upset and I apologize for calling the woman you raped a hooker. I can tell she means a lot to you."

He nodded calming down, but it still felt like James was somehow mocking him. "Apology accepted. Her name's Monique and we're in love."

"I can tell and I'm happy for you. You mentioned Sarah, how's she doing?"

Arguing with James and the mere mention of Sarah further darkened his expression. "She has some weird notion of broadcasting her voice and gathering the Human population at Winter Haven. That dumb clone."

James smiled deepening Byron's rage. "That's brilliant," he said. James' sudden cheerfulness sickened Byron making him want to rip his lips off. "All right, calm down Byron, your eyes are getting dark. Help Sarah and give her what she needs. Take your time and have everything fabricated then found by her salvagers. When you're done, come home. I won't bug you for a while. You can go on a vacation with Monique, have some fun and rest up. How does that sound?"

He released a long heavy sigh then said, "Real good." He paraphrased, "I do one more thing, have Monique then take her away." James nodded then disconnected the transmission.

Byron stood dusting himself off then walked into a small clearing and dissolved his data pad. He felt a presence behind him and spun, ready to unleash all the rage James instilled in him, but stopped. The woman who accompanied Kole was standing alone a short distance away. Her piercing blue eyes froze him in place. She stepped closer, almost floating, emanating power that Byron couldn't conceive. He felt a cocoon of power wrap around him, squeezing him tight before he could escape.

"You reek of the Shadow, the string puller. Every connection in life that we make puts a finger print on us. I also see that you've written your power to your bones." She chuckled. "Silly child, you are a living reflection of the Universe and you choose to turn yourself into a thing. You have a dark soul and in my time you'd be an ugly deformed imp of a man. You can't even see that all the pain that you've inflict on the world will never sate the emptiness within you." Byron tried to speak, but could only wheeze. "I guess," she continued, ignoring his attempt to argue, "I have the power to extract revenge for all those you've hurt, but what would that accomplish? When you kill someone you reek of blood, a smell that diminishes the light of your soul. And that's what it's all about, your soul. You've already suffered enough pain in your life to turn you into a thing, what more can I do to you? I can manifest a huge cock and rape you against a tree, but what would that act do to me? It would only add to your pain and you'd be drawn to another person to express it. I could kill you, but the pain in your soul will ripple through space and time into your next existence, unless you deal with it now. The cycle begins again further drawing you into darkness." She looked passed him into the forest. "I came here to erase your memory of me and having your Alchemy blocked. Later, after you've calmed down you'd think about me, and I don't want that. To be truthful, I can only take your conscious memories, but we carry everything within us, so you'll always remember me and what I'm going to do to you. The only thing I can do in the form of punishment is bless and curse you by telling you that it's your pain that resonates with another, both sets of vibration drawing together to act out its manifestation. In the end, you're only hurting yourself, over and over again. Like a junkie in a crack shack passing a pipe. You think that you're hurting others? You are manifesting your life one moment at a time and you choose..." she waves her hand across him. "This."

A little while later, Byron was standing in a clearing trying to remember what he was doing and why an impotent rage filled him. Something had made him feel helpless and small. His mind thrashed his memory until he remembered his talk with James and the one last task he had to do before he could return home to Monique. He calmed slightly, but couldn't shake the feeling of helplessness.

Chapter

20

After they maximized the carrying capacity of the flat bed with silver logs, Kole waited for Nick to survey his claim and for Kyra to return with Eric from counting all the dead Werewolves. He watched Enora a short distance away, her head tilted back, eyes closed basking in the sunlight. He still didn't trust her, but there was nothing he could do about her. He decided that he was wasting energy thinking about it. He walked over and stood beside her. "Now that you're free, what are your plans?"

She remained silent, but just before Kole repeated himself she replied, "I could feel you thinking about me from over there. It felt like you were arguing with yourself." Kole didn't respond. "We are like iron rods and if we have loud thoughts, it's like we emit a magnetic field that other rods can pick up."

"Do you know what I'm thinking?"

She tilted her head toward him, looking at him from the corner of her eye. "I can't read your mind and I don't want to. Do you know how busy a mind can be, all the layers of thought?" She closed her eyes and faced the sun. "But," she added. "If I were in your shoes I'd argue between action and inaction then accept the fact that I released something into the world that I'm powerless to do anything about. I'd want to try to reason with that person to see what they want. That's common sense and to answer your question, I'm waiting and enjoying the warmth of the sunlight. I forgot how penetrating the light can be."

"Waiting? Waiting for what?"

"The manifestation of my destiny and for the moment, I'll be traveling with you until it's time to change direction." She looked into the forest. "I've been out of a jar for less than a day and I'm already bored with your worry. You live and think in lies. You hide you true thoughts and feelings then speak, trying to evoke the correct emotional response in me to gain the illusion of an upper hand. Kole, cut the crap and be honest with me."

He debated the thought then went for it. "Fine, you scare me," he confessed. "I've seen and done things, but in all that time I've never felt what I feel off you. I try to maintain balance and do my part to keep this place together by stopping another Purge, but you come from a time of madness. When I look at you, my mind can't conceive what you are and I'm worried for the world."

"Thank you for your honesty and that wasn't so hard, was it?"

He turned to face her then spoke with a little heat, "My instinct is telling me to mess you up and I'm almost willing to try, so it's your turn to be honest with me."

"My child, I've been nothing but honest with you."

"Stop calling me that, I'm over five hundred years old. I'm not a child."

"Stop," she gently commanded. "You're behaving like a spoiled child. The vibration of that word and the loving energy that I put behind it is not disrupting you, but I understand that you want respect. Very well, but know that we are eternal and I see you as a child because you haven't moved out of the infantile state of Alchemy and if it's your destiny to stop another Purge then the Universe will put you in the right place and time to do so. All you're doing is telling the Universe that you'll do the task and become its instrument. You're running around worried about the thoughts of others hemorrhaging energy, making yourself weak, to be used by others and for what, to protect the world from something that's completely out of your control?"

"Wow, you're such a..."

"Am I?" she interrupted. "If I didn't care, I wouldn't waste my breath on you. Perhaps I care too much."

"Care too much?" he doubted. "What do you know about the world? You've been in a jar for a thousand years."

She gave a slight smile. "We haven't changed in over ten thousand years, it's not hard to predict. And I was never alone, the Universe was right there with me. I was never separated from the world."

He ran his fingers through his beard then gently tugged releasing his frustration. "I didn't want to argue with you. I just want to know what you're going to do."

"All things happen the way they're meant to. Try not to read more into it than that. Your uncertainty amassed a bit of energy that was released the way you needed it to and I wanted us to get to know each other better, so we came together in a moment of honesty."

He scrutinized her. "You're completely insane and I don't trust you one bit. The sooner you get away from us the better."

She nodded and Kole wasn't sure if anything that he said had registered with her, which annoyed him more, but before he could storm off protesting her presence, Nick cleared his throat. Kole turned and met Nick's hesitant gaze.

"Everyone's back and we're almost ready to go," Nick said. He called out to Eric and Kyra, "Over here you two, group huddle." He watched them a moment longer then called out, "Stop dragging your asses and hurry up." When the two finally joined them Nick continued, "I'm glad that we're all starting this new adventure together and you are all my employees, including you Enora." She turned to face them. "I have one rule," he said. "We work hard together, we slack off together and we all take home equal pay with bonuses to those who do extra. Kole, I overheard some of your and Enora's conversation and Kole, you're way more powerful than me and I take it that she's more powerful than you." He pointed to Him then to Enora and Eric. "All of you Alchemists can go bat shit crazy and there's nothing that I can do about it. So Kole, join my club and get over it. She has done nothing to warrant your attitude. Now, when we get back to town I'll negotiate price with Roy for the silver and the bodies."

"What bodies?" Enora asked.

Kole's mood darkened remembering what he did.

Eric spoke up, "We're being paid per Werewolf sample. There was supposed to be only three out here."

"And now Zombies," Nick chimed in. "Roy is going to pay us for that too, but I'm going to lie about their numbers and say fifty because I'm not going back into that smelly tunnel to count bodies. Just thinking about it makes me want to puke." He scrunched his eyes shut and wiped his mouth.

"No one's asking you to go back there," Kyra soothed. "And no one cares if you lie about that. Well Roy might, but he can come out here and count them himself."

Nick relaxed then nodded. "How many samples did you collect?"

Kyra shrugged. "There were explosions and…"

"It was messy," Eric finished. "We've collected enough."

"Enough," Nick repeated sounding pleased. "We saved Pine View and that's how I'm going to sell it. We'll be heroes. I'll start the negotiations with Roy on the way back so he'll have the payment ready when we arrive."

Kole was tired of standing around and wanted to get Eric away from Enora, but also thought about what she had said. He was eternal and nothing bad was happening in the moment, but he was itching to get back to town, his transport was there. He could take Eric and get far away from Enora in case she turned out to be crazy. He also didn't have a reason to run and it wasn't killing him to let Nick have his fun. But something inside him itched and he almost interrupted Nick to get everybody going. He forced himself to relax and listened to Nick assign everyone a position on his Barge.

On the ride back, Kole sat in the isolated rear gunnery position watching the forest pass by listing to the crew's cheerful chatter over the com, their laughter soothed his urge to collect Eric and disappear into the waste. He originally sought out civilization for Eric, which has been a success, but now he had to face the pressure to flee. He thought back to his teacher, with him it always felt like he was running from something. Always moving, hiding and now there's no reason for Kole to behave that way. He hated the paranoid part of himself that had ruined the good things in his life, but helped in the bad. He didn't know when, or how to trust. His teacher had never shown him that.

After they had arrived, Kole listened to everyone make plans to go to the pub for the evening as the gates of the Pine View closed behind them. He heard and almost felt the loud clag of metal and the multiple clicking of its locks. He sighed in relief thinking about his transport, wanting to sit in his chair and be wrapped in his refuge from the world. He was grateful when they finally came to a stop and left through the side hatch running into Enora and the rest of the crew as they walked toward town.

Kole asked Enora, "Can I help you find your way?"

"I'm with you," she replied.

"I'm not doing anything. I'm going to run a couple of diagnostics on my transport then turn in."

"That sounds good."

He cocked his eyebrow trying to figure out what she wanted then gave up. "Fine, come on," he muttered then walked away, forcing her to match his pace, but when they reached his spot his transport and tent were gone. "You got to be kidding me!" Kole yelled.

"What's wrong?"

"Someone stole all my stuff!"

Roy rushed up to him skidding to a halt with his arms flailing out to catch his balance. He straitened then fixed his jacket and turned his hat into place making Kole wait for an explanation. "Calm down Kole, everything is going to be okay," he soothed.

Kole gestured to where his transport used to be. "What, two or three days? I was here for a couple of days and someone stole my transport and all my stuff. Tell me that this is a joke and that it's a ploy to make Eric and I stay."

He shook his head. "No, I'm sorry. Someone stole it and now the town council wants you gone. You did things on the mountain that we didn't think you were capable of. Your file said one thing, but... Well, we're willing to take a loss and call your debt to Pine View even."

Enora grinned. "See, I'm glad I came with you. We just had this conversation. You wanted me to move on for the same reason. You can't say that the Universe doesn't have a sense of humor."

Kole closed his eyes trying to reign in his frustration. "Yes Enora, thank you for pointing that out," he growled as the images of slapping Enora and making Roy eat his hat flashed through his mind. "Who stole my transport?"

"We don't know, but a scummy Human male came through asking questions about you just before your transport slipped out with one of our merchants. I tried to get his image off the mainframe, but our security was hacked twice and all the feed was erased." He placed his hand on Kole's shoulder. "I know your loss is painful, but can you just whip up another transport?"

"No!" he roared. "I can't just whip up another one. That was my home, I have history there and it smells like me."

"Regardless, you're too dangerous to have around. You'll have to move on."

Enora stepped closer to Roy standing with a posture of authority. "That's not going to happen. We're going to stay, you'll wipe his debt clean and people are going to forget about us."

"Who are you?" Roy demanded. "Are you going to make people forget? Can you do that?"

"It doesn't matter who I am," Enora pressed. "We're now part of a salvage company and Kole will shave, get a haircut and wear a uniform. The people will forget that he was even here and with the silver rush there'll be plenty of new faces for everyone to look at. Now run along and tell your council that he and Eric went away."

Roy huffed. "I don't take orders from you, missy."

"Sir," she soothed. "No one truly cares if he's here or not and once you tell everyone that he's gone, they won't even look for him."

Kole took a moment to think about Enora's and Roy's point of view then decided for himself. "You're not being fair Roy," he said. "You want to get rid of us after we risked our lives to save your town. Go up the mountain and you'll see for yourself that those Werewolves were coming here to fatten their numbers before terrorizing the land." He waved Roy away. "I'm just not feeling it right now. We're staying until we decide to move on."

Roy's face turned a shade red. "I'm going to add your noncompliance and what you did on the mountain to your file and everyone's going to know," he seethed then stormed off.

He gazed at the patch of dirt where his transport had sat and felt defeated. "I don't know what just happened. Everything was going well and now it has all fallen apart."

Enora folded her arms and relaxed her posture. "I don't get it. Why would killing the Werewolves be bad enough to get a reprimand?" She chuckled. "Your file sounds like a criminal record."

"There're a couple of reasons why, mainly that I didn't kill the Werewolves their way. I didn't run back to town and consult them, or drum up a small force to have a shootout. I'm guilty of excessively using my power without cleaning up the mess. If I would've dissolved the silver and bodies then claimed that there were only three Werewolves out there, even though they probably knew what was going on, everything would still be fine. Now I'm refusing to leave, basically holding the town hostage in their eyes, but if I do what you say and change my appearance, disappearing into the world, they won't care because they would've killed my name." He laughed. "I feel sorry for the bastards who stole my transport because the next town they show up at will shoot first. I might get to be declared dead."

"Well then you're free now," she said facing him. Her hands moved through his shield to rest on his shoulders. "Let me help you find your true self." She touched his face dissolving his beard. Her hands felt soft against his skin, a gentle caress. Kole could feel the love within her intent as she trimmed his hair. He looked deep into her eyes, lost in her gaze. He could feel the warmth of her hands before him as she remade his clothes, the same layered grey rode that she wore. "There, finished," she chimed stepping back to give him room.

"Do I look different?"

"Yes. Now if you can, let go of your emotional crap so you can feel different. From internal to external, once you change inside, the way you move will change and your transformation will be complete. Soon, not even Roy will recognize you."

"It's too bad that they have us on their security. They'll use the footage to reference us and see the new me. And I'd like to see if you're right, that they'd forget me."

She smiled then confessed, "I've been emitting a frequency that interferes with their security and once Roy finds out, he'll want eyes on us, so let's change the color and look of our robes." She touched his chest and their clothes both changed into a matching set of red coveralls with reflective stripes. She took his hand and gave him a gentle tug. At first he resisted then wanted to please her. He gripped her hand not wanting to let go, allowing her to guide him to the town's interior hatch. She smiled giving him a sideways look then slid her fingers between his stepping close and walked shoulder to shoulder down a path toward town.

Chapter

21

Nick reached out and leaned against the shower wall feeling the hot water flowed over him. He had washed four times, but the rotten stench of Zombie still lingered. His mind flashed back to the cave, he could still hear their moans, the chorus of their sick song of hunger. He shuddered at the memory. He grabbed the bar of soap and lathered again, scrubbing his skin afraid that he was infected, imaging the Zombie disease eating away his skin turning him into one of them. But it was Kyra that had saved him and pulled him out of the darkness yet again, once as children and then now. Where would he be without her? What would he be? He owed her everything and she wanted nothing in return. One day he'd repay her for everything. The thought of her smile brightened his mood and rinsing for the fifth time, he finally felt clean.

He was late, taking too long in the shower, but you can't rush perfection. Kyra was probably pissed off again whining about how long it took him to get ready. He quickly grabbed some tight clothes trying to make time, but slowed squeezing into them then flashed himself his favorite "Oh Yeah" look in the mirror. He trotted to the lobby of the apartment complex then took his time getting to the pub because he didn't want to get sweaty on the way, besides he was already late.

He was planning to have a lot of fun blowing the credits Roy gave him for the kills and silver. He'd never been so rich and Roy went on and on about Kole, but Nick tuned him out, all he could see was that white card that was loaded with a small fortune.

He was getting close to the pub and could hear the music. He quickened his pace almost skipping then sidestepped a couple hogging the sidewalk. A pale woman with bright red lips and striking blue eyes and a handsome guy with a hard face, romantically strolling with their arms interlocked. "Lucky gal," he thought, but they were both dressed in dreadful looking red garbage sacks. It was always sad for him to see beautiful people dressed in drab.

"Hey Nick," the guy said with Kole's voice.

He wanted to ignore the guy and keep going, but that might be Kole. He stopped then turned around taking a moment to visualize the guy with a beard. "Is that you Kole?" he asked.

"Told you so," Enora flirted.

Kole grinned at her then asked Nick, "You going to the pub?"

Nick couldn't bend his mind around how different Kole looked, but something else was going on. "You two seem awfully cozy. On the mountain I thought you were going to kill each other. I even separated you two for the ride home and now you look like a cute couple on a date."

She looked at Kole's profile. "We connected and worked some things out."

Kole agreed. "We'll have to get everyone together tomorrow and have a talk."

He suddenly felt bored and looked for an out. "I'm late, I got to get going, or Kyra's going to be pissed."

"Oh," Enora said. "We passed them a couple of minutes ago. She seemed to be happy."

"Them?" he asked not wanting to know the answer.

"Yeah, Eric's keeping her company."

"That's odd," Nick said imagining Eric and Kyra laughing, holding hands and skipping to the pub. Faces of all those losers that Kyra had dated in the past flashed in his mind. She had always left them and waited for him, pounding on one door or another, yelling for him to hurry. Those other guys had never taken her away, but Eric's a good one and might come between them. He didn't like his negative thinking. His first thought should've been of her happiness. He glanced toward the pub then said, "She usually waits for me. It's our thing we do before going out."

Kole patted Enora's arm giving it a slight caress. "We're going to take off. I hope you have fun tonight."

All of a sudden the vibe between them got weird. "Will do," he said feeling awkward trying not to think about what they'd be doing later then continued on.

Tonight the pub was crowded and the warmth from all the bodies was more comforting to him than an open fire. He stood in the entrance basking in the energy from all the laughter and good will listening to the blaring Dwarven techno. The music pumped and the people on the dance floor bounced with their arms in the air following the pulse, shaking the floor. He pressed himself into the crowd and was greeted with smiles and raised glasses. Everyone had heard of the silver and told him how lucky he was to make the claim. People he'd never seen before reached out and grabbed his shoulder congratulating him, making him feel like a hero. Strangers bought him drinks wanting to be near him and he reveled in their attention, eventually making his way to the bar where Granny and her grandson filled orders. Nick flashed a smile to the grandson who clearly wasn't interested then ordered a few of shots to keep things moving. He soon found himself on the dance floor, body against body feeling close to everyone then was handed a little something to make everything feel like the music was flowing through him. It was an orgy of movement and he lost where his body ended and the crowd began.

He didn't know how long he had been dancing, but he had to rest. His skin was hot and prickly and his throat was dry and puffy. The music continuously flowed between various Dwarven, Elven and Human artists that allowed him to lose himself, but he needed water which at the moment happened to be more expensive than alcohol. After hydrating, he saw Eric across the bar then followed him untill he spotted Kyra. The pub was so packed he had to jump up to see over people, but he found them sitting in a booth. They looked happy and he thought of bumping into them telling them that he had just got there, but didn't want to know if Kyra didn't mind. He was always late and she was always annoyed, but tonight she was happy or even more than that, content. He felt small and weak then went back, making his way to the bar not wanting the evening to end. He pulled out his white card and bought rounds for his new friends. He was a hero and everyone loved him.

Later, a pretty fella with tight fancy clothes dragged him away promising to take him to a place very few in town get to see, but he had to follow blindfolded. He loved the man's gentle attention as the blindfold went on and couldn't resist the man's cooing voice as he was led into the cold quiet night through town to a place underground where the laughter, bells and dings were muffled.

The blindfold came off and once his eyes adjusted to the light he focused on a smiling Dark Elf. The man was dressed in a red suit with white pin stripes and matching red shoes. The Elf's long strait white hair was pulled back into a tight ponytail and he leaned with both hands on a black cane topped with a silver ginning skull. He stood between two large gold statues of people in victory poses. "Welcome," he announced. "To Fast Eddies Casino, I'm your host Fast Eddie and if you have the money, anything can be yours." Behind him, chandeliers hung from the rough rock ceiling while gambling tables and machines filled the large spacious room. Gold colored carpet with purple inlay filled the floor as a small group of young scantily clad men and women played tag around the tables. Nick smiled at Eddie, produced his white card and already forgot about the young man who brought him there.

The next morning, Nick struggled to wake. His skin burned, head pounded, tongue was stuck to the roof of his dry mouth and red light shone through his sticky eyelids. He struggled to move, but he was bound and his skin ached, feeling like it was cracking. He moaned from the pain then finally opened his dry eyes to the bright sunlight reflecting off the water of a small pond behind the pub. People on the shore pointed and laughed at him. He gathered enough senses to realize that he sat naked duct taped to a chair on a small raft made of scrap wood. The cool water on his toes felt nice, but the rest of him was sunburned turning his beautiful green skin brownish. He squinted looking himself over. One arm was taped to the arm of the chair holding his white card and the other was tapped across his chest with his index finger lodged to its second knuckle up his nose. He leaned his head back and painfully dislodged his finger thinking his nose would bleed, but it only felt like it did. He twitched his legs feeling that they were also tied to the chair and as he moved the raft bobbed threatening to topple him into the pond.

"I found him. He's at the pond behind the pub," Nick heard Kole say. Relieved, he shifted his head and watched Kole run to a rope anchored to the shore. Kole was still wearing his ugly uniform. He reached into the water and pulled the rope dragging him to shore. Kole tapped the com link in his ear then grabbed the back of Nick's chair dragging him off the raft. "What happened to you last night?" he asked.

"I don't know," Nick confessed while trying to penetrate the black canvas of a memory called last night. "I don't remember."

"We've been looking all over for you since sunup."

Kyra and Eric dressed in jeans and T-shirts ran across the grass down to the pond. Seeing them together made Nick's skin burn hotter. He didn't want Eric to see him like this, didn't want to give him ammo to whisper into Kyra's ear to take her away from him. She was more than his family. She was his protector, savior and best friend that would always be there to rescue him.

Kyra knelt beside Nick worried and looked him over. "This is horrible. Who did this to you?"

"I don't know," he mumbled, too ashamed to look her in the eye.

Enora was the last to arrive. She walked over and stood beside Kole sliding her hand in his.

Kyra pulled out a knife from her back pocket and cut the tape releasing him from the chair, but his skin hurt so bad he didn't want to move. "Let's lay him on the grass," she suggested.

"Wait," Nick protested then cried out as cold hands grabbed him.

They lifted him onto his feet ignoring his painful puffing and hissing then carefully spun him around leaving temporary hand prints on his skin. They lay him down on the cool pointy grass.

Tears ran down Kyra's cheeks. "I'm going to pull the tape off," she whispered then picked at an edge slowly peeling it, stretching his skin.

He clenched his jaw trying to take the pain. "Stop!" he screamed. "There has to be another way!"

Armed security guards surrounded as Roy sauntered into view. "It looks like it's time for you all to go."

Kole glared at Roy. "We're not going anywhere."

"That boy and I made an agreement yesterday," he said pointing at Nick.

Nick wobbled his head in disagreement.

Roy stood defiant with his fists on his hips. "Let me remind you," he growled. "I paid you for the silver and the Werewolf bounties then gave you double to leave."

"Is that true?" Kyra asked.

Nick felt everyone's eyes on him. Roy had said a lot of things to him that he had ignored when he held the white card. Then a memory flashed before his eyes. He nodded and his team groaned.

"What about the claim?" Eric asked. "We started a company."

Roy shook his head. "Last night the claim, your business and your new salvage barge changed hands," he informed them. "I looked into it and the card I gave you is now empty."

"Wait," Kole said. "Part of that was our pay."

"That's not my problem. I paid your boss and he's supposed to pay you."

Kyra lowered her head and closed her eyes. "Nick, tell me that you didn't spend all our money and lose everything?"

Nick didn't believe that the card in his hand was empty. He fought through the blackness remembering a casino and a Dark Elf named Fast Eddie. "Fast Eddie, he stole it all," he croaked.

"Fast Eddie," Roy repeated. "That's who you gave everything to."

He sat up leaning on his elbows then clenched his teeth fighting off the pain and nausea. "I didn't give him anything. I went to his casino…"

"We don't have a casino here," Roy interrupted.

"Yes you do. Fast Eddie the Dark Elf runs the place."

Roy laughed so hard that tears formed in his eyes. "A Dark Elf here? When you lie you lie big," he said then dried his eyes.

"I'm not lying. There were Dark Elves playing tag and…" he said trailing off then went quiet when the memory of gambling, drugs and being in an orgy pierced the blackness. He then knew that he'd paid for it all.

Roy and the security guards laughed at his expression of realization. Roy raised his hand quieting his men. He mocked, "Playing tag, that's the dumbest thing I've ever heard. It's real simple. I don't care what happened to you. We had a deal. I paid you, now leave."

Kyra stood and refused to look at Nick. "I'll meet you all at the gate," she sighed then left, pushing her way through the guards.

"You're lucky you're all messed up, or I'd slap the crap out of you," Eric threatened then calmed looking disappointed. "You blew our money, it's like stealing. You idiot! I'm sorry," he apologized. "You idiot!" he repeated. "I shouldn't call you that, I'm sorry. I'm going to go." He looked at Nick once more then yelled, "You idiot!" He finished then followed Kyra.

Kole let Enora's hand go then knelt beside Nick. "Let him be," Enora suggested. "Let pain teach him, or he'll never learn."

Kole smirked at her. "He's suffered enough." He touched the tape and caused it to lose its adhesion. "I'm sorry, I can't do anything about the sunburn or the looser printed in sunscreen on your forehead."

"Thanks. The tape really sucked, but I'll be okay," Nick said then grimaced as he pushed himself to his feet. "Roy, I'm going to my apartment to get my things."

"That won't be necessary. It's been a busy morning for me. Your apartment was broken into and all your things are gone."

Kole cursed. "You and your security suck. This is the worse town I've ever been in and I've been around." He pointed his finger at Roy. "If he says there's a Dark Elf in town who swindled him, then I believe him."

"Well," Nick corrected then confessed, "I kind of remember spending all the money."

Kole's expression soured. "Nick, you have some serious problems and Kyra does too. For some reason you're both in a symbiotic relationship and I don't know how to help you."

Nick didn't like Kole poking his nose into Kyra and his business, but chose to be nice. "I don't know what you're talking about," he denied then limped past the guards who parted for him. Kole and Enora followed as he made his way through town toward the gate ignoring everyone's stares, snickers and remarks.

Kole spoke up, "Do you want me to make you some clothes or something?"

"No, I don't care what these people think, they're all jerks. Beside I've been naked before."

"It's not for them. At least let me make you a loin cloth because we're tired of seeing your junk flop around."

Nick ignored him. "Don't worry about it Kole," Enora said. "He doesn't love himself."

Nick turned around as fast as his sore body allowed him. "Shut up Enora! I don't remember hiring you, so you have nothing to say here and I'm not ashamed of my nudity." He ignored the pain and gestured to his body. "I'm beautiful."

Enora blinked her annoying blue eyes at him. "You're ugly on the inside, besides I'm glad I don't work for you. You just ripped off your employees."

Nick chuckled, but wanted to laugh. "You don't know anything about anything."

They continued in silence. Nick's feet hurt slapping against the cement and his skin ached, he wanted the clothes, but he didn't want to give them the satisfaction of helping him. He did feel bad about spending all the money, but he couldn't help it. Last night, he wanted to stop, to say no to everyone after his money and to do the right thing, but he needed to feel special.

Nick looked up at the towering gate that separated him from the waste and thought about the other Barges they had left behind on the mountain. They could each grab one, trade the bad ones and gather enough materials to become merchants. The idea excited him and he thought of different ways to present the idea while waiting for Kyra and Eric. When the two finally showed up he was ready, but had to know about their relationship. "Are you two seeing each other?" he asked.

Kyra looked at Nick shocked. "No, we're just friends."

Eric's expression dropped like he was slapped across the face with a soiled towel and Nick felt ecstatic. He wanted to do the dance of joy, waving his fingers in the air while kicking up dirt, but quickly hid his feelings. "I was curious. Lately you two have been spending a lot of time together."

"Is that what this is about?" she asked. She looked like she was piecing things together. "I can't believe it. It's Jorsville all over again."

Nick scoffed. "I don't know what you're talking about."

"I was getting close to a guy named Buzz and you pulled the same crap then. How could I have been so stupid? I see it now, all those times that we seem to get ahead then you have an accident. I didn't think you were doing it on purpose."

"No," Nick soothed. "I love you, I'd never hurt you. I just want to make sure that he'd treat you right."

"I'm right here," Eric reminded. "If I was more than a friend, I would treat her good."

Kyra looked at Eric. "Not now."

Nick pressed, thrilled that he was breaking them up before they started. "Why not now, is there something wrong with him?"

"No, there's nothing wrong with him," she said defensively. "He's just not my type."

Enora placed her hand on Eric's shoulder. "Let her go Eric, you disserve better."

"Excuse me?" Kyra asked, insulted.

Nick glared at Enora. "He'd be lucky if Kyra touched him."

Kole laughed then became dangerously serious. "Everyone shut up! You're all acting like a bunch of children." He waved to the Gate controller and the gate banged and creaked open just wide enough for them to get through. "All this madness ends here. Let's go," he ordered. He walked past Nick into the waste. They followed and the gate closed behind them with a large bang and clicking locks.

Chapter

22

Sarah held her breath resting on the bottom of the pool feeling the warmth and pressure of the water. She pushed off the bottom slowly emerging from the bath. She opened her eyes and took a deliberate breath focusing her mind before standing. She waited listening to the water trickle off her slender body then waded through the waist high water tracing her fingers across its surface. She walked up the stairs and stood between two servants dressed in white robes. They waited, eyes averted, kneeling, facing each other and when she stopped, they produced towels to dry her off. Once dry they clothed her in the same white robe that they wore while she admired her large luxurious bathroom. The ancient marble reclaimed from a ruined mansion lined the floor and pool cooling her feet. Violet silk drapes hung from the ceiling along the walls and throughout the room creating pockets of privacy. Once dressed, the servants held open a path through the curtains to a vanity. She sat and enjoyed the daily routine waiting for them to comb and braid her hair. Beautiful golden flowers were painted on the tops of her feet and the backs of her hands and once they finished they carefully guided her feet into her open slippers. She stood then gracefully walked toward the closed door giving one of her servant time to go ahead and open the door for her. She walked down the hall into the living room. The servant closed the door behind her then helped the other drain and wash out her huge pool preparing it for tomorrow.

She stopped before Byron who sat sprawled out on her couch with his muddy, tan boots on her coffee table. He looked miserable. Unkempt hair, stubble and tattered forest green shirt and black pants. "It's about time," he growled. "What were you doing back there? I've been waiting forever."

Though his demeanor told her that he thought little of her, she didn't care. She looked at the muddy boot prints he left on her spotless floor. "Where's the servant who was taking care of you?"

"I told him to get out before I shove my boot up his ass. He wouldn't even look me in the eye, the coward. He kept smiling while he asked if he could get me anything. It was creepy."

"I see," she said. "Thank you for the mud you rudely traipsed through my home."

He looked around his legs at his feet. "Whatever. I thought the plan was to make people think I'm normal." He lifted his leg then shook off more mud before dropping his foot back onto the table with a thud. "Speaking about plans, I didn't realize that you needed to live in a temple to do your job."

She smiled. She didn't want to play his game, his empty words, but for now to get what she wanted, she needed to explain herself. "I didn't ask for any of this. The townspeople gave it to me. They made a pyramid of stairs and placed my home higher than any other so that I can look out any window and see everyone."

He scowled. "Don't give me that crap you're turning people into slaves."

"They're not slaves, they're volunteers. They want to give me love and for me to accept their love the highest compliment I could give. People can get offended if you reject their gifts and I'm trying to unify everyone."

"I was just in the streets and the way people are talking about you, it's like you're running a cult. They're now calling you Mother Sarah."

"You're witnessing the love of unity."

Byron groaned. "Save it," he argued. "I set up your stupid broadcast tower, some drones and got you a cannon that fires anti-alchemy rounds, compliments of James."

"Thank you, Byron."

"Stuff it," he said. "You're lucky James still backs you, or I'd gut you. Never forget what you are. You're not real. You were whipped up in a jar."

She saw no difference between herself and anyone else and could almost hear him grinding his teeth. "I hear your anger, but we were all made in one jar or another. I'm here therefore I'm real. I will do my job and bring unity to every man, woman and child. In this city there is no crime, people give freely to one another and the anger that you're spewing is nonexistent."

He rolled his eyes. "That's great. How are these people supposed to rise up against the Non-Humans when they're brainwashed into passivity?"

"Anger is a mental illness. It consumes you, blinds you and makes you traipse through a home with muddy boots. Do you realize that one of my servants, out of love will clean up after your mess? Your display of contempt doesn't hurt me, it only separates you from us. Your anger will infect my servants and they will hate you for not loving me."

"You actually believe the crap you're spewing. As for love, I should get one of your slaves to get down on their knees and please me. Maybe I should do that to you, teach you a thing or two."

"You just answered your earlier question. When someone comes to hurt one of us, we will all rise up like a wave and destroy them. Go ahead Byron hurt me, attack their way of life, their unity and see what they'll do. When the time comes the Human race will rise up, not out of anger, but necessity. Not to destroy the races, but to remove their way of thinking. It was the seeds of anger that created the Purge and anyone that holds that seed will die."

Byron's eyes widened. "That's crazy. You're not making any sense. Attacking the anger in people? I guess it doesn't matter why you're killing the other races as long as you do what you're told." He scrutinized her asking, "Does James know you're running a cult?"

"I'm getting results and people are no longer killing each other. That's all James cares about. Thank you Byron for your contribution and give my regards to James. It is time for me to go out and touch my people. You can let yourself out." She turned her back to him, ignored his protest and walked outside down the stairs that surrounded her home. She knew what she was and why she was created, but didn't care. She felt for the Human race and wanted to gather them up into her warmth and heal the world, it didn't matter to her that her feelings were manufactured. Everyone has been manufactured and there was nothing Byron could say that would change the fact that she existed. She also knew that she couldn't reach Byron and he would never change. Somehow he needed to be eliminated for the future and well being of the Human race.

A chilling breeze opened the loose folds of her robe telling her that the seasons were changing and all she had to do was casually mention a chill and she'd have blankets and winter attire delivered to her home. She smiled at the thought and was grateful for all the people's love and support. She didn't like having dark thoughts, but Byron's darkness is very deep and it was hard for her to deal with him.

She met a small group of her servants at the bottom of the stairs. They had insisted on escorting her through the streets despite her protest, but she came to accept their protection as another form of love. She gave her escorts the route she wanted to walk and allowed people to touch her and be touched by her. She needed her thought, intent and vibration to be carried in her words and ripple through the gathering mass. Her greatest enemy was an individual's self hate, the debilitating emotion that blinds them. People wept and she touched them. She heard their pain and told them that they're not alone. It was a process she needed to repeat daily, taking a lot of her energy to create the habit of light within the mass. Others smiled then told her good news and she listened then encouraged them, sharing their love. Through her uplifting words she used her gift to guide their feelings, increasing their morale and shift their awareness into the light.

She was almost finished her route when a soldier dressed in urban camouflage stepped in front of her. The young man stood stiff and full of purpose. "What can I do for the city?" she asked.

"Mother Sarah, the broadcast tower and artillery cannon are ready. Conveniently an Alchemist has entered range. What would you have us do?"

Members of the crowd whispered, "Alchemist," sparking fearful murmurs.

She raised her hand getting the people's attention and met most of their scared looks with calm reassurance. "Conveniently?" she repeated. "I guess so. This new cannon has double the range of anything else that we have?"

"Yes Mother, but is more artillery than cannon."

She ignored his correction. It didn't matter to her what the weapon was as long as it fulfilled its purpose. "Who is it?"

"We've identified the Alchemist Kole's transport. He's been operating out of Pine View."

"Kole?" she asked surprised that Byron hadn't killed him then for a moment wondered why. "It's time to test our new weapon."

People in the crowd gasped then urged her not to attack in fear of reprisal.

She calmed the people. "It's time to show the world who we are and what we stand for. We will not allow any Alchemist, or those deformed by Alchemy to come near us." She turned her attention back to the soldier. "Fire!" she commanded.

The soldier touched his ear and repeated her command then in the distance she heard the weapon fire. They waited then the soldier nodded, excitement touched his eyes. "Direct hit," he declared. "And our sensor drones don't detect any life. It looks like the special ammunition works, but we'll send out scouts to confirm his death."

The crowd's murmur sounded of shock and hope.

She addressed the crowd. "Tell everyone what you've heard today. We have weapons that can kill Alchemists and we'll no longer cower in fear. We don't need them and we don't care where the Alchemists run to as long as they stop messing with the Human race."

The crowd, swept up in the power of her words cheered and it pleased her.

Later that night, Sarah dressed in her silk nightgown slipped out of her king sized bed and walked, gliding across the room to activate her wall mounted com. James' face appeared on the screen. "Good evening James," Sarah said.

"Hello Sarah. How are things progressing?"

"Very well, thank you. I've had a positive development." She waited a moment for James to prepare himself for her news. "I've killed the Alchemist Kole and his apprentice."

James laughed. "That's a very good sign. When Byron convinced me not to kill him, I wondered why, but now I see that it was flow of the Universe."

She gave a pleasant smile and enjoyed his laughter, but wanted Byron eliminated which meant that she had to carefully plant a seed. "Perhaps Byron wanted to manipulate Kole into contradicting your plan. I'm just glad that I've killed him. Kole's death has advanced my plans and I've sent men out to spread the word that we're going to take the world back from the Alchemists. We just need more weapons."

He frowned. "Kole destroyed all the weapons that I was going to send you, but I have some in reserve." His face relaxed. "It's fitting that you've killed him, you would've had an army at your fingertips."

"Perhaps it is good that we start off slow. I can send out small teams to hunt down and assassinate loner Alchemists while building the army."

James agreed. "Well done Sarah. You'll get whatever you need."

She bowed. "Thank you James. Everything seems to be going so well except for my dealing with Byron. He's getting more patronizing and his presence is disrupting my work. People are questioning why I'm working with him and why he can't see the love that I offer. It won't take long before they see him as different and turn on him."

"I'll keep him away from you. Do you need anything else?"

"No," she said. "Now we wait."

Chapter

23

Morning came and Kole was the first to wake. Enora lay in his arms curled up against him with her head on his chest and arm draped across his belly. They had slept in their clothes uncovered on the ground while everyone else slept in warm cozy sleeping bags. Enora's alchemy was pure art, she had made sleeping bags and a large granite igloo for everyone to sleep in, but even though Kole couldn't feel the ground or the cold though his shield he still liked sleeping in a bed, it made him feel normal. Still groggy, he watched her sleep, enjoying her warmth and restful breathing. She smelled like warm strawberries and at first, he was unnerved that she could penetrate his shield, but now he enjoyed her touch, her softness, even missed her when she wasn't close. He reached up and rubbed his face feeling stubble remembering that Enora had shaved off his beard. He didn't want to get up and leave her, but his bladder was ordering him to move. He gently rubber her shoulder until she stirred rolling away from him. He slowly got up, stepped over the fire pit and crawled out the narrow opening.

The sun had risen over the mountain peaks, but the forest looked chilly with a little bit of frost in the shadows. Last night they had made camp just off the clear cut trail that they traveled to find the Werewolves. Their plan was simple, they were to walk up the mountain and take a vehicle. He would've kept walking into the night if it weren't for Nick's constant whining. At first Nick argued like a child refusing clothing, then night came and he couldn't put layers on fast enough. Once warm, he then whined about the food and a place to sleep. Soon his whining became contagious until the three children forced him to stop.

Kole could still hear Nick's voice repeating in his mind like a bad song. "Kole, why are we walking so fast?" he whined. "No one knows about the vehicles up there. We can take out time, or you can just make us a new one."

Kole ditched the memory focusing, hearing the hum of antigravity engines coming toward them and just as Nick's words repeated in Kole's mind one last time, their former Salvage Barge loaded with silver passed followed by a convoy of Werewolves' vehicles. In frustration, Kole wanted to kick Nick awake then grab him by the throat and squeeze till his head popped off, but realized that they wouldn't have made it up the mountain in time anyway. Instead he collected some wood then went back inside the igloo. He started a fire then manifested the materials to make coffee and pancakes. He manifested plain yogurt, maple syrup, honey and sliced strawberries in individual wood bowls to be used as toppings.

The smell of cooking roused everyone and when they gathered around the breakfast table Eric asked, "What's the occasion? You only make pancakes when you're in a good mood." He grabbed a plate and filled it.

"I've never had pancakes," Kyra said. "They smell good."

"Load up Kyra," Eric prompted. "If you spread the yogurt on first, the pancake won't suck up the syrup."

Nick stood with his arms crossed eyeing the table.

"Are you going to have some, Nick?" asked Kole.

"I don't like pancakes. I'll eat the toppings though."

Kyra scoffed. "Don't be stupid. How can you hate something that you've never tried?"

He ignored her. "I'll eat a bowl of yogurt covered in syrup, maybe with some strawberries too."

Kole shrugged. "Eat what you want, more for the rest of us."

Enora stepped past him helping herself.

Nick finally grabbed his portion allowing Kole to fill his plate.

"I wasn't expecting such an ordeal this morning," Nick complained. "Those Werewolf vehicles won't steal themselves."

"The Werewolf vehicles are gone," Kole said between bites.

"What?" Nick and Kyra asked in unison with their mouths full.

Kole cut his pancake then ate before answering. "They drove by earlier this morning when you were sleeping. I'm glad I saw them, or we'd still be on our way to get one." Kole was surprised at how quiet Nick was being then added, "Oh, I also saw a shipment of silver go by."

"I guess we're free to do whatever we want," Enora said. She smelled her coffee then took a sip.

"On foot without any real gear," Kyra argued.

Nick moaned. "Why don't you guys make something more than pancakes and get us out of here?"

Kole finished then grabbed a rod and poked the fire. "In the forest, I listened to you Nick, but I should've dissolved all the silver and now this region is out of balance."

Enora finished her meal and coffee then placed her hand on Kole's shoulder. "That's not true."

He enjoyed her touch and wanted to lean into her to reciprocate her warmth, but chose to be serious. "What are you thinking?"

She pulled her hand away leaving him feeling cold then explained, "Nick is a wheel that wobbles and his path is never strait. Agreeing with him set events into motion and right now those events look negative, but they may not be. I suggest that we all let go of yesterday and move on."

"Wobbling wheel?" Nick doubted then shoveled the last of his yogurt in his mouth.

"I can see that," Kyra said looking at Nick. "And I think she's being polite."

"Fine," Eric agreed. "I was still a little miffed at you Nick, but I guess I can let that go."

Nick's face scrunched. "Oh geez Eric," he said. "I don't need your pity."

"Why are you mad at me? You're the one who wrecked everything."

"You're all ganging up on me. I see what's going on. Just say the word and me and Kyra are gone."

Kyra chuckled. "Nick, its Kyra and I," she corrected. "Leave me out of this and stop being silly."

Nick gasped. "You too?" he accused.

Kole rubbed his temples feeling a headache coming on. "Everyone calm down," he said. "I'm tired of fighting. We'll make a new rust bucket, travel to the next town and trade it for something not made from Alchemy."

"Why can't you make something nice for us all to live in?" Nick asked.

"Because I have a bad feeling about those Rippers we found. Just one shot from one of those and we'd be blown apart."

"But you said those guns are rare," he reminded.

"All right Nick, let's think about what's rare and we can talk about our luck. Running into a huge pack of Werewolves with mining equipment and pet Zombies is very rare. Finding a decrepit Ripper is also very rare, but finding six new fully charged Rippers is impossibly rare."

"Do you think there are more Rippers out there?" Eric asked.

Kole nodded. "A long time ago my teacher warned me that the Rippers would resurface and that another Purge worse than the first would happen."

"So wait," Nick said. "If someone shot at this igloo it'd explode killing us?"

"Duh," Eric mocked.

Nick grabbed a handful of his clothes and looked frightened. "These can explode too?"

"Nick," Enora soothed. "Don't worry about your clothes. If you were shot by a Ripper you'd explode because you are a creature of Alchemy, much like those Zombies. You're lucky you didn't accidentally shoot yourself."

Eric slapped his knee laughing then looked at Nick's sour expression and laughed harder.

Kole thought Enora was being cruel, but her expression hadn't changed. She was stating fact. "Stop laughing Eric, this is serious," Kole said.

"I'm sorry," Eric apologized wiping his eyes.

"We're going to get dense unmodified body armor to protect ourselves from the Rippers."

Enora looked at him giving him a tingling feeling his stomach. "Kole, I get why you're being cautious and..." She placed her hand on Nick. "We appreciate it, but do you think thicker body armor will work?"

"It can't hurt. Thicker armor might absorb the Ripper's energy."

"Oh, that's just great," Nick complained. "Don't get shot, that's your advice?"

Kole shrugged agreeing. "That's good advice for anyone."

Later, Kole made a transport and some bars of precious metals for trade before they left traveling for a couple of days into the prairies to an open town named Rock Fall. It didn't take long for him to trade everything he had made for a Small Battle Barge in decent shape and some town currency. He divvied up the remainder of money into cards, and as he handed them out he said, "Buy the best equipment you can find, remember nothing augmented and try to stay together, this place can get rough, I'm not kidding. If someone thinks they can take something away from you, they'll try and I'll go out after I've change the security protocols on the Barge."

"If this place is so bad, why are we here?" Kyra asked.

"Look around," Eric suggested. "We're in the wild and this is a trading hub, you can find anything you want, but even the kids have guns."

Kole looked past their tight circle at some of the people pretending not to watch them. He had parked at the edge of town where the dry grass met the cracked street thinking that they'd have more privacy, but guessed wrong. Small hover cycles and cars glided down the cluttered streets in the distance while people in various grades of body armor and weapons walked the trash packed sidewalk. The battered buildings looked tough, all heavily fortified and made from duracrete bricks with metal roofs but, broken bricks, shattered wood and various bits of debris lined the buildings spilling onto parts of the sidewalks. A thin layer of dust coated everything giving the place a rustic look and oddly homey feel. "Eric, don't forget to pick up some grooming tools," Kole added remembering the loss of their transport and possessions.

Eric groaned then as if reading Kole's mind said, "I hope the bastard who stole our stuff gets what's coming to him. Do you think we'll see our transport again?"

"It's a small world. We'll eventually find it," he said. "Time is on our side."

Nick cupped his hands holding his card. "Thank you Kole for trusting me with this. I'll buy equipment and nothing else. Well," he corrected. "Maybe some ale with what's left."

"We shouldn't linger here," Kole insisted. "Go," he said and flicked his wrists.

"Come on guys let's move," Kyra said grabbing Nick and Eric's pulling them away.

Kole turned to Enora. "What are your plans?"

She smiled. "I'm waiting for you. I'm excited about buying body armor and guns. I think it'll make me look bad ass."

Kole thought about how others would see her, a clean unarmed woman in a dress in the middle of the waste. Somehow her demeanor seemed scarier than a heavily armed Ork. "In a way, you already look bad ass," he said smiling back at her.

"I guess you haven't noticed that we're going to need a few extra things."

He thought about it, but nothing came to mind. "Like what?"

"Pillows, bed sheets, blankets, feminine products, a pair of shoes for Kyra, food, drink, kitchen ware and everything in between."

Kole moaned. "I don't have enough money for all that. Wait, shoes for Kyra?"

"All she talks about is her lost collection and it'd mean a lot to her if we got her a new pair."

He didn't want to upset Enora, or wreck what was going on between them, but had to know. "Why are you still with us?"

"I was wondering when we were going to have this talk."

"Can you blame me? You're the most powerful person I've ever met and you want to travel with us. It makes me wonder what you're getting out of this."

"When I was in the jar, I took it as an opportunity to learn about my true self, in truth there was nothing else I could do. Your body and how others perceive you make up a lot of who you are. It's all reflections, but when that's taken from you, what do you have? I tore down and rebuilt myself many times and because I had no one to converse with, the language in my mind evolved to the point that I barely understood what you were saying when I was freed. Even my dreams turned the color black, fragmented and empty. To answer your question, I wanted to stay with you because there was a lot that I had to remember, body language, facial expressions and conversational tone as well as the condition of the world."

Kole thought for a moment. "I have a feeling that you're not telling me everything. You can learn all those things in time from people watching, you don't need us. I just want to make sure that you're with us for the right reasons."

"I don't want to hurt anyone," she reassured. "And I understand your caution. I'm learning to reconnect with the world and you're right, I can do that anywhere." Her eyes intensified and lips slightly puckered. "But, the real reason that I'm here is because I felt something between us when we met and I've decided to claim you as mine."

Excitement flushed through Kole heating his skin deepening his desire for her. "I was thinking that you'd want to bunk in Kyra's room, but now you'll be bunking with me," he dared. He was about to pull her close, hold her tight against his body, kiss her deeply, running his hand down her body to grab her ass then pick her up and throw her over his shoulder. He wanted to carry her off to the bedroom, rip her dress off and take her to bed, but remembered that they needed a bed to play on.

"Hey sexy," a gravelly voiced man yelled disrupting Kole's desire, aggravating him.

Kole cursed then poked his head out of the Barge's hatch. The people down the street had disappeared and six armed men walked toward them. They were armed with two automatic rifles, three pistols and a spiked club. All their brown armor had the look of being looted off three different corpses, but somehow the men all matched. A massive man led the group holding the spiked club that rested on his shoulder. The man was the ugliest person Kole had ever seen. He was bald with a blue tinge to his skin, a scar down the left side of his face, no neck and beady eyes that were too close together. He looked like the forced union of a Human and Troll with nothing but bad luck thrown in for good measure.

The Troll thing and his men stopped. When he spoke his teeth looked too big for his jaw, "I own all of you." Kole could barely pull his eyes away from the man's hideousness to notice that all his men we're half breeds of a kind, all of them super ugly and mean looking.

Enora leaned against him and hung her arm over Kole's shoulder. She whispered, "Look at these broken souls."

He was trying to mentally change gear to fend off the interlopers, but her breath on his ear fueled his desire, like she was enticing him on purpose. "They're not broken," he said. "They're inbred, or one of their parents was raped."

"Should we send them to prison?"

"There aren't any prisons."

"Shut up!" the half Troll shouted then pointed his club at Kole. "We're going to use you and your woman till we're sick of yah then we'll sell her to the Dark Elves and you to the Trolls."

Enora stepped past Kole. "Why are you bothering us? We were having a moment."

The gang laughed and Kole focused on the one guy who sounded like a hyena. He'd heard that type of laugh before, out of the trouble makers who mouth off and picks fights for other people to deal with. The half Troll rested his club on his shoulder. "Get them boys," he ordered. His men twitched like they were trying to move, but were held in place.

Confused, Kole watched them. "Is this a joke that I missed? What are you idiots playing at?"

"I can't move boss," the half Elven Ork said.

"I can't either," another said.

"Silence, "Enora commanded, her voice sounding heavy and powerful. She turned to Kole. "What should I do with them?"

"You're doing this?" he asked.

She nodded. "These men are evil and give only pain to the world. They could chose any path in life, but choose this one. Should I kill them, or let them go?"

"Why are you asking?"

"Because, I want you to tell me your truth and show me the real you, I won't judge."

He didn't want to say it, or think the thoughts he was having, but she wanted the truth. "If I were alone," he admitted. "I would've already killed them, starting with the one who laughs funny and ending with the leader. Because," he reasoned, "They're scum and the world doesn't need them."

She smiled. "Are you so special that you can decide what the world needs?"

Her question drove the fire out of him and he no longer wanted to kill them, but another truth was that she was more powerful than him. Her confidence made him think that she knew what she was talking about. "I don't want to kill them anymore, but if we let them go, they'll hurt someone else."

"Most likely, but that's their place in life and not your responsibility."

"But we're strong. We can do so much good for the world destroying one bad guy at a time."

"What good have you actually done? If you took everything that you've done back, would the world be any different? For the world to find light, we all must simply let go of the dark."

"Fine, let those guys go, but if they attack us, we kill them. We've wasted enough time on them and I still have to set everything up. I'd also like to finish out talk. I was feeling really good about where it was going."

She pressed herself against him with her lips close to his. "We can talk later, but for now we have to deal with these guys." She backed away. "Let's have some fun. Get the Barge ready and I'll alter their memories. We can follow them around and see what they get up to."

He reached out and took her hand missing her closeness. "We don't have time to linger, trouble will find us."

"Dwelling on the trouble will only bring it to you, think happy thoughts. Besides, we're Alchemists. All we have is time to linger."

Chapter

24

Jelek the half Troll squinted, watching the Small Battle Barge disappear into the distance. That Barge was going to be his ticket out of here and he had such plans, but that little Human stole his property. He growled a low rumble in his chest then turned to face his gang, wanting to take his frustrations out on someone. He tightened his grip on his club and looked at Kole. A Human ran away with his property, it's fitting that a Human should be punished, but remembered that Kole had been with him forever and had helped form the gang. The gang was a home for outcasts, people that didn't fit into the world, but Kole and Enora were the exception. They both helped him every step of the way and he couldn't punish them. Kole made him the very club that he used to pulverize Onourk's skull allowing him to carve out his territory and Enora nursed him back to health the day he almost died. He trusted them with his life.

"That sucked!" Jelek yelled. "Those weak Human made us look pathetic!" He spun around searching the street for witnesses. Just one smile from an idiot and he'd start a shootout to protect his reputation. "I tried to take it all, but next time we shoot fist, we can always take slaves later." He waved his hand beckoning his men to follow as he marched down the street.

"When are we going to get a hover car, Jelek?" an Orkish Elf asked.

He stopped and looked out the corner of his eye at him. "You tell me, you wrecked the last one I stole." He tightened his grip and was about to swing his club at the stupid Ork, but was interrupted.

"Where are we going now?" Kole asked.

He spun and faced everyone. "You bunch of whiny bitches, why are you all questioning me? Shut up and follow, that's all you have to do." But he felt compelled to answer Kole, "Were going back to the warehouse, my woman has lines on a job."

"What sort of job?"

He laughed a rumbling chuckle. "I'd forgotten how nosy you are. I thought when we started the gang that you trusted me."

"I do trust you," Kole said then pointed his thumb at Enora. "We want to duck out for a bit."

"No. I need you with me. My woman says that someone's hiring all the gangs for honest work."

"Honest work?"

He laughed. "I know. I tried to tell her that being a bad guy is way more fun, but she nagged the crap out of me. Networking she says."

When he took possession of the abandoned warehouse in the north end of town they all spent time clearing debris and putting up makeshift walls made from plywood and loose brick, but now the generator is out of fuel leaving his home dark and cold.

"Who are they?" a mixed Human Dwarf woman asked pointing at Kole and Enora. She shook her head, blinked a couple of times then laughed. "Sorry about that. I didn't recognize you. She turned to Jelek asking, "Did you get the Barge?"

She always knew how to twist his nuts. "No," he growled. "The Humans ran once they saw us." There were times when she made him so angry that he wanted to slap her, but didn't dare. She knew how to cut him up in a way that be painful, but allow him to heal quickly.

"Did you get any fuel? I'm sick of sitting in the dark freezing my ass off." He didn't answer. "I didn't think so, but I have a solution," she said widening her stance telling him that she wasn't going to take no for an answer. "Things have been a little slow for us and our gang has fallen on hard times. We can do some honest work to buy fuel so we won't freeze this winter."

He thought about arguing to reassure her that something will come up, but wanted her to sleep in the same bed with her that night. Yolanda was many things and being a mini heater for the cold nights was one of them. He could curl up around her in a cuddle and be warm, but when she left the bed, it was so cold. "Kole, Enora, come here, Yolanda has a plan."

Yolanda led them to their wobbly dinner table made from half rotten wood pallets. She handed him a piece of crumpled paper with charcoal writing across it. He recognized it as her writing, but was only capable of reading some of it. "This looks like it has potential," he said pretending that he understood. "Give us the run down."

This was his favorite part to watch. She took a deep breath and blurted her plan, "There's a guy out East named The Lollypop King. He's been gathering up all the gangs and getting them to sell candy. We buy it off him for a low price and sell it for whatever we want. I tried the candy and it's good. Being a gang we can pool our money and buy equipment so we can steal better equipment later."

"Selling candy?" Jelek asked, not fully understanding.

"That's the first part. When we sign up we'll also be in contact with other gangs from all over. We can be on the ground floor to something new, an honest network of crime."

The last thing she said didn't make sense to him, but he ignored it. "With The Lollypop King running everything. What's in the candy?"

"There's no drugs, it's just really good candy and once I tried it I wanted more."

"Do you want more now?" he asked looking for signs of addiction, but didn't see any.

"Can I see the candy?" Kole asked.

"I ate all the free samples," she sheepishly replied.

Jelek teased, "You didn't share, my greedy little piggy."

She clutched her hands and fidgeted. "That's what I'm saying, it was that good. Normally I would've shared, but I couldn't stop."

He didn't understand why she was acting strange and didn't care that she had eaten all the candy, but her plan was important to her. He put himself in her shoes then understood what she was going on about. "You think the candy will be that popular, but it's not a drug, Alchemy?"

She nodded. "They're the only ones who can make something normal addictive." He growled, but before he could go on an anti Alchemist tirade, she soothed, "It's only candy and if we don't eat any, it's mostly profit for us."

He slipped a veil over his anger and donned his best grin then laughed. "You're right," he replied. "It's a good plan. What's next?"

She grinned. "We meet the guy at The Lucky Hobo, neutral ground."

Later that day, Jelek flung open the double doors of The Lucky Hobo then strutted into the dimly lit bar with his most trusted people, Yolanda, Kole and Enora. The warm air held the sweet scent of stale ale and unwashed Human reminding him of profit and good fortune, but that was the Troll side of him. His grin widened seeing the sorry state of the run down rabble crying into their wooden mugs wallowing in their weakness making him feel, motivated. The Humans think they can hide from his gaze in the layers of shadow, but he could see everyone in this hole that looked like a saloon from the old movies. Wood planks creaked and bowed under his weight as he made his way to their contact who sat at a small table in the center of the room with a bowl of red wrapped lollypops, but his contact wasn't alone. He slowed his pace seeing Slim Jake and Slick Pete. All Human which didn't bode well for him, they seemed to stick together, but both Pete and Jake were backstabbing lying scum. They were who they were and he could trust them to do what they do. He secretly liked them both and even considered them friends that he had tried to kill on occasion.

Slim Jake wore light armor under a set of heavy to make himself appear bigger, but it looked more cumbersome and ridicules with his tiny bald head sitting on an inflated body. Slick Pete on the other hand had slicked back black hair and wore a cheap red plaid suit trying to look respectable.

Pete saw him first. His dark beady eyes narrowed and a smile spread across his face. "I was wondering if you'd show up Stinky."

Jake moaned. "Why is he here?"

His contact was a young average looking man dressed in clean clothes, but nothing fancy. He waited for him to take a seat before saying, "As I was saying, this is a great opportunity to join my employer as he unites organizations across the continent. Together you can set up a small distribution facility and sell our candy. Pool all your resources and imagine what you can do together."

"And if we don't?" Pete asked.

"Well…" he said. "You can go about your business, but if you interfere with any of our associates, you and your resources will be removed."

Jake laughed. "What if none of us sign on?" he challenged.

The Contact smiled. "Your loss, we're coming regardless, but your participation is a bonus for us. You're all established and we won't have to reallocate our resources here."

Jelek didn't like the way the man was talking, but understood the threat he represented. The sand was shifting and he liked being the king of his realm, but true power was coming. The sand will shift again, maybe next time in his favor. "I'm in," he said.

Pete scoffed then looked sideways at Jelek. "You lumbering ox. You don't' know anything about this guy. What we should do is unite against him."

Jake laughed again. "You're funny Pete. I think you say we unite, but then you unite with this new guy behind our backs and have help wiping us out."

"You're one to talk about betrayal," Jelek said, remembering last Christmas when Jake killed three of his best men.

Jake glared at him. "You killed my boys then beat me with your club leaving me for dead."

"I knew you were still alive, you stabbed me in the back with a spear and stole my narcotics. I had breathing problems for two weeks. I just wanted to share my pain."

"Those were my narcotics," Pete corrected. "You regenerate, so that didn't count."

"It still hurt, besides you got even. You blew up my transport."

Pete grinned.

Jake glare at Pete then took on a threatening tone, "Wipe that smile off your face, you woman stealing bastard!"

Pete looked at his nails. "It's not my fault that you can only get trashy women."

Jelek tapped his fingers against the table drawing their attention. "The three of us have shared our blood, pain and greed. We can always kill each other later, but for now I want to know where this candy is coming from." He reaches and cups the bowl of candy in his fingers then said, "If it's made by Alchemy."

The Contact placed his hands together and asked, "Does it matter?"

"Alchemists change the rules making the world unpredictable. You see, I can trust these two men to be who they are, but if you add Alchemy, I get concerned."

Jake and Pete both nodded.

The Contact eyed each of them. "Yes," he confessed. "There is a tiny component of Alchemy, but have you heard the good news?"

Jelek slowly shook his head asking him to continue.

"There are now weapons out there that can kill Alchemists. One has been killed with his apprentice."

Kole stepped forward. "Who were they?" he asked.

The table fell silent as all eyes focused on Kole before The Contact spoke, "Since you care, his name was Kole and he died outside of Winter Haven." He smiled. "A lot of people are celebrating. World change is coming."

Kole reached past Jelek and grabbed a lollypop.

"Who's this clown?" Pete asked Jelek, referring to Kole.

Jelek tried to think, but his mind clouded over in a sudden release. He didn't know who Pete was talking about and when he turned around only Yolanda was there, the way it should be.

Chapter

25

Kole was in a daze. He went through the motions of buying equipment for Enora and himself, but couldn't believe that people were celebrating his death after all that he had done for the world. He played their game, kept the balance and helped where ever he could, but none of it mattered, they all hated him. He didn't know what to feel. They carried their equipment back to their Barge then waited at the entrance for his team to arrive.

The waning sun changed the colors of the street and building making them sort of pretty to Kole. "I don't get it," he said to Enora.

"That they are celebrating your death?" she asked then leaned into his shoulder interlocking their arms.

"Yeah, how did you know?" he asked surprised that she knew what he was thinking.

"You've been sad since you heard, but at least you found out what happened to your transport," she said giving him a reassuring smile.

"I don't care about that."

"Do you want the truth or a lie?"

He rested his cheek on her soft blond hair and smelled strawberries. "The truth," he dared enjoying her warmth.

"Life comes then goes and the Universe turns. People want to be where they are and you can't save anyone because all you'll be doing is interfering with their destiny. You can only interact with events intersecting your path and seeking out events brings imbalance. The only safe path is to follow the Universe."

He thought about all the years he had tried to help people and bring a positive change only to get grief. But, who said what he was doing was positive? He thought so at the time, but looking back at when he had stuck his fingers into all those different pies, made him wonder what he was actually doing. He wasn't invited and when he offered to help, people used him. "Do people just suck?" he brooded.

She chuckled. "No. Everyone follows the Universe in their own way."

"How do you follow the Universe?"

"The Universe only understands energy, it doesn't understand good, or bad. You are in a symbiotic relationship with it and need to be careful where you put your energy. Look at your life. You're now believed dead and you're upset about it, but it might be a good thing. You were used by the world then discarded, but now you're free to do whatever you want. The world will continue to breathe life and death."

"You think there's something going on, a greater purpose?" he asked trying to understand what she was saying.

"There's something going on, but it's just something, a breath that involves us in a tiny moment. We infiltrated a gang looking for purpose and you took some candy. What do you want to do?"

He was so wrapped up in other people pissing on his memory that he'd forgotten about the candy he had taken and how Enora was able to befuddle the gang. He kissed Enora's fore head. "I guess we should look at the candy then."

He held up the lollypop so they both could see it then peered inside, searching for the tiniest fragment of Alchemy and was surprised to find two different fingerprints of the Alchemists who had made it. The first imprint was made by someone he had never met, but the second one he knew. He remembered encountering a child clone made by a small demented man and when Kole had tried to end his evil, the man narrowly escaped. He then looked for the two fragments purpose, but they seemed incomplete.

"Very interesting," she said.

"I don't get it," he confessed.

"They're waiting for an alchemical mate, I've seen it before and these ones are rather artful, but without the second parts I can only guess what this candy was made to do."

Stumped, he pulled his sight out of the lollypop in time to see a green hand snatch the candy away.

Nick laughed. "I'm surprised that worked. I thought your mighty shield would've stopped me." Kole dropped his hand then looked past Enora at Nick, Kyra and Eric who carried their new gear over their shoulders, but before he could stop Nick, he pulled off the wrapper and popped it in his mouth then asked, "How does it feel to be dead Kole?"

Aggravated, he wanted to slap him and yank the lollypop from his mouth, but realized that all the answers are being given to him. "How many of those candies have you eaten?" he asked.

"Six or seven," he said then rolled his eyes. "They're so good I can't get enough." He locked eyes with him and used the lollypop in a sexual manner which disgusted Kole.

Eric nudged Nick to make him stop. "I had one lick, but it tasted funny and gave me the creeps."

"It's a taste-o-gasm," Kyra corrected Eric. "That's probably why Nick loves them so much." She put a lollypop in her mouth.

"Now I see," Enora said interrupting their banter. "The first fragment is designed to build up in a person's system and make Non-Humans sterile." She pointed at Nick stomach. "But it doesn't do anything to Kyra, but the second fragment has an addictive mind altering effect, which is affecting her."

Nick stopped mouthing the lollypop and staring suggestively at Kole then shrugged. "I'm not into making babies and I don't know about her, but I feel just fine."

"You and babies, that's good news, the world can only handle one of you," Eric teased.

Kyra stopped sucking on her lollypop and touched her belly. "This is serious. They're evil and have to be stopped!"

Eric looked surprised at her outburst then suggested, "We can put the word out and hopefully stop everyone from eating the candy."

Enora disagreed, "It takes too long to build up in a person's system to see the results. No one will believe us and the people behind this will hide away putting the poison in something else."

Kyra frowned then continued to suck on her lollypop. "So we track them down and destroy them, or Kole can make them pancakes. These lollypops are so good."

Kole took Enora's hand, turned and faced his team. "The Alchemist Kole is dead, but Kole the Human is alive and I think I can help the world better this way. Kyra, I'm surprised by your passion and agree that they should be stopped, but you need to stay away from those candies. Now everyone put your things away, it's time to save the world."

Nick spat the candy's stick out then agreed, "Yeah, let's be heroes."

Kyra gently shoved Nick. "Let's save the future's children." She crunched the remainder of her candy under her teeth then spat out the stick.

"Can't we do both," Eric said. He smiled at Kole.

Enora gave Kole's hand a slight squeeze then let go. "I'll charm The Lollypop's representative and find out where his King is."

Kole watched her leave enjoying the sway of her hips then went inside the Barge to gear up. Safe in his room he dropped his shield exposing himself to the room's cool and stale air. He looked at his knucklers thinking that always carrying them around made him look silly. Enora didn't need charms to protect herself, why did he? Maybe he felt satisfied using them to beat the crap out of someone, especially if they were allergic to silver. He undressed and the thought of looking like a normal person who had seen good fortune instead of a person one step up from a beggar, felt empowering. He dressed then extended his shield to encompass his new armor. He grabbed his automatic rifle, set his helmet's com to their group channel then waited outside for Enora, sure that she wouldn't return empty handed and was surprised to see Jelek with all his men come around the corner.

"We have company," Kole said over the com.

Nick scoffed. "Is the company friendly for once?"

"I think, company's coming is the positive phrase," Eric said.

"Do you need help?" asked Kyra.

"I'll be fine, they can't hurt me," Kole said.

"We'll be ready if you need us," Eric said.

Jelek wore a grim smile and stopped a fair distance away, his club resting against his shoulder. His gang of half breeds, all armed for a fight, fanned out around him. Yolanda, his half Dwarf woman was also there looking mean, armed with a small mini-gun. Kole still couldn't wrap his mind around that couple whose people were sworn enemies.

Kole politely sang, "Can I help you?"

Jelek tightened his grip on his club then pointed its tip at the Barge before saying, "You can return what you've stolen from me."

"I bought it from a merchant. When was it yours?"

"It became mine when I saw it. You can hand it over, or we'll take it by force," he said then some of his men chucked menacingly.

Kole decided not to hold back, to choose freedom and not bother to dodge, or pretending that he could be hurt, but he needed to give them a chance. "I'm an Alchemist. Go home and live."

Yolanda laughed. "Fool!" she barked. "Alchemists don't wear body armor."

She pulled her trigger warming up her mini-gun, but Kole raised his rifle in one fluid motion and fired a round, shooting Yolanda in the face.

Chaos erupted. The gang scattered shooting on the run looking for cover. Some rounds hit Kole, but most ricocheted off the Barge's hull in the pinging sting of metal rain.

"Yolanda!" screamed Jelek, watching her body flopped onto the pavement.

Kole switched his rifle to burst, ignored Jelek who stood in the middle of the road focusing on a half Ork that sprang into the air, diving over a pile of broken bricks. Kole fired. His rounds went wide, a couple in a building and two into the Ork's rump. The half Ork landed on the jagged bricks screaming in pain as he slid down the other side face first into the building's wall.

Loud thumping told Kole that the Barge's side cannon had open up. Eric fired low, chewing up the street in a shower of asphalt to finally punch through a half Dwarf's back, shattering the corner of the building. Welds snapped, the building moaned and the reinforcements buckled as a potion of the structure fell into the street in a landslide of debris.

Children inside the building cried out and bystanders in the other buildings took up arms against Kole and Jelek. The block erupted into a huge shootout, but Kole stayed focused on the gang members targeting a half Elf who ran down a stairwell. The noise from all the gunfire was deafening and he was glad for his shield, without it he would've been turned into another stain on the road. Movement caught his eye and he was about to fire, killing the person running up the stairs thinking that it was the half Elf, but a homeless man emerged screaming about the his lost stuff. The man ran into the street, arms flailing and screaming incoherently.

Jelek charged toward Kole howling in rage as bullets from several directions pumped into him. He jerked with every step loosing blood and flesh then skid to a stop, poised to swing his club and take Kole's head off, but Kyra sprang out of the Barge's hatch and ran low wielding her two silver plated hand axes, intercepting him. Seeing her, Jelek shifted, losing chunks of flesh and redirect the handle of his club to come down on her, but she used him as a shield coming in close hacking her way up as she climbed his body to finally sink both axes into each side of his neck, severing his head. Entangled in Jelek's arms, Kyra took some rounds in her chest and head before Jelek's body fell on top of her.

Kole was stunned that Kyra would risk her life running into the hail of gunfire that had decimated Jelek's gang, ruined the pavement and mark up the side of his Barge. He wanted to help her, but if he pulled her to her feet, they'd shoot her. He waited for the people in the buildings to run out of bullets, or to realize that they weren't hurting him, but they kept shooting. He closed his eyes thinking about Enora and how she generated her shield and if he could manage, he could project his shield and help Kyra. He felt his shield's programming within his knuckler then reached out feeling the air and ground. He concentrated sensing the life energy around him, coursing through all things then felt a twinge. Someone on a roof fired a rocket at Jelek. Kole sent his awareness in the space between the layers of energy, creating a shield in the air that exploded the rocket half way to its target. The gun fire stopped. Kole opened his eyes. His emotions were flushed clean, leaving him feeling a level of contentment beyond peace.

He looked for people on the roof and in the windows that'd start shooting again, but the buildings had the feel of abandonment. Kole assumed that they had figured out what he was after the rocket had exploded then fled. The area felt painful to him, like he was standing in an invisible bubble born from spilled blood and venomous hatred, a scar in the energy of the world. Everything had taken damage, the street, his Barge and the buildings from stray and ricocheted rounds. No one cared what they were shooting at. It was an excuse to fight, an oil spill of hate contaminating everything.

"Is it over?" asked Eric. "I stopped shooting after I took out some of the building. These people are crazy."

Nick ran up beside Kole with his rifle in one hand and readjusting his body armor with the other. "What did I miss?"

Kyra worked her way to her feet then looked over her blood soaked armor. "Do you think I can return this and get a new one? It was just worn once."

Nick laughed. "Maybe if it was Human blood."

"I'll never get the smell out," she said shaking her head. "Damn, getting shot still hurts. Do you guys hear that ringing?"

"Then next time, shoot the Troll and you won't ruin your armor," Nick suggested.

"No," she disagreed. "Even if you shoot them in the head and leave a piece of lead in there, they'll wake up forgetting how to walk, or talk, but they do come back. I did the best thing."

"Then stop whining."

"Whatever. Shut up."

Kole felt someone standing behind him and turned to see Enora. "Is that mess Jelek?" she asked. Kole nodded. "That's too bad, I liked him."

Kole smiled. "Did you get the information you were looking for?"

"Yes. They have a distribution facility a two day ride from here and The King is coming for an inspection. There's also going to be a parade and town wide party with free candy."

"Free candy? Who in this world give anything away?"

"It does sound strange," Enora stated. "But parades are fun and if we leave now we can get there in time to watch it. The King's hosting and he'll be throwing candy into the crowd." She wiggled her eyebrows. "How fun is that?"

Kole laughed at her cute silliness then said, "I'd never imagine that a parade would excite you so much."

"Kole, we have all the time in the world to take out The King. Let's enjoy the small things, like the blooming flowers that are here one moment and gone the next."

"I guess so, besides it's you that'll make it fun, but I want you to gear up."

"Do I have to?" she asked pouting. "I can regenerate."

He nodded thinking about it. "That's interesting, but can you regenerate if your head's gone?"

"I don't know," she said. "If the body is a horse and the brain is its rider, then no."

Kole was intrigued by the implication of her statement, but dismissed his thoughts. "I know the armor must feel confining, but I'd feel better knowing that you're protected."

"I guess I do feel confined, like a person from the prairies moving to the mountains."

"Come on people let's go all ready." Nick said over the com. "I'm bored."

"We should get going," Kole said to Enora. "The kids are getting restless."

"Who's the adult here, them or you?" she asked. "We're having a nice moment, they can wait."

"Yeah, you're right. I'll tell Nick to be quiet."

She walked by. "Too late, the moment's gone. Let's move on," she teased.

Kole followed her then they were on their way to find The Lollypop King.

Chapter

26

Jas casually walked through the crowded back allies of the Dark Elf capital's slums. She didn't hide, ignoring the quick glances and ogling looks from the different races of men. It wasn't her fault that she was attractive with her long wavy black hair reaching to her waist, fair completion, red full lips and bright violet eyes. Strength and confidence filled her petite frame and with each step she moved in feminine beauty. Though their eyes were hungry the men didn't bother her. A Human in the dark dressed in a tan blouse, black pants and dress shoes meant one thing, Alchemist.

She soon found what she was looking for, a small condominium with an alchemically locked door. She had a knack for feeling other people's work and if Byron hadn't ignored James' summons she wouldn't be there digging up that looser. She pressed into his lock and quietly opened the door controlling it as it slid open. She peered in and it looked like there had been a struggle. Broken furniture, possessions and half eaten food lay strewn across the floor. She moved though the apartment and noticed a woman's touch telling her that it wasn't one of Byron's hiding places, but she also found his clothes scattered over the floor with a ripped woman's dress. With Byron's reputation, it didn't take her long to figure out what had happened.

She paused at the bedroom door and felt another lock. She manipulated the lock and opened the door a crack peeking in to see Byron asleep on a bed. She quietly snuck in. A dark Elf woman lay beside him awake, chained to the bed frame naked and uncovered. Her oily hair was matted and multiple streams of dried tears marked her cheeks. She didn't speak, but her pleading eyes spoke volumes. Jas leaned closer to Byron, slowly penetrating his shield with her fingers then flicked his nose.

Byron snapped awake flailing his arms and in his confusion then blurted, "What the!"

Jas waited for his eyes to focus on her before saying, "James wants to see you."

He glared at her then got out of bed wearing nothing but a pair of socks. He followed her into the living room where she stopped, turning to face him. His eyes traveled her body before he stepped closer into her space. Towering over her, he displayed his hard excitement. "I don't want to see James, Jasmine," he whispered with hungry eyes. "Why did you come here looking the way you do? Your hair, your lips, your tight shirt, you tease."

She ignored his nudity and arousal keeping eye contact. "We're having an old argument Byron. I've told you that I knew what I wanted since I was eight, and men aren't it."

"You dress like a woman screaming for a man, you shouldn't look so good."

She tilted her head down and looked up at him letting her eyes tell him that he was half a step away from losing his junk. "I'm not going to change for anyone, or be pressured to let you violate me. The only reason that you haven't rapped me like that poor woman you have tied up in the bedroom is because I'm stronger than you, and that must burn your ass hairs."

He laughed. "You have me all wrong Jas, Monique and I are in love."

"You and the woman you've chained up in the next room are in love? Are you listening to me? You're standing here in her living room trying to lower me enough so I'll give you what you can't steal, and you're in love."

He rolled his eyes. "You don't get it. Why are you bothering me?"

"James wants to see you," she repeated.

"It hasn't been a month. He promised that I'd have time for me. Tell him, I quit."

She was going to question him about his decision but remembered that she hated him and didn't care. She walked out leaving him sputtering and made her way back to James thinking about what she'd do to Byron if he ever fell out of James' favor.

At James' door, she closed her eyes and stepped into the light of his office then waited for her eyes to stop stinging before quietly walking across the tiled floor. She found James looking as sharp as ever in his dark Elf suit sitting behind his oak desk. She stopped, waiting for James to invite her to sit in one of the hardwood chairs.

He waved her forward and she sat, his emotionless eyes met hers. "Where's Byron?" he asked.

"He's with Monique, a Dark Elf woman who lives in the slums."

"I know about her."

"He told me to tell you that he quit," she said.

"Quit? What a fool."

"He also said that he and Monique are in love, but it didn't look that way to me." She asked, "Who's this woman to him?"

He smirked. "I did a little digging and it wasn't hard to find her story. When Monique was a child, Byron raided her home for fun. He was high and I won't go into detail, but Monique's family didn't make it."

She remembered Monique chained to the bed. "I can imagine what happened."

"Monique isn't even her real name," James continued. "Anyway, she hid and witnessed it all. That night she became mute and an orphan and you know what happens to a Dark Elf without a name to back them. She was quickly snapped up and marked as a slave. Over the years she learned many arts to get near Byron. She studied him and found out what he liked before trying to kill him. When she failed, Byron became obsessed with her and now you know." He thought for a moment. "I've decided that I'll give him a little more time to think about his decision before I put the word out. He's made a lot of enemies and I don't think he'll last long without my protection."

She wondered why James was still protecting Byron then asked, "Do you actually think he'll change his mind?"

"He might. I'll give him another month to come around, but enough about him. You did very well uniting the Ork tribes and putting a controllable King in place."

She thought about her last mission. "Controllable, I wouldn't say that when it comes to Orks. His people know that he has a powerful backer and that gives him enough clout to keep things in our favor, until they forget and try to overthrow him."

"That doesn't matter, you did well."

"Thank you," she said grateful for his acknowledgement. "What's next?" she asked.

"There's nothing right now, go and relax. I have a feeling that I'll need you soon."

She thanked James then left his office taking her time weaving through the people making her way to her hover cycle trying to get Monique's pleading eyes out of her mind. She wanted to stop the ideas flooding her, but they were taking over pushing her along. Nervousness fluttered within her as she stopped off at a store that sold common household goods. She knew what she wanted and easily found the Kitchenware. She dragged her fingers across the hilts of the different sets of knives until she picked up a thin, but elegant Dark Elf blade with a leather sheath. She admired the blade's beauty in appearance and balance then purchased it.

She had more of a feeling then a plan to kill Byron and free Monique, but fought against the compulsion to do so even after she bought the murder weapon. She tried to bring reason to her senses, screaming in her mind that it was all happening because she was upset, that she hated Byron and that she felt that he finally fell out of James' favor, but none of that was true. She slid onto the enclosed seat of her cycle, tightened her grip on the controls and forced herself to stop. She could've stopped Byron at any time, she had the power, but Monique didn't. That was another lie she told herself, she didn't want to be the defender of the weak, if she was, she'd never get any rest. She started her cycle then sped off toward one of the cities' gate initiating her plan because she knew it was Byron's time to die and knew that she could get away with killing him and tip the balance of power in her favor. It wasn't about hate, or setting Monique free. It was about power and her need to have it.

James is the most powerful Alchemist that she'd ever met and somehow Byron, that bag of crap had maneuvered himself into a trusted position. Secrets were shared enhancing his power and now when he's gone and Monique blamed, those secrets will be hers. Her belly ached at the thought of having James' knowledge course through her body, she wanted it bad. She sped on into the night across black sand wasteland of the Dark Elf territory to James' hidden ammunition factory hidden in the Dragon Teeth Mountains.

Hours later, dawn came when she entered broadcast range and punched in Byron's code that she'd spied from him years before. She heard the confirmation chime then sped down a narrow opening of jagged rock in the side of a mountain just large enough for a small transport then slowed as she drove through an illusionary wall into a hanger bay. The hanger door rolled closed behind her with a thump that slightly echoed through the empty bay. She parked then waited for the dim emergency lights to flicker on and cast the room in a blue hew and when she stepped out of her cycle she expected dust, but the gray duracrete floor had been buffed to a shine telling her that the factory's cleaning machines were still working. She walked up the steps onto the loading dock then noticed that though the floor had been maintained, dust covered spider webs clung to the walls and ceiling. The pot lights in the hall leading to the factory floor flickered on then passed an intersection leading to the administration level, but continued on.

The factory floor's industrial yellow lights hummed, slowly getting brighter as she passed automated machinery, conveyer belts and several crates filled with Ripper power packs. She looked across the floor and found what she was looking for, a vat of the blue substance that'll change the world. She climbed a metal staircase and opened the vat then looked at the blue liquid imagining what a tiny drop would do to her. She collapsed her shield grabbed her new knife, but hesitated. She double checked the lip of the vat for residue thinking that it's be stupid to blow her arm off then carefully dipped the very tip of the knife into the blue gel.

She held the knife before her studying the tiniest amount of gel. "Just the tip to penetrate Byron, that's all she'll need," she whispered then sheathed the knife and formed her shield.

Excitement filled her and she raced halfway down the stairs before stopping. She wanted to run to her cycle and full throttle it back to Monique, but she grabbed the rail forcing her mind to focus. She needed to erase all evidence of being there, or James will find out that she went behind his back and killed his favorite pet. She took a deep breath and slowly exhaled reminding herself that she had the weapon and the perfect patsy to pull it off, but a part of her wanted to make Monique permanently disappear. After hearing Monique's story, it'd be merciful to take the pain of her life away from her. She then remembered how haunted Monique looked chained to her bed with that monster asleep beside her. Something in Monique's eyes had punched through her heart making Jas want to save her, to rescue the damsel in distress. She dismissed the violent thought of easing Monique's pain. She was kidding herself, Monique had suffered enough and it just wasn't in her to kill someone who didn't deserve it.

She went to the administration department and found the main computer room. The door slid open and the lights turned on. She stood in front of the main computer table planning what she needed to do. She touched a table activating a holographic monitor that appeared at the back edge of a table. She logged in as Byron, ran a level three diagnostic on the security system shutting it down then erased all evidence of her being there as well as setting the security system to reset after she had left, but when she was about to log off an alert caught her attention. Her finger touched the alert before she could stop it, what could it hurt? She now owned the system.

An alert window popped up informing her that a spontaneous contamination had occurred in one of the items and that the item has been isolated. Two buttons then appeared, scan, or destroy? She mocked the computer knowing that it wouldn't respond, "Should I destroy it?" She hit the scan button then waited for the results. A window appeared saying that the contaminant was a virus that had spontaneously appeared sixty-seven years ago during the last production phase.

The message annoyed her. "What does that mean?" she asked. But if it has to do with a virus, it could be bad for the world especially if it's inside Ripper ammunition. She cursed then complained, "How can a virus live in a battery?" She searched for related events, but found none. She then tasked the computer to investigate the virus then thought that Byron was behind it. While the computer was working on her request, she checked the security logs and learned that the event happened two years after Byron had started production. The computer came back with inconclusive information and asked again to scan, or destroy the item. "Stupid piece of crap computer!" she spat then used it to locate the item.

This was the last thing that she wanted to do. She was supposed to be on her way to help murder Byron not investigate a virus that she knew nothing about. She grumbled to herself all the way to the production floor and found the battery on an offshoot of the conveyer belt. Right away she saw that the battery light was cobalt blue instead of the normal glowing blue. In her anger she didn't stop to think that the virus had already escaped the battery and contaminated her when she had dropped her shield. She sighed at the thought.

She looked into the battery and was relieved to see that the virus was contained, but had a hard time seeing the actual virus. She pushed her awareness into the gel, but the virus fought her pushing her back. She struggled with it then realized that it wasn't fighting, but consuming the energy that she was using to see it. Her first instinct screamed for her to run to the computer room and have the virus destroyed, but logic told her that it was contained and couldn't hurt her.

"What would this virus do to a person?" she asked herself then thought about the medical equipment in her safe house and some tests she can run. She'd need a normal person and an Alchemist from every species, preferably a bad person that won't be missed. She of course would have to dispose of them afterward. She licked her lips then whispered, "With this virus I could kill James and become the most powerful Alchemist on the planet. That is after I've taken all of his secrets." Saying it out loud made her feel that it was going to become a reality. She reached for the battery, but recoiled as her shield was ripped off her body and consumed by the virus. She collapsed and smashed her knees on the cold duracrete floor then fell onto her side curling up into the fetal position. She gasped and fought to calm her trembling body as droplets of sweat formed on her forehead. Again she feared contamination, but was able to look within and know that she was clean.

A couple of minutes passed before she was able to gather herself up and try a second time. Tentatively she reached for the battery fighting her habitual instinct to form another shield and peer into it thinking that another slap from the virus might kill her. She disengaged from the world and pulled her awareness into herself making her feel blind as her finger slid across the battery's cool metal surface. She felt funny, not herself, lop sided without the use of her power and at that moment realized how much Alchemy has dominated her life. She picked up the battery and slipped it into her pocket before returning to the computer to tell it to destroy the now phantom item. The computer went through the procedure then logged the information that Jas was happy to expunge from the database.

After returning everything she had touched back to the way she'd found it, she left the factory and raced back the Dark Elf capital. She didn't want to carry the virus with her, but it was far too valuable to leave tucked away in her cycle. A quick scan would detect it and there were plenty of good thieves around to try and steal it. She altered her sight to see in the dark, but didn't dare engage her shield. Feeling naked she entered the grind. The warm cavern air felt muggy and stank of heavy incense with the slight under tone of body odor. She carefully made her way through the thick crowd pretending she had her shield, but changed her path every time a person grabbed a good handful of her ass. In the past she never knew how many people had molested her, but mostly they ignored her. By the time she made it close to Monique's she had been elbowed, poked by armor, crushed between people and felt up by quick hands. She found a dead pocket where she collected herself taking inventory of her ripped blouse, frizzy hair, clammy skin, gross underarms and sticky lips that tasted of dirty smoke. All she wanted to do was go home and take a long hot shower to wash away the disgusting film on her skin, but first she had to see Monique.

Jas followed the railing to the back side of Monique's condo then leaned against the wall and waited by Monique's narrow bathroom window. She expanded her senses through the wall and carefully directed the energy so it wouldn't bother the virus then waited for Monique. Once she felt Monique's presence then heard the toilet flush, she tapped on the glass. Monique cracked the small window and peeked at her before opening it a little wider.

Jas leaned closer whispering, "Do you still want to kill Byron?" Monique quickly nodded. Her eyes welled with hope. Jas slipped her the knife telling her, "This blade will piece his shield, it might surprise you, so don't hesitate. You'll only get the one chance to put that monster down. Do you understand?" Monique nodded again then unsheathed the knife holding in front of her. Jas watched her notice the blue residue on its tip. "I trust you have an escape plan?" Monique's eyes darkened and her face grimed before she slowly nodded.

Jas left her, trusting that she'd succeed then took a different route through the grind back to her cycle. She sped into the waste planning ways to get to know her new virus.

Chapter 27

Kole woke beside Enora on their Barge in their new bed. He smiled thinking about the fun that they had the night before and listened to her pleasant snoring. He slowly slipped his arm under her pillow snuggling close, pressing his chest against her naked back feeling her soft skin against his. He ran his other hand down her arm finding her hand and interlocked his fingers with hers. She woke for a moment turning her head toward him with a slight smile then fell back asleep. He leaned his cheek against the back of her head smelling her hair then closed his eyes and lay on the edge of sleep, but realized that the vibration of the antigrav engine was missing. They had stopped moving and he argued with himself trying to decide if he should get up and get the day going, or stay warm and snug with Enora.

She moaned. "I can feel you thinking." She arched her back pressing into him.

Surprised he asked, "You can hear my thoughts?"

"No, your thoughts feel like static that fills the room. Why don't you get up, or calm your mind and cuddle some more. If you stay with me, I'm sure I can be very distracting."

He chuckled. "I wouldn't call you distracting. Enticing and beautiful come to mind. I liked the way we played last night, the feel when you tremble, tense and gush. You left me wanting more."

She rolled over and faced him smiling, her blue eyes sparkling. She whispered, "I like what we did and I felt what you did the other day in the fight with Jelek. You projected your shield and stopped a rocket. You were so excited I thought that you would share it with me."

The memory of the fight killed his excitement. He wanted to do other things than talk about what had happened, but he did bury the experience. They lay there looking into each other's eyes. She searched his eyes waiting. He licked his lips feeling exposed, naked and hurt. "I guess," he started. "I've hid what I know and who I am for so long, its habit. People suck and they try to take everything away from me, so I hide."

"You don't have to hide any more. I want to be with the real you."

He gently placed his hand on the side of her head dragging his thumb down her ear and giving her earlobe a slight pinch. Her eyes intensified. "I won't hide from you anymore," he promised. "When I stopped that rocket I opened up and felt multiple layers of matter and energy, it was very personal."

She slightly nodded then pulled his arm down to hold his hand. "The only truth is that, there is no truth. Everyone has a different relationship with the Universe and what works for you won't work for anyone else. The things that you think you know, will work for you until they don't."

He snuggled closer to her touching his forehead against hers. "I think we both know what works for me," he hinted.

She smiled and turned his arm over pointing to his moles. "Did you know that you have the constellation of Orin on your arm?"

He looked at his arm. "Oh, I guess so."

"I think you're handsome and I like all your parts."

He opened his heart to her then rolled her onto her back thinking about the one part he wanted to give her, but started with kisses.

Later that morning he decided that he wanted to be nice and make everyone pancakes, in truth it was the only thing that he knew how to cook. He kissed Enora's cheek, slipped out of bed then started his day with a shower.

After everyone was filled with pancakes and camaraderie they suited up. Kole started the Barge then flushed the sanitation tank over some bushes while Enora routed navigation through her station.

Once everyone was at their posts they sped off and entered the plains leaving the sparse forest behind. Kole opened the throttle to see what the Barge could do and to his surprised, everything felt and sounded good. Enora confirmed his mechanical instinct then said that they could even squeeze five percent more out of the engine, but would create more ware. The Barge wasn't his transport, but he was happy to have found an unmodified gem with nice seats, a good engine and shiny buttons. The thought of his luck changing for the better made him want to stop and live in the moment, allowing the world to pass by and forget about him.

He told Enora his thoughts. She laughed then said, "The world won't let you be a farmer."

"I wasn't talking about being a farmer."

She explained, "You want to dwell in the bubble of your positive feeling and protect it from the world so that no one steals it. It's like being a farmer working a piece of land under the sky being touched by the sun eating what he grows."

"I guess so," he said. "I just feel that my luck has been fluctuating lately and I want to savor it when it's good."

"The hardest thing in life is to learn that when something seems negative it might be the best thing for you."

"It sounds like everything gets handed to you," he teased.

Her lips curved into a slight smile. "You still have to take responsibility for what you're manifesting. Celebrate what you want and acknowledge, letting go of what you don't."

"Now it sounds like a lot of work and I feel kind of lazy," he joked.

She took on a more serious tone saying, "With every thought, breath and movement you are in a constant state of manifestation."

"Well, all I want is good luck for the rest of my life."

She laughed. "Who thinks that you don't have good luck?"

"Enora, I'm messing with you. You don't have to turn every talk that we have into a sermon. You can just say that living in a luck bubble would be cool."

"I know. The more you know the harder life becomes. With just a handful of words I can sooth someone's pain, but they don't want it. They just want you to listen while they flounder. I can feel their energy and I wait for them to tell me the truth and ask me for what they want, but they don't. They just suffer expecting me to cater to their suffering." They sat in silence for a few minutes. "Maybe you're right. Maybe it's better to live life and not know."

"Enora, I like being with you and I hope we can be together for a long time, but we're Alchemists and manifestation is part of what we do and if everyone else was into it, they'd know about it too. Let everyone else fumble in the dark, that's what they do. They must like it, so be happy with what you have and leave the rest of the world alone."

She relaxed into her chair. "I like you too."

He looked across the sea of grass toward the horizon and smiled, happy to be with her then saw glimmering specks in the sky. "What's that up there?" he asked.

Enora touched her ear piece. "I'm picking up a lot of radio chatter. Oh, someone's calling."

Kole listened as a man with a gruff voice ask, "What's the pass code?"

"Give me the candy now," She replied.

He belly laughed. "Weak," he mocked. "You're not going to get any candy with that attitude. Access granted, park wherever you want."

"He disconnected, that was rude," she complained.

Kole joined the group chat. "We're coming up on our destination and I have a feeling that it's going to be another criminal town, so no one do anything stupid."

"Way to instill confidence in us, Kole," Nick joked.

"Kole," Eric said. "There's a lot of activity on our port side traveling parallel to us. Do you have them on scope?"

"No," Enora replied. "There's nothing on scope. Well, that's good to know it's broken."

Kyra asked, "Can I get the turrets looked at too? They stick, nothing major just a second delay."

"A second is a long time," Nick said.

"I know. I was being polite, Nick. You don't have to be so caustic."

"Focus people," Kole said. "Stay alert, I don't remember this town being here."

"Maybe it's the new Slaver base," Eric offered.

"Wait," Nick said. "It's fuzzy, but I remember hearing about the Elven Fleet attacking Slavers. There was a big party to celebrate with free drinks and loose morals. I had a blast."

Kyra asked, "They're all Slavers?" Then something clicked against her teeth and her mouth sounded full, "Let's nuke the bastards and wipe everyone out. We'll stop them and The Lollypop King in one shot. I hate Slavers."

Kole visualized a mushroom cloud and everyone effected by it. "We'll take a look to see who's there. Slaves and regular people don't deserve to get nuked."

There was a sucking noise. "But, you're saying okay if it's just Slavers?" she asked with a hint of hope.

"It's never just Slavers," Nick said. "Would we still be the good guys if we commit mass murder?"

"Who cares, if there's a chance to kill them all we should do it, but if they're peaceful we should give them a pass."

Eric asked, "Are you sucking on a candy, Kyra?"

"What, Kyra?" Nick asked. "You're not making sense, name a peaceful Slaver. It's not in their nature to hold hands and sing songs."

Kole commanded them to be quiet. "We're not nuking anyone. The world can't take it. Kyra put your helmet on and stop eating those damn candies."

"I'm trying to stop I just have a couple more. They're so good," she said then sounded distressed. "Nick, get out of here! Stop it, those are mine!"

Frustrated at their flippant behavior, Kole tightened his grip on his controls cracking his knuckles. He decided that saying anything wouldn't matter. He released his tension in a heavy sigh then looked at the growing city on the horizon. "Do you see the size of this place?" he asked Enora. "With all those people coming, getting out might be a problem." But when she didn't say anything he looked over. She stared back at him with a distant expression looking tough and sexy in her body armor. "What do you see?" he asked.

"I was watching you manifest."

He wasn't sure if he wanted to know but asked, "Good things I hope?"

"If you're into that sort of thing then good I think."

"That doesn't sound good."

"There is no good or bad, there's only energy and getting frustrated at the kids only tells the Universe that you enjoy their antics, which manifests more antics."

He returned his gaze back to the growing city. "They drive me mental. How can I not get upset with them?"

"It's because you don't understand manifestation. Nick and the other kids are tools and I'm not being sarcastic. There are moments when they'll interact with the Universe on your behalf and help with your manifestation, but they don't know they're doing it. Other times, they'll burn your energy manifesting a torrent of frustration."

Kole frowned. "I feel that it's arrogant to treat others as tools and you're going to lose your connection with people thinking that way. That's how the Purge happened."

"That's the way it is and there isn't a choice."

He didn't like thinking about people that way, but asked, "How do you know this?"

"Manifestation shapes the world."

"You lost me."

"What is inside is manifest outside and what is outward is manifest inward. We breathe."

He laughed. "Maybe you're right. I have no idea what you're talking about. You've been in a jar for a long time and I can see why you're disconnected. It's not nice to use people, they're not tools."

"You misunderstand. I'm not the one using people. The Universe is meeting all of my needs and all I have to do is keep my hands off and let it happen. Once something happens, I thank the Universe giving it energy to show it what I want and the direction I wish to go."

"Are you saying I should ignore the kids? I'm trying to keep them safe and they seem to throw themselves into danger. I can't sit and watch that happen."

"Accept Nick knowing that his destiny will happen regardless of what you want for him."

Kole disagreed saying, "Letting them go is not connecting with people."

"The Universe connects us all."

"Hey Kole," Nick interjected. "You've been awfully quiet. Are you still driving this crate, or are you and Enora getting busy?"

Kole opened his com. "I guess you're done stuffing you gaping maw with candy."

"You sound tense Kole," Eric worried.

Kyra laughed. "Enora probably told him something that he didn't like."

"Gaping maw," Nick complained. "I was told that I have a beautiful mouth."

Disgusted by Nick's insinuation, Kole said, "I don't want to know, don't care."

Nick huffed, "Whatever."

Kole slowed as they rode along the exterior wall of the city. The wall wasn't like any he had ever seen. Instead of a thick heavy permanent wall, it was a two story mess of rusty interlocking metal plates that had been reinforced with metal pipes and as they drove through a large hole that passed for a gate, he noticed that the city's defenses were an automated system of artillery and anti-air guns. He looked for a road, trail or marks in the dirt, but there weren't any, just various sized gaps between the collapsible dwellings made out of corrugated metal sheets. Kole quickly ran out of room and parked in a cluster of tightly packed vehicles that lined the inside of the wall.

"What a crap hole," Nick said.

"Look at the tags on the other vehicles," Kyra said. "This place is made up of different gangs and slavers from all over. These people shouldn't be together."

Eric asked, "Kole, do you remember the Elves taking out a slaver city? This could be the survivors."

"I knew it," Kyra hissed. "We should vaporize the lot while we have the chance."

Kole released his seat's harness then looked out his window at the crowd of people moving between the crap shacks that they use for housing. He blinked then took an honest look at their makeshift armor and gang colors, but there were also merchants in the mix. "They're not all Slavers, there for the candy," he said.

"Look at them," Kyra argued. "Smiling, everyone's getting chummy and over there, a group of Slavers are dancing."

Eric asked, "Where? How do you know they're Slavers? Oh wait I see them. Yeah they're Slavers."

Nick cleared his throat. "These people destroy lives and seeing them happy really pisses me off. I'm with Kyra. I vote we vaporize them."

"I think that's wise," Eric added. "What say you Enora?"

"Looking at the way they've built this place tells me that they plan to periodically relocate. I assume that it's a lesson learned from the Elves. It's now, or never. I'll make the three implosion devices for you and turn this place into a crater. And while you guys are planting the bombs, Kole and I will find The Lollypop King and make sure he's put down."

Kole looked at Enora. "You talk so calm, like you're ordering fruit from a vendor. There're innocent people here."

"Are you sure?" she asked. "They know the Slavers and support them."

"I don't like this idea."

"Don't like it somewhere else, we have work to do," she said then slipped out of her seat and left the room.

Nick laughed. "Enora, if I was strait, I'd be hard for you right now."

Eric and Kyra groaned in disgust.

"I didn't say anything bad," Nick said.

Later they secured their barge then split up to plant the bombs and find The Lollypop King.

Chapter

28

Hidden in the remnants of an underground medical facility, Jas leaned back in her computer chair and kicked her tight laced boots onto her console then studied a holographic screen hovering before her. The screen was divided into ten sections, each centered on a test subject. Dressed in white hospital garb a collection of men and women from each race amused themselves in their confined rooms. In the past even them, the low end Alchemists could've broke free, but once Jas administered her virus their power was rendered inert. The computer recorded the time it took for each race, Trolls were first and the Humans last, but what frightened her was the virus' mutation. She had to decide on what to do with them now that the virus was airborne, each person a carrier and if one of them escaped, Alchemy would end. She couldn't let them go, but that only left two choices, destruction, or letting the machines take care of them for the rest of their lives. The thought of someone else stumbling onto the facility and releasing them by accident pushed her toward destruction.

She distracted herself by thinking about the virus. The computer at the manufacturing plant called its creation a spontaneous event, poof a virus. "Nonsense," she muttered. "Something happened during the clip's construction. Dirty material, air exposure, or that idiot

Byron had a lingering fart that somehow got mixed up in there."

She thought about gassing her subjects then incinerating the room, but decided to keep them alive a little longer to see if the Non-Humans would regress into Human form. She wondered, "Could they?" Then visualized the world remade with smiling Human faces until her eyes moved to the Trolls.

"Hey Bob," she mocked. "I used to be a flesh eating smelly Troll, now I live in the suburbs. No psychological damage here. What? No, I wasn't the one who ate your baby. That was my wife."

A flashing light on her console caught her attention. She tapped the light and James' face appeared on her screen.

James asked, "Jas, where are you?"

"I'm here taking a break."

Annoyance flashed in his eyes. "I know that you're on your well deserved break, but I couldn't find you in the system and if you were far away I wouldn't have bothered you."

"Oh," she replied. "Do you have a task?"

"Byron has been murdered. I need you to look into it."

A tingle of joy ignited in the center of her chest that she quickly buried. "Do you know who did it?"

"I have a Dark Elf investigator on it, but I suspect it was alchemic in nature."

"I'll leave right away send me the Elf's details."

James nodded then sent the information before disconnecting.

She read the name of the investigator and knew him by reputation then thought about the download. She had gone through a lot of trouble hiding her safe house, but now James might know about it. In the past she wouldn't have cared, but now she has her experiment and if James found out, she wasn't sure what he'd do. She knew that he used to work in genetic manipulation and could use his help, but something deep within her wanted to keep the virus safe, away from his hands. If she could manipulate it so it wouldn't spread she could become Queen of the world by making her enemies inert.

The virus was hidden away and now she had to protect her work. She entered a code, released lethal gas into her test subject's room, watched them die then incinerated the evidence.

Later in the Dark Elf capital, Jas met investigator Iztac at the crime scene. She walked through Monique's door and found him leaning against the living room wall waiting for her. His red eyes looked uninterested and didn't even give her the once over that she had hoped for. Charm went a long way when dealing with investigators who all looked the same in their blue uniforms and short white hair. Most of them didn't care and would take a bribe to look the other way, but Iztac was serious. James must be paying him well.

"Investigator Iztac?" she asked.

He nodded and allowed an awkward silence fall between them.

She ignored him and walked further in looking the place over, pretending to be fresh eyes.

"The body is in the bedroom," he said.

"I'm gathering information."

"There's not much to know. Byron was a client of the hooker known as Monique, but rumor says there was something personal between them and judging by the wound, I'd say so."

"I wouldn't know," she lied.

He examined his nails. "It's funny. Some would think that Monique murdered him."

She turned to watch him. "But you don't."

"She definitely had motive and was the one who did it."

She feigned annoyance then asked, "If you know she did it, then why don't you go get her?"

"In good time, we're Elves we live long. Besides Monique isn't an Alchemist and I find it odd that she was able to kill him without help."

"I'm sure James has a long list of Byron's enemies to give you."

"If you eliminate his Dark Elf enemies, the list is not that long and we know better than to cross James. So there's really one avenue of thought."

"And what's that?"

"Someone took advantage of Monique and supplied her with a weapon that she could kill Byron with. Not only that, Monique was able to pay her way out of the city." He looked up from his nails and met her eyes. "I wonder where she got the money."

Jas sighed in disappointment. "You're blaming me."

"I didn't say that," he said with a slight smile then went back to looking at his nails.

"What are you saying?"

"In my experience it's the victim's rival who's guilty and if I'm not mistaken, you're his only rival. That's why we Dark Elves patiently wait in the shadows because sooner than later our enemy's rival takes care of our problem. You've made a lot of people happy."

She laughed then mocked, "Is that what you have, a half brained theory?" She put her wrists together. "You got me, take me away."

He pushed himself off the wall then left.

Pretending the apartment was bugged, she said, "Accuse me without proof, what a jerk."

She continued to look around then made her way to the bedroom. The bed was a mess. Blankets strewn on the floor, blood splatter across the sheets and on the walls. Byron lay propped up on pillows naked in the middle of the bed on top of a pool of blood. His eyes rolled back and face frozen between surprise and pain. She examined the splatter on the walls and found a clean spot then visualized where Monique would've been, sitting on top of him. Jas stepped closer then understood everyone's suspicion then kicked herself for screwing up. The knife had punched through Byron's shield with ease then as a side effect, excavated his heart in an explosion that probably scared the crap out of Monique. She laughed at the thought then realized how they had found Byron so quickly. Monique must have fled in a hurry. Jas checked all the drains for blood and found none telling her that Monique hadn't cleaned herself up before running. She was a Dark Elf after all and was probably expecting to be terminated after the deed was done, taking the murder weapon for protection.

She walked back to the kitchen then opened the fridge and wasn't surprised to see it mostly empty with some leftovers that had gone off, a couple of bottles of water and a beer. She imagined the air smelling funny, like cool rot and smiled at her luck then grabbed the beer. She cracked the bottle, leaned against the counter and enjoyed the beverage thinking about James.

She sipped her beer, thinking that James knew what she had done and that the stupid dance with that investigator was a message from him telling her that he knows. She quickly planned her escape from the city then stopped, knowing that you're not caught until you're caught and without proof, James won't do anything. She then became afraid of Monique and what she knew. She should've tied up the loose end, but Monique had suffered enough. She filled her mouth with beer then swallowed hard feeling comforted. It was a mercy to let Monique live, but with her alive, it had become Jas' sin and as the investigator had said, they live a long time and the truth will eventually come out.

She finished her beer, left it on the counter then made her way to James. She walked into his sparse office and as she got closer to his desk he stood and looked happy to see her.

He walked around his desk and met her. "I still feel bad for calling you back," he said then gently placed his hands on her shoulders. She was surprise at how easily he passed through her shield. He had never touched her before. His face warmed. "What have you learned about Byron's fate?"

His warm hands and concerned eyes distracted her. "The investigator suspects Monique," she said.

He chuckled. "No he doesn't. Monique did do it, but Iztac suspects an Alchemist was behind Byron's murder." He sighed and looked disappointed. "I tried to help Byron get away from the drugs, to get him to clear his head, but his delusions were getting worse. And his obsession with Monique, he didn't know who she was. I don't think he cared who she was."

James had been kind to her in the past, but never this personal. She studied his expressions and he looked genuinely saddened by Byron's death. "I'm sure that he knew you cared about him," she said consoling him. "I didn't find the murder weapon, she must still have it."

"Do you know what it was?"

She shook her head and looked him in the eye then lied, "No, but I think it was a Ripper."

"You think? I was hoping that you'd know what happened," he said then made his way back behind his desk.

She was unnerved that he could penetrate her shield so easily and that his touch made her not want to disappoint him. "The wound wasn't that big, but the signs of a Ripper were there. Byron had exposure to the weapons and may have took some of it for himself," she said, pretending to speculate.

"I had a similar thought so I checked our closest manufacturing facility and found evidence that Byron had entered it without my permission."

"What was he after?" she asked hiding her nervousness and feigned surprise.

"I don't know. He was good at covering his tracks except that Byron hadn't left town since he shacked up with his pet. I guess it wasn't him unless he had a way to slip out of town without my knowledge."

She didn't bother thinking about what she had done to cover her tracks. She needed those thoughts buried to protect the illusion of innocents she had built. She knew that he was trying to bring her mind back to what she had done to cause her to slip up, besides if James had anything on her he wouldn't be fishing and flaunting the fact that he suspected her. "How do you know that Byron entered the facility?" she asked.

He shrugged dismissing the tension that had slowly built between them, that Jas had failed to feel until it was gone. "It doesn't matter now," he said. "For now they got away with it, but time will reveal the true murderer, once we find Monique."

Jas nodded. "What would you like me to do?"

He smiled at her. "Share my lunch with me."

"What?"

From behind his desk he pulled out a knife and a chunk of salt-cured ham and as he walked toward her he cut off a piece then presented it to her.

She took a bite. "This is good," she said. "What is it?"

"The Dark Elves call it something else, but I know it as prosciutto."

They ate their piece in silence then James said, "Over the years I've neglected you. Byron took up a lot of my attention and I could blame him, but it was my fault. When I found him all those years ago there was already darkness within him and at the time I thought he'd grow out of it with the right nurturing, but all I was doing was following him around as damage control." He sadly sighed then continued, "Our group is trying to give the world back to the Humans and in the past I had ordered him to remove some obstacles. I didn't know it would awaken the evil within him. I tried to break him out of his frame of mind. I yelled at him, pleaded, tried to distract him, rewarded his good behavior and took away his things when he was bad, but nothing had worked. He was addicted to drugs and violence. I wanted the best for him and to share our bright future, but that was me being sentimental."

He cut off another piece of meat then gave it to her. She said between bites, "I'm sorry for your loss and I wish I knew the Byron that you met so long ago, but he wasn't very nice to me. I'm just glad he didn't hurt our dream of a better world."

"I know that you two didn't get along and I could've defused the tension between you two, but I felt I'd be covering for him. I always hoped he'd pull his head out of his ass and see that there were people around him that cared about him. He just never healed the wounds that made him into a monster."

"Was it the drugs that made him lose his grip on reality, or was he always that way?" she asked.

"I don't know, I didn't pry into his past and there's no excuse for him being a dick to everyone," he said then shared the last piece of meat with her.

"I hope that you have as much faith in me as much as you did him."

"You've always been the good one and I've expected a lot from you. You've handled all the delicate tasks admirably and now that Byron's eclipse has passed, I can see you in the proper light. That's why I've decided to advance your power."

Excitement filled her and if she had known that killing Byron would've advanced everything in her life, she would've done it a long time ago, but it was always about the timing. In the past she might not have gotten away with it, but... she looked into James' eyes and wondered if he actually knew that she was the one who did it. Perhaps murdering Byron was test to prove that she could take his place and be better at it than he was. Byron was weak and she deserved to take everything that was his and one day she'll be strong enough to do the same to James, but something in her felt sad at the thought of ending James. She dismissed her ambition and said, "I hope that I'm worthy of this advancement."

"Remember that any advancement in knowledge that you haven't earned is hollow and can be taken from you," he warned then instructed, "Close your eyes and feel your identity, so that you can compare that to who you'll become. And once you can see the difference, you can build a bridge connecting you to that knowledge, owning it."

She closed her eyes and took inventory of her personality then asked, "Will that work? Can I build that bridge and own your gift?"

He said nothing and cupped the sides of her head with his hands, placing his thumbs on her forehead. A bright light flashed within her mind stinging her eyes then she felt something new swirl within her, but before she could understand what was happening, she had forgotten who she used to be and lost her place within herself. The swirling slowed and as everything settled. She felt different, but didn't know how.

He dropped his hands to her shoulders then pulled her in for a hug. "You've accepted my gift. I'm so proud of you."

She relaxed into his warmth and returned his embrace feeling his shield across his back then said, "Thank you. I didn't know what to expect and I tried to hold on to my memory, but I can't remember who I used to be. I have nothing to compare your gift to, I lost it."

He gently pushed her back to look in her eyes. "You've tried to remember the wrong thing. You are your power, now look within and understand."

She listened and found more alchemical symbols written into her bones, different from her old ones. When she had first met James she was like every other Alchemist using trinkets to channel her power, but trinkets could be lost, or stolen. He had convinced her to write her knowledge to her bones so that it would always be there and she could hide what she was from those who would fear her. But comparing the new writing with her old, she could see how sloppy and weak her writing was. "You're right," she murmured as a wave of fatigue washed over her. "I can see the difference. I need time to meditate."

"Whoa, you look pale. You're going to have to wait," he said and guided her to his chair. "Sit and rest."

She lined herself up then fell into his cozy chair closing her eyes. She could now remember all the times he had been nice to her, but at the time she had thought there had been an ulterior motive behind it. She smirked, amused that she couldn't see it before, but it was always her fear that had driven her ambition. She needed favor, position, and power to feel safe in the world, but all she did was create more reasons to be afraid. She started to dream, but for the first time she felt safe.

Chapter

29

Kole forced himself to relax in his tan colored body armor. He leaned against the Barge trying to look like he owned the place while he waited for Enora, wondering what was taking her so long. The others had gone off to plant her implosion devices, but now he wasn't sure that the bombs would be powerful enough. People of all races were still arriving in droves, dressed in various fashions from partial rags to full body armor. Now forced to park outside the walls, they walked in hooting and hollering, shooting their guns in the air. Kole had a feeling that they'd have a problem leaving and was grateful that Enora had listened and made a remote detonator instead of setting timers that Nick wanted. At first he didn't like the idea of using the bombs, being the executioner of people who'd be guilty by association then remembered seeing all the destroyed lives left in the Slaver's wake. Everyone around him looked normal and jovial which aggravated him knowing that they all had profited off the misery of the world. Feeling justified, he pushed the thought of the bombs out of his mind, saddened that these choices and actions have become his norm.

Enora asked, "Are you all right?"

Surprised, even through his body armor she could tell that he was upset, he blinked looking at the black eyes of her helmet, wishing he could see her face. "Yeah, I was just wondering when all this had become my reality. I had the quiet life of a drifter, what happened?"

Her voice and posture hardened. "How far are you willing to go? A long time ago I wanted to know the truth, to see behind the veil of reality, but when I did I learned that there is only one truth, that there is no truth. It's all energy," she said. "Out of our group, you're the only one wondering why, and if you decide to be a good guy then destroy the bad guys, embrace who you are."

He stepped closer, hooked his arm in hers and moved them into the crowd. "What about the whole jar thing? It wasn't a nice thing that happened to you."

She laughed. "That experience freed my mind."

"I'm serious," he said as people in more of a hurry bumped him as they passed.

"The hardest thing you're going to learn is that you imprison your mind with your own judgment. Just because you think something is bad doesn't mean that it is."

"If that's true, how is it possible that I can affect anything?"

"You have enough power to through a rock into a river and make a splash, don't you?"

"That reminds me, we should get a move on. Today we're to make a big splash."

"Are we?" she asked in a tone that hinted she knew more than him.

"Of course," he said not really wanting to hear her thought. "People will sleep easier when these Slavers are gone."

"None of that matters right now. We need to focus and find The Lollypop King."

"Why? We're going to make a big crater and kill everyone here. If he's not here, we can get him later."

He chuckled at her lack of foresight. "I'd like to make only one crater, thank you very much. So we need to confirm that he's here."

The crowd got thicker forcing him to hold her hand and take the lead. A live Ork band thrashed their instruments in the distance as waves of people bounced with their arms in the air and screamed with the music. He changed direction and pulled her out of the crowd into an alley having no idea where he was going.

"That band had an interesting sound," she commented. "In my time, Orks were new and didn't yet have a voice."

Further in, the ally was filled with smoke from the multiple drug dens. "Yeah," he said. "I can only handle so much rough love and blood, but if you don't focus on the words, it sounds happy."

They left the ally and pushed through a tight line of people then stopped. Kole stared in disbelief at people marching in master and slave leather outfits, sparkling tights and gang colors while holding their new automatic rifles in the air. "What is this?" he asked.

"Oh," she cheered. "It's a parade." She pointing further down at the giant balloons shaped in the different races. "Balloons and floats are coming. Maybe The King's on one."

The cartoon balloons passed and the first float featured a gold throne on a hill of small candy wrappers. In front of the throne danced an average sized man wearing a red and purple smiling demon mask. Kole couldn't hear any music, but the man gyrated in a gold sequin tuxedo jacket and black pants while twirling a curved handled candy cane that could be used for walking. He stopped, held the cane above his head in both hands and gave a pelvic thrust as several small hidden cannons fired off, showering the spectators with candies.

"Have my love," The Lollypop King yelled. His words were carried by alchemy.

The spectators reached out, caught some candy then cheered as Kole said, "Eww!"

As the float passed by Enora said, "That's him, let's blow this joint."

"How do you know that was him?" he asked then saw his name on the back of the throne. "Oh. But there's a ring of vehicles blocking us, how are we going to get out of here?"

"We grab our stuff and walk out then steal something else to get away. We're completely free right? Besides, they're bad guys and expect that sort of thing."

It finally sunk in. Kole knew then that their plan was going to happen and that if he stopped the implosion all these criminals would spread across the land and continue to hurt the world. He listened to the noise of the spectators and watched the floats pass by thinking about his place in the world then decided to be a good guy no matter the cost. His decision gave him enough peace to enjoy the moment and listen to Enora laugh and comment on the parade. He wondered what it was like in her crazy little head then said, "Fine, let's do this, but we need to make sure The Lollypop King dies tonight."

"Are you sure? He seems rather flamboyant. If we miss him he'll gather more people around himself and make it easier to kill off more bad guys. It'll be like scum fishing with him as bait and we have all the time in the world. We can smoke his friends, go on vacation then come back and do it again."

"You're joking right?" he asked hoping she was. "I can't tell. I can't see your face."

Nick interrupted them through group chat. "Where are you guys? We're back and Kole you're going to be proud of me, I walked through an orgy and didn't join in."

"Only you'd be able to find an orgy in all this mess," Eric said.

"We should hurry," Kyra suggested. "I found the slave pens and opened them after I planted my bomb. They weren't even guarded."

A series of fireworks erupted over head. "Wow," Kole said.

"These guys know how to party, it's too bad they're jerks," Nick said.

Eric asked, "What are we doing? Are we going to detonate, or join in?"

Kole watched the fireworks a moment longer making a decision. "Change of plans. We're going to take out The King then leave."

"Why?" Kyra asked.

"That sounds like a bad idea," Nick said.

"I'd be easier to hit and run," Eric said.

"This all sounds like arguing. He's an Alchemist and might survive, we need to be sure."

"I figured you'd want to take him out, so I created a tracking device on his pant leg. I know exactly where he is," Enora said.

"Excellent, great thinking Enora, pass the coordinates on and when we all get close, we'll meet up."

Chapter

30

The King stood on the balcony of his panel two story house watching the fireworks. "What is going on out there?" he asked through his mask. He spun on his heels walking bare foot into his living room across the polished mahogany floorboards avoiding various colored floor pillows to where his assistant waited. "I'm not feeling it," he said then clutched his chest. "I want to feel the explosions deep inside of me. Make them closer, I want my teeth to rattle."

The assistant brushed his long black hair out of his eyes then worked his data pad. "But sir, how can you feel it through your shield?" he asked then pulled on his white suit.

The King watched him fidget then stepped closer and adjusted his assistant's pink tie. "He's an adequate assistant," he reminded himself in a low tone. "Put those bad thoughts away and think happy. Now…" he struggled to find his assistant's name then gave up. "Assistant, I want more booze and drugs out there. I want people to party for a week. I want this to be the biggest event the world has ever seen."

"And more candy?"

"Yes!" he yelled. "I want so much debauchery out there that half the people will be puking in the streets then other half slipping in it." He shook his fists in the air then yelled, "I want everyone covered in

GOLD INTO LEAD

puke because you're not really messed up until you're puking!"

"Of... course Sir. That sounds like a good time."

"Shut up! You don't know anything. You should be anticipating my needs. I want more prostitutes out there, the good kind, not the scrawny drug addicted cheap ones with sores and chattering teeth."

His assistant sighed. "I'll get nothing but the best for your guests, Sir."

He suddenly felt silly and didn't like his assistant's poor attitude. "Are you mocking me?" he asked. "Do I need to slap a ball gag in your mouth and spank you black and blue again?"

He snapped to attention then stammered, "N, no Sir."

"You do this to yourself, right? I pay you well and you seem competent." He stared at him for a moment then decided what to do about his poor attitude. "I'm tired right now, but tomorrow we're going to start off with a whipping, it seems that it's the only way to get the best out of you. But don't worry, as a reward for tonight's work, I'll let you choose the gag."

His assistant closed his eyes looking like he was about to cry. "Thank you, Sir," he said cringing.

The King spun around then looked out the window. "That's better," he sang. "Now do what I said, more drugs, booze and prostitutes for everyone, and bigger fireworks, I want to feel them. Now get out before I find the strength to beat you, little bastard."

The King calmed his mind then thought about his assistants declining performance tracing it back to about a week, but couldn't figure out the cause. He thought harder then remembered taking his assistant's bed away and making him sleep on the floor. He had forgotten that he did that. He laughed at the memory, but thought the punishment wasn't harsh enough. He decided to do something fun, he'd manifest a clothes trunk that'd be place at the foot of his bed. His assistant can sleep in there, until he gets his crap together. He grinned at his ingenuity then heard a floorboard creak in the next room. He reached out with his awareness. His servants were out partying leaving him alone as five unwanted guests crept through his home. Excited, he planned to have more fun, but calmed to savor the moment.

Though the outside of his home looked like several crack shacks strung together, the luxurious interior was lined with maple wall panels decorated with ancient paintings, arched high ceilings and elegant chrome light fixtures. He retrieved his candy cane walking stick then strolled over to his massive sound system and cranked its volume, pumping sitar, tabla and zil music throughout his house. He spun, dancing to the center of the room. He shuffled side to side twirling his cane from hand to hand feeling the depth of the music, getting into the mood.

With the sharp cracking of wood, his tall double doors were dramatically kicked in crashing against the door stops. Without losing the beat, The King sprang, soaring across the room toward a person wearing heavy tan body armor. He felt like he was floating and everything slowed into a moment of beautiful silence, then with his cane he brushed the person's automatic rifle to the side striking his helmet with enough force that it broke its eye piece. He saw green skin and a red eye before continuing to beat him back with a flurry of blows to his limbs. In the middle of his beating, the Ork's rifle went off strafing the wall.

The Ork fell and The King stood over him thinking about the gun fire and his beautiful home. The King turned around and saw his favorite painting was riddled with smoking bullet holes. He screamed, "My painting! You monster, do you know what you just did? That was the original Mona Lisa by the renaissance man Leonardo Dicaprio!" He trembled with rage. First the annoying Ork kicked in his doors instead of opening them then shot up his priceless masterpiece and worst of all, damaged his state of mind. He wanted to make him pay.

On his back, the Ork leveled his rifle between his knees then fired destroying his crystal chandelier. "You're not even aiming at me!" The King screamed. He sidestepped, hooking the Ork's knee with his cane jerking the Ork forward out of the doorway. The King dropped his weight and struck the Ork's hand with the back of his cane then took the Ork's rifle away with his free hand, throwing it across the room, but before he could thrash the living crap out of the Ork, another person in stained tan body armor with bullet holes, attacked him from behind.

His new attacker danced with feminine grace wielding two silver hand axes trying to cut him up. Her movements excited The King and his shield held, allowing him a moment to enjoy the attempt on his life. He danced with her, blocking leg to leg and arm to arm slowly charging his body with power. He thrust outward with an open palm strike sending her flying across the room and into the wall. She crumpled to the floor then bounced to her feet. "Wow," he approved. "You move like a goddess. I just popped a chub." He looked her over. Her body armor didn't give him much, but she had all the curves in the right places. "Who are you?" he flirted. "I'd love to have you for dinner. We can discuss why you want to kill me."

But before she could be swayed by his charm, she rolled to her side as three bursts of energy struck his back pushing him into the wall. He spun away dancing to the center of the room as the third attacker wearing the same body armor helped the Ork to his feet. The King reached out sensing the unrefined alchemy within his new attacker then felt the wood dowel. The dowel was older and not made by his attacker. "New to the game?" he asked the third attacker. "You're not reaching the full potential of your dowel. Let's see what you can do without it." He flicked his hand making the programming within the dowel inert. The boy flung the dowel across the floor, pulled out his rifle, aimed then fired. The Ork had retrieved his rifle joining in and The King watched his art and home become peppered with holes.

Unimpressed, he was sick of them destroying his home and decided to finish the dance. He connected with his music again then sprang toward the girl. The Ork and boy followed him unloading their weapons, hitting everything but him. He laughed at them while they reloaded then proceeded to quicken his pace, showing the girl his true skill. The dance was quick. He stepped in and when she blocked, he pressed, tilting his wrist, sliding his cane under her arm. He alchemically charged his body as he dropped his weight, driving the head of his cane into her ribs. She fell back and he followed driving up under her chin then stabbed downward with the other end of the cane into the top of her leg. With her reeling back, he palm struck her again sending her crashing through the wall.

The Alchemist boy dropped to the floor trying to perform a transmutation, but failed. The King was no longer amused. Power flowed through him, no thought, or emotion, just the void. He moved. He was in front of the boy. He raised his knee throwing his body and power into the movement striking the boy's upper chest. His knee slid up into the boy's neck under his chin, lifting him into the air. Together they soared upward till the boy crashed halfway into the ceiling. His legs dangled as The King hit the floor.

The Ork turned to run, but The King was on him. The king hooked the Ork's leg with his cane, tripping him. The Ork slid head first into the six inch base boards with a loud thump. The King wanted this one to pay for the doors and the destruction of his most prize possession, the Mona Lisa. The Ork floundered trying to get up as The King beat him with his cane, striking his knees, elbows, back, head and legs. The thrashing continued long after the Ork had stopped moving, until his cane cracked.

Breathing heavy, he felt the last two people walk into the room. He collected himself and flipped his cane holding the hook in his hand, then pointed its end at them. He felt ruffled and sweaty, but still needed to entertain his unwanted guests. He struck a pose looking cool then fired his disguised Ripper at them. One of the assailants dove away leaving the other to take the hit, but nothing happened. He could feel that they were both Alchemists, but his Ripper did nothing telling him that they wore their armor over their shields. He laughed finding a reservoir of energy to meet their challenge then embracing the moment. Balancing life and death within himself, he sprang forward attacking the Alchemist that had the feel of femininity. Once they joined he struck her with his cane and she moved with him using his momentum to return his hits through his shield. At first he didn't realize that she was touching him, driving her fingers deep between his muscles hurting him as they danced, adrenaline drove him and as he became fire, she became water. He changed his tactic trying to hook her, but she stepped in landing an upper cut, shattering his mask and lodging tiny ceramic fragments into his face. The mask fell from his face pulling out a couple of strands of his black hair and in that moment, he felt her knee against his. He pushed forward locking her knee then jolted, sending her backward.

He glared his dark eyes at her then brushed the ceramic fragments out of his brown skin. She felt like void and could hurt him, but he didn't have time to think about it, the other Alchemists had moved in to engage. The King didn't want to find out if this one could hurt him as well and decided to blow a hole in the floor, dropping down. He landed on his debris covered pool table that he had used to entertain prominent Slave Masters and slipped on the eight ball. He fell landing hard on the floor, grateful that his shield still functioned. The Alchemist followed, landing firm. The King sprang to his feet, sweeping his cane, trying to take out the Alchemist's legs, but the Alchemist kicked out stuffing the cane. The Alchemist jumped down landing on him, driving his fist through his shield into his forehead. A flash of light then stars flooded The King's vision. He flailed trying to block, waiting for his vision to return. The stars cleared and he grabbed the Alchemist's armor then pushed him away. Seeing his end, The King's appetite for destruction had been sated. He opened a hole in the ceilings to the night sky, but before he could escape, launching himself like a missile, the Alchemist wasted his last attack and struck his cane.

The King shot upward through the holes passing the woman who watched him soar high into the sky. He sailed through the fireworks that looked amazing and over biggest party that he had ever seen. The day had gone well turning into the best day of his life until those five interlopers wrecked it. The fight flashed through his mind, but the last attack seemed out of place, nagging him. He finally gave in and looked at the cane. The crack in his cane had fractured and now a glowing blue substance was getting brighter as it ate its way through the inner wall. He watched it for a moment then realized what was happening and in a panic, he tried to throw the cane away, but it exploded.

He couldn't scream, the air was sucked out of his lungs, but he continued to soar in darkness. A hot numbness filled him from head to toe as he felt for his right arm that was now gone, touching bone. He finally got his lungs to work taking in a cold breath and felt the sensation of falling. He focused on remaking his shield, pushing through the fog of pain and dipped into his pocket finding the panic button that James had given him. His drive to stay alive focused his mind allowing him to create his shield a moment before his hit the ground, skidding to halt. His energy dipped collapsing his shield dropping him onto rocks and mud that felt soothing. He searched through his fading mind and found the fingerprints of the five people who had ruined his life. He started to dream, but before he lost consciousness he swore to himself that if he survives, he'll make them pay.

An annoying voice pulled him out of sleep. "Come on, wake up," James insisted.

Inside of his eyelid was bright red from the morning sun and his body was too heavy to move. He unstuck his tongue from the bottom of his mouth then managed to moan before he opened his eye to look at a blurry figure now blocking the sun. He cleared his throat. "Dad, is that you?"

James sighed. "Give it up. I'm never going to say it."

"Come on," he whispered. "Say it. Say, I'm your daddy," he joked.

"Laugh it up flam bay, you almost died. What happened? Half of your body is missing."

"I was attacked and my cane blew up," he said, listening to bird chirping in the distance.

"You weren't the only one who got blown up, or imploded, whatever."

He closed his eye. "Are you going to fix me?"

"I'll restore you, but it'll take time to get your new limbs working."

"Good," he said, thinking about revenge. "Is the party still going? It was epic and the fireworks were perfect, I bet everyone could feel them."

"Everyone's dead. It looks like three implosion devices went off and destroying everything. What's going on out here? All my plans are turning to crap. It's a crap-capade!"

James' voice was stressed and sounded upset, but The King thought it'd be a good time to cheer him up. "Have you seen my assistant?"

"He's... dead," James stressed.

"But he had my day planner."

"Your day planned is gone, everything is gone, my plans are falling apart and all my people are dying!"

"But, I'm still alive."

"You're not going to be if you don't stop screwing with me!" James fumed.

"All right, calm down, I'm not going anywhere. Pop a squat and tell Uncle King your problems," The King said, giving James the time he needed to calm down and put his crazy away.

"Byron's dead," he finally said, "and I can't prove it, but I know Jas did it."

The King knew that James had a soft spot for Byron, but didn't know why. Every encounter with Byron was agitating and he was always dark and moody. And as he went through his memories of Byron he added drug addicted and delusional rapist to the list of complaints then had difficulty sounding empathetic. "I'm sorry to hear that," he lied trying not to further anger James. He didn't want to be left in the woods as vulture meat.

If James knew he was insincere, he didn't show it. "I think of you all as my dysfunctional family and Byron was a troubled son. I had always imagined you all with me when this is over. The Human race restored and the world made whole with each of us in charge of their own territory, to do as they please. Now it's like the Universe has turned on me after a thousand years of moving things into place." They were quiet for a moment and The King was happy to feel a cool breeze against his skin then James continued, "Maybe Byron's death was a good thing. The people in his territory would've suffered."

The King opened his eye again and James was still a blur. "Speaking about suffering," he hinted to James that he should fix him.

James scoffed. "Stop whining, you're fine. You're not dying anymore."

"That's a load off my mind. I was afraid I was going to have a limp for the rest of my life."

"You selfish bastard, I'm pouring my heart out and all you can think about is yourself."

He relaxed into the rocks and dirt again then apologized, "I'm sorry James, I know you're hurting, but the Universe is a lot bigger than us and it's at least ten moves ahead. How do you know that things aren't progressing the right way?"

"Because people messing up my plans, first some idiot named Kole almost derailed Sarah, killed my Werewolf army and then blew up one of my Ripper factories. Now, after all the trouble we went through having the Elves to attack the Slaver city, we waste our time prepping the survivors, recruiting town to town to have people distribute our candy, then they all get imploded. What's all that?"

"Cid's dead too? He was insane and I just knew he was going to turn on us, but it seems that everything related to the Rippers is going bad. Maybe we should abandon them."

"Where did you get that from? You're just saying that because your candy cane turned you into gristle."

"No, there's something weird about them, it's a feeling," The King said. "Where is this Kole?" he asked hoping he had a name to focus his revenge upon.

"Dead, Sarah took care of him. Why, what are you thinking?"

"Five people attacked me last night, three of them were Alchemists. I felt them and have their spiritual fingerprints in my head. There was a woman, I think their leader. She was powerful, a moving void and they knew about the Rippers."

"How do you know?"

"They wore armor over their shields. Even if the armor as a disguise to get near me, one of them jumped out of the way when I fired my cane. They knew, and I'm willing to bet that it's all connected to the events around Sarah. We let the existence of the Rippers be forgotten and hid them for what, eight hundred years and now, all of a sudden someone knows? I think that Kole had friends." He let a heavy silence fall between them. "Fix me, I'll hunt whoever down and get our revenge."

Chapter

31

Mother Sarah sat cross legged on her meditation mat dressed in an off white loose fitting shirt and harem pants. She was relaxed and focused on her breathing when the cities warning alarm went off startling her. Shaken, she listened, hearing the thumping of running and could almost feel a new tension in the air. She remained focused, trusting that her people knew what they were doing and was about to return to a state of relaxation when a light knocking on her door beckoned her.

"Mother Sarah?" asked Rae, Sarah's latest servant. "An Ork army is nearby and the Governor wants your advice."

She slowly inhaled. "Fetch my outdoor attire and have my hover car readied."

"Yes Mother," she said speaking through a small gap in the doorway. "Do you like it? I mean, it must be nice to have the only hover car in the city."

She didn't like the feel of the question and thought about firing Rae, but remembered that she was young and new. "Do you like serving me?"

"Yes Mother," she said then asked, "Did I offend you?"

She slowly inhaled filling her lungs focusing on the air passing through her nose. "The shape of your questions comes from a negative place."

"I don't understand."

"Your questions are born from jealousy. You must have seen the car and wished it was yours to fly around in, to possess the freedom to go wherever you want because you have none. You reach for the sky because you feel stuck in the dirt, trampled by the world. You first question begs for me to justify owning the car by saying that it was a gift from the Governor, because he wanted me to quickly respond to the needs of the people. Your second question places me lower than you, begging me to reassure you that I wasn't offend. Answering you gives you permission to question me whenever you wish. You have also delayed me in this time of crises telling me that you want to feel more important than everyone else because you are empty inside."

"Nothing you said is true," she said sounding hurt. "I asked because I'm scared."

"What are you afraid of? We're not under attack, now fetch my outdoor attire and have my hover car readied."

"Yes Mother," she said then closed the door.

Shortly after, Sarah left her servants waiting with her car on the roof of the Governor's building which followed ancient architecture of a stone structure. Built on an elevate platform so everyone had to look up to see it and climb a hill of stairs to enter, giving it domination in a person's psyche, but that didn't matter to her. She walked past the Governor's secretary sitting at her desk then waited for the secretary to get up to open the office door. The middle aged Governor with slicked black hair dressed in a gray suit and red tie sat at his large oak desk sitting with his back to the window listening to the two Militia leaders who occupied the other seats. She was pleased to see that his baby blue walls were decorated with various pictures of him with city workers. Happy pictures of smiles and growth, teamwork and the sharing of common goals.

"Ah, Mother Sarah," the Governor said then flashed a grin before getting up. "Here, take my chair."

She graciously sat in his large chair while he stood off to the side.

She wiggled herself forward then watched the surveillance recordings. "Where did they get the flying vehicles?"

An older man with white hair and a gravelly voice dressed in a green uniform spoke, "We suspect that they've always had it. Our spies have reported that the Ork tribes have been recently united under a self proclaimed King, or great chieftain, whatever those things call their leader."

A younger Militia man with a brown crew cut spoke sharp and quick asking, "What should we do? We've evacuated the farms that they're now looting and burning. Are we going to attack?"

Sarah quickly visualized the result then said, "No. They don't want us yet. Look at where they're going, this is an invasion force heading for the Elves and they have more than enough Battle Barges, troops and aircraft to easily wipe us out."

The older man said, "They're going to establish a supply lines then harass us, taking whatever they can get and our people will starve. We have to show the Orks our strength. It's the only thing those beasts understand."

"I agree," Sarah said. "But we need to stay neutral in their war. This reminds me of a joke, what do you do if a bear is humping your leg? You let him finish." She let them chuckle then suggested, "We let the Orks pass and set up their lines while we establish our defenses. The Elves and Orks have done nothing for us in the past and have treated us like rodents, so all we're going to do is defend our people. Let them kill each other while we gather people and resources to destroy the survivors, if need be."

The older man laughed. "You're right, they don't see us as a threat and maybe that's what saved us. Our people are scattered, disorganized and weaker than them and whoever wins their war will take everything including our land."

Sarah smiled. "We can use this to our advantage. We need to reach out to our neighbors and make trade agreements, alliances, and any other thing you can think of before they become complacent thinking that the Orks are only interested in the Elves."

"I see," the younger man said. "We can profit off their fear and rally enough people to build a nation."

The older man theorized saying, "We don't know how long this war will drag on, or what other races will get involved and if we do it right, we can become a real Winter Haven."

"Oh, I like that," the younger man said. He explained to Sarah, "The Ork war will make it cold like winter out there and we'll be a haven for the Human race."

"Yes," Sarah said. "I got that."

He blushed. "I... meant no disrespect," he stammered.

The Governor looked out the window. "How many people do you think will come?"

Sarah felt the power within herself that James had given her. "We offer a safe home and an Alchemist free land which has attracted many, but with the Orks close by we shouldn't use fear as a tool. We need to trigger everyone's instinctive fight, not flight. We'll start a campaign saying that the Orks are stupid animals that can be easily outsmarted and destroyed."

"Yes," the young man agreed. "We can make posters." His hands fluttered as he struggled to find words. "Like with one of those people, um, circus animal tamers with a whip and chair forcing a slouched, dumb looking Ork to jump through a hoop."

Sarah nodded. "Any idea that'll change fear into hope, glory, or purpose, but hate is off the table. Our focus should be unity not superiority, so on your poster you can add a second tamer."

"But, in the past I think there was only one tamer, that's what made it special. One man commanding a beast to do what he wants."

"Yes, everyone knows that, but second tamer hits their psyche," Sarah explained. "They'll stop and know something's off. They'll see Humans getting an Ork to do what they want and it'll make them feel safer in numbers. Then we'll have the military posters inspiring purpose and joining something that'll make a difference, one soldier changing the world."

The older man added, "We'll send out recruiters, but we'll need more than posters."

"We can make movies, like in the old days with heroes crushing villains. We can show whatever we want." He stuck his thumbs together making a finger window. "Picture one side with their war torn land filled with sick and abused children and have their evil overlord pushing his primitive army into our beautiful land, murdering those who want peace. We can make it sound like we're making an army to rescue and free the defenseless Humans."

Sarah nodded pleased with their brainstorm and happy that James' plan is becoming manifest. "I will include propaganda in my broadcasts and soon more people will come leaving their pain and fear behind."

The Governor touched her shoulder. "We are all happy that you've come to Winter Haven. Your broadcasts have inspired us all to become better people and I can see us expanding. And when the time is right, the Human race can take back our planet so we can finally have peace."

The two Militia men smiled at the thought.

"Thank you Governor," Sarah said. "That's all I want for the Human race."

Late in the privacy of her home, Sarah reached out to James and placed a call. James answered looking rough around the edges saying, "Hello Sarah, I'm surprised to hear from you."

With the way he looked and the stress in his voice, Sarah could tell something was wrong. "I wanted to report that an Ork army has marched by heading into the Elven lands."

"Yes," he said. "I have to expedite my plans."

"Why?"

"I'm really trying to see things as being positive, but all my plans have fallen apart except for that one. I guess that's the proper path."

She soothed, "Sometimes something that seems negative isn't."

"Byron's dead," he said, shifting their conversation. "He was such a pain and I can't help but feel bad about it."

She wanted to console him, but couldn't help asking, "How did he die?"

He saddened. "A prostitute stabbed him to death."

She almost laughed envisioning Byron slumped in a filthy ally with a knife in his back and his pants around his knees. "I'm sorry for your loss, but I'm not surprised."

Hurt crossed his face, but was quickly released. "At least you're honest," he said. "I think I'm the only one who's going to miss him."

She said nothing, allowing that portion of their conversation to die then prompted him asking, "Your other plans have fallen apart?"

"Yes," he said then cleared his throat. "The King thinks that the Alchemist Kole had friends and that they are behind it, but you told me that Kole and his apprentice were dead."

She had forgotten about Kole then remembered ordering the artillery strike. "They were passing by Winter Haven in his transport and I used a Ripper round to destroy them," she explained. "My scout confirmed that there were no survivors, but that's unimportant, there's someone out there messing up your plans and it doesn't matter who."

"I guess not," James agreed. "At first all the loss had annoyed me because I put a lot of work into the world. I just wish the Universe had shown me the correct path in the beginning."

"Some of your lost plans may have been needed to create the ripples that are now propelling us forward."

"A World War is our only path now, that's why I had the other plans. I thought that I might be able to avoid all the mass destruction, but I guess I can't, so I'll work to get the other races involved. I'll have the Trolls supply weapons to the Orks and the Dwarves supply humanitarian aid the Elves while the Humans stay neutral. Later the Dark Elves will attack the Dwarves and the Dwarves will attack the Trolls."

She smiled. "I'm happy for you. Your plan is finally taking on a life of its own."

"I might not look it, but I'm ecstatic. I put enough energy into my plans nudging them along and removing those who create eddies. Waiting for the manifestation to take was the hardest thing I had to do."

"I can only imagine, but we're now at the point where things are going to pick up speed. I'm concerned about one thing though, the Orks are close by and if they take a heavy loss they'll use us as an easy victory to boost troop morale."

He frowned. "I can see that. I'll send what you need to defend your people, but don't be afraid to slap the Orks around. With every victory over the Orks, your renown will grow and people will see you as a strong leader."

The thought of reaching more of the down trodden warmed her. "That's what you made me to do," she said thanking him.

Chapter

32

Kole was grateful for the fireworks that went on for what seemed like forever, lighting up the party that had gotten out of hand. The outside noise had covered their fight with The Lollypop King and the messed up partiers made it easy for them to escape in a fast moving skiff of a transport. Once they were at a safe distance, the haunting flash from the massive implosion looked like hollow light that blanketed the barren landscape. Nick, half conscious had protested before their escape, arguing that they should've taken something big and luxurious. Through his swollen face, he declared that he owned everything there because all the owners would soon be dead, but Kole just wanted to get out of there before more things went wrong.

The fight with The Lollypop King severely aggravated Kole because nothing went as planned. Nick had recklessly attacked early, getting himself thrashed, forcing Kyra to rescue him, but for a mundane against an Alchemist, she did well by surviving. Kole had planned to be the first one in, he may have been able to surprise The King and take him down with less of a fuss, but instead, after the children got pummeled, he enjoyed watching Enora fight. He would never admit it, but he felt rather cheeky when he damaged the candy cane a moment before The King had fled, though it bothered him that he didn't have a body to confirm the kill. But he still felt satisfied when he looked up through the hole in the ceiling and saw The King's silhouette in the cane's explosion. He smiled at the memory, a dark pleasure.

Enora asked, "What are you thinking?" She sat in co-pilot seat looking at him.

The skiff was narrow and compact like a hover plane without wings, or a tail, made for three people, but was faster than his old transport. The tight cockpit somehow comforted him after he climbed up the footholds in the hull and slipped in through the canopy. He pushed the memory of the explosion away. "I think that you might be right, I like being a good guy and I was thinking that what we did was ultimately a good thing."

She waited saying nothing.

"I mean," he said, glad that the others weren't there to hear him. "It was mass murder, but why not? They were all bad guys, though I can't help but feel that my moral compass is bent."

"You're over thinking," she said. "You did it, now let it go. You see, a person can justify anything, so you're beating yourself up over nothing." She was quiet for a moment. "Perhaps you're asking the wrong person because I don't see what we did as good, or bad. It just was."

Her answer didn't help him. "What do you feel?"

"I feel contentment, which can also be seen as peace because my bowl is empty and an empty bowl has an infinite amount of use, but once it's filled, that is all that it'll be. In other words, if you fill your bowl with upset, that's all you'll be."

"But, do you feel emotion? You sound cold."

She laughed. "I feel emotion, you big dope. Think of what I do as a wine tasting, I experience emotion then release it. I don't consume it, sucking on a piece of food until it loses its flavor becoming bland. When I do move out of peace I feel so deeply that I can weep from the beauty of watching a falling leaf, but what you want to know is what I felt when we destroyed those people."

"Yeah, that's what I want to know," he confirmed, noticing the light change signaling dawn's approach.

"I felt nothing because those people choose to be broken, but they do serve a purpose. The world can be a bowl too, filled with what the world wants. We are all connected with everyone serving a purpose, yin and yang. The world is a concert of broken pieces glued together to make a picture," she said. "Honestly, killing them did nothing in the world. It would've been better to have left them alone, now others will just take their place because you didn't fix why they existed in the first place."

Kole imagined the world as one big bowl filled with everyone's energy. He watched the people consume that energy, becoming it, multiply it, manifesting for the world. "I think I'm starting to understand you," he said. "The only way to change the world is for everyone to clean their bowl, then the world's."

"Yeah," she agreed. "But that's easier said than done. The world is the way it is because people want it this way. Just enjoy yourself doing what you feel is right as long as you don't hurt anyone else."

"Except for the bad guys we just destroyed, right?"

"At the time it felt like it was the right thing to do," she said then the console beeped. She pressed a button, listened then said, "A small southern farming village is under attack from the Orks."

"Orks?" Kole asked. "Orks don't come this far north, it's a trap."

"Does it matter? I thought that you wanted to be a good guy."

He scoffed. "I do, but I'm not stupid."

"I guess if you don't spring the trap, someone else less capable will," she teased, adding, "Poor buggers."

Kole groaned. "Fine, pass me their info." He saw the directional marker on his screen then altered course. He then opened his group com and said, "We've picked up a distress call claiming that Orks are attacking. We're going to check it out."

"Trap?" asked Eric.

Nick complained, "In this thing? We could've taken anything, but you had to have this. Its cramped back here, my legs and ass are asleep. Now you want me to jump out and fight? I don't think so."

Kyra grunted then cursed. "Get off me Nick! There's enough room for you, stay on your side, but Nick does have a point. Orks don't pack light and a direct hit will blow this can apart. Maybe we should come back when we have something better."

"I don't think they're going to wait around for us to find a new ride, if the distress call's real," Eric said.

"Real or not we're going to check it out," Kole said, spotting four columns of smoke in the distance. "I don't think it's a trap. Nick, wake your ass up and Eric, prep the tail gun."

"Sure, I guess we're doing this," Eric said. "But I don't think this vehicle is in combat shape."

Kyra spoke, "I've been thinking. Fighting Orks sounds fun, but since we've teamed up there's been a lot of fighting and I think we can all use a vacation."

"I can see that," Nick agreed. "I got banged up pretty bad. The last guy put a lot of heat into bashing my face in."

"It's like he knew you," Eric chimed.

Kole half smiled. "I hear what you're all saying, but do you know what's funny? I know a place where we can relax and have a good time except that the fastest way there is through those Orks. So why don't we pack away our complaints and go rescue some farmers."

Nick mumbles something under his breath.

Kole jumped on it asking, "What was that, Nick?"

"I said that I think rescuing those farmers will be fun."

Kole knew crap when he heard it and teased, "Yeah, I think so too. That's the spirit."

The small village sat on the edge of a valley divided by a river that the villagers use to pipe water up into their farms on the lower plateaus and as Kole approached he realized that it hadn't always that way. The old buildings were stained, covered in grit and the valley hadn't always been there. Collapsed ruins littered the valley walls telling him the story of a painful past.

There were more Orks than he had thought. A Battle Barge with modified armaments sat idle on the main street protecting a slave ship while two scout crafts patrolled the perimeter. It looked like the Orks had already sacked the village and piled everything worth stealing onto the street to sort through later. They were now focused on collecting the villagers, pulling them from their hiding places and enslaving them. Some villagers had put up a small fight and now their bodies lay in the sun.

Kole slowed seeing what awaited them then decided that Nick and Kyra may have been right, they weren't equipped to handle the Orks. He and Enora would survive, but Nick and Kyra wouldn't and Eric had yet to master his shield, putting him in the maybe pile. He thought about running, protecting his crew, but he had the power in that moment to stop their tyranny.

Kole came to a stop out of the range of their guns then unfastened his safety harness. "Enora and I will take care of this," he said. "Nick and Kyra get up here, I want you guys at a safe distance and Eric, you go with them." He climbed out of the cockpit, grabbed his rifle then jumped, landing on the ground that was more gravel than grass.

Nick hung his battered face out the side door and looked down the main street. "They're taking slaves now? Did we just leave this party?"

Kyra grabbed a hold of Nick's armor, looked around him. "I guess we're going to have to kick their asses too."

Nick asked, "Kole, what are the Orks doing? They know we're here, they're looking at us."

"We're acting like Alchemist and they're waiting for us to make the first move. Normal people in our situation would've run by now."

Kyra laughed. "Normal people wouldn't have shown up."

Nick looked at him. "Since they think some of us are Alchemists, could we talk them into buggering off and leaving these people alone?"

Enora walked around the front of the skiff carrying her rifle. "Are we going to follow them back to their territory making sure that they don't attack anyone else? That sounds boring and self-righteous."

"Yeah," Kole reluctantly agreed. "That does sound boring. I guess it's decided, we take them out. You guys stay safe. Enora you're with me."

Kole and Enora walked toward town while Nick darted away driving the skiff.

"Kole," Nick said. "I found some music for you. It's from those ancient western movies."

"I'm not really into that right now."

He played the music. "Just put this in your head when you're facing off with the bad guys," he said then whistled along.

Kole lost his focus and became annoyed. "Why do you have to be such an Ork dork? I'm trying to focus and get my game on," he fumed as the two Ork scout transports sped off after Nick.

Enora waved her hand and one of the scout ship's engine exploded turning it into a tumbling mess of metal, flames and smoke.

"You have to teach me how to do that," Kole said, watching a fighter plane launched off the back of the Battle Barge. Its metallic oval body and crescent wings banked toward Nick.

"You already know. Just try," Enora suggested then waved her hand again causing the second scout to explode.

Kole reached out to the fighter trying to destroy it, but an image of Troll hands building it flashed in his mind. "I tried to take out the fighter, but I saw something instead. I guess I needed some sort of contact with it."

"Your perception of distance and connection caused your failure," she said then shrugged.

He huffed, "I had a snide comment for you, but I put it away because I like you so much."

"Thank you, that's the most romantic thing you've ever said to me."

Kole's smile was hidden by his helmet, but as they approached, the Orks ignored them. They went back to forcing the villagers onto the Slave Barge. "It's weird that they're not attacking," he said a moment before the forward mounted cannon of the Battle Barge fired giving Kole a second to feel the Ripper round before it exploded between them. Kole was thrown into the air then tumbling across the grass and gravel skidding to a stop. He pushed himself up noticing that half of his body was covered in shrapnel and that he was missing sections of his leg armor, exposing his shield. He picked himself up and ran toward the back of the closest building, putting it between him and the Barge, but that didn't stop the Orks. One of their side guns opened up, pumping Ripper rounds through the walls of the building. Kole dove under the Ork's salvo that spat shattered wood, drywall and chunks of insulation over him. He crawled, hearing and feeling the sharp creeks and jittering moans of the building until it finally collapsed in one final thunderous crackle of wood, toppling onto the Battle Barge.

Kole scrambled to the second building then threw himself, diving through a window and knocking over a shelving unit full of preservatives. Soaked in vinegar he sprang to his feet and looked out the front window to see the Battle Barge backing up. Suddenly the front door's bell range as the door was kicked in. All Kole saw was green skin and black armor before he reacted. He ran sideways to a curtain strung across a doorframe with sign above it saying employees only while he fired a small burst at the Ork's face. The Ork went down and the others didn't waste time forcing their way in. They fanned out in front, shooting up the wall and doorframe, but by then Kole found the stairs leading up.

"Enora, are you all right?" he asked, finding a moment to breath.

"Yes, I was thrown down the hill. Some armor was blown off and I had a stick through my calf. I haven't felt pain in a long time and I could've lost a limb."

"That doesn't sound okay."

"I healed myself. They have my attention and I'll be there soon."

Kole made it to the roof and stood on its edge looking down then fired at six Orks in the street as Nick in the smoking bullet riddled skiff ran over four of the Orks. Metal screeched and sparked as Nick sideswiped the Battle Barge on the valley side. He struggled to turn back to the street, but the Battle Barge fired its main cannon through the building's rubble hitting the skiff dead center. The skiff exploded tearing in half. Its front end rolled crashing through a wall into a building while the back end was sent bouncing down the valley wall.

Kole screamed, "Eric!" He jumped off the roof, flipping his rifle around in the air using it as an axe, shattering an Ork's skull his rifle's butt. He hit the pavement hard folding into the fallen Ork then sprang, throwing the body aside, knocking the last Ork's rifle away before planting his hand on the Ork's armor making his chest explode out his back. The Battle Barge's tail gun quickly found him, firing, but Kole rolled forward slapping his hand on the Barge's hull. He envisioned the walls within the Barge turning into long metal spikes killing everyone inside, but before he could run to Eric, the Barge exploded in a massive flash of light.

Chapter

33

Nick smiled at being called an Ork's dork thinking that his influence was finally rubbing off on Kole. He opened the throttle wondering how far he had to go to be safe and wait out the Ork's impending doom.

Eric laughed. "Ork dork," he echoed and opened a separate channel for them.

Kyra sat in the co-pilot's seat. "What is wrong with you, Nick?"

"You know," he replied. "Maybe it's because my dad raped my mom and my mom abandoned me on the doorstep of that hell hole. Maybe because I was a mistake and no one loved me, or maybe a person has to be a little crazy to have a bit of fun in this world, who knows?"

"Speaking about fun," Eric said, "We have a fighter coming in."

"The Orks have a fighter?" she asked sounding surprised.

"Orks are people too, you racist bitch, why wouldn't they have one?" Nick asked. "Besides, they know I'm here so they sent their best."

Kyra gasped. "I'm not a racist!"

Nick heard the clicking of the rear gun opening up. "Evade!" Eric ordered.

Nick jerked the controls in time to see the ground erupt beside them as the fighter's guns tracked them. The fighter paused and Nick slowed, evaded again then punched the throttle.

He heard more clicking. "You're doing good Nick, keep it up," Eric said.

Nick saw the fighter's shadow then turned as the fighter strafed, punching holes through the cockpit's canopy, cargo and tail section. Kyra screamed and the skiff shook, rattling Nick's controls. The engine pinged and smoked, warning alarms beeped and lights flashed before the port stabilizer failed, turning them on their side, dipping the skiff closer to the ground. Nick struggled flexing his entire body fighting his shuddering controls desperately trying to keep the skiff from buying it while Kyra frantically worked her controls rerouting power, putting out fires.

Eric yelled, "Die Ork scum!"

Nick heard the clicking of the gun and could almost feel Eric's murderous intent. He quickly flicked opened a side window bleeding the smoke filling the cockpit then held fast his shaking controls, hoping that Eric would score a kill because he could no longer evade. His arms jiggled and he was losing strength, but managed to turn back toward town. "If we're going down," he snarled. "We're going to take some of these bastards with us."

Eric cheered, "I got him. I got him. Die you sons of dogs!"

Nick smiled through clenched teeth watching the town come up fast. He killed the throttle intending to land and walk in, but nothing happened. He toggled the throttle hoping that it would fix itself, but there was a loud bang, the pinging stopped. He shot around a building at the edge of town heading for the main street. Suddenly a portion of his control went slack. He jerked, dipping the skiff and grazing the ground, but was able to gain control a moment before he ran over four Orks standing in the middle of the street. The sounds of their meaty thumps against his hull made him wanted to laugh, but he was barely able to avoid their Battle Barge, sideswiping it. The screech of metal was deafening. Nick pulled away, but the Barge's side gun opened up blowing off the rest of his canopy. A round struck the side of his head, ripping off his helmet. His head knocked against the hull and he almost let go of his controls, but managed turn again. Numbness squeezed the crown of his head and his neck burned. He blinked then there was a flash of light in his cockpit. His controls went dead and they sailed sideways then hit the ground, rolling. They crashed through a wall of a building coming to a sudden stop. Nick's chest hurt, but felt better when he hit the release to his safety harness. His face and head hurt with blood flowing into his left eye. Kyra was limp.

    He imagined springing to his feet and pulling Kyra to safety, but his body didn't move and the cockpit grew darker. Human hands reached for him then darkness and the pain from being dragged across rubble woke him. A man propped him and Kyra against a wall leaning them against each other. Nick's eye focused on three frightened Humans holding each other, an older man, an older woman and a boy. They all wore soiled plaid shirts and tan overalls, but before he could thank them, a massive explosion shook the ground shooting chunks of shrapnel through the remnants of their building.

    The woman stared at him unaffected by the destruction while the others fearfully cried out. "Nick?" she asked.

    He tried to place her face thinking that he owed her credits, but was sure that he'd never met her before. "Do I know you?" he asked.

    Her face contorted between anguish and relief as she left the man's embrace to grab him, holding him close. "I've spent so many years searching for you, I never gave up," she blubbered.

    He had cooled down and his body ached. It felt like someone threw a condom over the wrong head and it took a couple of second for him to connect the dots. "Are you my mother?" he asked.

    Tears flowed down he cheeks. She clutched him tighter, slightly rocking as if he were a little boy then smiled. "Yes," she sobbed. "I'm your mother." Her heart pounded in Nick's ear as she spoke of her horrible past. "The Orks raided my village, killed my husband and two children," she explained. "They forced me to watch then raped me. They burned my home and left me staked to the ground, hoping that the sun would bake me to death. I was rescued, but didn't want to go on. I lost everything. When I was told that I was pregnant, I wanted to live for you and I had you because I wasn't sure if you were my husband's child. During labor I passed out and when I woke, they told me that you were a Half Ork and were still born. I named you Nick after my father." She wiped her eyes and cheeks. "I didn't care what you were, you were mine," she said. "But, they stole you and hid you away. Everyone had lost someone to the Orks during that raid and they took you away because you were a reminder of their pain. Years later…" She shuttered. "I found the truth, but the man who hid you had already passed on, so I had nothing. They didn't even apologize. So I went into the world searching orphanages, but by the time I found the right one, you were gone." She whispered, "I'm sorry that I was never there for you."

The man and boy sat there watching, giving her space to tell her story and the first thing Nick wanted to do when she confessed that she was his mother, was punch her in the mouth, but his arm didn't work. Then after hearing her side, he didn't know where to put his heartache. He had blamed her for so much, all those years of darkness and pain had ruined his life, but seeing her lost and broken opened an emotional floodgate of sorrow and regret. "I thought you had abandoned me," he gushed. He managed to push her back. "That you hated me because I'm ugly."

Tears flowed unchecked. "No… no," she comforted, cradling his face in her hands. "I could never ever do that. You were my boy, my last hope to survive, a ray of light that I clung to for my salvation and sanity. I never gave up hope that I would find you and you are beautiful. When they told me that you were still born, a piece of me died and the rest of me darkened. I became a shriveled husk until I found out that you actually lived and those… those monsters who called themselves Human, doctors, were responsible for our heartache." She clutched at the front of her shirt twisting the fabric trying to sooth her broken heart. She reached for him again and he collapsed into her motherly embrace. All his anger and grief melted away and his body protested as he embraced her.

They wept in each other's arms and he never wanted to let her go then with a crash and splintering wood, a group of Orks kicked in the back door to their hiding place, spilling in. Nick tried to move, to hide his mom from them, but was too weak. The Orks paused seeing the farmers then laughed. They lumbered forward collecting the man and boy then an Ork thrust out his hand and roughly grabbed his mother by her hair. She screamed. Her eyes were filled with terror while Nick and his mother clawed and clung to each other trying to hold on. The Ork pulled, wrapping his arm around her waist. Their fingers slid down each other's arms then suddenly she was ripped from Nick's grasp and dragged away. The last Ork stopped in front of Nick, uttered an insult then kicked him in the face breaking his nose. His eyes cried and the Ork laughed at the blood running down Nick's face. The Ork leaned across him and yanked Kyra's helmet off, throwing it across the room. The Ork picked her up then shook her, but she remained limp. He dropped her then laughed again at Nick before walking out.

This wasn't the first time that Nick had been kicked in the face. He spat out a mouth full of blood then fell onto his side worming his way to Kyra. He placed his ear near her mouth and listened to her breath then smiled knowing that together they could do anything, even find his mother. His mother never gave up on him and even if he had to go alone, he would find her. Again, he dropped his face into the rubble and succumbed to the darkness.

Chapter

34

Enora had been walking beside Kole when the Ork cannon fired, exploding a round close enough to send her cartwheeling through the air. She enjoyed the moment feeling like she was floating. Her mind slowed, watching the world spin, sky, dirt, sky, dirt. She fell into the valley hitting the ground tumbling over debris until she slammed into a pile of rotted wood and plaster. She lay in a tight cocoon of garbage until she transmuted the waste into oxygen. Now free she decided to spring to her feet and run up the hill to help Kole, but her leg felt strange, tingly. She struggled to place the sensation then finally looked to see that a stick had impaled her calf. She wondered how that had happened then thought back to the explosion deducing that the Orks were using rounds dipped in Ripper residue. Her shield hadn't collapsed, but it had moved exposing her leg, allowing the explosion to blow off some leg armor and embed shrapnel into her side making her look sparkly. She lay there watching her leg bleed listening to the echo of popping machinegun fire then reached down and transmuted the stick, repairing her leg.

She jumped hearing Kole's voice. "Enora, are you all right?" he asked. The worry in his voice touched her.

"Yes," she answered. "I was thrown down the hill. Some armor was blown off and I had a stick through my calf. I haven't felt pain in a long time and I could've lost a limb."

"That doesn't sound okay."

She thought about how it sounded, realizing that she had been intrigued by the experience. "I healed myself," she said. "They now have my attention and I'll be there soon."

She cleared her mind, felt the air around her and was about to fly high into the sky and rain death upon the Orks when a small explosion sent the back end of the skiff shooting into the valley. At first she didn't know what the smoking contraption of twisted metal was. Nick had left, that couldn't be them, but watching it bounce its way down the valley wall and land in the river she had a bad feeling about it.

She decided that Kole could handle himself then flew down to the river's edge, gently touching down on a bed of rocks. She reached out, found the wreckage and transmuted it into water releasing Eric into the river. She waved her hand and made the river spit him out onto the shore. She knelt beside him then took off his soaked helmet and was about to check his vitals when his body jerked spitting out water. She was happy that Eric was alive and turned her attention back to the Orks when a massive explosion shook the ground sending chunks of flaming metal soaring across the valley into the neighboring dwellings.

She flew up the valley's wall and landed at a crater's edge where the blackened hover matrix of the Battle Barge now lay. The explosion had decimated that side of the village leveling most of the buildings and setting the other side of the valley on fire. She stood in an eerie silence. The Orks were gone, she'd forgotten about the Slave Barge and Kole was missing. She reached out and felt Nick and Kyra a short distance away. Worried, she stretched further out fighting to stay focused. Kole should've been standing around acting cocky or digging Nick and Kyra out of the rubble. Her worry damaged her calm and she was barely able to feel him.

She rushed, flying then landed beside his mutilated body. The blast had torn his clothes off and taken his left arm and right leg leaving his torso riddled with holes. On the surface he was dead, but she looked deep within him, finding an ember of life. She thought about letting him go, returning him to the Universe, but if it had been his time, he would've already left before she had got there. She went to work, slowly feeding the ember and rebuilding his body, but knew that he wouldn't be the same. Portions of his brain had been damaged and she couldn't remake the pathways built from a person's experience. Instead she repaired his brain leaving the holes in his pathways for him to rebuild. Soon, she finished repairing his body then took a moment to look him over. She remembered lying beside him in bed learning his body and from memory, remade all the blemishes that made him beautiful. She swelled feeling love for him then dressed him before picking him up and flying back to the crater.

Kyra and Eric were waiting for them lounging on various seats that they had pulled from the ruins while Nick paced in front of them. She laid Kole on the ground. "You two look cozy," she said, hiding her concern for Kole. "All you need is a fire pit and we can be camping."

Eric shot out of a bucket seat, rushed to Kole's side kneeling beside him. "What happened?" he asked.

But before she could answer Nick blurted on the edge of panic, "Did you stop the Slave Barge?"

"No," she said, watching Nick fidget, plucking his hands. "By the time I got up here they were already gone." She met Eric's eyes. "Kole was hurt badly and almost died, but I repaired what I could."

Kyra stood behind Eric. "What do you mean, what you could?"

Nick leaned over Eric's shoulder. "He looks fine," he said. "We need to go rescue those slaves. Enora, make us some weapons and a ride."

Kole was still unconscious and that worried Enora. "I'm not going anywhere without Kole," she said. "What do the slaves have that you want?"

Nick slapped his hands to his sides becoming ridged. "It's not what I want, but who," he blurted.

"Forgive him, Enora," Kyra said then explained, "He found his mom after all these years then the Orks took her away. We think she's on the Slave Barge."

Nick rubbed his neck looking miserable. "If I wasn't so messed up and I had my rifle, I might've been able to stop them."

Worried about Kole, Enora assessed everyone's injuries and determined that they'd heal then ignored their fussing. She knelt beside Kole placing her hand on his chest. His body now had enough energy resting below the surface to tell her that he was asleep. She gently rocked him, encouraging energy flow.

Kole woke groggy. "What happened?" he groaned

The worry left Eric in laughter. He joked, "You got blown up."

Kole stirred reaching over grabbing his new arm. "This isn't mine, my leg too. They're not responding properly and my head feels funny."

Enora touched his shoulder getting his attention. "You were badly hurt and I had to remake parts of you. Everything's there, but because I'm not you, I couldn't wire your brain properly. You'll have to relearn how to use those limbs."

He looked his limbs over then snickered. "You're so sweet. You remade the moles on my arm that made the constellation of Orion."

"I did my best."

"Thank you Enora, for putting me back together, but did you happen to give me a little extra?" he teased then wiggled his eyebrows.

She groaned. "No, you're fine the way you are."

He laughed then focused on Nick. "What's wrong with him, he looks like someone shot his favorite pet?"

Nick was quiet. Eric spoke for him, "Nick found his mom then the Orks took her."

Kole looked confused. "There were Orks? Oh yes I remember now." He clutched his chest. "My chest hurts, am I having a heart attack?"

Enora looked into him. "No, you're fine."

"Something's different. I feel things, I think they're emotions."

Eric looked worried then brightened. "I know. This will put you back to normal. I was thinking about keeping a Pixie for a pet and naming it Little Kole. What do you think?"

Kole looked up at him. "That's a horrible name," he said. "Pixies are sentient and keeping one as a pet is slavery. That idea is bad all the way around."

"Doesn't that make you mad? Pixies killed your teacher, remember?"

"I remember, and I'm at peace with that."

Shocked, Eric looked at Enora. "What did you do to him?"

"He had brain damage. We have to be gentle with him until he adjusts."

Kyra fretted. "You mean that he's a different person? That's major, he's a walking weapon. Will he go nuts and kill us all?"

"I'm right here," Kole said. "That's not nice, Kyra."

Nick grunted. "Kole, it's better to get it all out in the open. We've seen you do some scary things and we have the right to know if you're going to go psycho. At least give us a head start if you do."

Kole struggled to get up then Enora and Eric helped him. He slung his new arm over Eric's shoulder then wrapped his arm around Enora, looking at her with such warmth and affection that it made her tingle inside. His eyes didn't leave hers when he spoke to the group, "I understand your concern, but I'm not going to hurt any of you. I remember everything that we've done, but I feel different about it." He smiled at Enora then looked at Nick. "If you and Kyra are that concerned about me, we can go our separate ways, but I'd really like to help you find your mom and all the other villagers."

Nick trembled then wiped eyes, relieved.

Kole smiled warmly. "Time's wasting and I have a choice for you. We can find something to chase after the Orks, or we can repair that Ork fighter. It's better to fly in the long run."

"I can't wait that long," Nick blurted. "They could be hurting her right now."

Kole stepped away from Eric and Enora and limped closer placing his hand on Nick's shoulder. "We'll find your mom, no matter long it take us," he said reassuring him. "Now, let's find a ride. We have people to rescue."

Kole's Apocalyptic Pancakes

1 ½ cups of Milk
1 ½ cups of Flour
1 Egg
1 tbsp of Baking Soda
1 tbsp of Corn Starch
1 tbsp of Non-Alcoholic Organic Vanilla Extract
1 tbsp of 100% Natural Raw Sugar

To eat like a wasteland scavenger,
apply a layer of Greek Yogurt across
the surface of the pancake then cover with
Maple Syrup.